EXULTANT

DESTINY'S CHILDREN: BOOK 2

EXULTANT

DESTINY'S CHILDREN: BOOK 2

STEPHEN BAXTER

GOLLANCZ

LONDON

Copyright © Stephen Baxter 2004

The right of Stephen Baxter to be identified as the
author of this work has been asserted by him in accordance
with the Copyright, Designs and Patents Act 1988.

First published in Great Britain in 2004 by
Gollancz
An imprint of the Orion Publishing Group
Orion House, 5 Upper St Martin's Lane,
London WC2H 9EA

A CIP catalogue record for this book is
available from the British Library

ISBN 0 575 07428 0 (cased)
ISBN 0 575 07429 9 (trade paperback)

Typeset at The Spartan Press Ltd,
Lymington, Hants

Printed in Great Britain by
Clays Ltd, St Ives plc

www.orionbooks.co.uk

To Gregory Benford

ONE

In the past we humans, struggling to comprehend our place in the universe, imagined gods, and venerated them.

But now we have looked across the width of the universe, and from its beginning to its end. And we know there are no gods.

We are the creators of the future. And the only entities worthy of our veneration are our own descendants, who, thanks to our selfless striving, will occupy the gods' empty thrones.

But we have a Galaxy to win first.

The Doctrines of Hama Druz
(CE 5408; Year Zero of the Third Expansion of Mankind)

CHAPTER 1

Far ahead, bathed in the light of the Galaxy's centre, the night-fighters were rising.

From his station, Pirius could see their black forms peeling off the walls of their Sugar Lump carriers. They spread graceful wings, so black they looked as if they had been cut out of the glowing background of the Core. Some of them were kilometres across. They were Xeelee nightfighters, but nobody in Strike Arm called them anything but flies.

They converged on the lead human ships, and Pirius saw cherry-red light flaring.

His fragile greenship hovered over the textured ground of a Rock. The Rock was an asteroid, a dozen kilometres across, charcoal grey. Trenches had been dug all over its surface, interconnecting and intersecting, so that the Rock looked like an exposed brain. Sparks of light crawled through those complex lines: soldiers, infantry, endlessly digging, digging, digging, preparing for their own collisions with destiny. It was a good hour yet before this Rock and Pirius's own greenship would reach the battlefield, but already men and women were fighting and dying.

There was nothing to do but watch, and brood. There wasn't even a sense of motion. Under the *Assimilator's Claw*'s pulsing sublight drive it was as if he was floating, here in the crowded heart of the Galaxy. Pirius worried about the effect of the wait on his crew.

Pirius was nineteen years old.

He was deep in the Mass, as pilots called it – the Central Star Mass officially, a jungle of millions of stars crammed into a ball just thirty light years across, a core within the Core. Before him a veil of stars hung before a background of turbulent, glowing gas; he could see filaments and wisps light years long, drawn out by the Galaxy's magnetic field. This stellar turmoil bubbled and boiled on scales of space and time beyond the human, as if he had been caught at the centre of a frozen explosion. The sky was *bright*, crowded with stars and clouds, not a trace of darkness anywhere.

And through the stars he made out the Cavity, a central bubble blown clear of gas by astrophysical violence, and within *that* the Baby Spiral, a swirl of stars and molecular clouds, like a toy version of the Galaxy itself embedded fractally in the greater disc. *That* was the centre of the Galaxy, a place of layered astrophysical machinery. And it was all driven by Chandra, the brooding black hole at the Galaxy's very heart.

This crowded immensity would have stunned a native of Earth – but Earth with its patient, long-lived sun, out in the orderly stellar factory of the spiral arms, was twenty-eight thousand light years from here. But Pirius had grown up with such visions. He was the product of a hundred generations grown in the birthing tanks of Arches Base, formally known as Base 2594, a few light years outside the Mass. He was human, though, with human instincts. And as he peered out at the stretching three-dimensional complexity around him he gripped the scuffed material of his seat, as if he might fall.

Everywhere Pirius looked, across this astrophysical diorama, he saw signs of war.

Pirius's ship was one of a hundred green sparks, ten whole squadrons, assigned to escort this single Rock alone. When Pirius looked up he could see more Rocks, a whole stream of them hurled in from the giant human bases that had been established around the Mass. Each of them was accompanied by its own swarm of greenships. Upstream and down, the chain of Rocks receded until kilometres-wide worldlets were reduced to pebbles lost in the glare. Hundreds of Rocks, thousands perhaps, had been committed to this one assault. It was a titanic sight, a mighty projection of human power.

But all this was dwarfed by the enemy. The Rock stream was directed at a fleet of Sugar Lumps, as those Xeelee craft were called, immense cubical ships that were themselves hundred of kilometres across – some even bigger, some like boxes that could wrap up a whole world.

The tactic was crude. The Rocks were simply hosed in towards the

Sugar Lumps, their defenders striving to protect them long enough for them to get close to the Lumps, whereupon their mighty monopole cannons would be deployed. If all went well, damage would be inflicted on the Xeelee, and the Rocks would slingshot around a suitable stellar mass and be hurled back out to the periphery, to be re-equipped, re-manned, and prepared for another onslaught. If all did not go well – in that case, duty would have been done.

As the *Claw* relentlessly approached the zone of flaring action, one ship dipped out of formation, swooping down over the Rock in a series of barrel rolls. That must be Dans, one of Pirius's cadre siblings. Pirius had flown with her twice before, and each time she had shown off, demonstrating to the toiling ground troops the effortless superiority of Strike Arm, and of the Arches squadrons in particular – and in the process lifting everybody's spirits.

But it was a tiny human gesture lost in a monumental panorama.

Pirius could see his crew, in their own blisters: his navigator Cohl, a slim woman of eighteen, and his engineer, Enduring Hope, a calm, bulky young man who looked older than his years, just seventeen. While Cohl and Hope were both rookies, nineteen-year-old Pirius was a comparative veteran. Among greenship crews, the mean survival rate was one point seven missions. This was Pirius's fifth mission. He was growing a reputation as a lucky pilot, a man whose crew you wanted to be on.

'Hey,' he called now. 'I know how you're feeling. They always say this is the worst part of combat, the ninety-nine per cent of it that's just waiting around, the sheer bloody boredom. I should know.'

Enduring Hope looked across and waved. 'And if I want to throw up, lift the visor first. That's the drill, isn't it?'

Pirius forced a laugh. Not a good joke, but a joke.

Enduring Hope: defying all sorts of rules, the engineer called himself not by his properly assigned name, a random sequence of letters and syllables, but an ideological slogan. He was a Friend, as he styled it, a member of a thoroughly illegal sect that flourished in the darker corners of Arches Base, and, it was said, right across the Front, the great sphere of conflict that surrounded the Galaxy's heart. Illegal or not, right now, as the flies rose up and people started visibly to die, Hope's faith seemed to be comforting him.

But navigator Cohl, staring ahead at the combat zone, was closed in on herself.

The *Claw*, was a greenship, a simple design that was the workhorse of Strike Arm; millions like it were in action all around the war zone. Its main body was a bulbous pod containing most of the ship's systems: the weapons banks, the FTL drive and two sublight drive systems. From the front of the hull projected three spars, giving the ship the look of a three-pronged claw, and at the tip of each prong was a blister, a clear bubble, containing one of the *Claw*'s three crew. For greenship crews, nobody else mattered but each other; it was just three of them lost in a dangerous sky – *Three Against the Foe*, as Strike Arm's motto went.

Pirius knew there were good reasons for the trifurcated design of the greenship. It was to do with redundancy: the ship could lose two of its three blisters and still, in theory anyhow, fulfil its goals. But right now Pirius longed to be able to reach through these transparent walls, to touch his crewmates.

He said, 'Navigator? You still with us?'

He saw Cohl glance across at him. 'Trajectory's nominal, pilot.'

'I wasn't asking her about the trajectory.'

Cohl shrugged, as if resentfully. 'What do you want me to say?'

'You saw all this in the briefing. You knew it was coming.'

It was true. The whole operation had been previewed for them by the Commissaries, in full Virtual detail, down to the timetabled second. It wasn't a prediction, not just a guess, but foreknowledge: a forecast based on data that had actually leaked from the future. The officers hoped to deaden fear by making the events of the engagement familiar before it happened. But not everybody took comfort from the notion of a predetermined destiny.

Cohl was staring out through her blister wall, her lips drawn back in a cold, humourless smile. 'I feel like I'm in a dream,' she murmured. 'A waking dream.'

'It isn't set in stone,' Pirius said. 'The future.'

'But the Commissaries—'

'No Commissary ever set foot in a greenship – none of them is skinny enough. It isn't real until it happens. And *now* is when it happens. It's in our hands, Cohl. It's in yours. I know you'll do your duty.'

'And kick ass,' Enduring Hope shouted.

He saw Cohl grin at last. 'Yes, *sir*!'

A green flash distracted Pirius. A ship was hurtling out of formation. One of its three struts was a stump, the blister missing. As it sailed by,

Pirius recognised the gaudy, spruced-up tetrahedral sigil on its side. It was Dans's ship.

He called, 'Dans? What—'

'Predestination my ass,' Dans yelled on the ship-to-ship line. 'Nobody saw *that* coming.'

'Saw what?'

'See for yourself.'

Pirius swept the crowded sky, letting Virtual feeds pour three-dimensional battlefield data into his head.

In the seconds he'd spent on his crew, everything had changed. The Xeelee hadn't stayed restricted to their source Sugar Lumps. A swarm of them speared down from above his head, from out of nowhere, heading straight for Pirius's Rock.

Pirius hadn't seen it. Sloppy, Pirius. One mistake is enough to kill you.

'This wasn't supposed to happen,' Cohl said.

'Forget the projections,' Pirius snapped.

There were seconds left before the flies hit the Rock. He saw swarming activity in its runs and trenches. The poor souls down there knew what was coming too. Pirius gripped his controls, and tried to ignore the beating of his heart.

Four, three, two.

The Xeelee – pronounced 'Zee-lee' – were mankind's most ancient and most powerful foe.

According to the scuttlebutt on Arches Base, in the training compounds and the vast open barracks, there were only three things you needed to know about the Xeelee.

First, their ships were better than ours. You only had to see a fly in action to realise that. Some said the Xeelee *were* their ships, which probably made them even tougher.

Second, they were smarter than us, and had a lot more resources. Xeelee operations were believed to be resourced and controlled from Chandra itself, the fat black hole at the Galaxy's very centre. In fact, military planners called Chandra, a supermassive black hole, the Prime Radiant of the Xeelee. How could anything we had compete with *that*?

And third, the Xeelee knew what we would do even before we decided ourselves.

This interstellar war was fought with faster-than-light technology, on both sides. But if you flew FTL you broke the bounds of causality: an FTL ship was a time machine. And so this was a time-travel war, in which information about the future constantly leaked into the past.

But the information was never perfect. And every now and again, one side or the other was able to spring a surprise. This new manoeuvre of the Xeelee had *not* been in the Commissaries' careful projections.

Pirius felt his lips draw back in a fierce grin. The script had been abandoned. Today everything really was up for grabs.

But now cherry-red light flared all around the Rock's ragged horizon.

On the loops, orders chattered from the squadron leaders. 'Hold your positions. This is a new tactic and we're still trying to analyse it.' 'Number eight, hold your place. *Hold your place.*'

Pirius gripped his controls so tight his fingers ached.

That red glare was spreading all around the Rock's lumpy profile, a malevolent dawn. Most of the action was taking place on the far side of the Rock from his position – which was itself most unlike the Xeelee, who were usually apt to come swarming all over any Rock they attacked.

The *Claw* would be sheltered from the assault, for the first moments anyhow. That meant Pirius was in the wrong place. He wasn't here to hide, but to fight. But he had to hold his station until ordered otherwise.

Pirius glimpsed a fly standing off from the target. It spread night-dark wings – said to be not material but flaws in the structure of space itself – and extended a cherry-red starbreaker beam. The clean geometry of these lethal lines had a certain cold beauty, Pirius thought, even though he knew what hell was being unleashed for those unlucky enough to be caught on the exposed surface of the Rock.

Now, though, the rectilinear perfection of the starbreaker beam was blurred, as a turbulent fog rose over the Rock's horizon.

Cohl said, 'What's that mist? Air? Maybe the starbreakers are cutting through to the sealed caverns.'

'I don't think so,' said Enduring Hope levelly. 'That's rock. A mist of molten rock. They are smashing the asteroid to gas.'

Molten rock, Pirius thought grimly, no doubt laced with traces of what had recently been complex organic compounds, thoroughly burned.

But, for all the devastation they were wreaking, the Xeelee weren't coming around the horizon. They were focusing all their firepower on one side of the Rock.

Still Pirius waited for orders, but the tactical analysis took too long. Suddenly human ships came fleeing around the curve of the Rock, sparks of Earth-green bright against the dull grey of the asteroid ground. The formation had collapsed, then, despite the squadron leaders' continuing bellowed commands. And down on the Rock those little flecks of light, each a human being trapped in lethal fire, swarmed and scattered, fanning out of the trench system and over the open ground. Even from here it looked like panic, a rout.

It got worse. All across the Rock's visible hemisphere implosions began, as if its surface was being bombarded by unseen meteorites. But the floors of these evanescent craters broke up and collapsed, and through a mist of grey dust a deeper glow was revealed, coming up from *inside* the Rock. It was as if the surface was dissolving, and pink-white light was burning its way out of this shell of stone. The Xeelee, Pirius thought: the Xeelee were burning their way right through the Rock itself.

Enduring Hope understood what was happening half a second before Pirius did. 'Lethe,' he said. 'Get us out of here, pilot. Lift, lift!'

Cohl said weakly, 'But our orders—'

But Pirius was already hauling on his controls. All around him ships were breaking from the line and pulling back.

Even as the Rock fell away, Pirius could see the endgame approaching. For a last, remarkable instant, the Rock held together, and that inner light picked out the complex tracery of the trench network, as if the face of the Rock was covered by a map of shining threads. The asteroid's uneven horizon lifted, bulging.

And then the Rock flew apart.

Suddenly the *Claw* was surrounded by a hail of white-hot fragments that rushed upwards all around it. The greenship threw itself around every axis to survive this deadly inverted storm. The motions were rapid, juddery, disconcerting; even cloaked by inertial shields, Pirius could feel a ghost of his craft's jerky motion deep in his bones.

Everybody on the Rock must already be dead, he thought, as the ship tried to save him. It was a terrible, monstrous thought, impossible to absorb. And the dying wasn't over yet.

Pirius's squadron leader called for discipline, for her crews to try to regroup, to take the fight to the enemy. But then she was cut off.

Cohl shrieked, '*Flies*! Here they come—'

Pirius saw them: a swarm of flies, rising out of the core of the shattered rock like insects from a corpse, their black-as-night wings unfolding. They had burned their way right through the heart of an asteroid. Some greenships were already throwing themselves back into the Xeelee fire. But the Xeelee deployed their starbreaker beams; those lethal tongues almost lovingly touched the fleeing greenships.

Pirius had no meaningful orders. So he ran. The *Claw* raced from the ruin of the Rock. The cloud of debris thinned, and the jittery motion of the *Claw* subsided. But when Pirius looked back he saw a solid black bank, a phalanx of Xeelee nightfighters.

He had no idea where he was running to, how he might evade the Xeelee. He ran anyhow.

And the Xeelee came after him.

CHAPTER 2

The battle at the centre of the Galaxy was watched from far away by cold eyes and orderly, patient minds.

Port Sol was a Kuiper object, a moon of ice. It was one of a hundred thousand such objects orbiting in the dark at the rim of Sol system. It was not the largest; there were monstrous worldlets out here larger than Pluto. But it was no closer to other planetesimals than Earth was to Mars.

This immense belt was a relic of the birth of Sol system itself. Around the fast-growing sun, grains of dust and ice had accreted into swarming planetesimals. Close to the fitfully burning young star, the planetesimals had been crowded enough to combine further into planets. Further out, though, out here, there had been too much room. The formation of larger bodies had stalled, and the ancient planetesimals survived, to swim on in the silent dark.

Port Sol's human history had begun when its scattered kin had first been populated by a rum assortment of engineers, prospectors, refugees and dissidents from the inner system. More than twenty thousand years had worn away since then. Now Port Sol's great days were long past. Its icescapes, crowded with immense ruins, were silent once more.

But still, lights sparked on its surface.

This lonely worldlet had been home to Luru Parz for far longer than she cared to remember. Sometimes she felt she was as old as it was, her heart as cold as its primordial ice. But from here she watched the activities of humanity, from the bustling worlds of Sol system all the way to the heart of the Galaxy itself.

And now she watched Pirius, Dans and their crews as they strove to evade their Xeelee pursuers. The incident, brought to her attention by patient semi-sentient monitors, unfolded in a Virtual image, a searing-bright slice of Galaxy centre light, here on the rim of Sol system.

Faya, her cousin, was with her. 'They're lost,' Faya sighed.

'Perhaps,' Luru said. 'But if they find a way to live through this, or even if not, they might discover something useful for the future.'

'There is always that.'

'Watch . . .'

The tiny, remote drama unfolded.

CHAPTER 3

Aboard the *Claw*, a strange calm settled. The loops were all but silent now, save for the ragged breathing of Pirius's crew. But behind them that black cloud of Xeelee ships closed relentlessly.

Another ship came alongside the *Claw*. It had taken a lot of damage. One strut had been crudely amputated, and a second blister looked cloudy; but the pilot's blister was a bright spark of light. Pirius looked back, but nobody else followed: just the two of them.

Pirius recognised the other's sigil. 'Dans?'

'Large as life, Pirius.'

'I recognised your lousy piloting.'

'Yeah, yeah. So why aren't you dead yet?'

'Shut up.' It was Cohl. 'Shut *up*.'

'Navigator, take it easy.'

'Do we have to endure this garbage, today of all days?'

'Today of all days we need it,' Enduring Hope said.

Pirius said, 'Dans, your crew—'

'I'm on my own,' Dans said grimly. 'But I'm still flying. So. Every day you learn something new, right? Those Xeelee always have something up their sleeves. If they have sleeves.'

'Yes. In retrospect it's an obvious tactic.'

So it was. The Xeelee's usual approach was to swathe a Rock with fire, trying to scour out the trenches and get to the monopole cannons, all the time harassed by greenships and other defensive forces. This time they had focused their assault on one side of the Rock, easily perforating the defensive forces there. And they had used their starbreakers to burrow *straight through* the asteroid and out

13

the other side, thus destroying the Rock itself and hurling themselves without warning on the remaining defenders.

'It's going to take some counter-thinking,' Pirius said. 'We'll need scouts further out, perhaps.'

'Yeah,' Dans said. 'And flexible formations to swarm wherever the first assault goes in.'

'It won't be us doing it,' said Cohl grimly.

'You aren't dead yet, kid,' Dans called. She was twenty, a year older than Pirius and a veteran of no less than six missions before today.

Cohl said, 'Look at that crowd behind us.' The flies were still closing. 'We can't outrun them,' the navigator said. 'In fact we shouldn't be trying; we have orders to stand and fight. We are already dead. It's our duty to be dead. "A brief life burns brightly." '

It was the most ancient slogan of the Expansion, said to have been coined by Hama Druz himself thousands of years before, standing in the rubble of an occupied Earth. In a regime of endless war it was prideful to die young and in battle, a crime to grow old unnecessarily.

Under such a regime the highest form of humanity was the child soldier.

But Dans said rudely, "I knew you were going to say that.'

Pirius heard Cohl gasp.

Dans said, 'So report me. Look, navigator, a brief life is one thing, but neither Hama Druz nor any of his legions of apologists down the ages told us to throw away our lives. If we took on that crowd of flies *they wouldn't even notice us*. Now what use is that?'

'Pilot—'

'She's right, Cohl,' Pirius said.

'But whatever the orthodoxy,' Enduring Hope said, 'can I just point out that they are *catching up*? Three minutes to intercept . . .'

Pirius said tensely, 'Dans, I don't want to boost your ego. But I suppose you have a plan?'

Dans took a breath. 'Sure. We go FTL.'

Cohl snapped, 'Impossible.'

This time it was the technician in her talking, and Pirius knew she was probably right. The FTL drive involved tinkering with the deepest structure of spacetime, and it was always advisable to do that in a smooth, flat place, empty of dense matter concentrations. The Galactic centre offered few such opportunities, and safe FTL use here needed planning.

Dans said rapidly, 'Sure it's risky. But it beats the certainty of death. And besides, the chances are the Xeelee won't follow. They aren't as stupid as we are.'

Enduring Hope said, 'Which way?'

Virtuals flickered in their blisters, downloaded by Dans. 'I say we cut across the Mass to Sag A East . . .'

The bulk of the Galaxy's luminous matter was confined to a flat sheet, the delicate spiral arms contained in a plane as thin in proportion to its width as a piece of paper. But at its heart was a Core, a bulge of stars some five hundred light years across. This region swarmed with human factory worlds and military posts. Within the Core was the Central Star Mass, millions of stars crammed into a space some thirty light years wide. The two brightest sources of radio noise within the Mass were called Chandra – or, officially, Sag A*, the black hole at the very centre – and Sag A East, a remnant of an ancient explosion.

Such names, so Pirius had once been told by an over-informative Commissary, were themselves relics of deeper human history. The soldiers to whom the Galaxy centre was a war zone knew this geography. But few knew that 'Sag' stood for Sagittarius, and fewer still that Sagittarius had once referred to a pattern in the few scattered stars visible from Earth.

'Two minutes to closing,' Cohl reported edgily.

'Short hops,' Dans insisted. 'Forty minutes to cross a few dozen light years to East. Maybe we'll find cover there. We regroup, patch up, go home – and die another day. Come on, what is there to lose? For you it will be easy! At least you still have a navigator.'

Starbreaker beams flickered around Pirius. The nightfighters were getting their range; at any moment one of these beams could touch his own blister. He would die without even knowing it.

'We do it,' he said.

Dans quickly downloaded a synchronisation command. 'The two of us, then. On my mark. Two – one—'

Space flexed.

The nearby stars winked out of existence. The general background endured, but now a new pattern of hot young stars greeted Pirius, a new three-dimensional constellation.

Space flexed.

Again he jumped, to be faced by another constellation.

And again, and yet another blue-white supergiant loomed right in front of him, immense flares working across its broad face, but it disappeared to be replaced by another set of disorderly stars, which disappeared in their turn . . .

Jump, jump, *jumpjumpjumpjump* . . .

As the jumps came more frequently than Pirius's eyes could follow, the ride settled down to an illusion of continuity. There was even a sense of motion now, as distant stars slid slowly past. It did him no good at all to remind himself that with each jump spacetime was pivoting through its higher dimensions, or that even millennia after the technology's first use the philosophers still couldn't agree whether the entity that emerged from each jump was still, in any meaningful way, 'him'.

First things first, Pirius.

He glanced over his systems and his crew. 'Everything nominal,' he said. He raised a thumb to the pilot of the second ship, and through a blister's starred carapace he saw a gesture in response.

'We're still breathing,' Enduring Hope said. 'But take a look out back.'

The cloud of Xeelee ships had vanished. But a single dogged craft remained, its wings spread black and wide, a graceful sycamore-seed shape.

Dans said, 'Stubborn bastards, aren't they?'

Hope said, 'At least we bought some time.'

'Yes. We've still got thirty minutes before East,' Pirius said. He waved his hands through Virtual consoles, initiating self-diagnostic and repair routines to run throughout the ship. 'This is a chance to take care of yourselves,' he told his crew. 'Eat. Drink. Take a leak. Sleep if you have to. Use your med-cloaks if you need them.'

Cohl said blankly, 'Eat? Sleep? *We're going to die.* We'd do better to review why we have to die.'

Dans said, 'Lethe, child, there are no Commissary arses to lick out here. Don't you find the Doctrines cold comfort?'

'On the contrary,' Cohl said.

Pirius glanced down at Cohl's blister. He imagined her in there, wrapped up in her skinsuit, swaddled by machines, clinging to the pitiless logic of the Doctrines.

Thousands of years had worn away since the first human interstellar flight, and since humanity had begun the mighty march across the Galaxy called the Third Expansion. The Expansion was an ideological programme, a titanic project undertaken by a mankind united by the Doctrines forged by Hama Druz after mankind's near-extinction. In the fierce light of human determination lesser species had burned away. At last only one opponent was left: the Xeelee, the most powerful foe of them all, with their concentration at the very centre of the Galaxy.

It was already millennia since the Third Expansion had closed around the centre. But the Xeelee responded in kind, just as resolutely. The Front had become a great stalled wave of destruction, a spherical zone of friction where two empires rubbed against each other. And seen from factory worlds scattered a hundred light years deep, the sky glowed pink with the light of endless war.

The Xeelee would not engage with mankind in any way but war. There was no negotiation, no rapprochement, no contact that was not lethal. To the Xeelee humans were vermin – and they had a right to think so, for they were superior to humans in every way that could be measured. And so, only if each human were prepared to spend her life without question for the common good would humanity as a whole prevail. This was the Doctrinal thinking taught in seminaries and cadre groups and academies across the Galaxy: if humans must be vermin, humans would fight like vermin, and die like vermin.

For millennia humans, fast-breeding, had toiled to fill the Galaxy. Now, whichever star you picked out of the crowded sky, you could be confident that there was a human presence there. And for millennia humans had hurled themselves into the Xeelee fire, vermin fighting back the only way they had, with their bodies and souls, hoping to overcome the Xeelee by sheer numbers.

Pirius knew a lot of fighting people thought the way Cohl did. By keeping mankind united and unchanged across millennia, it had self-evidently worked. Many soldiers feared that if the Doctrines were ever even questioned, everything would fall apart and that defeat, or worse, would inevitably follow. Compared to that risk, the remote notion of victory seemed irrelevant.

Dans said breezily, 'So what about you, Tuta?'

'My name is Enduring Hope,' the engineer said, apparently not offended.

'Oh, I forgot. You're one of those infinity-botherers, aren't you? So what do you believe? Is some great hero from the far future going to swoop down and rescue you?'

Pirius had tried to stay away from Enduring Hope's peculiar sect, who called themselves 'Friends of Wigner'. Pirius thought of himself as pragmatic; he was prepared to put up with nonsense names if it kept his engineer happy. But the Friends' cult violated Doctrinal law just by its very existence.

'You can mock,' Hope said. 'But you don't understand.'

'Then tell me,' Dans said.

'All of this' – Hope made an expansive gesture – 'is a first cut. Everybody knows this. In this war of FTL ships and time travel, we stack up contingencies in the Library of Futures on Earth. History is a draft, a draft we change all the time.'

'And if history is mutable—'

'Then nothing is inevitable. Not even the past.'

'I don't understand,' Pirius admitted.

Dans said, 'If you can redraft history, everything can be fixed. He thinks that even if he dies today, then history will somehow, some day, be put right, and all such unfortunate errors removed.'

'Hope, is that right?'

'Something like it.'

Dans snapped, 'Pirius, the creed is anti-Doctrine, but it's just as much a trap as the Doctrines. A Druz junkie thinks death and defeat reinforce the strength of the Doctrines. A Friend believes defeat is irrelevant because it will all be erased some day. Either way, *you don't fight to win*. You see? Why else has this damn war stalled so long?'

Pirius felt uncomfortable with such heresy – even now, even here.

With a trace of malice Hope said, 'But you're as doomed as we are, pilot Dans.'

Cohl said, 'What about you, Pirius? What do you want to achieve?'

Pirius thought it over. 'I want to be remembered.'

He heard slow, ironic applause from Dans.

Cohl muttered, 'That is just *so* anti-Doctrinal!'

Hope murmured, 'Well, you might be about to get your chance, pilot. Sag A East is dead ahead. Dropping out of FTL.'

Jumpjumpjumpjump jump – jump – jump . . .

As the FTL hops slowed, they passed through a flickering barrage of stars, and electric-blue light flared around them: the pilots called it FTL light, a by-product of the energy the ship was shedding, coalescing into exotic evanescent particles. Pirius, relieved to get back to practical matters, tested the controls of the greenship and burped its two sublight drives – including the GUTdrive. This was a backup, a venerable human design, and one you would light up only in the direst of circumstances for fear of attracting quagmites . . .

While Pirius worked, the others had been looking at the view. 'Lethe,' Dans said softly.

Pirius glanced up.

Sagittarius A East was a bubble of shocked gas, light years wide, said to be the remnant of an immense explosion in the heart of the Galaxy. Suddenly Pirius was at the centre of a storm of light.

Dans called, 'And look at that.' She downloaded coordinates.

A pinpoint of crimson light glowed directly ahead, embedded in the glowing murk. It was a neutron star, according to their first scans, a star with the mass of the sun but only twenty kilometres across.

Dans said, 'That's a magnetar. And I think it's going to blow.'

Pirius understood none of that. 'What difference does that make—?'

'Here come the Xeelee,' Cohl snapped.

'Split up,' Dans called.

The greenships peeled away from each other. The single night-fighter, emerging from its own sequence of FTL jumps, seemed to hesitate for a heartbeat, as if wondering which of its soft targets to pursue first.

It turned towards the *Claw*.

'Lucked out,' Enduring Hope said softly.

'Hold on to your seats,' Pirius said. Lacking any better way to go, he hurled the ship towards the neutron star.

Still the Xeelee followed.

As the *Claw* squirted across space Pirius called up a magnified visual. The neutron star was a flattened sphere, brick red, its surface smooth to the limits of the magnification. Blue-white electric storms crackled over its surface.

Cohl said, 'That thing is rotating every *eight seconds*.'

Dans was standing off, Pirius saw from his tactical displays, watching the fleeing *Claw* and the dark shadow of her pursuer. 'Help me out here, Dans,' Pirius muttered.

'I'm with you all the way. When you flyby, take her in as close as you can to the surface of the star.'

'Why?'

'Maybe you can shake off the Xeelee.'

'And maybe we'll get creamed in the process.'

'There's always that possibility . . . The crust is actually solid, you know,' Dans said. 'There's an atmosphere of normal matter, no thicker than your finger. You can get as close as you like. Your shields will protect you from the tides, the radiation flux, the magnetic field. It's worth a try.'

'OK, guys,' Pirius said to Cohl and Enduring Hope. 'You heard Dans. Let's set a record.'

That won him ribald comments. But he could see that both Cohl and Hope were calling up fresh displays and hunching over their work. For a manoeuvre like this all three of them would have to work closely together, with Pirius controlling the line, Cohl monitoring *Claw*'s altitude over the star's surface, and Hope attitude and the ship's systems. As they settled to their tasks – and so put aside their Doctrine manuals or illicit prayer beads or whatever else they turned to for comfort – Pirius felt reassured. This was a good crew, at their best when they were committed to what they had been trained to do.

Light flared over his Virtual displays. 'Whoa . . .'

The star's surface had changed. Cracks gaped, and a brighter light shone from within. For a few seconds there was turmoil, as the whole surface shattered and melted, and remnant fragments swam. But as suddenly as it had begun the motion stopped and the crust coalesced once more, settling down to a new smoothness.

'Dans – what was *that*?'

'Starquake,' said Dans briskly.

'Maybe it's time you told me what a magnetar is . . .'

When this remnant was hatched out of its parent supernova explosion it happened to be spinning very rapidly – turning a thousand times a *second*, perhaps even faster. For the first few milliseconds of the neutron star's life the convection in the interior was ferocious, and where the hot material flowed it generated huge electrical currents. The whole thing was like a natural dynamo, and those tremendous currents generated an intense magnetic field. As the star lost energy through gravity and electromagnetic radiation, the spin slowed down. But a good fraction of the tremendous energy of that spin poured into the magnetic field.

Dans said, 'The field is still there, lacing the star's interior. The field will decay away quickly – "quickly" meaning in ten thousand years or so. But while the star is young—'

'And the crust quake?'

'The magnetism laces the solid surface, locking it to the interior layers. But the star is slowing down all the time, and the whirling interior drags at the solid crust. Every so often something gives. Happens all the time – like, hourly. But every so often the magnetic field collapses altogether, and the star flares, and . . . Lethe.'

'What?'

'Pirius, I've got another plan.'

'Make your flyby over these coordinates.' Data chattered into the *Claw*'s systems.

'Why?'

'Because a flare is about to blow there.' She downloaded a rapid Virtual briefing: a major collapse of the planet's magnetic field, more faulting in the crust – and a huge fireball punching out of the star's interior, a fist of compressed matter exploding out of its degenerate state. The magnetic field would hug the fireball to the star's surface, whirling it around in a manic waltz.

The energy released by this event, it seemed, would be enough to cause ionospheric effects in the atmospheres of planets across the Galaxy. 'Think of it,' Dans breathed. 'This flare will batter the upper air of Earth itself – though not for twenty-eight thousand years or so. And you are going to be sitting right on top of it.'

'Tell me why this is good news,' Pirius said grimly.

Dans paged through Virtual data, copying everything to Pirius. 'Pirius, in the middle of that flare the structure of spacetime itself is distorted. Now, we know Xeelee ships fly by swimming through spacetime, that their essence is controlled spacetime defects. Surely not even a Xeelee can survive that.'

'And so—'

'So you fly through the middle of the flare. See how it will arch through the magnetic field? If you pick your course right you can avoid the worst regions, while leading the Xeelee right into it.'

'But if a Xeelee can't survive,' Enduring Hope pointed out reasonably, 'how can we?'

Pirius said, 'We don't have a choice right now.'

'Four minutes to closest approach,' Dans said.

Pirius swept his fingers through Virtual displays. 'Cohl, I'm sending you Dans's coordinates. Let's aim for that flare. We can't end up any more dead, and at least it's a chance. Dans – we'll need time to plot the manoeuvre. How long will the flare last?'

Dans hesitated. 'Only a second or so at its fullest extent. Pirius, a neutron star is a small, very energetic object. Things happen *fast* . . . Oh.'

For a moment Pirius had actually allowed himself hope; now that warm spark died. It was just too fast. 'Right. So that millisecond is all we will have to compute our course, to lay it in, *and* to execute the manoeuvre.'

Cohl said. 'It would take our on board sentient tens of seconds to compute a course like that. Even if we had prior data on the shape of the flare. Which we don't. Of course a Xeelee could do it.'

'Three minutes,' Hope said evenly.

Pirius sighed. 'You know, just for a moment you had me going there, Dans.'

Dans snapped impatiently, 'Lethe, you guys are so *down*. Maybe there's a way even so. Pirius, have you ever heard of a Brun manoeuvre?'

'No.'

'Pilot school scuttlebutt. Somebody tried it, oh, a year or more back.'

Pirius hadn't heard of such a thing. But the turnover in pilots at the Arches Base was ferocious; there was little opportunity for field wisdom to be passed on.

'It didn't work.'

'That's reassuring.'

'But it could have,' Dans said. 'I looked into it – ran some simulations – thought it might be useful some day.'

'Two minutes thirty.'

'Pirius, listen to me. Stick to your course; make for the flare. But keep listening. I'll compute your manoeuvre for you. A way through the flare.'

'That's impossible.'

'Sure it is. And when I download the new trajectory you'd better be prepared to splice it into your systems.' Dans peeled away.

'Where are you going?'

'If this doesn't work out, don't touch my stuff.'

'Dans!'

'That's the last we'll see of her,' Enduring Hope said laconically.

'Two minutes,' Cohl said. 'One fifty-nine . . .

Pirius shut her up.

As the *Claw* fell through space there was no noise, no sense of motion. The Xeelee's slow convergence was silent, unspectacular. Even the neutron star would be invisible for all but a few seconds of closest approach. It was as if they were gliding along some smooth, invisible road.

The crew continued to work calmly, the three of them calling out numbers and curt instructions to each other. The *Assimilator's Claw* was drenched with artificial intelligence, sentient and otherwise, and its systems were capable of processing data far faster than human thought. But the systems were there to support human decision-making, not to replace it. That was the nature of the greenship's design, which in turn reflected Coalition policy under the Doctrines. This was a human war and would always remain so.

There was no sense of peril. And yet these seconds, which counted down remorselessly inside Pirius's head, would likely be the last of his life.

There was a flare of blue light, dead ahead, FTL blue – and then a streak of green. It was a greenship, cutting across his path. Suddenly data was chattering into the *Claw*'s systems. It was a new closest-approach trajectory.

Pirius saw Cohl sit up, astonished. 'Where did that come from? Pilot—'

'Load the course, navigator.'

A Virtual coalesced before Pirius: Dans's head, disembodied. Her face was small, round, neat, with a wide, sensual mouth, a mouth made for laughing. Now that mouth grinned at Pirius. 'Boo!'

'Dans, what—'

'It's not me, it's a downloaded Virtual. The real Dans will be hitting the surface of the star in—' She closed her eyes, and the image wavered, blocky pixels fluttering, as if she was concentrating. 'Three, two, one. Plop. Bye-bye.'

Pirius felt a stab of regret through his fear, bafflement, adrenalin rush. 'Dans, I'm sorry.'

'There was no other way – no other trajectory.'

'Trajectory from where?'

'From the future, of course. Pirius, you're twenty seconds from closest approach.'

He glimpsed a splash of red, wheeling past the blister. It was the neutron star.

Dans said, 'You need to cut in your GUTdrive. On my mark—'

'Dans, that's insane.' So it was; the antiquated GUTdrive was a last-resort backup system.

'I knew you'd argue. Your sublight won't work. Do it, asshole. Two, one—'

In the heart of the GUTdrive, specks of matter were compressed to conditions not seen since the aftermath of the Big Bang; released from their containment, these specks swelled immensely. This was the energy that had once driven the expansion of the universe itself; now it heated asteroid ice to a frenzied steam and forced it through rocket nozzles. A GUTdrive was just a water rocket, a piece of engineering that would have been recognisable to technicians on pre-spaceflight Earth twenty-five thousand years before.

But it worked, even here. A new light flared behind the ship, a ghostly grey-white, the light of the GUTdrive.

Dans winked at Pirius. 'See you on the other side.' The Virtual collapsed into a cloud of dispersing pixels.

The neutron star cannonballed at Pirius, suddenly huge. It was a flattened orange, visibly three-dimensional, its surface mottled by electric storms. It slid beneath *Claw*'s prow, and for a moment continents of orange-brown light fled beneath Pirius's blister. All these impressions in a second, less. But now a stronger light was looming over the horizon, yellow-white: it was the site of the flare, a grim dawn approaching.

And in the same instant the *Claw* juddered, shook, its drive stuttering. *What now?* Diagnostics popped up before Pirius. Around a Virtual of the GUTdrive core, shadowy shapes swarmed, Quagmites, he saw: the strange entities that were attracted by every use of a GUTdrive in this region – living things maybe, pests for sure, feeding off the primordial energy of the GUTdrive itself, and causing the mighty engine to stutter.

'The fly's on us!' Cohl cried.

When Pirius glanced at the reverse view he saw the Xeelee fighter. Its night-dark wings flexed and sparked as it swam through space after him. He had never seen a Xeelee so close, save in sims: he didn't know anybody who had, and lived. It was more than inhuman, he thought, more than just alien; it was a dark, primeval thing, not of this time. But it was perfectly adapted to this environment, as humans with their clumsy gadgetry were not.

And it was still on his tail. All he could do was fly the ship; there was absolutely nothing he could do about the Xeelee.

Ahead, light flared. Over the horizon came rushing a massive flaw in the star's crust, a pool of blue-white light kilometres wide from which starstuff poured in a vertical torrent, radiating as much energy in a fraction of a second as Earth's sun would lose in ten thousand years. An arch, yellow-white, was forming above the star's tight horizon, kilometres high. In places the arch feathered and streamed, tracing out the lines of the magnetic field that restrained it.

On a neutron star, events happened fast. The rent in the surface was already healing, the arch collapsing almost as soon as it had formed, its material dragged down by the star's magisterial gravity field.

And the *Claw* flew right underneath it.

Pirius's blister shuddered as if it would tear itself apart. Those mottled surface features whipped beneath, and the arch loomed *above* him. He had never known such a sensation of sheer speed. He might not live through this, but Lethe, it was quite a ride.

There was a punch in the small of his back, the ghost of hundreds of gravities as the *Claw* kicked its way out of the star's gravity well.

The neutron star whipped away into darkness. The arch had already collapsed.

And in the last instant he glimpsed the Xeelee, behind him. No longer an implacable, converging foe, it was folding over, as if its graceful wings were crumpled in an invisible fist.

The *Assimilator's Claw* hung in empty space, far from the neutron star. The crew tended their slight wounds, and tried to get used to still being alive. They saw to their ship's systems; the encounter with the quagmites had done a good deal of damage to the GUTdrive.

And they reconstructed what had happened during those crucial moments at the magnetar.

At its heart the magnetic field embracing the flare had been as strong as any field since the first moments of the universe itself. At such field strengths atoms themselves were distorted, forced into skinny cylindrical shapes; no ordinary molecular structure could survive. Photons were split and combined. Even the structure of spacetime was distorted: it became *birefringent*, Pirius learned, crystalline.

It was this last which had probably done for the Xeelee. Nobody knew for sure how a nightfighter's sublight drive worked. But the drive *seemed* to work by manipulating spacetime itself. In a place where spacetime crystallised, that manipulation could no longer work – but the *Claw*'s much cruder GUTdrive had kept functioning, despite the quagmites.

All that was straightforward enough. Just physics.

'But what I can't get my head around,' Pirius told Dans's Virtual, 'is how you appeared out of nowhere and squirted down the right evasive manoeuvre for us, based on a knowledge of the flare's evolution *before it happened*.'

Dans said tinnily, 'It was just an application of FTL technology. Remember, every FTL ship—'

'Is a time machine.' Every child learned that before she got out of her first cadre.

'I pulled away. Out of trouble, I watched the flare unfold, recorded it. I took my time to work out your optimal path – how you *would* have avoided destruction if you'd had the time to figure it out.'

Pirius said, 'But it was academic. You got the answer after we were already dead.'

'And I had to watch you die,' said Dans wistfully. 'When the action was over, the Xeelee out of the way, I used my sublight to ramp up to about a third lightspeed. Then I cut in the FTL.'

Cohl understood. 'You jumped back into the past – to the moment just *before* we hit the flare. And you fed us the manoeuvre you had worked out at leisure. You used time travel to gain the time you needed to plot the trajectory.'

'And that's the Brun manoeuvre,' Dans said with satisfaction.

'It's some computing technique,' Cohl mused. 'With the right vectors you could solve an arbitrarily difficult problem in a finite time – break it into components, feed it back to the source—'

Pirius was still trying to think it through. 'Time paradoxes make my head ache,' he said. 'In the original draft of the timeline, *Claw* was destroyed by the flare and you flew away. In the second draft, you flew back in time to deliver your guidance, and then you – that copy of you – flew into the neutron star.'

'Couldn't be helped,' Dans said.

He could see she was waiting for him to figure it out. 'But that means, in this new draft of the timeline, we survived. *And so you don't need to come back in time to save us*. We're already saved.' He was confused. 'Did I get that right?'

Hope said, 'But there would be a paradox. If she *doesn't* go back in time the information that future-Dans brought back would have come out of nowhere.'

Cohl said, 'Yes, it's a paradox. But that happens all the time. A ship comes limping back from a lost battle. We change our strategy, the battle never happens – but the ship and its crew and their memories linger on, stranded without a past. History is resilient. It can stand a little tinkering, a few paradoxical relics from vanished futures, bits of information popping out of nowhere.' Cohl evidently had a robust view of time-travel paradoxes. As an FTL navigator she needed one.

But Pirius's only concern was Dans. 'So can you save yourself?'

'Ah,' Dans said gently. 'Sadly not. More than one Xeelee chased us after all. If I hadn't hung around to work out your course I might have got away. I'm all that's left, I'm afraid. Little pixellated me . . .'

'Dans—' Pirius shook his head. 'You gave your life for me. *Twice*.'

'Yeah, I did. So remember.'

'What?'

She glared at him. 'When you get back to Arches, leave my stuff alone.' And she popped out of existence.

For long minutes they sat in silence, the three of them in their blisters.

'Here's something else,' Cohl said at last. 'To get back to Arches from here we'll have to complete another closed-timelike-curve trajectory.'

'A what . . . Oh.' Another jump into the past.

'We'll arrive two years before we set off on the mission.' She sounded awed.

Hope said, 'I'll meet my past self. Lethe, I hope I'm not as bad as I remember.'

'And, Pirius,' Cohl said, 'there will be a younger version of Dans. A third version. *Dans won't have to die*. None of this will be real.'

Pirius really did hate time paradoxes. 'Time-loops or not, *we* lived through this. We will remember. It's real enough. Navigator, do you want to lay in that course?'

'Sure . . .'

Hope said dryly, 'You might want to delay a little before kicking off for home, pilot. Take a look.' He projected a Virtual into their blisters.

It was a shape, drifting in space. Pirius made out a slender body, crumpled wings folded. 'It's the fly,' he breathed.

Hope said, 'We have to take it back to base.'

Cohl said, 'We captured a Xeelee? Nobody ever did that before. Pirius, you said you wanted to make your name stand out. Well, perhaps you have. We'll be heroes!'

Hope laughed. 'I thought heroism is anti-Doctrinal?'

Pirius brought the greenship about and sent it skimming to the site of the derelict. 'First we need to figure how to grapple that thing.'

As it turned out – when they had got hold of the Xeelee, and with difficulty secured it for FTL flight and had hauled it all the way back to the base in Arches Cluster – they found themselves to be anything but heroes.

CHAPTER 4

This was the energetic heart of a large galaxy, a radiation bath where humans had to rely on their best technological capabilities to keep their fragile carbon-chemistry bodies from being fried. But to the quagmites it was a cold, dead place, in a dismal and unwelcoming era. The quagmites were survivors of a hotter, faster age than this.

They were drawn to the neutron star, for in its degenerate-matter interior there was a hint of the conditions of the warm and bright universe they had once known. But even here everything was frozen solid, comparatively. They were like humans stranded on an ice moon, a place where water, the very stuff of life, is frozen as hard as bedrock.

Still, every now and again there was a spark of something brighter – like the firefly speck which had come hurtling out of nowhere and skimmed the surface of the neutron star. The quagmites lived fast, even in this energy-starved age. To them the fractions of a second of the closest approach to the neutron star were long and drawn-out. They had plenty of time to come close, to bask in the warmth of the ship's GUTdrive, and to feed.

And, as was their way, they left their marks in the hull of the ship, the ghostly, frozen shell that surrounded that speck of brilliance.

When the ship had gone the quagmites dispersed, ever hungry, ever resentful, searching for more primordial heat.

On Port Sol, Luru Parz turned to her cousin with a quiet satisfaction.

'I knew they would survive,' she said. 'And in the technique they have stumbled upon I see a glimmer of opportunity. I must go.'

'Where?'

'Earth.' Luru Parz padded away, her footsteps almost silent.

CHAPTER 5

If you grew up in Arches, meeting your own future self was no big deal.

The whole point of the place was that from the moment you were born you were trained to fly FTL starships. And everybody knew that an FTL starship was a time machine. Most people figured out for themselves that that meant there might come a day when you would meet a copy of yourself from the future – or the past, depending which end of the transaction you looked at it from.

Pirius, a seventeen-year-old ensign, had always thought of meeting himself as an interesting trial to be faced one day, along with other notable events like his first solo flight, his first combat sortie, his first sight of a Xeelee, his first screw. But in practice, when his future self turned up out of the blue, it turned out to be a lot more complicated than that.

The day began badly. The bunk bed shuddered, and Pirius woke with a start.

Above him, Torec was growling, 'Lethe, are we under attack? – oh. Good morning, Captain.'

'Ensign.' Captain Seath's heavy boot had jolted Pirius awake.

Pirius scrambled out of his lower bunk. He got tangled up with Torec, who was climbing down from the upper tier. Just for a second Pirius was distracted by Torec's warm, sleepy smell, reminding him of their fumble under the sheets before they had fallen asleep last night. But soon they were standing to attention before Seath, in their none-too-clean underwear.

Seath was a stocky, dark woman, no more than thirty, and might once have been beautiful. But scar tissue was crusted over her brow, the left side of her face was wizened and melted, expressionless, and her mouth drooped. She could have had all this fixed, of course, but Seath was a training officer, and if you were an officer you wore your scars proudly.

Astonishingly, Torec was snickering.

Seath said, 'I'm pleased to see part of you is awake, ensign.'

Pirius glanced down. To his horror a morning erection bulged out of his shorts. Seath reached out a fingernail – bizarrely it was manicured – and flicked the tip of Pirius's penis. The hard-on shrivelled immediately. Pirius forced himself not to flinch.

To his chagrin, *everybody* saw this.

To left and right the great corridor of the barracks stretched away, a channel of two-tier bunks, equipment lockers and bio facilities. Below and above too, before and behind, through translucent walls and ceilings, you could see similar corridors arrayed in a neat rectangular lattice, fading to milky indistinctness. Everywhere, the ranks of bunks were emptying as the recruits filed out for the callisthenics routines that began each day. This entire moonlet, the Barracks Ball, was hollowed out and filled up with a million ensigns and other trainees, a million would-be pilots and navigators and engineers and ground crew, all close to Pirius's age, all eager to be thrown into the endless fray.

Arches Base was primarily a training academy for flight crews. The cadets here were highly intelligent, physically fit, very lively – and intensely competitive, at work and off duty. And so the place was riven with factions which constantly split, merged and reformed, and with feuds and love affairs that could flare with equal vigour. Today it was Pirius's bunk that Captain Seath was standing before, and from the corner of his eye Pirius could see that everybody was looking at him with unbridled glee. His life wasn't going to be worth living after this.

Seath was walking away. 'Pirius, put your pants on. A ship's come in. You've got a visitor.'

'A visitor? . . . Sorry, sir. Can I ask what ship?'

Seath called over her shoulder, 'The *Assimilator's Claw*. And she's been in a scrap.'

That was enough to tell Pirius who his visitor must be. Torec and Pirius stared at each other, bewildered.

Seath was already receding down the long corridor, here and there snapping out a command to an unfortunate ensign.

Pirius scrambled into his pants, jacket and boots. He held a clean-cloth over his face, endured a second of stinging pain as the semi-sentient material cleaned out his pores and dissolved his stubble, and hurried after Seath. He was relieved to hear Torec hurrying along in his wake; he had a feeling he was going to need some familiar company today.

Pirius and Torec bundled after Captain Seath into a flitter. The little ship, not much more than a transparent cylinder, closed itself up and squirted away, out of the Barracks Ball and into space.

All around Pirius, worlds hailed like cannonballs.

The Barracks Ball was one of more than a hundred swarming worldlets that comprised the Arches Cluster Base. Beyond the rocks, of course, hung the hundreds of giant young stars that comprised the cluster itself, tightly packed – in fact, the largest concentration of such stars in the Galaxy. Above the stars themselves was a still more remarkable sight. Glowing filaments, ionised gas dragged along the loops of the Galaxy's magnetic field, combined into a wispy inter-stellar architecture constructed on a scale of light years. The character-istic shape of these filaments had, it was said, given 'Arches' its name.

The Galaxy centre itself was just fifty light years away.

It was a stunning, bewildering sky – but Pirius, Torec and Seath had all grown up with it. They made no comment as the flitter laced its perilous route through the shifting three-dimensional geometry of the base.

Besides, Pirius had more on his mind than rocks and stars.

Torec looked composed. She was a little shorter than he was, a little broader at the shoulders. She had a thin face, but a full mouth, startling grey eyes, and brown hair she wore in rows of short spikes. Her nose was upturned, a feature she hated, but Pirius thought it made her beautiful. They had been each other's squeezes, in barracks argot, for a couple of months now – staggering longevity in the fevered atmosphere of the barracks. But, despite the taunting from their colleagues, they showed no signs of falling out. Pirius was glad that Torec's calm presence was with him as he faced the strangeness to come.

It was standard policy for any data FTL-leaked from possible futures to be presented immediately to any individual named in that data. Some of Pirius's friends even knew when and how they were going to die. And so Pirius already knew, everybody knew, that in future he was destined to pilot a ship called the *Assimilator's Claw*. But the *Claw* hadn't yet been commissioned. If a version of the *Claw* had come into dock – and a captain had taken the time to come get him from his bunk to meet a visitor – that visitor could only be one person, and his heart hammered.

The fiitter's destination was a dry dock. Perhaps a hundred kilometres across, this Rock was pocked by pits where ships nestled. They were all shapes and sizes, from one-person fighters smaller than greenships through to ponderous, kilometre-wide Spline ships, the living vessels that had been the backbone of the human fleet for fifteen thousand years.

And in one such yard sat a single, battered greenship. It must be the *Assimilator's Claw*, and as Pirius first glimpsed the scarred hull of his future command, his breath caught in his throat.

Torec nudged his elbow and pointed. A cluster of ships hovered maybe half a kilometre above the Ball's surface in a cubical array, and Pirius saw the flicker of starbreaker beams and other weapons. Within the array he glimpsed a sleek shape, caged within that three-dimensional fence of fire, a shape with folded wings, black as night even in the glare of the cluster's huge suns.

'Lethe,' he said. 'That's a Xeelee ship.'

'And that,' said Seath coldly, 'is the least of your troubles.'

There was no time to see more.

The flitter dropped into a port. Even before the docking was complete Seath was walking towards the hatch.

Pirius and Torec followed her into a bustling corridor. It was only a short walk through a hurrying crowd of engineers and facility managers to the *Claw*'s pit. And at the airlock Seath slowed, glanced at Pirius, and stood back to allow him to go ahead first.

This was Pirius's moment, then. His pulse pounding, he stepped forward.

Three crew waited by the lock: one woman, two men. Dressed in scorched and battered skinsuits, their chests adorned with a stylised claw logo, they were clutching bulbs of drinking water. Pirius glanced at the woman – short, wiry, a rather sour face, though with a fine, strong nose. Pale red hair was tucked into her skinsuit cap. One of the men was heavy-set. His face was broad and round, his ears protruding; he looked competent, but somehow vulnerable. They were both grimy and hollow-eyed with fatigue. 'Cohl', he read from their nametags, and 'Tuta' – or 'Enduring Hope' according to a hand-lettered addendum. He had never met them, in his timeline, but he already knew these names from the foreknowledge briefings: they were his future comrades, who he would choose for his crew, and with whom he would risk his life. He wondered who they were.

He was avoiding the main issue, of course.

The other man, the pilot, wasn't tall, but he topped Pirius by a good half-head, and, under the skinsuit, was bulkier. Scath had told him that *this* version was aged nineteen, two years older – two more years of growing, of filling out, of training. At last Pirius looked the pilot in the face.

Time was slippery. The way Pirius understood it, it was only the speed of light that imposed causal sequences on events.

According to the venerable arguments of relativity there wasn't even a common 'now' you could establish across significant distances. All that existed were events, points in space and time. If you had to travel slower than lightspeed from one event to the next, then everything was OK, for the events would be causally connected: you would see everything growing older in an orderly manner.

But with FTL travel, beyond the bounds of lightspeed, the orderly structure of space and time became irrelevant, leaving nothing but the events, disconnected incidents floating in the dark. And with an FTL ship you could hop from one event to another arbitrarily, without regard to any putative cause-and-effect sequence.

In this war it wasn't remarkable to have dinged-up ships limping home from an engagement that hadn't happened yet; at Arches Base that occurred every day. And it wasn't unusual to have news from the future. In fact, sending messages to command posts *back in the past* was a deliberate combat tactic. The flow of information from future to past wasn't perfect; it all depended on complicated geometries of trajectories and FTL leaps. But it was enough to allow the Commissaries, in their Academies on distant Earth, to compile libraries of possible futures, invaluable precognitive data that shaped strategies – even if decisions made in the present could wipe out many of those futures before they came to pass.

A war fought with FTL technology had to be like this.

Of course foreknowledge would have been a great advantage – if not for the fact that the other side had precisely the same capability. In an endless sequence of guesses and counter-guesses, as history was tweaked by one side or the other, and then tweaked again in response, the timeline was endlessly redrafted. With both sides foreseeing engagements to come for decades, even centuries ahead, and each side able to counter the other's move even before it had been formulated, it was no wonder that the war had long settled down to a lethal stalemate, stalled in a static front that enveloped the Galaxy's heart.

For Pirius, it was like looking in the mirror – but not quite.

The architecture was the same: a broad face, symmetrical but too flat to be good-looking, with sharp blue eyes and a mat of thick black hair. But the details were different. Under a sheen of sweat and grime the pilot's face was hard, the eyes sunken. It was as if the bones of his skull had pushed out of his flesh. He looked much older than nineteen, much more than two years older than Pirius.

In that first glance Pirius quailed from this man. And yet he was so familiar, so like himself, and he felt drawn.

He held out his hand. The pilot took it and clasped firmly. It was an oddly neutral feeling, like holding his own hand; the pilot's skin seemed to be at precisely the same temperature as Pirius's own.

'I saw the Xeelee ship you brought back,' Pirius ventured. 'Quite a trophy.'

'Long story,' said the pilot. He didn't sound interested, in the Xeelee or in Pirius. His voice sounded nothing like Pirius's own, in his head.

'So I get to be a hero?'

The pilot looked mournful. 'I'm sorry,' he said, apparently sincerely.

That bewildered Pirius. 'For what?'

There was a heavy hand on his shoulder. He turned and found himself facing a bulky man with the long black robes and shaven head of a Commissary.

'Pirius – *both* of you! – I've been assigned as your counsel in the trial,' the Commissary said. 'My name is Nilis.'

Even at this moment of confusion Pirius stared. Arches was for young people; with white stubble, his face jowly, his skin pocked with deep pores, this Commissary was the oldest person Pirius had ever seen. And he was none too smart. His robe seemed to have been patched, and its hem was worn and dirty. Behind him were two more Commissaries, who looked a lot less sympathetic.

Nilis's eyes were strange, blue and watery, and he looked on Pirius and the pilot with a certain soft fascination, 'You're so alike! Well, of course you would be. And both so young . . . Temporal twins, what a remarkable thing, my eyes! But how will I tell you apart? Look – suppose I call *you*, the older pilot, Pirius Blue. Because you're from the future – blueshifted, you see? And *you* will be Pirius Red. How would that suit you?'

Pirius shook his head. *Pirius Red*? That wasn't his name. Suddenly he wasn't even himself any more. 'Sir – Commissary – I don't understand. Why do *I* need a counsel?'

'Oh, my eyes, has nobody explained that to you yet?'

The pilot – Pirius Blue – stepped forward, irritated. 'Come on, kid, you know the drill. They're throwing the book at me for what happened aboard the *Claw*. And if they are charging *me*—'

Pirius had heard rumours of this procedure but had never understood. 'I will be put on trial too.'

'You got it,' said his older self neutrally.

Pirius was to be tried for a crime that he *hadn't even committed yet*. Confused, scared, he turned around looking for Torec.

Torec shrugged. 'Tough break.' She seemed withdrawn, as if she was trying to disengage from him and the whole mess.

Pirius Blue was looking at him with revulsion. 'Do you have to let your jaw dangle like that? You're showing us both up.' He brushed past Pirius and spoke to Captain Seath. 'Sir, where do I report?'

'Debriefing first, pilot. Then you're in the hands of Commissary Nilis.' She turned and marched him away; the battle-weary crew of the *Claw* followed.

Nilis touched Pirius Red's shoulder, 'You come with me. I think we need to talk.'

Nilis had been assigned quarters in a Rock the ensigns knew as Officer Country. To get there from the dry dock, with Pirius, Nilis endured a short flitter hop through the swarm of captive asteroids that made up the base.

In the sky outside the hull, worldlets plummeted like fists.

Planets were rare, here in the Core of the Galaxy; the stars were too close-packed for stable systems to form. But there was plenty of dust and ice, and it gathered into great swarms of asteroids. Some of the base asteroids were unworked – just raw rock, still the lumpy aggregates they had been when tethered and gathered here. The rest had been melted, carved, blown into translucent bubbles like the Barracks Ball. Worked or not, they were all wrapped in stabilising superconductor hoops, like presents wrapped in gleaming electric blue ribbon, and they all had Higgs-field inertia-control facilities mounted on their surfaces. The Higgs facilities gave a gravity of a standard unit or so on the worldlets' surfaces, and provided stable fields in their interior: tiered for a Barracks Ball, more complex in other Rocks depending on their uses.

And the generators drew the Rocks to each other. Mutually attracting, they swooped and swirled about each other in an endless three-dimensional dance, mad miniature planets free of the stabilising influence of a sun. Some of the Rocks swam so close to the flitter that you could see maintenance crew working on the surfaces, crawling over the tightly curved horizons like bugs on bits of food.

Pirius saw, bemused, that Nilis kept his eyes closed all the way through the hop.

Pirius had his mind on bigger issues. So his whole life was suddenly defined by whatever that arrogant clone of himself had done downstream! He wished he could meet Pirius Blue alone to have it out.

Nilis's room, deep in the belly of Officer Country, was small. It was unfurnished save for a low bunk, a desk with a chair, and a nano-food niche. Pirius sat awkwardly on the bunk, and declined an offer of food or drink. Nilis himself sipped water. The walls of the room were translucent, as were all the walls throughout the Base, but they were buried so deep in this warren of offices and conference rooms that the sky beyond could barely be glimpsed.

'Which is the way I prefer it, I'm afraid,' Nilis said with a rueful smile. He sat on the room's single chair, his robes awkwardly rucked up to expose scrawny shins. 'You have to understand that I'm from Earth, where I live as humans did in primitive times – I mean, on an apparently flat world, under a dome of sky scattered with a few distant stars. Here the worlds fly around like demented birds, and even the stars are glaring globes. Of course only the most massive stars can form here; conditions are too turbulent for anything as puny as Sol . . . It's rather disorienting!'

Pirius had never thought about it. 'I grew up here. Sir.'

'Call me Nilis.'

But Pirius was not about to call a Commissary, even a soft eccentric Commissary like this one, anything but 'sir'. He said, 'Arches doesn't seem strange to me.'

'Well, I suppose it wouldn't.' Nilis got to his feet, cup of water in his liver-spotted hand, and he peered out through layers of offices at the wheeling sky. 'A self-gravitating system – a classic demonstration of the n-body problem of celestial mechanics. And chaotic, unstable to small perturbations, never predictable even in principle. No doubt this endless barrage has been designed as conditioning, to get you proto-pilots used to thinking in shifting three-dimensional geo-metries, and to programme out ancient fears of falling – an instinct useful when we descended from the trees, not so valuable for a star-ship pilot, eh? But for me it's like being trapped in some vast celestial clockwork.'

Irritated, distressed, Pirius blurted, 'Forgive me, sir, but I don't understand why I'm here. Or why *you're* here.'

Nilis nodded. 'Of course. Cosmic special effects pale into insignific-ance beside our human dilemmas, don't they?'

'Why must I be punished? I haven't *done* anything. It was *him* – he did it all.'

Nilis studied him. 'Has your training not covered that yet? I keep forgetting how *young* you all are. Pirius, what Blue has done is done; it is locked in his timeline – his personal past. He must be punished, yes, in the hope of eradicating his character flaws. Whereas *you* are to be punished in the hope of changing your still unformed timeline. We can't change *his* past, but we can change *your* future, perhaps. Do you see? And so you must suffer for a crime you haven't yet committed.

'At least, that's the logic of the system. Is it right or wrong? Who's to say? We humans haven't evolved to handle time-travel paradoxes; all this stretches our ethical frameworks a little far. And, you know, I really can't imagine how it must be for you, Pirius Red. How does it feel to confront a version of yourself plucked out of the future and deposited in your life?'

'Sir, we train for it. It's not a problem.'

Nilis sighed. He said, with a trace of steel in his voice, 'Now, Pirius, I am here to help you, but I'm not going to be able to do that if you're not honest with me. Try again.'

Pirius said reluctantly, 'I feel – irritated. Resentful.'

Nilis nodded. 'That's better. Good. I can understand that. After all, your own future has suddenly been hijacked by this stranger, hasn't it? Your choices taken away from you. And how do you feel about *him* – Pirius Blue, your double – regardless of what he has done?'

'It's difficult,' Pirius said. 'I don't like him. I don't think he likes *me*. And yet I feel drawn to him.'

'Yes, yes. You are like siblings, brothers; that's the nearest analogy, I think. You are rivals – the two of you are competing for a single place in the world – you might even grow to hate him. And yet he will always be a part of you.'

Pirius was uncomfortable; this talk of 'brothers' was seriously non-Doctrinal. 'Sir, I wouldn't know about brothers. I grew up in cadres.'

'Of course you did. Popped from the birthing tanks, placed in a training cadre, plucked out and moved on, over and over! You don't know what it's like to have a brother – how could you? But I know,' he said, and sighed. 'There are corners, even on Earth itself, where people find room to do things the old way. Of course I had to give all that up when I joined the Commission. How unfortunate for you; if only your cultural background were richer it might help you cope better now. Don't you think?'

None of this meant much to Pirius. 'Sir, please—'

'You want to know what an old buffoon like me is doing all the way out here.' He smiled. 'I volunteered. As soon as I heard the particulars of the case, I knew I had to get involved. I volunteered to act as counsel to you and your twin.'

'But why?'

'You know that I'm a Commissary.' That meant he worked for the Commission for Historical Truth, the grand, ancient agency dedicated to upholding the purity of the Druz Doctrines – a task it performed with persuasion and force, with zeal and dedication. 'What you probably don't know is that the Commission itself has many divisions. The Commission is thousands of years old, Pirius. Astonishing when you think of it! The Commission has lasted longer than many of Earth's civilisations. And it has grown into a very old, very tangled bureaucratic tree.

'I work for a department called the Office of Technological Archival and Control. We're a sort of technological think tank. If somebody gets a bright idea on Alpha Centauri III, we make sure it's passed on to Tau Ceti IV.' These were places Pirius had never heard of. 'But the name says everything: "Archival and Control". Not a word about innovation, eh? Or development? The Commission's cold hand is at our throats, and our opportunity to *think* is restricted. Because that's the last thing the high-ups want us to do. Oh, yes, the very last. And *that's* why I'm here. Do you see?'

Pirius tried to pick his way through all this. 'No, sir, I don't.'

'I heard about your heroics – or rather, Pirius Blue's. I knew that to have captured a Xeelee, even to have survived such an encounter, he must have *innovated*. He must have found some new way of striking back at our perennial foe. And I've come to find out what that is. Of course I'm unqualified for the job, and from the wrong corner of the Commission. I had to fight my way through a few administrative thickets to get this far, I can tell you.'

Out of all that, one word stuck dismayingly in Pirius's mind: *unqualified*.

'But why is all this so important to you – to Earth?'

Nilis sighed. 'Pirius, have you no sense of history? Perhaps not – you young soldiers are so brave, but so limited in your horizons! Have you any idea at all how long this war has been going on for – how long this Front has been stalled here? And then there are the deaths, Pirius, the endless deaths. And for what?'

'The Xeelee are powerful. FTL foreknowledge leads to stalemate—'

Nilis waved a hand dismissively. 'Yes, yes. That's the standard justification. But we have got *used* to this stasis. Most people can't imagine any other way of conducting the war. But *I* can. And that's why I am here. Listen to me. Don't you worry about this absurd trial. I'll get you both cleared, you and your older twin. And then we'll see what we will see – eh?'

Pirius stared, bemused. He was no fool, and in fact had been selected for pilot training because of his capacity for independent thought. But he had never in his life come across anybody as strange as this Commissary and could make nothing of what he said. Bewildered, disoriented, he longed only to be out of here, out of Officer Country, and back in the great orderly warmth of the Barracks Ball, safe under his sheets' coarse fabric with Torec.

*

Pirius had to wait an agonising week for the trial to be called. He tried to immerse himself in the mundane routines of his training.

Arches was under the control of the Training and Discipline Command, jointly run by the Navy and the Green Army, and every child hatched here was born into the Navy's service. Most were destined to live out their lives performing simple services, administrative or technical support. But at the age of eight a few, a precious few, were filtered out by a ruthless programme of tests and screening, and submitted for officer training.

Pirius had made it through that filtering. Now his life was crammed with instruction in mathematics, science, technology, tactics, games theory, engineering, Galactic geography, multi-species ethics, even Doctrinal philosophy – as well as a stiff programme of physical development. But at the end of it was the prospect of serving the Navy in a senior and responsible role, perhaps as technical or administrative ground crew of some sort, or better yet in one of the prized flight roles – and best of all, as Pirius already knew was his own destiny, as a pilot. After that, if you prospered, there was the possibility of moving on to command, or, if you were invalided out, you could expect a role on the ground, or even in Training Command itself, like Captain Seath.

For young people primed from birth with the importance of duty, no better life could be imagined.

But none of this would come to pass if Pirius flunked his training, no matter what destiny FTL foreknowledge described for him. So Pirius tried to keep working. But his mind wasn't on it, and as rumours spread about his predicament, his friends and rivals – even Torec – kept their distance.

He was relieved when the trial finally started. But, despite Nilis's confidence, it didn't go well.

The hearing was convened in a dedicated courtroom, a spherical chamber close to the geometric centre of Officer Country. The judges, officers of the court, advocates and counsels, witnesses and defendants took their places in tiered seats around the equator of the sphere. The central section was left open for Virtual displays of evidence. As mandated by custom and enshrined in Coalition law, the judging panel contained representatives from many of the great agencies of mankind: the Commission, of course, the Green Army, who governed the destinies of the millions of Rock-bound infantrymen, and the Navy, of which Pirius Blue's Strike Arm was a section.

Before the trial opened, the president of the court, a grizzled Army general, gave a short instruction about the formal use of language: specifically, the use of historic tenses to describe events occurring in the 'past' of Pirius Blue's personal timeline, though they were in the future of the court itself.

Nilis leaned to Pirius Red. 'Even our language strains to fit the reality of time paradoxes,' he said. 'But we try, we try!'

At first it wasn't so bad: it was even interesting. Prompted by an advocate, Pirius Blue, the Pirius from the future, talked the court through a Virtual light-show dramatisation of the incident in question, drawn from the ship's log and the crew's eye-witness accounts. The court watched Pirius's withdrawal under fire from the line around the Rock barrage, his flight to Sag A East, the spectacular showdown with the Xeelee. From time to time he referred to his crew, Cohl the navigator and Tuta the engineer, to clarify details or correct mistakes. The show was stop-start, and if a clarification was conceded it would be incorporated into the draft of the Virtual sequence and that section run again.

Pirius himself – Pirius Red – watched intently. He felt intimidated that a version of himself, only a few years older, had been capable of *this*.

He tried to assess the reaction of the court members. Despite the legalistic setting, the members of the court watched, rapt, as miniature Virtual spacecraft chased each other across the spherical chamber. It was undoubtedly a dashing, daring episode, and it seemed to touch something primitive in people's hearts, whatever their roles here today.

But Pirius Red's heart sank at the grim expressions on the panel's faces as they heard one example after another of how Pirius Blue had disobeyed orders: when he failed to hold the line as the Xeelee broke through the Rock, when he failed to turn back to face the fire of the pursuing nightfighters. Even Dans, obviously a maverick, had shown a closer adherence to duty by ensuring that she sent back a FTL beacon containing data on the engagement to the past, giving the military planners a couple of years' notice of the Xeelee's new Rock-busting tactic.

Nilis seemed unperturbed. He nodded, murmured notes into Virtual receptors, absorbed, analytical, his blue, rheumy eyes bright in Virtual light. He seemed most animated, in fact, at the dramatisation of Dans's ingenious counter-temporal manoeuvre. He whispered to Pirius Red, 'That's it. That's the key to the whole incident – *that's* the way to out-think a Xeelee!'

When the reconstruction was over, the panel conferred briefly. Then with a curt, dismissive gesture, the president of the court summoned Nilis to make his response.

As he gathered his robes to stand up, Nilis whispered to Pirius Red, 'See that look? He thinks the case is already over, that my defence is just a formality. Hah! We'll show them – just as Blue showed that Xeelee.'

Pirius turned away, his heart thumping.

Nilis immediately conceded the accuracy of the reconstruction. 'I'm not here to pick holes in a story told fully and honestly by three very honourable young people. And I'm not here to question, either, the central charge against Pirius: that he disobeyed orders both standing and direct in the course of the action. Of course he did; he doesn't deny it himself. I'm not here to ask you to set aside self-evident fact.'

The old general asked dryly, 'Then why are you here, Commissary?' Muffled laughter.

Nilis rose up to his full height. 'To ask you to *think*,' he said grandly. 'To think for yourselves – just as Pirius did, *in extremis*. We must think beyond mere orders. Why obey a pointless order if it will cost you your life, and the lives of your crew, and your ship, and gain absolutely nothing? Isn't it better to put aside that order, to flee, to return – as Pirius self-evidently has done – and to fight again another day? Isn't it obvious that Pirius disobeyed his orders the better to fulfil his *duty*?'

Pirius was shocked. If one thing had been drummed into him more than anything else since his birth it was: *orders are everything*. He could tell from the thunderous expressions on the bench how well that sort of sophistry was going down with the service personnel.

Nilis went on in detail to analyse Dans's use of the 'Brun manoeuvre' – he described it as 'the ingenious use of a closed timelike curve in a computing algorithm' – which he considered the crux of Pirius's innovatory tactic. 'Thanks to these two brave pilots, Pirius and Dans, at last we have a way, at least in principle, of overcoming the

Xeelee's single biggest advantage over us: their computing resource. This will need further investigation, of course, but surely you see that that alone is an achievement far beyond the dreams of most warriors in this endless war. And then, on top of that, *Pirius brought home a Xeelee*, a captive nightfighter! The information we will acquire may – no, *will* – transform our prospects in this conflict.' He paused, breathing hard.

Pirius had never heard a speech like this. Nobody talked about victory – not victory any time soon, anyhow. The war wasn't to be won, it was to be *endured*. Victory would come, but it was for future generations. The brass on the bench weren't impressed by Nilis's grandiose declarations either.

And Nilis proceeded to make things a thousand times worse.

'Sirs, once again I urge you to *think*. Rise above yourselves! Rise above your petty rivalries! Isn't it true that soldiers of the Green Army habitually resent Strike Arm for the perceived luxury of their bases? Isn't it true that Navy officers traditionally imagine that the Commission knows nothing of the pressures on warriors, even though the Commission plays such a significant role in running the war? And as for we of the Commission, are the Doctrines really so fragile that we fear their breaking even in such an extraordinary case – even in a case where a brave officer is simply overriding a pointless order for the sake of prosecuting his duty more effectively? . . .'

And so on. By the time Nilis was done insulting everybody, Pirius knew that the case, if it had ever had any chance of going his way, was lost.

The panel's deliberation was brief. The president of the court took only a few seconds to announce its verdict.

For his gross violation of orders Pirius Blue was to be demoted, and transferred to a penal unit at the Front. Pirius Red knew, everybody knew, that such a posting was tantamount to a death penalty. It was scarcely more of a shock when the court announced that Pirius's crew, Cohl and Tuta, would be transferred along with him for their 'complicity' in his 'crimes'.

And, in an almost causal afterthought, the president announced that Pirius Red, the pilot's younger version, would likewise be transferred to a penal Rock. There were reassignments, lesser punishments, for the younger versions of Cohl, Tuta and Dans.

By now Pirius understood the theory of temporal-paradox law. But he found this impossible to take in.

Once the president had finished speaking Nilis was immediately on his feet again. He announced his intention to appeal the verdict. And he requested that in the interim he have both Pirius Red and Pirius Blue assigned to his personal retinue. He would act as guarantor of their behaviour, and he would seek to make best use of their services in the betterment of mankind's greater goals.

The panel conferred again. It seemed some bargain was done. The judges did not dispute Nilis's right to appeal. They would not allow Pirius Blue, as prime perpetrator of this anti-Doctrinal lapse, to escape the sentence passed down, but as a gesture of leniency they placed Pirius Red, the younger copy, in Nilis's care.

Nilis got up one more time, to make a final, angry denunciation of the court. 'For the record let me say that this shameful charade is in microcosm a demonstration of why we will *never* win this war. I refer not only to your sclerotic decision-making processes, and the lethality of your inter-agency rivalry, but also to the simple truth of this case: that a man who defeated a Xeelee is not lauded as a hero but prosecuted and brought down . . .'

It was stirring stuff. But the automated monitor was the only witness; the court was already emptying.

Pirius stood, bewildered. He saw faces turned to him, Torec, Captain Seath, even Pirius Blue, his older self, but they seemed remote, unreadable, as if they were blurred. So that was that, it seemed: Pirius's life trashed and taken away from him in a summary judgement, for a 'crime' he hadn't even had the chance to commit.

He shouted down at Pirius Blue, 'This is all your fault.'

Pirius Blue looked up from his lower tier and laughed bleakly. 'Well, maybe so. But how do you think I feel? Do you know what's the worst thing of all? That mission, my mission, is *never even going to happen.*'

Then he was led away. Pirius Red didn't expect to see him again.

Here was the broad, crumpled face of Nilis, like a moon hovering before him. 'Ensign? Are you all right?'

'I don't know. It doesn't seem real. Sir, I don't want to be placed under your supervision. I only want to do my duty.'

Nilis's expression softened. 'And you think that if I pull you back from the Front, that pit of endless death, I'll be stopping you from doing that? You think your duty is only to die, as so many others have before you?' The old man's eyes were watery, as if he was about to cry. 'Believe me,' Nilis said, 'with me you *will* fulfil your duty – not by dying, but by living. And by helping me fulfil my vision. For I, alone of all the fools and stuffed shirts in this room, *I* have a dream.'

'A dream?'

Nilis bent close and whispered, 'A dream of how this war may be won.' He smiled. 'We leave tomorrow, ensign; be ready at reveille.'

'Leave? Sir – where are we going?'

Nilis seemed surprised at the question. 'Earth, of course!' And he walked away, his soiled black robe flapping at his heels.

CHAPTER 6

Nilis's corvette was a sleek arrow shape nuzzled against a port, one of a dozen strung along this busy Officer Country gangway.

Captain Seath herself escorted Pirius Red to the corvette. They were the first to get there; they had to wait for Nilis.

Pirius wasn't sure why Seath had brought him here herself. It wasn't as if he had any personal effects to be carried; he had been issued a fancy new uniform for the trip, and anything else he needed would be provided by the corvette's systems, and it would never have occurred to him to take such a thing as a souvenir. Officially, she said, Seath was here to make sure Pirius 'didn't screw up again'. Pirius thought he detected something else, though, something softer under Seath's scarred gruffness. Pity, perhaps? Or maybe regret; maybe Seath, as his commander, thought she could have done more to protect him from this fate.

Whatever. Seath wasn't a woman you discussed emotions with.

He studied the corvette. It was a Navy ship, and it bore the tetrahedral sigil of free mankind, the most ancient symbol of the Expansion. He said, 'Sir – a Navy ship? But I'm in the charge of Commissary Nilis now.'

She laughed humourlessly. 'The Commission doesn't run starships, ensign. You think the Navy is about to give its most ancient foe access to FTL technology?'

'The Xeelee are the foe.'

'Oh, the Navy and Commission were at war long before anybody heard of the Xeelee.' It was disturbing to hear a straight-up-and-down officer like Seath talk like this.

48

There was a reluctant footstep behind them. To Pirius's surprise, here came Torec. She was as empty-handed as Pirius was – but like him she wore a smart new uniform. A complex expression closed up her face, and her full lips were pushed forward into a pout that looked childish, Pirius thought.

'You're late,' Seath snapped.

'Sorry, sir.'

Pirius said, 'Come to say goodbye?' He felt touched but he wasn't about to show it.

'No.'

'Pirius, she's going with you,' Seath said.

'*What?*'

Torec spat, 'Not my idea, dork-face.'

Commissary Nilis came bustling along the corridor. Unlike the two ensigns he did bring some luggage, a couple of trunks and two antique-looking bots which floated after him. 'Late, late; here I am about to cross the Galaxy and I'm late for the very first step . . .' He slowed, panting, 'Captain Seath. Thank you for hosting me, thank you for everything.' He beamed at Pirius. 'Ready for your new adventure, ensign?' Then Nilis noticed Torec, 'Who's this? A friend to wave you off?'

'Not exactly,' Seath said. 'This is Ensign Torec. Same cadre as Pirius, same generation. Not as bright, though.'

Torec raised her eyebrows, and Pirius looked away.

'And why is she here?'

'Commissary, I've assigned her to you.'

Nilis blustered, 'Why, I've no desire to take another of your child soldiers. The corvette isn't provisioned for an extra mouth—'

'I've seen to that.'

'Captain, I've no use for this girl.'

'She's not for you. She's for Pirius.'

'Pirius?'

Seath's face was hard, disrespectful. 'Commissary, take my advice. You're taking this ensign out of here, away from everything he knows, dragging him across the Galaxy to a place he can't possibly even imagine.' She spoke as if Pirius wasn't there.

Nilis's mouth assumed a round O of shock, an expression that was becoming familiar to Pirius. 'I see what you mean. But this base is so —' He gestured. 'Inhuman. Cold. Lifeless. The only green to be seen anywhere is the paintwork of warships!'

'And so you imagined our soldiers to be inhuman too.'

'Perhaps I did.'

Seath said, 'We're fighting a war; we can't *afford* comfort. But these children need warmth, humanity. And they turn to each other to find it.'

Pirius's cheeks were burning. 'So you knew about me and Torec the whole time. Sir.'

Seath didn't respond; she kept her eyes on the Commissary.

Nilis seemed embarrassed too. 'I bow to your wisdom, Captain.' He turned his avuncular gaze on Torec. 'A friend of Pirius is a friend of mine. And I'm sure we'll find you something gainful to do.'

Torec stared back at him. For the ensigns, this was an utterly alien way to be spoken to. Torec turned to Seath. 'Captain—'

'I know,' Seath said. 'You spent your whole life trying to get to officer training. You made it, and now *this*. Well, the Commissary here assures me that by going with him Pirius will fulfil his duty in a manner that might even change the course of the war. Though I can't imagine how,' she added coldly. 'But if that's true, *your* duty is clear, Ensign Torec.'

'Sir?'

'To keep Pirius sane. No discussion,' Seath added with soft menace. 'Yes, *sir*.'

Nilis bustled forward, hands fluttering. 'Well, if that's settled – come, come, we must get on.' He led the way through the open port into the ship.

Captain Seath stared at the ensigns for one last second, then turned away.

Pirius and Torec followed Nilis aboard the corvette. Sullenly, they avoided each other's eyes.

They had both been aboard Navy vessels before, of course – transports, ships of the line – for training purposes. But they had never been aboard a ship as plush as this before. And it was clean. It even *smelled* clean.

In the corridor that ran along the ship's elegant spine, there was carpet on the floor. A two-person crew worked in the tip of the needle hull, beyond a closed bulkhead. In the central habitable section the outer hull was transparent, and if you looked into the sections beyond the rear bulkhead you could see the misty shapes of engines. But two compartments were enclosed by opaque walls.

Nilis ushered his hovering cases into one of these cabins. He looked uncertainly at the ensigns, then opened the door of the other opaqued compartment. 'This cabin was for you, Pirius. I suppose it will have to do for the two of you.' There was only one bed. 'Well,' he said gruffly. 'I'll leave you to sort it out.' And, absurdly embarrassed, he bustled into his own cabin and shut the door.

In the cabin there was more carpet on the floor. The room was dominated by the bed, at least twice as wide as the bunks they had been used to. Pirius glimpsed uniforms in a wardrobe, and bowls of some kind of food, brightly coloured, sat on a small table.

They faced each other.

'I didn't ask to be here,' said Torec. She sounded furious.

'I didn't ask for you.'

'I've better things to do than to be your squeeze.'

Pirius snapped, 'I'd rather squeeze that fat old Commissary.'

'Maybe that's what he wants.'

They held each other's gazes for a second. Then, together, they burst out laughing.

Torec crammed a handful of the food into her mouth. 'Mm-m. These are *sweet*.'

'I bet the bed's soft.'

Still laughing, they ran at each other and began to tear off their clothes. Their new uniforms were not like the rough coveralls they had been used to on Arches; Officer-class, the uniforms crawled off the floor where they had been carelessly dropped, slithered into the wardrobe, and began a silent process of self-cleaning and repair.

The room had everything they needed: food, water, clean-cloths, even a lavatory artfully concealed behind panelling. 'Evidently officers and Commissaries don't like to admit they shit,' Torec said dryly when they discovered this.

For hours they just stayed in the room, under the covers or on top of them, eating and drinking as much as they could. They knew they had to make the most of this. Soon enough somebody would come for them and take all this stuff away; somebody always did.

But nobody did come.

'How long do you think it will take to get there?'

Pirius was cradling her head on his arm, and eating tiny purple sweets from her bare belly. 'Where?'

'Earth.'

He thought about that. Even now, more than twenty millennia since humanity's first interstellar jaunt, a trip across the face of the Galaxy was not a trivial undertaking. 'Earth is twenty-eight thousand light years from the centre.' Everybody knew that. 'FTL can hit two hundred light years an hour. So—'

Torec had always been fast at arithmetic. 'About six days?'

'But we can't get so far without resupply, not a ship this size. Double the time for stops?'

She stroked the centre line of his chest. 'What do you think it will be like?'

'Earth? I have *no* idea.' It was true. To Navy brats like Pirius and Torec, Earth was a name, a remote ideal – it was what they were fighting for. But they had never been told anything about Earth itself. What would be the point? None of them was ever going to go there. Earth was a totem. You didn't think of it as a place to *live*.

'So what does Nilis want you to do?'

'Win the war.' He laughed. 'He doesn't tell me anything.'

'Maybe the Commissary is working out a training programme for us.'

'Yes, maybe that.' It was a comforting thought. They were used to having every waking second programmed by somebody else. Everybody moaned about the regime the whole time, of course, but Pirius admitted to himself it would be reassuring when they heard a brisk knock on the door and the Commissary issued them their orders.

But twenty-four hours went by, and still they heard no such knock.

They began to grow uncomfortable. It was hard even to sleep. They weren't used to being enclosed, isolated like this. Back at Arches, where they had grown up, they had spent their whole lives in vast open dormitories, like the ones in the Barracks Ball, places where you could always see thousands of others arrayed around you, eating, sleeping, playing, fighting, bitching. Again everybody complained, and snatched bits of privacy under the covers of their bunks. But the fact was it was reassuring to be cocooned in a vast array of humanity – to have your little slot, and to fill it. Now they had been ripped out of all that, and it was disquieting.

Already Pirius could see Captain Seath's wisdom. If not for the presence of Torec, somebody he could share all this with, he probably would go crazy. The two of them clung to each other for reassurance. But it wasn't enough.

*

At the end of that first twenty-four hours they felt a soft judder – probably a docking, causing a ripple in the corvette's inertial field as it interfaced with a port's systems. They surely couldn't be at Earth yet, but they were *somewhere*.

They jumped out of their tousled bed, pulled on uniforms and hurried out of their cabin, leaving it for the first time since Arches.

Through the transparent hull they saw a plain of metal that softly curved away, like a plated-over moon. The corvette had nuzzled against a dock on this metallic worldlet, and to left and right they could see more ports, receding beyond the metal world's tight horizon, complex puckers within which more ships rested.

There was no sign of the corvette's crew. But Commissary Nilis stood here, gazing out. He hadn't noticed the ensigns. He had his hands behind his back, and he seemed to be *humming*.

Torec and Pirius glanced at each other, Pirius stood to attention and plucked up his courage, 'Sir—'

Nilis was startled, but he smiled. 'Ah, my two ensigns! And how are you enjoying the trip? Well, we've barely started, If there's anything you need, just ask.' He turned back to the window. 'Look over there – remarkable. I think that's a Spline ship.' So it was, Pirius saw. The great living vessel nestled in its dock; it looked like a bulging eyeball.

Torec nudged Pirius, who asked, 'Sir – Commissary – can you tell us where we are?'

'Well, this is Base 528, 1 believe,' Nilis said. 'We're here for our first provisioning stop.' He glanced at them. 'And what does that number tell you?'

Pirius was confused, but Torec said: 'Sir, that it's an old base. Arches is 2594. The older the base, the lower the number.'

'Quite so. Good. Now, come, *see*.' He walked past them to the other wall.

Pirius saw ships: many ships, of all shapes and sizes, criss-crossing before his vision. The nearer ships shuttled into docks, or left them. Beyond there were many more, just sparks too remote to make out any detail, a shifting crowd that sorted itself into streams that swept away. The ships were beyond counting, he thought, stunned, and this vast streaming must continue day and night, all from this one base.

But Torec was looking beyond the ships to the stars. 'Pirius. The sky is *dark*.'

The sky was dense with stars, many of them hot and blue. But in every direction he looked, between the stars the sky was black, black as velvet. 'We aren't in the Galaxy centre any more,' he said.

'Quite right,' Nilis said. 'We are actually in a spiral arm – the Three-Kiloparsec Arm, the innermost arm of the Galaxy's main disc.'

'Three-Kilo,' said Torec, wondering. 'I've heard of that.'

'Many famous battles were fought here,' Nilis said. 'But long ago. Once this base was on the front line. Now it is a resupply depot. The Front has since been pushed deeper into the heart of the Galaxy, deeper towards the Prime Radiant itself. In this part of the Galaxy there are ports, dry docks, graving yards, weapons ships: it is a belt of factory worlds that encloses the inner centre, a hinterland that spans hundreds of light years.' He sighed. 'I've travelled here a dozen times, but the scale of it still bewilders me. But then a war spread across a hundred thousand light years, and spanning tens of millennia, simply cannot be grasped during a human life spanning mere decades. Perhaps it isn't surprising that the idea of *winning* this war is beyond the imagination of even our most senior commanders.'

Torec said hesitantly, 'Commissary?'

'Yes, child?'

'Please – what do you want us to *do*?'

Nilis laughed. 'Why, nothing. You must relax – treat this as a holiday, for believe me we will have plenty to do once we get to Earth.' He slapped them on their shoulders. 'For now, just enjoy the ride!' And he disappeared into his cabin.

Pirius and Torec shared a bewildered glance. For Navy brats, leisure was an alien concept. They stared out at the streaming ships.

The next leg of the journey would be the longest, a straight-line cut through the spiral arms of the Galaxy spanning six days and no less than fifteen thousand light years, before they reached a resupply depot at the Orion Line.

In the humming womb of the corvette, Pirius and Torec still had nothing to do.

By the end of the second day the rich food began to make them feel bloated. There was always sex, of course, but even the appeal of that faded. Pirius came to suspect uneasily that the fact that they could screw as much as they liked here took away a lot of the appeal of their under-the-blanket barracks fumbles.

In quiet moments on the third day, Pirius tried to analyse his feelings for Torec.

Obviously Seath had assumed they were a stable couple, that their relationship was strong. But the truth was that Torec had only ever been a buddy. For now she was his favoured squeeze, and vice versa, but that might have changed overnight, without hard feelings or regrets. In the Barracks Ball, there was a lot of choice, and a *lot* of bunk-hopping. Sex was all about athletics, and a bit of comfort. Surely they weren't in *love*. Were they doomed to spend their lives together even so?

Of course there was nobody to discuss this with – certainly not the Commissary, and they hadn't even seen the crew. The ensigns had nobody but each other.

And so, naturally, on the fourth day they turned on each other.

By the fifth day, after hours of screaming rows, they were exhausted and regretful. In their striving to hurt each other they had both said many things they hadn't meant, the most hurtful for Pirius being the charge that he had ruined Torec's life, for it held a grain of truth.

They came back to each other for comfort. The day became a good day, a day of tenderness. Having endured the storm, Pirius sensed they had moved to some new level in their relationship. Perhaps he began to wonder, eventually they really would find love.

But then the sixth came, just another day in this unwelcome luxury, and still the journey dragged on.

At the end of the sixth day Torec escaped into sleep. But Pirius was restless. He slipped out of bed, sponged down with a clean-cloth, and pulled on a uniform. Torec stayed asleep, or at any rate pretended to.

Pirius found Nilis sitting in a chair before the transparent hull, working at a data desk propped on his knee. The Commissary smiled at Pirius and waved him to another chair.

Pirius sat stiffly, and gazed at the panorama out of the window.

The corvette's FTL drive, working smoothly and silently, was making many jumps per second, and it seemed to Pirius that the scattered stars were sliding past his field of view. But after each jump the corvette was briefly stationary relative to the Galaxy's frame of reference. So there were none of the effects of velocity you'd expect from a sublight drive, no redshift or blueshift, no aberration; they crossed the Galaxy in a series of still frames.

For Pirius it was a strange sky. Far from the Core now, they were moving out through the Galaxy's plane. They were passing through the Sagittarius Arm of the Galaxy, one of its richest regions outside of the Core itself. There were plenty of stars, but they seemed scattered and remote – and, remarkably, *not one* of them was close enough to show a disc. Even between the stars the sky was odd, black and empty. It seemed a quiet, dull, low-energy sort of environment to Pirius.

Not only that, you could actually tell you were embedded in a sheet of stars. If Pirius looked straight ahead his eyes met a kind of horizon, a faint band of grey-white light that marked the position of the Galactic equator: the light of millions of stars muddled up together. Away from the plane, overhead or down below, there were only scattered handfuls of nearby stars – you could immediately see how thin this disc was – and beyond that there was only blackness, the gulf, he supposed, of intergalactic space.

The corvette wasn't alone. It was one of a stream of ships, a great thread of swimming sparks that slid across the face of the Galaxy. If he looked around the sky he could see more streams of light, all more or less parallel to this one, some of them passing back to the centre, others running out to the periphery. Occasionally a companion ship passed close enough to make out detail. These were usually Spline vessels, vast meaty spheres pocked with glistening weapons.

Nilis was watching him. Pirius started to feel self-conscious.

Nilis waved a hand, 'Marvellous, isn't it – all this? A human Galaxy! Of course, if you were to drop at random into the plane of the Galaxy, chances are you'd see little enough evidence of human presence. We're following a recognised lane, ensign, a path where ships huddle together in convoys for mutual protection – this convoy alone is hundreds of light years long. And you can see the Navy Splines assigned to guide and shield us. We've driven the Xeelee back to their Prime Radiant in the Core, but they are still out there – in the galactic halo, even in other galaxies – and they are not averse to plunging down from out of the disc to mount raids.'

Pirius glanced up uneasily at the dark dome of the sky.

Nilis went on, 'But even so, even on a galactic scale, you can see the workings of mankind. Think of it! On hundreds of millions of worlds right across the Galaxy's disc, resources are mined, worked, poured into the endless convoys that flow into the Core – and there on the factory worlds they are transformed to weaponry and fighting ships, to be hurled inward and burned up, erased by the endless friction of the Front itself. Of course, after so long, many worlds are dead, used up, exhausted and abandoned. But there are always more to be exploited. So it goes on, it seems, until the Galaxy itself is drained to feed the war, every bit of it devoted to a single purpose.'

Pirius wasn't sure what to say. 'It's remarkable, sir.'

Nilis raised an eyebrow. 'Remarkable? Is that all?' He sighed. 'The Coalition discourages the study of history, you know. That's according to the Druz Doctrines, in their strictest form. There is no past, no future: there is only *now*. And it is a now of eternal war. But *I* have looked back into the past. I have consulted records, libraries, some official, some not, some even illegal. And I have learned that we have been devoted to this single cause, to expansion or war, for *twenty thousand years*. Why, the human species itself is only some hundred thousand years old!

'It's been too long. We have become rigid, ossified. There is no development in our politics, our social structures, even our technology. Science is moribund, save for the science of weaponry. We live out lives identical in every respect to those of our forebears. You know, there used to be more innovation in a *decade* than you see in a thousand years now.

'In a way the Xeelee themselves don't matter any more – no, don't look so shocked, it's true! You could replace the Xeelee with another foe and it would make no difference; they are a mere token. We have forgotten who we are, where we came from. All we remember, all we know, is the war. It *defines* mankind. We are the species that makes war on the Xeelee, nothing else.'

'Sir – is that such a bad thing?'

'Yes!' Nilis slammed his fist on to the arm of his chair. 'Yes, it is. You know why? Because of the *waste*.' He reeled off statistics.

Around the Front there were a hundred human bases, which supported a billion people each, on average. And the turnover of population in those bases was about ten years.

'That means that ten billion people a year are sacrificed on the Front, Pirius. The number itself is beyond comprehension, beyond empathy. *Ten billion*. That's more than three hundred every single second. It is estimated that in all some thirty *trillion* humans have given their lives to the war: a number orders of magnitude higher than the number of stars in this wretched Galaxy we're fighting over. What a waste of human lives!

'But there is hope – and it lies with the young, as it always did.' Nilis leaned forward with a kind of aged eagerness. 'You see, at Sag A East, despite a lifetime of conditioning, when it came to your crisis you – or at least your future self – threw off the dead imperative of the Doctrines. You improvised and innovated, you showed initiative, imagination, courage . . . And yet, such is the static nature of this old people's war, you are seen as a threat, not a treasure.'

Pirius didn't like the sound of that 'conditioning'.

'*That* is why I asked for you, ensign.' Nilis looked out at the swimming stars, the silent, ominous forms of the Spline escorts. 'I reject this war, and I have spent most of my life seeking ways to end it. That doesn't mean I seek defeat, or an accommodation with the Xeelee, for I believe none is possible. I seek a way to win – but that means I must overturn the status quo, and *that* is enough to have earned me enemies throughout the hierarchies of the Coalition. It is a lonely battle, and I grow old, tired – and, yes, afraid. I need your youth, your courage – and your imagination. Now, what do you think?'

Pirius frowned. 'I don't want to be anybody's crutch, sir.'

Nilis flinched. But he said, 'That brutal honesty of yours! Very well, very well. You will be no crutch but a collaborator.'

Pirius said uneasily, 'And I don't see why you're alone. What of your – family? You said something about a brother.'

Nilis turned away. 'My parents were both senior Commissaries, who made the unpardonable error of falling in love. My family, and it *was* a family of the ancient kind, was as illegal on Earth as it would have been on Arches Base. The family was broken up when I was small – I was taken away.

'Of course my background is the key to *me*; any psychologist will tell you that. Why, the Doctrines deny women the right to experience giving birth! What a dreadful distortion that is. You yourself, Pirius, you were *hatched*, not born. You grew up in a sort of school, not a home. You have emerged socialised, highly educated. But – forgive me! – you are nothing but a product of your background. You have no *roots*. My background is, well, more primitive. So perhaps I feel the pain of the war's brutal waste more than some of my colleagues.'

This made little sense to Pirius. On Arches, there was contraceptive in the very water. Men *could* get women pregnant – the old biology still worked – but it would be a pathology, a mistake. A pregnancy was like a cancer, to be cut out. The only way to pass on your genes was through the birthing tanks, and you only got to contribute to them if you performed well.

Nilis went on, 'Since I lost my family I have been neither one thing nor the other, neither rooted in a family or comfortable in a world of birthing houses and cadres.' He glanced at Pirius. 'Rather like you, Pirius, I have been punished for a crime I never committed.'

Pirius heard a soft sigh. Glancing back he saw Torec, standing behind a half-open door. She was wearing a shapeless sleeping gown, and her face was puffy with too much sleep.

Nilis looked away, visibly embarrassed.

She said, 'You're teaching him to talk like you do, Commissary. Pretty soon he won't sound like Navy at all. Is that what you want?'

Pirius held his breath. Back at Arches Torec would already have earned herself a week in the can

But Nilis just said, flustered, 'No. Of course not.'

'Then *what*? Six days we've been on this stupid toy ship. And still you haven't said what we're doing here.'

Pirius stood up, between Torec and the Commissary. 'Sir, she just woke up . . .'

She shook him off. She seemed infuriated. She hitched up her gown, showing her thighs. 'Is this what you want? Or *him*? Do you want to get into our bed with us, Commissary?'

Pirius used main force to shove her back into the cabin and pushed the door shut. He turned uncertainly. 'Commissary, I'm sorry—'

Nilis waved tiredly. Pirius saw that the skin on the back of his hand was paper-thin. 'Oh, it's all right, ensign. I do understand. I was young once too, you know.'

'Young?'

Nilis looked up at him. 'Perhaps you don't think of yourself that way. The human societies of the Core really are very young, you know, Pirius – those bases are swarms of children. The only adults you see are your instructors, I imagine. But *I* see you with a bit more perspective, perhaps. You have the bodies of adults, you are old enough to love and hate – and more than old enough to fight, to kill and to die. And yet you will suddenly throw a tantrum, like Torec's;

suddenly a spike of childhood comes sticking up through the still-forming strata of adulthood. I do understand, I think.

'And besides, she's right to ask such questions. After all I have turned your lives upside down, haven't I?' He smiled.

Yes, you have, Pirius thought uncomfortably. And he wondered if Torec had seen through to the truth. Maybe all these words about the philosophy of war were meaningless: maybe the truth was that this was just a silly old man who needed company.

Two days out from Earth, the corvette burst out of the crowded lanes of the Sagittarius Arm, and passed into the still emptier spaces beyond.

Pirius looked back at Sagittarius. It was a place of young stars and glowing clouds, hot and rich. The outer edge of this spiral arm was the famous Orion Line, where an alien species called the Silver Ghosts had resisted humanity, and the Third Expansion had stalled for centuries. The storming of the Line had been a turning point in human history. Since then, like an unquenchable fire, humanity had roared on, consuming all in its path, to the centre of the Galaxy itself.

But they were leaving all that behind. The corvette was approaching the Galaxy's ragged outer edge now, and the stars were scattered thin. Earth's sun, he learned, wasn't even in a proper spiral arm at all, but in a curtailed arc of dim, unspectacular stars.

Their last stop before Earth would be at a system called 51 Pegasi.

As the corvette cruised towards the system's central star, Torec came out of their room to stand before the transparent hull. Since her outburst, or maybe breakdown, Torec had been subdued. But the Commissary made no comment: it was as if the incident had never happened.

'There.' Nilis pointed. 'Can you see? The sailing ships . . .'

The planetary system here was dominated by one massive world, a bloated Jovian that swept close to the sun, a world so huge its gravity pulled its parent star around. It was that jiggling, in fact, which had led to the world's discovery from Earth, one of the first extrasolar planets to be discovered. Humans had come here in their crude slower-than-light starships, in the first tentative exodus called, retrospectively, the First Expansion.

'I used to come here for vacations,' Nilis murmured. 'The sky was always full of sails. I used to watch them at night, schooners with sails hundreds of kilometres wide, tacking this way and that in the light.

You know, systems like this are a relic of the history of human advance. Technology tends to get simpler as you approach the source, Earth. It took so long to get to more remote regions that humanity had advanced by the time they got there; each colonising push was overtaken by waves of greater sophistication. The Xeelee are different, though. All over the Galaxy their technology is at the same stage of development. So they must have arrived all at once: they must be extra-galactic . . .'

'Commissary,' Pirius asked hesitantly, 'where is Earth?'

The Commissary glanced around the sky, blinking to clear his rheumy eyes. Then he pointed to a nondescript star hanging in the dark, barely visible. 'There.'

Pirius looked up. For the first time the light of humanity's original sun entered his eyes.

CHAPTER 7

Pirius Blue and the crew of the *Claw*, stranded in their own indifferent past, were taken away from Arches Base.

The transport was a heap of junk, a battered old scow whose best days were long past. They had to keep their skinsuits sealed the whole time, and the Higgs-field inertial control had hiccups, making the gravity flicker queasily. You couldn't even see out through the hull.

But then this wasn't a Navy boat, as Enduring Hope had pointed out as they had dragged themselves aboard. Its hull was painted Army green, making it even uglier. 'And,' said Hope the engineer gloomily, 'everybody knows how good the Army is at running space-ships.'

Cohl wriggled on a heap of sacking, trying to get comfortable enough to sleep. 'Welcome to your new timeline,' she said.

Pirius was still consumed with guilt for having landed them in this – Cohl and Hope, and their younger selves, including his own. He had no idea how he was going to find the strength to endure what was to come. He could think of nothing to say to his crew.

After two days of living in their skinsuits, two days of sucking emergency rations through straws and stretching their suits' relief systems to their stinking limit, the scow lumbered to a landing. The ship's inertial field switched off, plunging them into microgravity, but their training had prepared them for such things, and they all grabbed handholds before they went drifting off.

Without warning the hull popped open to reveal grey, trampled ground, a sky crowded with stars.

An Army private in a scuffed green skinsuit appeared at the door. He was wearing a bulky inertial-control belt. 'Out,' he ordered.

Pirius led the way. He picked up his bag and loped out of the broad hatchway, letting himself drift to the ground. He looked around. He was on a Rock – a small one by the feel of its gravity. He was standing in a crater, a walled plain, its surface heavily pitted by footsteps and broader scars where the bellies of ships had touched. The sky was crowded with massive stars, and behind that speckled veil the centre of the Galaxy was a wall of light, too diffuse to cast a sharp shadow.

Cohl asked, 'Where do you think we are? Those stars are dense enough for it to be a cluster.'

'Not Arches,' said Enduring Hope bleakly. 'I suspect we're a long way from *there*.'

'Shut up,' the Army private said without emotion. He went along their little line, handed them inertial belts like his own, and took away their bags. 'You won't be needing that shit any more.'

Pirius knew this was likely the last they would see of their gear, all he had left of his life at Arches. Everybody had heard the scuttlebutt that buck privates believed Navy flyers were well off compared to them, and he had expected theft, but not to lose his kit so quickly; it was shocking, denuding. But perhaps that was the idea.

An Army officer stood before them – a captain, according to the stripes on her shoulder. Her skinsuit was battered and much repaired, and through its translucent sheen Pirius saw the gleam of metal down her left side, her leg and torso and arm. She had her hands behind her back, and her face was shadowed, but brown eyes regarded them somberly – and, Pirius saw, startled, a fleck of silver gleamed in each pupil. 'Put on your belts,' she said.

Pirius snapped to attention. 'Sir, I am Pilot Officer Pirius of—'

'I don't care who you are. Put on your belts.' They hesitated for one heartbeat, and she yelled, '*Do it.*'

Pirius's inertial belt was battered and the fabric was stained dark, perhaps with blood, though the colour was indistinct in the pale Galaxy light. As he snapped it on weight clutched at him, dragging him to the asteroid dirt. It had been preset to what felt like more than a standard gravity. He reached for the clasp.

'Don't touch that control.'

Pirius snapped back to attention.

'My name is Marta,' the captain said. 'This is a base at the heart of the Quintuplet Cluster. We know it as Quin.' Pirius knew that this was indeed a long way from Arches. 'Let me begin your re-education right now. This is an Army base, and I am an Army officer. You are still Navy personnel, attached to what we call the Navy Division, but you are under my command. You will be trained for work in the Service Corps.'

Pirius's heart sank. The Service Corps: the shit-shovellers. He said, 'Sir, what will our duties—'

'Shut up.'

'Sir.'

'That is the *last* question I want to hear from you. It is not important what you know, only what you do. And you do only what I tell you. Is that clear?'

The three of them mumbled a reply: 'Sir.'

She took a step closer to them, and Pirius saw that she walked, not stiffly, but a little unnaturally; the systems that had replaced her left side worked smoothly, but not quite as an intact human body would. 'Lethe, you're unfit.' She prodded at Enduring Hope's belly. 'I'm truly sick of having you fat wheezing flyboys dumped on me.'

She stood back. 'Let's get this straight from the start. I don't want Navy rejects here. *Nobody* wants you. But here you are. The work you will be assigned will be the dirtiest of dirty jobs, and the most dangerous. I've no doubt you'll foul it up, but soon you'll die, and then you'll be out of my hair. Until then you will do what I tell you without question or complaint.'

'Sir.'

She had a data desk in her shining left hand. 'Let's check you are who you're supposed to be. Pirius.'

'Pilot Officer Pirius, sir.'

'You're not a pilot any more, Pirius.'

'Sir.'

'Cohl.'

'Sir.'

'Tuta.'

Enduring Hope didn't reply.

Marta didn't look up from her desk. 'Tuta.'

'Sir, my name is—'

Pirius broke in. 'He's Tuta. Sir.'

Marta tapped her desk. 'Fine. So you're loyal to each other. You can all share Tuta's punishment.' She touched a control at her chest and suddenly the pull of false gravity on Pirius climbed, reaching twice standard. 'Three circuits,' she said. It turned out she meant them to run three circuits of the crater rim; Pirius guessed it would amount to ten kilometres. 'Your fitness work starts here,' she said.

Pirius said, 'Sir. We've lived in these suits for days already.'

'Four circuits,' she said evenly. And she turned her back and walked towards her transport.

Without another word Pirius turned away and began to plod towards the crater wall. Cohl and Hope fell in beside him. He saw that Hope was already sweating. Hope mouthed silently, *I'm sorry.*

The way wasn't hard to follow. All around the eroded rim of the crater there was a path where the asteroid ground had been beaten flat by the passage of uncounted feet. But to run under the false weight of their belts was brutal, and their skinsuits, designed for the comparatively light use of greenship crews, were not intended for this kind of hard labour. Soon Pirius's feet started to blister, and the suit chafed at his groin and armpits.

Enduring Hope managed two circuits before his legs gave way. Pirius and Cohl had to support him the rest of the course.

When their punishment run was done, Pirius, Cohl and Hope, exhausted, their skinsuits covered in charcoal-grey asteroid grime, were shoved through a hatchway in the ground.

They found themselves in a shabby underground receiving area. Here orderlies briskly stripped them of their skinsuits, and the rest of their clothing. Uncomfortable as their skinsuits had become, they were unhappy to see these last contacts with their past disappear into the black economy of this nameless Army Rock.

Shivering, naked, they were put through a brisk barrage of showers and radiation baths. Every hair on their heads, faces and bodies was burned off, and the top layer of skin turned into a powder that they could brush away with their fingers. Clumsy, aged bots probed at them, working at their teeth and ears and eyes. Fluid was pumped into their mouths and recta, only to spill out from both ends, humiliatingly, bringing the contents of their guts with it. After that they were subjected to a battery of injections that went on until their arms and thighs ached.

Pirius understood the need for such precautions. The human bases studded around the Front were closed communities, isolated by light years, and tended to develop their own strains of bugs and mites. Pirius and the others could easily pick up a disabling plague from Arches, to which they might have no immunity. But despite all these injections he suspected that a lot more care was being taken to ensure that Quin Base wasn't infected by *them*.

When the cleansing was done, the three of them were led out of the receiving area. Then they were pushed out through a bulkhead hatch into a much larger chamber beyond. It was a barracks, a noisy high-roofed chamber crowded with people – and *they were still naked*, to Pirius's sudden horror; the medics hadn't given them so much as a blanket between them.

A grinning cadet, female, very young looking, met them at the bulkhead. She wore a bright orange coverall, and she greedily eyed Cohl's breasts, which the navigator vainly tried to cover with her hands. 'Come on. I'll show you your pit.' And she turned and led them into the big chamber.

Pirius tried not to be self-conscious, to give a lead to his crew. But of course it was impossible; he walked hunched over, his hands clamped over his genitals.

This underground habitat was basically a barracks, like the Barracks Balls at Arches. But it was much less orderly, crammed with tottering heaps of bunks that climbed from floor to rough-hewn ceiling. The air was hot and muggy and stank of stale food and sewage.

And everywhere there were people. They crowded the alleys, they clambered on the bunks, they stared as the flyers passed. Some of them wore official-looking coveralls, like the girl who had met them, but others were bare to the waist, or wore shorts and shirts improvised from worn-out coveralls or blankets. And some of them just ran naked, as unashamed as the flyers were mortified. They ran and shouted, they wrestled on the floor, and couples and threesomes enjoyed noisy sex in the bunks, skin against glistening skin. And they all looked *young*, even compared to the population of Arches Base.

It was a swarming mass of youth and energy, an animal mass; Pirius had never seen anything like it. It was more like a nursery than a barracks. But some of these children were already veterans of combat. You could tell, he was starting to learn, by the gleam of metal in their eyes.

They reached a little block of bunks. One of the bunks was occupied by a man who lay on his back, hands locked behind his head. He said, 'Welcome. Pick a bunk! It doesn't really matter which . . ' He was *old* – at least twenty-five, old compared to the population of this chamber anyhow. He even had a little grey at his temples.

On three of the bunks sat small stacks of clothing, coveralls, underwear, a skinsuit each. The clothing was clearly ancient, much patched, and lacked any sentience whatsoever, just a one-size-fits-all design with crude expansion joints at elbows, knees, waist and neck. You even had to do up the fastenings yourself. But the coveralls were at least clothes, and the flyers grabbed at them.

The swarming cadets crowded around, grinning, curious, malicious, heads shaven, their faces slick with sweat. Pirius towered over them. Some of them were so young he couldn't tell if they were male or female. As small hands plucked at his coverall, he forced a grin. 'Sorry to disappoint you. The surface crew took everything we had – hey!' Somebody had grabbed his balls. He backed up quickly and closed his coveralls.

Although the others were just as mortified, neither of them had raised a hand at the swarming cadets, which really would have been disastrous. He felt obscurely proud of them.

The older man on the bunk swung down his legs, stood up and clapped his hands. 'Come on, give them a break.'

'Fresh meat,' one cadet giggled. She, or maybe he, had sharpened teeth.

The man stepped forward, arms extended. 'Yeah, but they'll be almost as fresh tomorrow. Come on, come on . . .' He herded the recruits away, like guiding unruly children, and they reluctantly acquiesced. But a circle of them stayed, staring at the newcomers and whispering.

'You'll get used to it,' the older man said.

'I doubt it,' said Enduring Hope, as he struggled into a coverall that refused to fit.

Cohl was investigating her blankets. 'These aren't clean. Lethe, they're *warm*.'

'You'll get used to that too. There's a rather high turnover here.'

Cohl said, 'What happened to her?'

'Who? Oh, the last person to sleep in those blankets? . . . You don't want to know.' He wore a green-grey coverall, open to the waist; his body was taut, fit. He was handsome, Pirius supposed, with a lean, well-drawn face, a small nose, thick hair he wore swept back from his brow, and a quick smile. Pirius's immediate impression was of weakness, oddly, despite his appearance. But his manner was relaxed as he welcomed the crew. And, like the other veterans here, his eyes shone silver.

Pirius walked up to him, hand extended. He introduced himself and his crew.

'I used to be a flyer too,' he said, 'before I found my calling shovelling shit on this Rock. My name is Quero.'

Hope was staring at him, 'No, it isn't.' He lumbered clumsily up to Quero, and, hesitantly, touched his sleeve. 'I know your true name. Everybody does.'

Cohl growled, 'I don't.'

Quero said, 'I call myself "This Burden Must Pass".'

Cohl said, 'Oh, terrific. Another Friend.'

Burden laughed. 'Why do you think I got busted down here? And why I keep on being busted back?'

'You're a heretic. You deserve it.' Cohl threw herself back on her bunk bed. She covered her face against the glare of the drifting light globes, turned on her side and curled up.

'If you say so,' Burden said gently.

Hope was captivated. 'Pirius, you don't know who this is, do you? This Burden Must Pass is the leader of the Friends.'

Burden admonished him gently. 'Now, you know we don't have leaders. But I'm flattered you know me.' He placed a hand on Hope's shoulder, and gazed into his eyes. 'You've had a tough time. I can't promise you it's going to get any easier. It never does. But just remember, none of it matters. And at timelike infinity—'

Hope's eyes were wide. 'Yes. *This burden must pass.*' Pirius saw his lower lip was trembling.

Burden turned to Pirius. 'I take it you're not a believer.'

'No. And you're very trusting to break Doctrine in front of three strangers.'

Burden shrugged. 'Look around. What else can they do? And are you going to inform on me?'

'No,' said Pirius. He glanced at Hope, who was sitting on his bunk, blank-faced. 'If you can keep him happy, that's fine by me.'

'You're loyal to your crew. And wise. I like that.'

'I don't need your approval.'

'Of course you don't.'

'And if I was wise I wouldn't be here—'

Cohl yelped and sat up. She pointed at a row of bunks opposite. 'Did you see that?'

Pirius turned, saw nothing. 'What?'

'*A rat!*'

Burden laughed gustily. 'Oh, you'll soon get used to the rats!' A klaxon sounded harshly, and the lights briefly dipped to green. Burden said, 'Have you eaten? How long were you travelling? . . . Well, it doesn't matter. I'd advise you to get some sleep.'

'Why?'

Burden started pulling off his coverall. 'You'll need it. In the morning your training will start in earnest. It's usually quieter in here at this hour; you created a stir.' He glanced at Pirius warningly. 'This isn't a pilot school. It's not exactly intellectually demanding. But—'

'We already had a taste of it.' Pirius began to explore his grubby blankets, and wondered how he could get them washed.

He checked on his shipmates. Cohl, still curled up, might not have been sleeping, but if not she was faking it well. Enduring Hope, physically exhausted and now apparently emotionally drained by his meeting with this enigmatic spiritual leader, slumped into his bunk.

Pirius lay back and closed his eyes. But the light was shifting and bright, the noise clamouring and disorderly. He had never thought of an Arches Base Barracks Ball as particularly peaceful, but so it seemed compared to this. He forced his aching muscles to relax, and he tried not to count down the minutes until he had to rise again.

In the hour before reveille the general clamour seemed to subside. The talking, screwing and wrestling was done for the night, it seemed, and people were drifting into sleep.

And in that last still hour, Pirius heard an odd noise. It was a scratching, a rustle, a whisper. Then a soft piping rose up from all around the dorm, a chorus of tiny voices joined in near harmony.

Later Burden told him it was the rats, calling to each other from around the barracks. Having travelled with humans twenty-eight thousand light years from Earth, the rats had learned to sing, and humans who had never heard birds had learned to enjoy their song. For the rats it was a survival tactic; they had become lovable.

When the klaxon sounded the soft singing was overwhelmed.

CHAPTER 8

As Nilis's corvette approached Sol system, even while it was still under FTL, it was bombarded by a whole series of Virtual messages. The Virtuals were like shrieking ghosts, liable to erupt into existence anywhere in the corvette at any time. Some of these messages were sanctioned by the various authorities; others, it seemed, were not, but had been able to punch their way through a Navy boat's firewalls anyway. Torec was freaked by the whole experience.

It took Pirius Red some time to understand that many of these clamouring entreaties and demands were aimed, not at Nilis, but at *him*, the boy who had captured a Xeelee.

'Don't let it worry you,' Nilis said with a smile. 'You're already famous, that's all!'

Of course that was disturbing enough in itself. Pirius had always harboured a guilty desire to do something spectacular, to be remembered. But he didn't want to be notorious for something *he* hadn't done, and, now that history had been edited, never would.

And anyhow personal fame was utterly non-Doctrinal. Pirius had expected that here, close to the centre of humanity, adherence to the Doctrines would be stronger than ever. But that, it turned out, was naïve.

'In many ways things are simpler out where you come from,' Nilis said gently. 'Here in Sol system, and especially on Earth – despite the best efforts of the Commission for Historical Truth – everything is very crowded, very old, and very messy. *Nobody* is in control, really, and never could be. You'll see!'

Like much of what Nilis had to say to him, Pirius found it best not to think too hard about that. But the messages continued to come, and as the light of Sol grew brighter, his heart beat faster.

The corvette stopped briefly at Saturn. Pirius and Torec knew that name, for this immense gas giant had famously been requisitioned long ago by the Navy as its largest base in Sol system.

Pirius peered out in awe. Around the cloud-draped planet, ships and facilities orbited in swarms. Even the moons bristled with factories and weapons emplacements – though it turned out that many of the smaller moons had been broken up for raw materials, water-ice of mantles and rock of cores.

Nilis waxed nostalgic about this world. He even showed Pirius Virtuals of how it had been before the arrival of humans, when it had been circled by a spectacular system of ice rings. But the rings had been too tempting a mine for the first settlers of the system, and too fragile to withstand the fires of the first wars fought here.

Scenery didn't interest Pirius much. As a Navy brat he was much more intrigued by military hardware. So he watched a steady stream of ships plunging into the planet's clouds. Nilis said that the ships were descending to Saturn's rocky heart, itself a planetoid about the size of the Earth and immersed in a hydrogen ocean thousands of kilometres deep. In the atrocious conditions of that deep murk, out of sight even of the rest of humanity, huge machines were being built.

Earth, this remote speck of rock at the Galaxy's rim, was still the logical centre of humanity. The Interim Coalition of Governance exerted a tight control on a Galaxy full of human beings, and the epicentre of that control was here, on Earth. If the worst came to the worst – if the Xeelee ever broke out of the Galaxy's Core and struck at Sol system itself – Saturn would be the bastion of the last defence of Earth, and those mighty engines would come to life.

The corvette was here because the Xeelee nightfighter captured by Pirius Blue had been hauled across the Galaxy and placed in orbit among Saturn's moons.

'There was really no other choice,' Nilis murmured. 'Bringing back a Xeelee has been enough of a sensation as it is. At least here it will be under Navy guard. If we took it deeper into the inner system we'd be asking for trouble.'

Pirius said, 'You mean the risk to Earth would be too great?'

'Oh, no, Pirius, not that. We have come here not to protect

mankind from our Xeelee, but to protect the Xeelee from *us.*' He winked.

After six hours the corvette slid cautiously away from Saturn and its cordon of technology. As it was carrying celebrities of various degrees of reluctance, the corvette's crew were granted permission to shorten the remainder of the trip by using their FTL drive within the boundaries of Sol system.

So Pirius saw Saturn wink out of existence, to be replaced immediately by a wall of light, blue-white, that flooded the corvette with dazzling brilliance.

At first Pirius and Torec couldn't understand what they were seeing. It was an immense shield of blue-grey, almost like metal, that curved smoothly away on all sides. It even looked polished, for Pirius saw a dazzling highlight from the sun. And yet the surface was subtly textured, and there were flaws, darker masses scattered irregularly across the shining surface. Each such mass was surrounded by a fringe of paler blue, flecked with white. Other objects crawled across the shield, trailing arrow-shaped wakes behind them.

Nilis seemed to have anticipated their difficulty. Rather than explain, he encouraged them to use the corvette wall's magnification facility to explore the view and figure it out for themselves. Slowly the strange truth of what they were seeing opened up in Pirius's mind.

He was looking down at a planet, a hemisphere dominated by a single great ocean – an ocean of water, *open to the sky*. It was kept liquid not by technology but by thermodynamic equilibrium, its curved surface not shaped by human design but following a simple gravitational equipotential. Even the wispy clouds he saw were water vapour. Although humanity had by now mapped the Galaxy, this was still, remarkably enough, the largest open-water ocean encountered anywhere.

This was Earth.

Those crawling forms were ships, scudding like insects over the ocean's surface. But some of the larger forms looked oddly familiar. They turned out to be Spline, which had themselves evolved on a watery world, and now gambolled ponderously in the deep-ocean waves of the Pacific. After millennia of war, the seas of Earth had become a nursery for living starships. But the Spline schools weren't the strangest thing Pirius saw.

He focused on an island, one of the irregular masses of rock that protruded into the air from the ocean's patient hide. He peered down at buildings, docks, landing strips. He could even see people moving between the buildings. One little girl, skipping down a path to a beach, glanced up at the sky, as if she could see him staring down at her. Her face was a tiny button. And she was quite naked; the child wore no mask, no skinsuit, no protection of any kind – *naked and in the open*.

It was too much. Pirius and Torec fled to the enclosed security of their cabin, where they clung to each other, trembling. But they could feel the corvette shudder subtly as it dipped into the air of Earth.

After their landing at a spaceport, a small bubbletop flitter took them in a short suborbital hop to their final destination, Nilis's home.

As the flitter shot briefly back out of the atmosphere Pirius saw that the primary spaceport had been at the heart of one of the larger landmasses. Now the flitter took them over a strip of ocean to a large offshore island. On this island Pirius spotted crumpled hills and rocky outcrops, obviously natural formations, no use to anybody. In the lowlands, though, and near the coasts and along the river valleys, the land was covered by wide green rectangles and cut through by arrow-straight canals.

But this cultivated land was marred by clusters of silver-grey, irregular, bubbling masses, like blisters. You could see these were not the work of humans, for they lacked both the symmetry of deliberate human design and the more organic patterns of unplanned settlements. But these alien scars were the cities of mankind, Pirius learned; they were called Conurbations.

Conurbations were officially referred to only by numbers. Thus the corvette had landed at the fringe of Conurbation 2807, while the flitter would bring them to Conurbation 3474, a sprawling city surrounding a broad, languid river. These numbers had been assigned by the long-vanquished Qax – pronounced 'Kh-axe', the alien occupiers of Earth in the years before Hama Druz. The huddling domes of the Conurbations, bubbles of blown rock, were essentially Qax designs; they had been preserved as a kind of permanent memorial of that dreadful time. But Nilis, with a wink, told them that the locals referred to their cities by much older, pre-Occupation names, though not a trace of those older settlements had survived the time of the Qax. Thus they had first landed at *Berr-linn*, and Nilis's base was in a city called *Lunn-dinn*.

They landed by the bank of the river, close to one of the great domes of Lunn-dinn. As they prepared to leave the flitter Pirius glimpsed the river itself, sparkling in the low sun. Even that was a stunning sight: *open water*, billions of tonnes of it just sliding by in miraculous equilibrium with an atmosphere that was itself open to space.

It was a short walk through a covered passage from the pad to Nilis's apartment, which was just inside the skin of the dome. Nilis briskly walked through dusty rooms, maintenance bots clustered in Nilis's wake demanding instructions, and self-proclaiming 'urgent' Virtuals fluttered around him, evanescent and noisy. There was a musty smell, a faint staleness. It had evidently been some time since he had been home.

Nilis showed the ensigns to the room he had assigned them. Thankfully it was without windows to the outside. Torec simply pulled off her uniform, threw it to the floor and climbed into the single wide bed.

Pirius followed her, a little more slowly. In this strange new place fear and curiosity warred in him, making him restless. But he held Torec until her trembling had stopped and she slept.

He woke after two hours. Torec was sleeping soundly; for now she had escaped from the strangeness.

Pirius watched her for a while. The curving skin of her shoulder was smooth, flawless, and her small face, turned away from him, was blank, as if she was a child, unformed. He felt a surging warmth towards her, an urge to hold her so they could protect each other in this bewilderingly strange place.

If you'd asked him before they left Arches, he thought, he'd surely have said Torec was no more than a squeeze to him, and vice versa. Now she seemed a lot more. Was his feeling for her because they were alone here, the only bit of familiarity for each other so far from home? Had he felt this way about her, underneath, even before they had left Arches? Or maybe the crisis they had been through on the ship had drawn them together, as if they'd been through combat.

It was complicated. He wasn't used to digging into his own emotions so deeply; in a Barracks Ball you didn't get a lot of quiet time to think.

There was plenty to distract him here, of course. He slid carefully out of bed.

He explored the room. He found doors to a lavatory, and a shower room – not a clean-cloth store, but a place where *running water* came pouring out of a slot in the roof at his commands. Pirius tried it. Though it was hot and clear, the water left him feeling vaguely unclean; perhaps it came from the safety of a recycling tank, but it could have come from the river, or the ocean. He didn't imagine he would ever enjoy this strange experience.

He dried off and dressed in a fresh uniform.

He stepped to the door and hesitated. He hadn't come all the way to Earth itself to hide. He tapped the door; it slid open silently, and he left the room.

The apartment was astoundingly big, and astoundingly empty; Pirius thought you could have lodged five hundred ensigns in a space this size, but it was all devoted to one fat Commissary. As he wandered, small maintenance bots scuttled silently after him, scuffing at the carpet, removing all traces of his presence as he passed. The apartment was just under the outer skin of the dome, and large picture windows had been cut into the outer wall. The rooms were flooded with light that poured unfiltered from the parent star. Pirius, trying to acclimatise, shied away from the light.

Some of the rooms had functions that seemed obvious. One contained a long conference table, for instance, flanked by rows of chairs. Pirius touched the surface of the table. It was pale brown and textured with a kind of grain, a material he had never seen before. Other rooms seemed designed for leisure; typically they had chairs and low tables set up before the windows.

Every room was cluttered, full of artefacts, memorabilia perhaps, or the objects of Nilis's study. Some of this stuff was Virtual, complex three-dimensional sketches left half-finished, hovering in the air. But there were much older technologies too. In one room Pirius even found a row of *books* – though he would learn that word only later – blocks of paper you held in your hand.

One room held a kind of display: certificates and plaques covered the walls, and in open cases medals and little statues shone. There was even a Virtual display, a double-helix representation that whirled and sparkled. Many of these items bore small plates marked with lettering. Pirius's reading was poor – in his line of work reading was just a backup data access system – but he recognised Nilis's name repeated over and over. It wasn't hard to see that these artefacts were prizes, awards, certificates: tokens of achievement, of congratulation. Once again this was horribly un-Doctrinal. You were supposed to do your duty for its own sake, not for recognition, not for *pride*. But the little tokens did not shout for attention; they were gathered here with a quiet, untidy pride, the marks of a life of achievement.

Indeed, the whole place was like a projection of Nilis's personality: rich, cluttered, fusty, baffling.

At last Pirius came to a room where, between two vast windows, the wall was broken by an open door.

Pirius stood on the thick carpet, frozen, ingrained panic rising. But this was Earth, the only world in the Galaxy where you could walk out of a dome without so much as a skinsuit and expect to live. He remembered the little girl on the island, who had shown no fear.

In the open space beyond the door, Pirius glimpsed Nilis. Barefoot, his Commissary's robe hitched up around his knees, he walked cheerfully through the bright light. He was carrying something green and complex, cradling it in his hands. Whistling, he passed on out of sight.

Pirius took a deep breath. After all he must already be breathing the unprocessed air of Earth. It seemed fresh, a little cool, and there were strange scents: a sharp tang, like nothing he had smelled before, yet somehow familiar even so. A *green scent*: the thought came to him unbidden. He didn't allow himself to hesitate further. He walked across the room to the door, out on to the platform beyond.

The light blasted his face, hot, intense, coming from a sun so brilliant he couldn't even bear to look towards it. But he made out something of the sky. It was *blue*, he saw, stunned. There were objects floating in that blue sky, fat, fluffy, irregular, shaded grey beneath. Surely the size of starships, they must be clouds, masses of water vapour.

Nilis was standing beside him. His hands, empty now, were grimy, black dirt trapped under his fingernails. He smiled. 'You're doing well, ensign,' he said.

'Yes, sir.' Pirius glanced about. He was on a terrace, a broad rectangle of concrete. Much of the terrace was given over to a series of troughs, each of which contained heavy black earth. Things were growing in there: plants, Pirius supposed, with leaves of green, blood red, black. Small hand tools were scattered about. Though maintenance bots hovered hopefully, Nilis, barefoot, sweating, black-nailed, had evidently been tending this little garden himself.

Beyond the lip of the terrace the land fell away to the river, which swept by, its surface glistening like the hide of some immense animal. Pirius felt dwarfed, naked.

'So,' Nilis said. 'What do you think?'

'The sky,' Pirius said.

'Yes?'

'It's *blue*. I wasn't expecting that.'

Nilis pondered that. 'No, I suppose you wouldn't.' He wiped his brow and lifted his face; the light of the sun seemed to smooth out the wrinkles etched in his brow. 'You could know everything about the physics of light, Pirius, but you would never guess a sky might be blue. Earth, drained as she is, continues to remind us of our limits, our humility.'

'Drained?'

'Look again, ensign. What else can you see, beyond the lid of sky?'

Pirius shielded his eyes from the sun. Everywhere he looked, sparks slid by. 'Ships,' he said.

Nilis pointed to a drifting tetrahedral form, faintly visible, white against blue. 'See that? It's a Snowflake. Its builders, who the Assimilators called "Snowmen", lived far out in the halo of the Galaxy. A billion years ago they built their giant artefacts to record the slow cooling of the universe. We destroyed the Snowmen and confiscated their technology. Now Snowflakes orbit Earth in a great shell as deep as the Moon's orbit: they are watch stations, I suppose, waiting for any threatening move from the Xeelee – and those huge eyes are turned on Earth too, seeking out signs of insurgence from dissident human factions. Oh, don't look so surprised, ensign; in any age there are always plenty of rebels.

'Now – see those streams of ships? At night it's easier to see their formations as they enter and leave orbit. You know, a surprising amount of the materiel for this war comes from Earth itself. At the equator there are mines that tap the liquid iron of the planet's core, for mass and energy. The home planet's very lifeblood is poured into the throat of the war! Already, so it is said, the structure of the core has been so distorted by such mining that the planet's natural magnetic field has been affected. But don't worry. The Coalition lifts great stations into low orbit to protect us from any magnetic collapse . . .'

Pirius had learned that Nilis wanted him to speak openly. So he said boldly, 'Commissary, I'm still not sure what you do all day.'

Nilis laughed. 'Nor are my superiors.'

'But your achievements must be significant.'

'Why do you say that?'

'Because they earned you trophies. And *this*.'

'The apartment? Well, perhaps, though those jealous idiots on the Conurbation Council always keep the best views for themselves!' He tapped his teeth. 'You don't know much about me, do you, Pirius? No reason you should. I suppose my enduring claim to fame is that I am the man who doubled the output of Earth's farmland – and, of course, of every food production facility in the Galaxy.' He patted his generous belly. 'It was long before you were born, of course. But every time you enjoy a hearty meal you should think of me and offer up thanks.'

'How . . . ?'

Ecology had long been deleted from the Earth. Outside of a few domed parks, the land was given over to nanotechnological machines, which, powered by sunlight, toiled to turn the raw materials of the air and the soil into the bland paste, nano-food, that was the staple diet of the whole of mankind.

'All I did was to double the efficiency of those labouring little critters.' Nilis sighed. 'The technology was simple enough. But still it was a marvellous day for me when the speaker of the Coalition's Grand Conclave herself brought a handful of nano-dust to a scraped-clean bit of ground – not far north of here, in fact – and released my food bots into the wild.'

Pirius didn't know how to phrase his questions; he had never met a scientist before. 'How did you figure out what to do?'

'By reading history, my boy. Who invented the nanobots that feed us, do you suppose?'

'I don't know.'

'Come, come. What *race*?'

'I – human, of course.'

'Not so.' Nilis shook his head. 'The Commission doesn't *lie* – that would be very anti-Doctrinal. But it is happy to allow certain inconvenient truths to fade into forgetfulness. Pirius, it was the Qax, our occupiers, who first seeded Earth with nanobots. They did it to make us reliant on them, and later as a deliberate act of the Extirpation: by destroying our ecology they sought to cut our links to our past. And then, when the Qax fell and the Coalition took over, there were simply too many mouths to feed, too much ancient knowledge lost, to resist using the bots to feed the liberated swarms.

'Nobody knows that Qax machines are feeding them! But *I* knew, because I was curious, and I dug into various old libraries and found out. Then I checked to see if the Expansion had yet reached the Qax home world. Of course it had, long ago. So I applied for a study grant from my Office. I learned that the Assimilation officers had gathered a great deal of data on Qax nanomachinery, though their studies had been allowed to gather dust for centuries. With that, it was straightforward for me to revisit the basis of the food nanobots and find ways to improve their operation. "Straightforward" – the work of ten years, but that is a mere detail.'

Pirius was impressed. 'It was a great contribution to the war effort.'

Nilis looked at him quizzically. 'Well, I suppose it was, though I didn't intend it that way. My nano-food got me this apartment, and a source of funding – and, more importantly, a power base, of a sort, at least a position of independence. Yes, I'm proud of my work, and I'm certainly not shy of shouting about it when it's useful. But I certainly didn't achieve it by *thinking* in the way we're all supposed to, with that peculiar mixture of arrogance and narrowness that characterises the Druz Doctrines. I was prepared to look into the murky corners of the past – I was prepared to accept the uncomfortable, paradoxical truth that though we have conquered a Galaxy we are utterly dependent on an alien technology!

'And, of course, the latitude I won as the Man Who Fed The Galaxy has allowed me to cultivate my garden. Come see. Don't worry; I won't ask you to get your hands dirty . . .'

Nilis's 'garden', confined to the concrete troughs, was unprepossessing, just tangles and clumps and spindles of green, crimson and black, some curled together. Everything was small, compact, tough-looking.

Nilis watched Pirius's reaction. 'So what do you think?'

Pirius shrugged. 'All I've seen of nature is rats and the algae you have to scrape out of air ducts, and nobody makes a pet of *that*.'

Nilis laughed. 'Well, my little gatherings here are nobody's pets either. I suppose you'd say they are weeds.' He picked up one scrawny growth, a green stem topped by a gaudy yellow flower. 'This is a native plant, obviously. Its chlorophyll green has become mankind's symbol, hasn't it? – even though we try to stamp it out wherever we find it. Ironic! We understand its biochemistry, of course, but we've long forgotten the name our forefathers gave it. I found it growing in the heart of the city – of Lunn-dinn, right here. Our Earth is supposed to be managed, ensign: paved over, milked as efficiently as possible by the nanobots. But even in the cities, where the concrete cracks, a little earth gathers. And where there is earth, plants grow, welcome or not.

'But look here.' From a tangle of vegetation Nilis pulled out leaves: one a neat oval shape but jet black, the other almost square and deep red. Nilis said, 'I found this black-leaf on Earth – but it's not a native! It's actually from a planet of Tau Ceti. And this red-leaf isn't a native either; it comes from a system a thousand light years away. I doubt if these little creatures were brought here on purpose; they travelled as spores in the recycling systems of starships, perhaps, or lodged in the sinuses of unwary travellers. Both come from worlds basically like Earth, though, worlds of Main Sequence suns and carbon-water chemistry, or else they couldn't survive here.

'But even on worlds so similar to Earth, life can develop in radically different ways. All these leaves are photosynthetic; they all gather energy from sunlight. But only Earth life uses chlorophyll; the others use different combinations of chemicals – and so they aren't green. Interesting; you would think that this black shade is actually the most *efficient* colour for a gatherer of sunlight . . . On each world life is born, like and yet unlike any other life in the universe. Once it's born it complexifies away, endlessly elaborating, until it has filled a world. And then we come along, with our starships and Expansions, and mix it up, complexifying it further.'

Pirius frowned. 'If their biochemical basis is so different they can't eat each other.'

'Well, that's true. But these plants coexist anyhow. At the very least they compete for the same physical resources – the sunlight, say, or room in the soil; whoever grows fastest wins. There may be reasons to eat something even if not for the biochemistry; a concentration of some essential mineral fixed by your prey, perhaps.

'And look at this.' He moved to another trough and showed Pirius a kind of trellis, no more than ten centimetres high, covered in tiny black leaves, with a green plant draped over it. 'The miniature trellis is a tree-analogue from the Deneb system,' Nilis said, 'and the green plant is a pea, from Earth. The pea has learned to use the frame as a support. And probably the trellis is using the pea for its own purposes, perhaps to attract other Denebian life forms; I haven't figured it out yet.' He smiled. 'You see? Cooperation. The first step to an interstellar ecology, and all happening by accident. It wouldn't surprise me to come back here in, oh, ten or fifty million years, and find composite life forms with components from biochemical lineages once separated by light years. After all our own cells are the results of ancient mergers between beings almost as divergent, between oxygen-haters and oxygen-lovers.'

As he pottered around the little plants, cupping each gently with his dirt-stained fingers, Pirius suddenly saw how lonely this man was.

'I'm not sure why you're showing me this, sir.'

Nilis straightened up, massaging his back. 'I wish I'd had these troughs built a little higher! Just this, ensign: we live in a universe of endless, apparently inexhaustible richness. Everywhere life complexifies, finding new ways to combine, to compete, to live, endlessly exploring the richness of the possible – indeed, as in this example, actually expanding that richness. Once human society itself showed the same tendency to complexify: no surprise, as we are children of this rich universe. But the Druz Doctrines deny that tendency. The Doctrines try to hold us static, in form, thought, intention – for all time, if necessary.'

Pirius said, 'The Doctrines have kept mankind united for twenty thousand years, and have taken us to the centre of the Galaxy.'

'There is truth in that. *But it can't last*, ensign. The Doctrines are based on a falsehood – a denial of what we are. And, in the weeds that grow through the tarmac of our spaceports, we see clear evidence of our lack of ability to *control*. In the social realm it's just the same – remember those Virtual fan messages you had! The world is much more messy than Commission propaganda allows us to believe.

'And *that* is my philosophical objection to the Doctrines, Pirius. *That* is why I have strained every sinew for years to find a way to win this war – before we lose it, as otherwise we inevitably must. You wouldn't think we are in peril, looking around. We have covered the Earth, enslaved nature, spread across a Galaxy. We are strong, we are united – but it is all based on a lie, it is all terribly fragile, and it could all fall apart, terribly easily.'

Pirius heard a soft tapping sound. He looked down, puzzled. The concrete platform was becoming speckled with dark little discs: water splashes. Then he felt a pattering of droplets on his bare skin, his hands, his brow, even his hair. Perhaps some climate-control system had broken down.

Nilis sighed and pulled the hood of his robe over his head. 'Oh, my eyes. Not another shower! I will never finish.'

Pirius looked up. One of those clouds hovered right over his head, its underside dark and threatening. And water was falling towards him, fat drops of it. By tracking back along their paths Pirius could see the drops were falling *out of the sky itself*.

It was too much; the last of his courage failed him. He turned and ran for the controlled environment of the apartment.

Later that night Pirius was restless again.

The apartment was dark. But as he walked through the rooms a soft light gathered at his feet, and washed into the corners of the room. It didn't dazzle his night-adapted eyes, but was bright enough for him to see where he was going.

A colder light came pouring in from outside, through the window: a silver light tinged with green.

He walked forward, not allowing himself to think about what he was doing. Maintenance bots followed him with silent, discreet efficiency.

The terrace door was closed. He pressed his hand to its surface, and it dilated.

There was no rain. It looked safe.

Pirius stepped forward. That cool light picked out the lines of the terrace, washed over Nilis's tiny garden, and sparkled from the broad back of the river beyond. It was an eerie glow that seemed to transform an already strange world.

Deliberately he looked up.

The source of the light was the Moon, of course, the famous Moon of Earth. It was a disc small enough to cover with his thumb. But it was a transformed Moon – and one of Earth's legendary sights, whispered of even in the Barracks Ball of Arches Base.

The face of this patient companion had gazed down through all of man's turbulent history. But the face was unchanged no more. Patches of grey-green were spreading across the pale highlands and the dusty maria, the green of Earth life rooting itself in the Moon's ancient dust. That was why Moonlight was no longer silver, but salted with a green photosynthetic glow.

And a great thread arced out of the centre of the Moon's face and swept across the night sky towards the horizon. Pirius thought he could see a thickening in that graceful arc as it swept away from the Moon towards the Earth. The arc was the Bridge, an enclosed tunnel that joined the Moon to the Earth – or at least to an anchoring station a few hundred kilometres above the Earth. The Bridge had been built with alien technology captured millennia ago; now the important folk of the Interim Coalition of Governance could travel from Earth to Moon in security and comfort, as easily as riding an elevator shaft.

The Bridge itself, defying orbital mechanics, was unstable, of course, constantly stressed by tides, and it had to be maintained with drive units and antigravity boxes studded along its length. The whole thing was utterly grandiose, hugely expensive, and quite without a practical purpose. Pirius laughed out loud at its folly and magnificence.

The next morning he tried to describe his feelings on first seeing the tethered Moon.

Nilis just smiled. 'We travel to the stars, but we still must build our pyramids,' he said enigmatically.

CHAPTER 9

Two weeks after his return to Earth, Nilis set up a meeting with a man called the Minister of Economic Warfare.

As he prepared for this meeting, Nilis made no secret of his nervousness, nor how much was riding on the outcome. 'I suppose you'd call Minister Gramm my champion. My nano-food innovation was fundamentally an economic benefit, you see, and so its deployment in the war effort came under the purview of Economic Warfare. Since then Gramm has supported me in my various initiatives – hoping I will pull out another gem!' He sighed. 'But it's difficult, it's always difficult. The Coalition is very ancient and has its own way of doing things. Mavericks aren't treated well. Without the shelter of Gramm's patronage, I'm quite sure I would have been sidelined long ago . . .'

And so on. Pirius and Torec listened patiently to this, for Nilis in his blundering way seemed to appreciate having someone to talk to. But it was hard to be sympathetic. To Pirius Red the bureaucratic problems of working at the higher levels of the Interim Coalition of Governance were somewhat esoteric.

On the day of the meeting, to their dismay, Nilis suddenly decided to take both ensigns with him.

Before they set off Nilis insisted on checking over their uniforms. It did Pirius no good to point out that the smart uniforms took care of themselves better than he or Torec ever could; Nilis nervously examined every seam, every centimetre of beading.

'Anyway,' said Pirius, 'I don't see what we can add to a meeting with a minister.'

'Oh, you're my secret weapon,' Nilis said, smiling edgily. 'You are unruly defiance made flesh! Even when tangling with the Coalition, you must never underestimate the power of psychology, ensign.'

Nilis insisted that they were going to walk to the Ministry building – walk across the Conurbation, an Earth city, in the open air. It was a dreadful prospect, but Pirius knew by now that it was no use arguing with the Commissary when he had made up his mind.

Still, Pirius and Torec hesitated on the doorstep of Nilis's apartment. Pirius had acclimatised to the point where he could sit out in the garden with Nilis, even *eat* in the open air, but Torec was further behind, and after all to venture out of doors without a sealed-up skin-suit violated every bit of conditioning drummed into them since before they could talk.

'But it has to be done,' Torec said grimly.

'It has to be done.' Hand in hand they took the first step, out into the light.

Nilis strode off along a road that arrowed between the hulking shoulders of blown-rock domes, straight to the heart of the Conurbation. His robe flapped, the watery sun shone from his shaven head, and a small bot carrying his effects laboured gamely to keep up. For all his insistence on checking the ensigns' appearance, Nilis himself looked as if he had come straight from his rooftop garden; he wasn't even wearing any shoes.

He didn't look back. The ensigns had to hurry after him.

The surfaces of the domes were smooth, polished, some even worked with other kinds of stone. One massive dome, coated with a creamy rock, gleamed bright in the sunlight. 'The Ministry of Supply,' Nilis called over his shoulder. 'Supplied themselves with marble readily enough!'

There wasn't much traffic, just a few smart cars. But there were pedestrians everywhere, even off the ground. Walkways connected the domes, snaking through the air at many levels in casual defiance of gravity and logic. People hurried along the ways, chattering; others were accompanied by shells of glowing Virtual displays, as if they carried their own small worlds around with them. In some places the walkways would tip up steeply, or even run vertically, but the crowds bustled over them blithely. The people were so immersed in their own affairs they didn't even notice the unfailing miracles of inertial engineering that enabled them to walk without effort straight up a wall.

Torec was muttering under her breath, some comforting nonsense. But she kept walking. She was doing well; and Pirius felt proud of her – not that he'd have dared to tell her so. You didn't look up at the open sky, that was the key. You didn't think about how exposed you were to the wild. You concentrated on the manufactured environment; you kept your gaze on the smooth surface of the road, or on the buildings around you.

But at one point Torec stopped dead. Through a crack in the road surface a bit of green showed, a weed. It was a bit of raw life pushing through a hole in the engineered reality around them. Pirius was more used to green things than Torec, thanks to Nilis's garden. But here in the wild it was an oddly terrifying sight.

As they pushed into the dense heart of the city, things got still more difficult for the ensigns. People started to notice them. They stared openly as the ensigns passed, and pointed, and peered down from the walkways. The ensigns' uniforms didn't help; their bright scarlet tunics stood out like beacons in the Conurbation crowds, who mostly dressed in plain black Commissary-style robes.

Nilis grinned. 'They've never seen soldiers before. And you're famous, Pirius!'

'Commissary, it wasn't even *me*—'

Nilis waved a hand. 'Never mind temporal hair-splitting. To these crowds *you're* the kid who beat a Xeelec. Don't let them worry you. They're just human, as you are.'

Torec frowned. 'Human maybe, but not like us.'

It was true, Pirius thought. In Arches Base everybody was the same – small, wiry, even with similar features, since most of them had been hatched from the same birthing tanks. 'But here,' he said, 'everyone is different. Tall, short. There are *old* people. And they're all *fat*. You don't see many fat people at the Front.'

'No,' Nilis said. 'But that's policy, you see. If you're kept hungry, if everything in your world is shabby, you have something to fight for – even if it's just an inchoate dream of somewhere safe and warm and with enough to eat.'

Torec said, 'So you let us fight for you, while you starve us and let us live in shit.'

Pirius was alarmed, but Nilis seemed to admire her outspokenness.

'Like it or not, that's the policy – and since very few front-line troops ever come here, to the heart of things, few people ever know about it . . .'

In the immensity of the city Pirius tried to keep his bearings. The whole of human society was like a great machine, so he had always been taught, a machine unified and dedicated to a single goal: the war with the Xeelee. The people around him, absorbed in their important and baffling bits of business, might seem strange, but they were parts of the greater machine too. He mustn't look down on them: they were warriors in their way, just as he was, as was every human being.

But he thought of Nilis's extraordinary ambition of ending this war. Perhaps he, Pirius, a mere ensign, would play a part in a revolution that would transform the lives of every human in the Galaxy – including every one of the confident, jostling crowd around him. In that case he had nothing to fear. Indeed, these people of Earth should fear *him*.

It was a deliciously non-Doctrinal thought. He always had wanted to be remembered.

'Ah, here we are,' said Nilis.

They stopped before another dome, as grand and busy as the rest. Nilis led them out of the glare of day into an antechamber. Much of this dome had been left open; there were partitions and internal walkways, but once inside you could look up and see the great rough sweep of the old Qax architecture itself.

They were subjected to a ferocious security check. Bots clambered over them, their identities were verified, they were scanned for implants, given quickfire tests for loyalty and mental stability, and subjected to many other examinations whose nature Pirius couldn't even recognise. Most of this was performed by automated systems, but a single human guard was there to overview the process, a blue-helmeted woman from the Bureau of Guardians. Nilis endured it silently, and Pirius and Torec followed his lead.

At last they were released. A small Virtual marker materialised before them and floated off. It led them to a roofless office, deep in the heart of the dome, with a long conference table and a nano-food niche. With a sigh Nilis ordered hot tea.

'And now we wait,' he said to the ensigns. '*We're* on time, but Gramm won't be. It's all part of the game of power, you know . . .'

This dome belonged to Gramm's Ministry of Economic Warfare, he told them. Aside from its specifically military arms, like the Navy and the Green Army and the Guardians, mankind's police force, and agencies with cultural goals such as the Commission for Historical Truth and the Ministry of Public Enlightenment, the three greatest ministries at the heart of the Interim Coalition of Governance were this Ministry of Economic Warfare, the Ministry of Supply and the Ministry of Production.

Nilis chattered on, 'Even though they all report in to a single Grand Conclave member – Philia Doon, the Plenipotentiary for Total War – to get anything done you have to deal with all three. Even Minister Gramm can't deliver anything by himself. But Economic Warfare's aim is to ensure the dedication of all mankind's resources to the great goal. To some extent it acts as an intermediary between the other two. And that gives Gramm some leverage. He can be a difficult man, but I couldn't ask for a more useful ally . . . Ah, Minister!'

Minister Gramm came bustling into the room. Even by the standards of Earth, Pirius thought, he was stupendously fat; his belly pushed out his grey cloak so that it hung over his legs, and his fingers, clasped before his stomach, were tubes of pasty flesh. His scalp was shaven and his cheeks heavy, so that his head was like a round moon.

He brought two people with him, both women. The first he briskly introduced as Pila, a senior advisor, who Nilis had evidently met before. Golden-haired, she was slim, beautiful, expensively dressed, and oddly detached, as if all this was somehow beneath her. She showed no interest in the ensigns.

The second person with Gramm was quite different. Small, round-shouldered, the shape of her body was hidden by the severe cut of her black robe. Her skin was an odd weathered brown, as if she had been irradiated. All her features were small, her nose a stub, her mouth pinched and her hair was just a grey scraping over her scalp. Pirius found it hard to judge her age. The smoothness of her skin had nothing to do with youth; it was as if her features had been worn by time. Indeed it wasn't until she spoke that Pirius was even sure this was a woman.

Nilis bustled forward to greet the Minister, his hand extended, his big bare feet slapping on the polished floor. But the small woman spoke first.

'So here are our young heroes from the Front.' She stood before Pirius. Her eyes were deep and dark, hidden in sockets that seemed to have receded into her head. 'I wish I could smell you – you have about you the burned-metal stench of vacuum, no doubt.' She reached out a small hand, and made to brush his cheek. To his shock her fingers passed through his flesh and broke into a swarm of blocky pixels. 'Yes, I'm a Virtual,' she said. 'An avatar, actually. I'm too many light minutes from here to be able to contribute. But I couldn't miss *this*.'

To Nilis, Gramm said uncomfortably, 'This is Luru Parz, Commissary. My – ah – consultant.'

Pirius had absolutely no idea who this woman was or what she wanted, and it baffled him that Gramm didn't even seem to want her here.

But there was no time to think about that, for now Gramm was looming over Torec. 'What an exotic little creature. The colour of her uniform – the texture of her flesh – why, she's like a little toy.' He reached out and laid his fat fingers on her shoulder.

Torec endured this, expressionless. But when his hand slid down her shoulder to her breast, she grabbed his finger and bent it back.

He recoiled, clutching his hand to his crotch. 'Lethe, I think she broke it!'

Luru Parz was laughing. 'No, she didn't. You deserved that, you fat fool.'

Gramm glared up at Nilis. 'I'll hold you responsible, Commissary.'

Nilis was trembling with anger, Pirius saw. 'Well, you have that right, sir. But I point out that it is "exotic little creatures" like these who are fighting and dying on our behalf, even as that Earth is more than a cess-pit of decadence. They certainly deserve more respect than to be treated as playthings, even by a minister.'

Luru Parz opened her mouth to laugh louder. Her teeth were quite black, Pirius saw. 'He has you there, Gramm!'

Gramm glared at her. 'Shut up, Luru; sometimes you go too far.'

The slim woman, Pila, watched all this with an air of detachment. 'If the pleasantries are over, shall we start?'

Still cradling his hand, Gramm slumped in a chair. 'Let's get it over.'

Nilis bustled to the head of the room with his bot.

Pirius and Torec cautiously took their seats as far from the others as possible. Luru Parz sat too, but Pirius saw that her Virtual wasn't perfect, and she seemed to hover above her chair.

A servant appeared – not a bot, Pirius saw, wondering, a *human* servant – with drinks and a tray of some kind of hot, spicy food, which he set before the Minister. Gramm pushed the fingers of his uninjured hand into the food and began to eat steadily.

A glass of water, Virtually generated, materialised before Luru Parz, and she picked it up and sipped it gently. She saw the ensigns staring at her, and she smiled. 'Here on Earth, children, there is even an etiquette for dealing with a Virtual guest. High culture, you see. Isn't that something worth fighting for?'

Nilis was ready to make his presentation. 'Minister, Madam Parz, Madam Pila, ensigns—'

Gramm growled, 'Get on with it, Nilis, you bumbling idiot.' The servant discreetly wiped grease from his mouth.

Nilis pointed dramatically at Pirius. 'I brought these child soldiers back from the Front for two reasons. First they symbolise our endless war. All across the Front, bright young people are fighting and dying in hordes. And it has been that way for three thousand years.'

Gramm asked, 'Is this to be one of your interminable moral lectures, Nilis?'

Nilis said urgently, 'Moral, you say? Don't we at least have a moral responsibility to *try* to curtail this endless waste? Wouldn't that be moral? And that's the second reason I brought these two home. Because this one, Pirius, will – or would have, in an earlier timeline draft – *would have* found a new way to strike at the Xeelee. You can see the results in the derelict I brought home to Saturn. Minister, Pilot Officer Pirius showed that we *can* think differently about the war, even after all this time.'

'Tell me what you're proposing, Commissary.' The Minister sounded languidly bored.

Nilis snapped his fingers. His bot unfolded a white screen and produced a clutch of styluses with a kind of flourish. And above its hide, a Virtual of the Galaxy coalesced. The central bulge was bright enough to cast shadows on the polished surface of the conference table, and its paper-thin disc sparkled with supernova jewels.

'Here is the Galaxy, with its four hundred billion stars,' Nilis said. 'I have consulted the archives of the Navy, the Green Army, and other military groups. And here are their current targets for military action.'

He snapped his fingers again. A series of bright green specks lit up across the Galaxy's image. 'You can see there are still a few in the disc – pockets of resistance we've yet to clear out – and more in the halo, beyond the range of this image. But the main action is of course at the Front.' This was a sphere, emerald green, embedded in the Galaxy's central bulge. 'It's an impressive disposition, the culmination of a grand military ambition. But our strategy is missing one crucial element.'

A new Virtual coalesced in the air, before the Galaxy image. It was another spiral, looking like a cartoon version of the star city behind it.

Pirius recognised it immediately. 'That's the Baby Spiral,' he said. 'It's inside the Front – the system at the very centre of the Galaxy.'

Nilis said, 'Quite right, ensign. But look here . . .' The image magnified until the centre of the Baby Spiral loomed large and bright and its crowded arms feathered off into the surrounding darkness. Nilis pointed to an unassuming speck of white light, just off-centre from the spiral's geometric heart. 'Ensign Pirius, can you tell us what that is?'

'That's Chandra. Sir, the Xeelee's Galactic Prime Radiant is based at the three-million-stellar-mass black hole at the centre of the Galaxy. The Xeelee seem to use it as their operational command post.'

Nilis nodded. 'Good, good.'

'Yes,' said Luru Parz. 'And a summary appropriately hedged with qualifications.'

Gramm glared at her. 'What do you mean by that?'

' "Seem to use it" for this and that . . . Don't you think it's extraordinary, Minister, that after three thousand years of siege warfare around this Prime Radiant we know so little about it, and indeed about our foe?'

Gramm turned away from her. 'Make your point, Commissary.'

Nilis said, 'My point is this.' He turned to the display dramatically. 'The Prime Radiant is surrounded by military targets, as you can see. *But the Prime Radiant itself is not a target.*' He looked at their faces, waiting for comprehension to dawn.

'And,' Gramm said around a mouthful of food, 'you're saying it should be.'

'Of course it should! The Prime Radiant is properly named, for it is in a real sense the source of the Xeelee presence in our Galaxy. And if we could strike at it—' He snapped his fingers again. Suddenly the centre of the Baby Spiral glowed emerald green, and one by one the other lights went out. 'Minister, take out the source and all these other targets, which are downstream of it in a logical sense, are essentially taken out too. Why, it's a question of economics. If you shut down the factory, you are saved the expense of picking off its products one by one. Take out the power plant—'

'Yes, yes. Get on with it, man.'

'This, sir, is how I believe we should be fighting this war. What I'm asking for is the initiation of a new project. Its ultimate goal will be specific: *the destruction of the Xeelee Prime Radiant.*'

Through the fog of his verbiage, Nilis's meaning suddenly became clear. Pirius felt a deep thrill run through him. To strike at the Prime Radiant itself!

The meeting was continuing. Pirius tried to focus.

Gramm picked his teeth. 'What a wonderful imagination you must have, Commissary. But is that all you have?'

'Minister—'

'Do you imagine that in the long millennia of this war that *nobody* has come up with such an obvious tactic? Don't you suppose that if it were ever possible it would have been done by now?'

'But if you won't even think it through—'

Unexpectedly Gramm turned to Pirius. 'Why don't you take the floor, ensign?'

'Sir?'

'You're the hero of the hour. You downed a Xeelee; that's why you're here. Why don't you explain to us why the Commissary's suggestions are a fantasy? If I asked *you* to take out the Prime Radiant, how would you respond?'

Pirius stayed where he was, uncertain and embarrassed. But Nilis shrugged and sat down.

So Pirius stood up, walked to the front of the room and thought for a moment. He waved his hand to banish Nilis's expensive Virtual displays, leaving only the white board, and he picked up a stylus. With an apologetic glance at Nilis, he drew a red asterisk at the right hand side of the board. 'Sir, I believe there are three fundamental problems. First, even if we could get through the Xeelee defences in the region of Chandra' – he tapped the asterisk – 'we don't have any weapon that can strike at a black hole, and whatever the Xeelee are doing with it.'

'Of course not,' said Luru Parz. 'How could we since we've put no effort into finding out what the Prime Radiant actually is? . . . Go on, ensign.'

Pirius drew a red circle around the asterisk. 'Second problem. We can't get through to Chandra anyhow, because if we could get close enough to engage the Xeelee's inner defensive cordon, they would surely out-fly us, out-think us. Their equipment is better than ours. Most important, their computing capability is superior.'

'And third' – Pirius drew a dotted line reaching back to the left of the asterisk, and cut it through with a vertical line – 'we can't even get that close, because of FTL foreknowledge. The Xeelee would see us coming and shoot us down before we left our bases.' He hesitated, looked at his sketch and went back to his seat.

He won an ironic slow clap from Gramm. 'Admirably summarised.' The Minister raised an eyebrow at the Commissary. 'Nilis? I hope you won't claim now that you have a solution to all these problems?'

'No, sir. Not all of them. But, thanks to Pirius and his companions, I can solve one.' He walked to the white board, picked up a stylus and tapped at the red circle Pirius had drawn around the Prime Radiant. 'We *may* have a way to beat Xeelee processing power. It's uncertain – Pirius Blue and his colleagues improvised it in the middle of combat – but we can take the concept and build on it. Minister, *we can out-think the Xeelee*. I know that's true because we've done it once already. And if one of these ancient obstacles can at least in principle be overcome, then perhaps we can defeat the rest. Suddenly we see a chink of light; suddenly we have hope.'

Luru Parz was nodding. 'Yes, yes. It was this strange news from the Front which drew my attention too. A new hope.' And that was why she had forced her way into this meeting, Pirius saw, apparently over the objections of a minister. Whoever this strange woman was she had power – and her ambition seemed to be a mirror of Nilis's.

Gramm glared at Nilis. 'And that's all you have to say? *This* is the case you're going to put? Can you not see, Commissary, how you will make an enemy of almost everybody in authority if you go around claiming that better minds than yours have, for millennia, pursuing the wrong targets – with the wrong weapons too?'

Pirius saw that Nilis was struggling to control his anger. 'Those "better minds" have been locked into a rigidity of thinking for those long millennia, Minister.'

'Don't go too far, Commissary,' Gramm said.

Nilis dismissed that with a wave. 'I'm well aware that it wouldn't be your decision alone, Minister, so let's not play games. All I want at the beginning is seedcorn funding, enough to get us to proof-of-concept of the pilots' new closed-timelike-curve computing paradigm. When that's successfully demonstrated, we can move to the next stage and ask for further funding to be released, stepwise. The political and financial control of the Coalition and the relevant Ministry over every stage of the project would be absolute—'

'You can bet your life it would,' Gramm shouted.

'Ask for more,' Luru Parz said immediately.

Nilis looked confused.

'Ask for more,' she said again. 'We work in ignorance. We've seen that today. We have to start a new programme of inquiry; we have to understand our enemy, at last. We can begin with your captive Xeelee, Commissary. But we have to find out more about them – especially their Prime Radiant – if we are to defeat them.'

Nilis had no choice but to nod. 'You're right, of course.'

Luru pressed Gramm. 'Minister, these requests are undeniably reasonable – and politically will be hard to refuse. After all Nilis and his heroes and his captive Xeelee have made an undeniable stir here on Earth. If there was no follow-up, questions would surely be asked. Even under the Coalition, public opinion counts for something.'

Gramm grunted. 'The power of the mob. Which the Commissary no doubt intended to stir up when he marched his two pet soldiers through the streets of the Conurbation.'

Pirius glanced at Nilis. Could it be true that Nilis had been so manipulative as to use them to further his own ends in such a way? There was much of the doings of Earth he had yet to understand.

But he had listened to this meeting unfold with increasing irritation. He felt bold enough to speak again. 'Minister, Commissary – I'm sorry – I don't understand this talk of control and caution and stepwise funding. Isn't winning the war what this is about? Why don't we just *do* this?'

Gramm raised his eyebrows. 'Bravely spoken,' he said with quiet menace. 'But no matter what gossip you've heard in your barracks at the Front, we don't have infinite resources, ensign. We can't do everything.'

'But it's not just that,' said Luru Parz. 'Ensign, my dear child, how sweetly naïve you are – but I suppose you have to be or you wouldn't be prepared to fight in the first place. Is winning the war *really* what we want to achieve? What would Minister Gramm *do* all day if there were no more need for a Minister of Economic Warfare? I'm not sure our system of government could withstand the shock of victory.'

Gramm glared at Luru Parz, but didn't challenge her.

Recklessly Pirius said to Gramm, 'I don't care about any of that. We have to try to win the war. It's our duty. Sir.'

Gramm looked at him, surprised, then threw his head back and laughed out loud, spraying bits of food into the air. 'You dare lecture a minister on duty? Lethe, this pet of yours has spirit, Commissary!'

'But he's right,' Nilis said, shaking his shaven head gravely.

Luru pressed again. 'So he is. You have to support this, Minister.'

Gramm growled, 'And I will be flayed in Conclave for it. I would have thought you would be the most conservative of all of us, Luru Parz.'

She smiled. 'I am conservative – very conservative. I just work on timescales you can't imagine.'

Gramm actually shuddered, hugely. Again Pirius wondered who this woman was, what hold she had.

Pila, Gramm's elegant advisor, watched this wordlessly, her lips upturned with disdainful humour. Throughout the whole of the meeting, as far as Pirius could remember, she hadn't said a single word.

When the meeting broke up Nilis came to the ensigns, his eyes shining. 'Thank you, thank you. I knew my hunch was right, to bring you here – you have made all the difference! "Project Prime Radiant" – that's what we'll call it – Project Prime Radiant was born today. And the way you spoke back to the Minister – I will be dining out on that for years to come!'

Torec glared at Pirius, who said dolefully, 'Yes, sir.'

'And now we have work to do, a great deal of work. The Minister has given us seven weeks to report – not long, not even reasonable, but it will have to do. Are you with me, ensigns?'

Pirius studied this flawed old man, a man who had dragged him from his training, from his life, had hauled him across the Galaxy and then paraded him to further his own ends – and yet, flawed though he might be, Nilis was working for victory. Pirius could see no higher duty. 'Yes, *sir.*'

Nilis turned to Torec. 'And you won't be worried about being turned out of your job, when we win the Galaxy?'

Torec smiled. 'No, sir. There are always more galaxies.' Her tone was bright, her smile vivid.

But Pirius saw Nilis pale at her words.

CHAPTER 10

On Quin Base you lived inside the Rock.

Once this Rock had been nothing but a lumpy conglomerate of friable rock, ice and dirt. Now it had been hollowed out and strengthened by an internal skeleton of pillars of fused and hardened stone.

The Rock's inner architecture was layered. You spent most of your off-duty time in big, sprawling chambers just under the surface. Here you ate, slept, fornicated, and, perhaps, died. Beneath the habitable quarters was another layer of chambers, not all pressurised, with air and water purifiers, and the nano-food bays which processed rivers of grunt sewage. Right at the heart of the Rock were more essential systems yet: weapons shops and stores, a dry dock area for small craft.

But Pirius Blue and his crew spent most of their time on the surface. As Service Corps recruits, their job would be to support infantry in combat conditions. And so their training began with basic infantry work.

Which turned out to be very basic indeed.

Under Captain Marta's watchful glare, in squads of a hundred or more, skinsuited cadets were put through hours of parade drill. Then there was the physical work: they bent, jumped, lifted, wrestled, endured endless route marches.

And they ran and ran and ran, endless laps of the trampled crater rim that seemed to be Marta's favoured form of torture.

Cohl, gasping, complained to Pirius, 'You'd train a rat like this.'

Pirius forced a laugh. 'If they could teach a rat to hold a spade you wouldn't need infantry grunts at all—'

'No talking!'

And off they ran again, glued to the asteroid dirt by their inertial belts.

It seemed as if every cadet on this Rock was younger than the Navy crew, save only This Burden Must Pass; every one of them was fitter, including Burden. It was galling that the *Claw* crew came last or near last in every exercise they were put through, and had more work inflicted on them as 'punishment'. The younger ones with their hard little bodies actually seemed to relish the sheer physical joy of it.

And it went on for hours. After a few days, sleep became the most important element in Pirius's life, to be snatched whenever he could in the brief hours they were left alone before reveille, or out on the surface between punishing routines. He even learned to catnap standing up.

It was very different to Navy training. Much of the training for flight crews was specialised, highly intellectual, with physical training focusing on fast reactions, fine control, endurance – it was a unifying of mind and body, so that both could work effectively and efficiently under the intense conditions of combat. The very geometry of Arches Base, with its n-body architecture of plummeting asteroids, was designed to stimulate, to train you from birth to be free of vertigo, to judge shifting distances and motions on an interplanetary scale.

But Army grunts didn't have to fly FTL warships. Here there was nothing more stimulating than dirt. Navy jokers always said that all grunts had to know how to do was dig and die, and now that Pirius was cast down among them he was starting to suspect it was true.

Nothing could help poor Enduring Hope, though. No amount of effort seemed to shift a gram of fat from his body, and he always trailed in last.

As Captain Marta inflicted her punishments on him, she always kept the rest of the training group, hundreds of them sometimes, waiting at attention in their sweat-filled skinsuits. As Hope slogged through his lonely circuits, their resentment was tangible.

For Pirius, things slowly got more bearable.

After a couple of weeks he could feel some of the fat falling off his body, and his muscles didn't ache quite so much as they had after his first outings. His body was still young and was responding to the exercise, and he was not deprived of food, which he ate ravenously.

He would never admit he enjoyed it. But he knew he was growing healthier, and he took some pleasure from the glow of his muscles.

He learned to use the correct Army rankings: colonel, not commander, sergeant, not petty officer. That at least lubricated the friction with the officers, none of whom had any time for Navy 'flyboys'. It turned out that most officers here belonged to the elite regiment known as the Coalition Guard, who even looked down on the rest of the Army.

The culture of these infantry troops was very different from the Navy, but slowly he began to perceive their fundamental pride. This war fought with starships had a surprisingly primitive base. There was ground to be held everywhere, on planets full of people and docks and weapons factories, on Rocks thrown into the battle zone. If the ground was lost, the battle was lost. And if you were infantry you held the ground; if you were infantry you *were* mankind's fighting force, and everybody else was just support.

Even the horror of their surroundings in the barracks began to wear off.

At first they felt as if they had been thrown into a pit of strange, subhuman animals. They were surrounded by smooth-skinned, lusty kids; it seemed to Pirius that whichever way you looked somebody had his dick out. 'It's like being in a Coalescence,' Cohl whispered, horrified, her eyes wide.

It certainly wasn't like Arches. There the instructors – combat veterans, even if they were invalided out – were role models for the cadets, and discipline was comparatively light. Most adults here were keepers, not teachers. It was all very dismaying.

But gradually, in their way, these strange swarming kids seemed to accept the *Claw* crew. Jabbering in their own strange, rapid dialect, the cadets would show them the way to the refectories and showers and delousing blocks. Others showed them simple tips on how to make your life easier: for instance if you saved some grease from your food and rubbed it into the inside of the joints of your skinsuit, the chafing was eased a lot. Once when Pirius stumbled during one of Marta's endless route marches, a couple of them came over and helped him up.

In the barracks one night, another offered to share her Virtual with him. It was a drama, a crude soap opera full of strong plot lines and tear-jerking emotions, one of a whole series pumped out endlessly by story-telling machines, all different yet all the same. Pirius watched a little to be polite, then slipped away when his host fell asleep.

And he became accustomed to visitors in the night: a smooth round face hovering over his, a brush of lips on lips, a small hand probing under his blanket. These approaches came from boys, girls and various combinations. Gently, with a smile, he pushed them away. He felt his life was complicated enough for now.

There was bound to be intense companionship here. After all this was the front line of a war zone. You grew up with the people around you, and you knew you might die with them.

Death seemed always near. The very architecture of the Rock reminded you that the Army wasn't in the business of preserving your life. If an attack were to come, the Rock's pressurised layers would crush down. The cadets were a shield of human flesh and blood that might protect the Rock's really valuable cargo, the weapons and ships at the core, a little longer.

People were expendable. Of course that was true across the Front, in every branch of the services. Pirius had been brought up to believe he wouldn't even have been given his life in the first place if not for the strength and steely will of the Coalition, and it was his duty to give up that life whenever he was asked.

But the economic logic of war was brutal. At least as a pilot, the extensive training invested in you made you worth something. Here, among these Army grunts, the training was a good deal cheaper; and the grunts were a lot more disposable as a consequence. It was a chilling, desolating thought, which no amount of Doctrinal justification made easier to bear.

And so these children turned to each other for comfort.

Anyhow the situation got better, bit by bit. But not for Enduring Hope.

Hope withdrew into himself; he became grey, oddly sickly, and was always exhausted. His broad, soft face, between those protruding ears, rarely showed a smile.

Pirius knew Captain Marta wasn't trying to destroy Hope but was attempting to break him down to build him up. But, he feared, she was getting it wrong. Pirius couldn't see a thing he could do about it.

It came to a head at a roll call.

*

It was the thirty-fourth day after Pirius's arrival here. Once again Enduring Hope had been the last to finish his run. The silence of the waiting cadets hid a wave of resentment that would break over Hope once he got back to the barracks.

But today, as he stood in his place in the line, wheezing, his body heaving with the strain of breathing, Pirius saw a spark of defiance.

Holding her data desk, Captain Marta called him. 'Tuta.'

'My name,' he said, 'is Enduring Hope.'

'Two more laps,' Marta said levelly. 'Increased load.'

Still gasping, Hope stumbled out of his place in the line and prepared to resume his run. Over the open loop Pirius could hear a barely muffled grumble as the cadets prepared to wait in their skinsuits even longer.

Enough, he thought. This is my fault, after all. He stepped forward. 'Captain Marta.' Every eye save the Captain's were on him.

Marta inspected her data desk. 'I told you, cadet. No questions.'

'His name is Enduring Hope.'

Hope heard him and stopped; he turned, astonished, hands on his knees. 'Pirius,' he said between gasps. 'Shut it.'

Marta said, 'If you're so keen to share his punishment, you can take it for him.' She touched her chest. The weight on Pirius's shoulders increased suddenly, like a heavy load being dropped on to his back. 'Three laps,' she said.

He walked stiffly out of line and began to plod towards the crater path.

Hope said, 'No, sir. I won't have him take my punishment for me.'

'Four laps, Pirius.'

'Captain—'

'Five laps, increased load.'

Again the burden on Pirius's back increased. He heard nothing more from Hope, who returned to his place in line.

Pirius traced the now familiar route, around and around this ancient splash in the Rock. His footprints shone pale in regolith that weathered quickly in this ferocious radiation environment, so close to the heart of the Galaxy.

He was already tired from his own training, and the increased load was the heaviest he had yet had to bear. Even after one lap his heart was thumping, his lungs pulling, a blistering headache locked across his temples, and his stressed knees were tender. But he kept on, and counted off the laps, two, three, four.

As he neared the end of his fifth lap Marta came to stand at the end of the course, her artificial half-torso gleaming by Galaxy light. He didn't acknowledge her. He ran right past her, ran past the finish line. She let him run on, but she increased the load again. And when he repeated the stunt after the next lap, she increased it again.

By the end of the tenth lap he could barely see where he was going. And yet still he raised one foot after another, still he pounded over the churned-up dirt.

This time, as he passed Marta, she touched a control on her chest.

His suit locked to immobility. Suddenly he was a statue, poised in mid-step, unbalanced. He fell, feather-slow. He hit the ground and finished up with half his face buried in carbonaceous dirt. His lungs heaved, but he could barely move inside the suit.

Marta crouched down so he could see her face with his one exposed eye. Over the voice loop he thought he could hear the whirr of exo-skeletal multipliers. She said, 'It's not my job to kill you, cadet.'

'Sir.'

She leaned closer. 'I know your type. I could see it in your face the minute you landed. That's why I've picked on your fat friend, of course. To flush you out.'

'Sir.'

She hissed, 'Do you imagine you're a hero, Pirius? Do you think you're special?' She waved a hand. 'Look at the sky. At any moment there are a billion human beings on the front line of this war. And do you imagine that out of all that great host *you* will be noticed?'

He struggled to speak. 'That's my ambition. Sir.'

She leaned back. 'If I release you, will you keep running?'

'Sir.'

'What do I have to do to keep you from killing yourself?'

'Artillery.'

'What?'

'There is an artillery unit, here on Quin.' It was true; Burden had told him. 'Send Enduring – uh, Tuta there. He's an engineer. With respect, sir.'

She grunted. 'I'll take it on advisement. But next time you pull a stunt like this, cadet, I'll let you kill yourself for sure.'

'Noted, sir.' She got up and walked away, leaving him lying in the dirt. Cohl, Burden and a couple of other cadets came to carry him back to the airlock, where they had to cut him out of his locked suit.

It took a couple of days to come through, but Enduring Hope's transfer to a platoon of monopole-cannon gunners was confirmed.

CHAPTER 11

Pirius Red's cockpit was just a jet-black frame, open to space, very cramped. Through the open frame he could see the pale yellow-gold stripes of Saturn's cloud tops turning with majestic slowness. There were no physical controls, only Virtual displays and guide icons that hovered before his chest. The only other light was the soft green glow of the suit's biopack. It was a lash-up.

But at least the cockpit was human-built, unlike the rest of his craft.

When he glanced over his shoulder he could see the sleek, slim form of the ship's main body, and the flaring, stunningly graceful shape of its wings. The hull was utterly black, black beyond any human analysis, so black it seemed that not a single infalling photon of Saturn light was reflected. This was the nightfighter disabled and captured by his own future self, Pirius Blue.

It was hard to believe this was happening. Today, six weeks after arriving on Earth, in the heart of Sol system itself, Pirius Red was to fly a Xeelee ship.

For a boy brought up at the centre of the Galaxy, the sky of Sol system was dismal, empty, its barrenness barely broken by the few stars of this ragged spiral-arm edge and the bright pinpoint of the sun. Even Saturn was surprisingly dim, casting little light; the immense planet might harbour the mightiest concentration of firepower in Sol system, but it seemed oddly fragile. He wondered briefly how it might have looked in the old days when its tremendous rings of ice and dust had not yet been burned up as fuel and weaponry. You couldn't even see the Core. Nilis had told him that from here the Galaxy centre should be a mass of light the size of the Moon, brighter than anything in Earth's sky save Sol itself. But Galaxy-plane gas clouds hid it. The earthworms didn't even *know* they lived in a galaxy until a few centuries before star flight began.

But today he didn't care about earthworms. To Pirius, sitting here, this bare Galaxy-rim sky was a wild, exotic space, and to be at the controls of a genuine nightfighter was an unimaginable adventure.

He said to himself, 'Life doesn't get any better than this.'

A scowling face, no larger than his thumbnail, popped into existence before his eyes. 'What's that, ensign?'

'Nothing, sir.'

This was Commander Darc, a sour, middle-aged, evidently competent Navy officer. The Navy hierarchy had insisted that one of their own be Pirius's only contact during the trial itself, and Pirius wasn't about to argue.

'You OK in that cage? If you want us to pull you out—'

'I'm fine.' Pirius smiled, making sure his face was visible behind the visor.

Darc growled, 'Yes, I bet you are. Shrunk to fit, eh, ensign?'

That was a jab about Pirius's compact frame. 'If you say so, sir.'

'Listen up.' The mission clock was counting down, and Darc began his final briefing. 'The cockpit we built for you is obviously normal matter, baryonic matter.' Pirius still wasn't sure what that meant. 'But the hull of the ship itself, including the wing stubs, is made of another kind of matter called a condensate. Now, condensate doesn't have normal quantum properties . . .'

Pirius flexed his gloved fingers experimentally; icons sparkled around Darc's disembodied, shrunken head.

If a chunk of matter was cooled to extremely low temperatures – a billionth of a degree above absolute zero, or less – the atoms would condense into a single quantum state, like a huge 'superatom', marching in step like the coherent photons in a laser beam. Such a state of matter was called a 'Bose-Einstein condensate', though Pirius had no idea who Bose or Einstein might have been.

'We don't know how to make such stuff at room temperatures,' Darc said. 'Or how to make it dense; our lab condensates are so thin they are scarcely more than vacuum. But condensate has useful properties. For instance if you add more atoms they are encouraged to join the condensate structure.'

Pirius thought about that. 'A condensate is self-healing.'

'The physicists would say self-amplifying. But yes; so it seems. You do understand that only your wing stubs are condensate. The wings themselves, when unfolded, are the basis of your sublight drive and are much more extensive. And they aren't material at all . . .'

There was a lot of tension with the Navy crew assigned to the Project. Darc had spent his career in the Solar Navy Group; Pirius had learned that he'd never been deeper into the Galaxy than the Orion Line. Solar would be mankind's last line of defence against the Xeelee in case of the final collapse, and was itself an ancient force whose officers were fiercely proud of their own traditions. But Pirius had heard a lot of muttering about the 'inbred little freaks' from the centre of the Galaxy who were getting all the attention.

But Pirius was in this seat, not any of them.

Pirius knew that Nilis was aboard one of the escort ships, no doubt listening to every word. And he wished Torec was here to see this. Torec had fought for the privilege of being pilot on these trials. Given where she had got to in her training back on Arches, she was in fact marginally better qualified than Pirius. But Nilis had assigned her to another part of the project, the development of his 'CTC computer', as he called it, his closed-timelike-curve time travel computing machine. Nilis made it clear that he regarded the CTC-processor work as just as important as experiments with the Xeelee ship, and she had had to accept the assignment.

Anyway in Pirius's mind there had never been any question about who should get this ship; in a sense it was already his.

Darc was still talking. 'The cockpit you're sitting in is all ours, a human construct, Pirius. You've got full inertial protection in there, and other kinds of shielding. And we *believe* we have achieved a proper interface of your controls with the ship's control lines. It was technically tricky, they tell me. More like connecting an implant to a human nervous system than hacking into any electromechanical device.'

'Sir, you're telling me you're not sure if it's going to work.'

'Only one way to find out, ensign.'

It was hard to concentrate, sitting here in this cockpit. Of course this wasn't all for Pirius's benefit; Darc, a career officer, was taking the chance to grandstand for audiences of his own.

The icons before his face were tantalising. *Only one way to find out.* Pirius was in the hot seat; for once in his life he had power over events – and here, not Darc, not Nilis, not even Pirius Blue could get in his way.

He spread open his hands.

*

There was a shiver, It was like a breath on the back of his neck, or the touch of Torec's fingers on his back when he slept.

He turned. The nightfighter's wings had opened. They swept smoothly out of their condensate stubs to become a billowing black plane, like a sheet thrown over some immense bed. He knew that these were not material, not even anything so exotic as condensate. They were constructs of spacetime itself.

And they *pulsed*. The ship seemed poised, like a tensed muscle. He could *feel* it.

Suddenly the ship was alive; there was no other word for it. And despite the worst predictions of the doom-mongers, even though he knew he was triangulated by a dozen starbreaker beams and other weapons, the ship waited to do his bidding. He laughed out loud.

Darc's face was hovering before him, a shining coin, purple with rage. 'I'll feed you to the recyclers if you try another stunt like that, you little runt!'

No, you won't, Pirius thought. You won't dare. In the Conurbations of Earth I'm a hero. It was an unexpected, delicious, utterly non-Doctrinal thought. He had the power – and Darc knew it.

'Awaiting permission to start the trial, sir,' Pirius said, carefully keeping his voice level.

Darc's mouth worked, as if he was chewing back his anger. Then he said, 'Do it.'

Pirius selected hovering icons and gathered them together with gentle wafts of his hands. Then he pointed.

The sparse stars blurred, turned blue. Saturn crumpled like a wad of golden tissue, vanished. Then the stars settled back, like a curtain falling, and it was over almost before he knew it had begun.

There should have been no kick in the back, no sense of acceleration; if the inertial shield failed by the slightest fraction he would have been reduced to a pulp. And yet he felt *something*, as if his own body knew it had taken a great leap.

'. . . hear me? Respond, ensign. Darc to Pirius, Respond—'

'Yes, sir, I'm here.'

There was a perceptible delay before Darc replied, 'Ensign, you travelled light seconds at around three-quarters lightspeed.'

'Just as per the flight plan.'

'You even stopped where you were supposed to.'

Pirius glanced back over his shoulder. Saturn, the only object in his universe large enough to show a disc, had been reduced to a tiny yellowish spot. He should have felt even more isolated, he thought, exposed. But all he felt was power. With this ship he could go anywhere, do anything.

And the test had barely begun.

'Sir, do you want me to bring her back?'

'You sit tight,' Darc snapped. 'That fly is going to get a thorough checkout before it moves another centimetre – as are you. We're coming as fast as we can.' And so they were, Pirius saw. Staring towards Saturn, he made out a small flotilla of ships, gradually drifting across the background stars.

He pressed his hands to his thighs, resisting the temptation to take off once more.

Nilis loomed huge over the nightfighter. With its wings furled the ship would have rested in the palm of the hand of this kilometres-high Virtual, Pirius thought.

It ought to have been an absurd sight, even a faintly revolting one; Nilis's head was the size of a Spline starship, every blocked pore in his aged skin a pit like a weapons emplacement. But Pirius was back in orbit around Saturn now, and the planet's subdued golden light oddly filled up the Virtual image. And wonder was bright in Nilis's tremendous eyes.

'Defects in spacetime,' Nilis said. 'That's what the wings of a nightfighter are. Flaws in the structure of spacetime itself. And look here.'

He waved his immense hands and produced another gigantic Virtual. This one showed the Xeelee nightfighter in flight, the beautiful, elusive, bafflingly complex motions of its wings of flawed spacetime. Nilis replaced the true image with a schematic. The ship was overlaid by a framework, a kind of open tetrahedron, with bright red blobs at its four corners. The tetrahedron went through a complex cycle of deformations. It closed like an umbrella, its legs shortening as they moved, then they would lengthen before the 'umbrella' opened again and the frame returned to its starting configuration.

'This is a schematic of the wings' motion,' Nilis said. 'See the way the wings change their shape. You have to think of spacetime as the

109

natural medium of the craft. It is like – like a bacterium embedded in water. To a small enough creature, water is as viscous as treacle, and in such sticky stuff swimming is difficult, because if your recovery stroke is the same as your impulsive stroke you pull yourself back to where you started. So what bacteria do is to adopt different geometrical shapes during the first and second parts of the stroke, to pull themselves forward. It's called a geometric phase, a closed sequence of different shapes.

'Pirius, the nightfighter is embedded in spacetime as surely as any bacterium in water. By pulsing through their sequence of shapes, the wings of the nightfighter are clearly using a geometric phase to control and direct the ship's motion. It's a shapeshifting drive – nothing like a rocket, no need for anything like reaction mass to be thrown out the back of your ship – really quite remarkable. And quite unlike the principles on which human sublight drives are based.'

Pirius understood, if vaguely. Human-designed drives pushed, not against spacetime itself, but against the vacuum, the seething quantum foam of virtual particles that pervaded space. At the heart of such a drive was an extended crystalline substrate, made to vibrate billions of times a second. As the substrate passed through the quantum foam, electric fields were induced in its surface by the foam's fluctuating forces, fields dissipated by spraying out photons. If you arranged things right, so Pirius had been told in cartoon-level lectures, you could use those shed photons to push you forward.

'Our drives work all right,' Nilis said, 'But they are slower than the Xeelee drive. And they break down constantly. Those crystals are expensive, and they shatter easily.'

Pirius knew that. You had to carry a rack of spares for a journey of more than a few light hours. 'And besides,' he said slowly, 'the Xeelee method sounds more—' He couldn't think of the word.

Nilis smiled hugely. 'Elegant?'

'I guess so.'

'Thanks to your brave work today we understand the source of that elegance a great deal better. But still there are questions. Swimming in spacetime is an *odd* way to do things. This is a method that would work best in regions of highly curved spacetime, where you can get more traction – say, around a black hole.'

'We know the Xeelee infest Chandra.'

'Yes, and that offers us all sorts of clues about them. But they also have to operate in environments like *this*, far from any dense con-centrations of matter, where spacetime is all but flat. In fact, if the spacetime was perfectly flat the drive couldn't work.

'And why use spacetime defects as the basis of your drive in the first place? There *was* a time, in the moments after the Big Bang singular-ity, when such things were common, for the orderly structure of the swollen spacetime we inhabit was still forming. There were points, loops, sheets—'

'The point defects are monopoles.'

'Yes. That's why monopoles are useful weapons – one defect can interfere with another. Spacetime was heavily curved too. I suppose if you were designing a drive system *then* you might naturally pick defects and spacetime-swimming as your way to work. It isn't nearly so obvious *now* – and hasn't been since microseconds after the singularity. So why use it? And then there is the question of the Xeelee themselves. Where are *they*?'

That leap confused Pirius. 'Sir?'

'No matter how closely I inspect this craft I can only find machinery, layer upon layer of it. No sign of a crew!'

'I don't know what that means.'

'Nor do I – not yet.' The immense ghostly Virtual leaned forward, and a glistening eye the size of a Conurbation loomed eagerly over Pirius. 'Still, I do think we're getting somewhere. The word "Chan-dra", you know, is very ancient – pre-Occupation. Some say the black hole is named after a scientist of antiquity. Others say that the word means "luminous". Well, if luminous it is, I don't think Minister Gramm is going to enjoy the sight of what Chandra is beginning to illuminate, for us!'

CHAPTER 12

Alone, her skinsuit stained dark grey by Moon dust, Torec clambered through the remains of an exotic matter factory.

This place had been built twenty thousand years ago by the Qax, alien occupiers of Earth. After the rebellion that had forced the Qax out of Sol system, all the equipment had been stripped out and the roof smashed open to the black sky. You could still see small blast craters and bits of wreckage left over from that ancient turmoil. And the gaunt walls remained, broken sheets of lunar concrete that cast long, sharp shadows over the undulating dust of the Moon ground.

While Pirius had been flying a nightfighter among the moons of Saturn, she had been stuck here a month already. There were three weeks left before the deadline Gramm had set, and the final demonstration of Nilis's prototype CTC-processor, his time travel computer, would be due. Torec longed for those weeks to be up.

Torec was always aware of Earth, high in the sky. The great arc of the Bridge was easily visible – stunning, unnatural, disturbingly defying logic. And she could see the layers of defences that surrounded the home planet: the circling Snowflakes, the crawling specks of patrolling warships. Even seen from its Moon, Earth bristled with fortifications.

It was only in these ruins, half an hour's hike from the development base, that she felt at ease. When she walked here Earth's bright blue was eclipsed by the broken masses of the walls, and she could imagine she was far away from here, not in Sol system at all. And the best thing was that the earthworm techs she had to work with never came here.

An alarm chimed softly in her helmet. The latest integration test was due to begin, a full-scale run of the CTC processor prototype. It would go ahead whether she was there or not, of course. But she had her duty.

She turned, made for the open sunlight, and began to bound across the plain, legs working together in a comfortable low-gravity style.

She took her place on the low ridge that had been designated as an observation area. A countdown was proceeding, she saw, a silent flickering of numerals ticking away on monitoring displays. Techs stood patiently and bots hovered, waiting for the test to begin.

The prototype CTC processor was a maze of ducts, pipes and tubes that connected anonymous silver-white boxes. It sprawled for more than half a kilometre over the dusty lunar plain. The ground was darkened by boot prints, but as the time of the test approached the area had been evacuated, and only monitoring bots hovered cautiously over the complex central tangle.

The prototype, gleaming silver and gold in the pure low sunlight of lunar morning, looked oddly beautiful, a scattered work of art. But Torec had come to hate this thing which governed her life.

Two Virtuals materialised, out of nothing. One was dressed in a skinsuit; the other, Nilis, was not. The Commissary, hovering a few centimetres above the lunar floor, wore nothing more than his customary scuffed robe, and his feet were bare. He had never been one for Virtual protocol, but this was actually illegal. Virtuals were supposed to 'dress' suitably for the environment they showed up in; it cost nothing more than a little extra computing power, and to do otherwise risked fooling a real-life inhabitant of the target environment about conditions that could be lethal. But it was typical Nilis, Torec thought. As he watched the patient countdown, his gaze was intent, his hands clasping each other, his eyes hollow.

The other Virtual was of a woman, dressed appropriately in a skinsuit. She was tall, somehow elegant despite her functional clothing. Seeing Torec she walked across to her, leaving no footprints in the lunar dust. 'You're the Navy child.'

Torec bristled. 'I'm Ensign Torec.'

'My name is Pila. I work in the Ministry of Economic Warfare.' Her face was smooth, ageless; she gazed at Torec, apparently mocking. It was a look Torec had become very familiar with on Earth, and had come to despise.

'I met you once. You work for Minister Gramm.'

'I'm one of his advisors, yes.' Pila waved a hand at the prototype. 'Very impressive. And it's all based on time travel?'

'Closed timelike curves, yes.' Torec pointed to the ducts. 'Pilot Officer Pirius – Pirius Blue – defeated the Xeelee because his fellow pilot used her FTL drive to bring tactical information back from the future. So we have miniature bots in those tubes. The bots are the components of the processor. They fly back and forth, and actually jump through short FTL loops.'

'Little starships in tubes! And these bots travel back in time and tell you the answer before you even pose the question?'

'Something like that.'

'How marvellous.'

The dummy problem they were hoping to run today concerned protein-folding. Proteins were the structural elements of life, but remained beyond the capability of humans to design optimally. There were more proteins a hundred components long than there were electrons in the universe; to work out how many ways a long protein molecule could fold up was an ancient problem, previously insoluble even in principle. 'But we hope to crack it,' Torec said. She pointed to a large blank Virtual screen. 'The results will be displayed there.'

Pila eyed her analytically. 'Are you enjoying your posting here, ensign? On the Moon, this project?'

'I'm here to do my duty, ma'am.'

She nodded, her mouth pursed. 'Of course. And you anticipate success?'

Torec had learned how to deal with smooth-faced bureaucrats and their slippery questions. Nilis had warned her severely that if she was pessimistic, or even overly optimistic, she could trigger the funding being pulled. 'This is only the first step. A proof of principle. Eventually we will have to cram this down into a unit small enough to be carried on a greenship.'

'A clever answer,' the woman murmured. 'And what is your key problem?'

Torec shrugged. 'Control of those flying bots, obviously. We've a list of issues.'

Virtual Nilis, who had ignored them both completely, now clapped his hands in agitation. Torec saw that the silent count was nearing its close; Nilis, projected from distant Earth, could barely contain his anticipation. Even Pila turned to look.

The count reached zero. The Virtual screen stayed blank, empty of protein schematics.

In that first instant Torec knew the trial had failed. After all the whole point of this FTL-computing exercise was to send the answer back in time to the beginning.

And an explosion flared at the centre of the complex. Torec was briefly dazzled. Silent, brief, the detonation kicked up an unspectacular flurry of Moon dust that, with no air to suspend it, collapsed immediately back to the ground.

Torec blinked and looked around. On the lunar plain, the techs were already converging on the ruin of their prototype. Some of them, she could hear on the open loop, were actually laughing.

The woman Pila had already gone.

The Virtual of Nilis was glaring at her. She had never seen him look so angry. 'In your quarters,' he snapped. '*Now.*' And he winked out of existence, leaving pixels sparkling briefly.

When she got back to her quarters she pulled off her skinsuit, dumped it in a hopper and climbed into her shower.

Big droplets of water squeezed out of the spigot with infuriating low-g slowness. It was typical of the earthworms to install such a luxury in a place where water couldn't even flow properly, where it would actually have been *better* to have been supplied with simple honest clean-cloths. But she slaked off her sweat, rinsed her hair and washed Moon dust out from under her nails.

The project's development was being carried out on the floor of an immense walled plain called Clavius. Though this had once been the site of a major industrial facility erected by the Qax, it was far to the lunar south, and so was still outside the scope of the current para-terraforming efforts, the vast domed colonies that were turning the Moon's face green around the equatorial foot of the Bridge between Earth and its satellite.

For a month Torec had been stranded in this airless, dusty place.

Nilis had given her a small team of scientists and engineers, to progress his designs for a revolutionary new computer. It had done her no good to protest that she had been trained as a pilot; she was a fighter, not some kind of double-domed tech. Nilis said it was important that one of what he called his 'inner team' be attached to this essential development.

So she had been put in charge of what was laughingly called the Project Office. It was her job, in theory, to make sure the techs here did their job to spec, to quality and on time.

At first she had actually welcomed the move to the Moon. Unlike the Earth the Moon was a *proper* world, in her view, a world without a freakish layer of unmodified atmosphere or surging bodies of open water. This was a world where, quite properly, if you stepped out of a dome you had to wear a skinsuit, and where if you fell over you weren't likely to break anything – if you wanted high gravity you set an inertia field; that was the way it was supposed to be. She had even liked the look of the scenery, when Nilis had shown her images of Clavius from orbit, a spectacular crater formation with mountainous walls surrounding a cluster of settlement lights.

But it hadn't turned out that way. For a start the Moon itself was *not* like the rocky worlds she had encountered in the Core, where, thanks to the stars' relentless crowding, few stellar systems were stable and worlds wandered where they would. The Moon had spent five billion years stuck at the bottom of a star's gravity well as the companion of a massive planet, and debris, sucked in by those overlapping gravity fields, had battered its surface until nothing was left. As a result, every mountain was sand-blasted to a dune-like smoothness, and every scrap of the ground was covered by a thick layer of dust that crushed under your feet where you walked, or kicked up behind you, and stuck to your skinsuit until it was almost impossible to get off, no matter how hard you scrubbed.

And then there were the people.

Incredibly she was the only person here born beyond the orbit of the Moon. Not only that, aside from a couple of essential systems and security types, she was the only Navy personnel here. The rest of them, Ministry folk, were bureaucrats – *and* they were double-domes. From the beginning they had looked on her as a bizarre, exotic creature from some alien realm, as if she wasn't human at all.

The double-domes had soon discovered that she knew little about their technical specialisms. When she tried to put her foot down they would bluster and baffle her with jargon. And they squabbled among themselves the whole time. From the beginning the development team was organised into groups corresponding to subcomponents of the CTC processor itself, or else stages of the project: scoping, design, component prototyping, subassembly, integration. No matter how Torec tried, those groups soon became clannish, to the point where many of them wouldn't even communicate with each other – even though their work would have to fit together seamlessly if the overall goal was to be reached.

It was a horrible frustrating mess. Soon Torec had come to hate the prototype, which developed into a baffling, maze-like complex of components that spread across the grey lunar dust. And she came to hate the techs in their expensive Ministry skinsuits as they clambered over their equipment, prodding, tinkering and arguing.

What was worse was that Torec really didn't care about any of this. This wasn't her life, her goal; she didn't want to be here. And when the techs picked up on that they began to ignore her altogether.

She was here for Pirius, not for herself. That was the basic truth. As it happened, she had had feelings for Pirius even before Nilis had shown up. She knew their relationship was special – though she wasn't sure *he* understood it. But now things were different. She knew the situation wasn't Pirius's fault, but it was *because* of him.

She hated the Moon, her work, the people she had to deal with. She was very confused about her feelings for Pirius. And what was worst of all was that he wasn't here.

When she came out of the shower, the Nilis Virtual was in the room.

His face was bathed in the light of an invisible sun, but he wasn't looking her way. He had been uncomfortable in her company since that row on the corvette. He said, 'Another disappointment, then.'

'Yes.'

The Moon-Earth time lag was small, but enough to be disconcerting until you got used to it. 'If only we could use wormholes!'

'Commissary?'

'I know you've taken to hiking over to the ruins of the old Qax exotic matter facility. But do you know why the Qax set up that factory? Because you can use exotic matter to make wormholes, superluminal bridges between two points in space and time. If you configure it correctly, a wormhole can be a tunnel to the past. In fact it was a *human* wormhole time-bridge that started our trouble with the Qax in the first place.'

Torec had heard some of the techs talking of those semi-legendary, pre-Occupation times, and of *Mi-chael Poole*, the great engineer who had built wormholes to open up Sol system, and past and future too.

'Yes. Now, imagine if we could use wormholes to close our processor's timelike curves, instead of these absurd toy spaceships we have flying everywhere! You know, it's a Druzite myth that our progress is forever upward; the merest glance at your ruins shows that. If only Michael Poole was alive now! I'm sure he would have our prototype up and running in a day. Ensign, do you ever think that the people of the past were giants – that we are stunted, small by comparison?'

'No, sir,' she said defiantly. 'We are the ones who are here, now. All we can do is our best.'

'Are you talking about duty again, ensign?'

'Yes, sir.'

' "Our best." ' He turned to face her. She wondered how she looked to him: just another Virtual ghost, she supposed, palely lit, hovering in the air in his Conurbation apartment. 'How do you feel about your work, Torec?'

She knew Nilis would not be satisfied with a bland evasion. 'I can't say I'm happy, sir.'

'You aren't?'

'This isn't what I'm trained for. I can see why you took Pirius to Earth; what he did – Pirius Blue – was astonishing. But I was only brought along to keep Pirius happy.'

Nilis sighed. 'You feel trapped. Perhaps, you think, without my intervention you would have ended your relationship with Pirius, moved on to somebody else . . . You were in the wrong place and the wrong time, and so have ended up here.'

'Something like that,' she said. She kept her face blank. What did this old fool know? Anyhow it was none of his business.

But as it turned out he did know rather a lot. 'In fact,' Nilis said dryly, 'you wouldn't have broken up with Pirius.'

Her face was hot. 'How can you know that?'

'Because I asked Pirius Blue. In that other, vanished timeline, Pirius Blue stayed with, ah, Torec Blue, shall we call her, until he left for his last fateful mission. For *two years*, ensign. That was a factor in Captain Seath recommending you to come on this mission. She knew too.'

Torec's feeling were very complex. She didn't like discussing her emotional life with this soggy old Commissary, and it made her uncomfortable to talk about a relationship she might have had but now never would. 'You're talking about two years *I* won't live through. Two years of choices *I* don't get to make.'

'True,' said Nilis. 'So how do you feel now?'

She thought it over. 'Just as trapped. More, maybe.'

He laughed. 'The curse of predestination! Well, if it's any consolation, it wasn't my idea to bring you to Earth.'

'Yes, sir.'

'But now you're here you have a job to do. You are at least satisfied that you're doing your best, are you?'

'Yes, sir—'

'*Don't lie to me.*' Suddenly his face was blazing.

She flinched. But it struck her that he must have timed that riposte to beat the time lag – he knew what she would say before he had heard her reply. 'Sir?'

'We failed again today, ensign, in case you hadn't noticed.'

'But it isn't my fault – the techs—'

'And if we fail in three weeks, when Gramm conducts his final review, then the plug will be pulled. No more funding. Everything will be lost. I suggest you start to do the job I entrusted to you.'

'Sir—'

'And don't tell me it's beyond you. Let me give you three pieces of advice. First, the bot control issue. That has plagued us since the beginning.'

'The techs say it might be intractable. The problem of controlling a crowd of FTL bots—'

Nilis waved a hand dismissively; Torec saw Earth soil under his fingernails. 'Then step around the problem. Think sideways, ensign. *Let the bots guide themselves.* As long as each bot is aware of the position of the other nearest, and follows the overall imperative, the solution will emerge. Tell your techs to let the bots swarm. Next, discipline. Even I, from half a million kilometres away, can see the open warfare that's broken out between some of your sub-teams.'

119

Torec said miserably, 'Sir, they all say the others are fools, or even saboteurs, who must be forced to do things *their* way. And when we come together on the test site nothing ever fits.'

He laughed. 'Well, you're not the first project manager who's faced that. Interface management, Torec. Change control. Look up those terms and apply them.' He stood up and brushed dust from his robe; when it left contact with his body it disappeared. 'Finally—'

'Sir?'

She saw fatigue in his deep eyes; she knew he was spreading himself thin, commuting between Earth and Saturn to give time to all the different, and all demanding, aspects of his project. 'Oh, my eyes, I don't have the words. The people here are soft-bodied technicians from the cities of Earth. They are softer than *me*! But you, you're a soldier from the Central Star Mass! And you're smart, I know that.' He waved his hands. '*Kick butt!* Is that how you'd put it?'

'Yes, sir,' she said dully.

He was staring at her, apparently still unsure if she had got the message. 'What do you imagine failure in this project will mean, ensign?'

'The war will go on.'

'Forget about the war. Forget about mankind's glorious destiny. What about *you*? Do you imagine you will be shipped back to the Front – that you will be carried back across the Galaxy? Do you imagine anybody would go to such expense, just to get a few combat weeks out of a cipher like you? Do you think that anybody cares that much? *Do you think the Coalition loves you, ensign?*'

She felt crushed.

He thundered, 'I'll tell you what will happen. You'll be sent to Mercury. That's Sol I, the planet closest to the sun. There are mines there, and solar energy farms. It's a factory world, ensign, a place of warrens where you never see the blazing sun, and you're grateful not to. And there you will die – not gloriously, not in combat with your comrades, but miserable and alone, when your youth and strength are used up. Do you want that?'

'Sir, my duty—'

'Oh, to Lethe with your duty!' he roared. '*Is that how you want to die?*'

'No.'

'What did you say?'

120

'No! Sir.'

'Then I suggest you ensure we don't fail.'

His Virtual snapped out of existence.

CHAPTER 13

Even though his training gradually morphed away from simple endurance and fitness work, day to day life as an infantry cadet was a lot harder than anything Pirius Blue had suffered in the Navy.

For one thing, he now spent his whole life in his Army-issue skinsuit. In a greenship blister, at least you could crack your faceplate from time to time and scratch your nose. Here, for hours on end, you just had to endure your itches, chafes and other discomforts.

You even got lectured at in your skinsuit, one of thousands standing on the surface of the Rock, by Marta or one of the other instructors.

'You need to grasp the basic logic of the Rocks,' Marta would say. 'The Xeelee have more firepower than we do. But somehow we have to soak up that firepower. And that's where the Rocks come in. We just throw Rocks, one after the other, in through the Front and into the Cavity around Chandra. The Xeelee come flocking out. But the big mass of a Rock absorbs all that Xeelee juice . . .' It was a crude strategy, but time-tested, said Captain Marta; human troopers riding the Rocks had kept the Xeelee bottled up inside the Front for three thousand years. And soon it would be the honour of these fresh troops to join them.

Bathed in the light of the Galaxy centre, the cadets stood in rows, their bio-packs shining green, listening to such stuff in attentive silence. As the hours wore by, Pirius would see rustles of movement as a cadet shifted her inertial-field weight from one booted foot to the other, or her body would subtly relax as she voided her bladder or bowels into her suit's system, all the time keeping rigidly at attention.

Woe betide you if you showed any physical discomfort – and fainting was rewarded by ten days of route marches.

The theory of infantry strategy didn't take long to impart, however. To a first approximation, Pirius decided, an infantryman's job was to dig.

Every day troopers would swarm in their thousands out of the great underground barracks and, under the brusque command of their officers, cut into the surface of the Rock. Much of the asteroid was already covered by lattice-works of trenches and foxholes and dugouts left by previous generations, but these were regularly ploughed over so you always had virgin areas to work.

And in these earthworks Pirius and Cohl learned how to dig.

There was actually an art to digging, if you had to do it on the surface of an asteroid in a skinsuit. The environment was micro-gravity, of course, with hard vacuum all around. The trick was to use your inertial belt to pin you to the ground, while digging into the dirt with your spade and trenching tools.

The upper few metres of asteroid dirt were generally loosely packed; most asteroids were coated with dust, the product of aeons of collisions and micrometeorite bombardment. Under the layer of dust you would eventually reach conglomerate, a rubble of boulders and pebbles, which was pretty much the story the rest of the way in: only the largest asteroids had solid cores. It was easy enough to collect a big spadeful of this stuff and hurl it out of the way; there was no air resistance, and the dust grains followed a spray of neat parabolas. But gravity was so low that it could take many minutes for the grains to fall back – and it took skill to aim your spade-load so that the debris didn't rain down on your neighbour, or even more embarrassingly back on top of you.

Inside the Front, the conditions would be worse still. There, as you dug your trench, you would be drenched by gamma rays and other hard radiation emanating from the exotic objects that crowded the Galaxy's centre. So the trainers sent up drones to pour gamma radiation down over the labouring cadets, and they had to wear stiffer, shielded skinsuits, which made the digging still more tricky. What was worse yet was that the radiation ionised the dust, which made the grains stick to each other and to your skinsuit, and a good proportion of your time was taken up just scraping debris off your suit. It took Pirius and Cohl a long time to get the hang of it.

A long trench being dug was an oddly beautiful sight, though. You would see neat lines of dust fountains, thrown up by the brisk, enthusiastic work of the cadets, and on the open loops you would hear them sing together as they worked. It was a strange juxtaposition: this very strange place, so far from Earth, with one of the most primitive human technologies.

As his muscles continued to build up, Pirius almost began to enjoy the endless labour. Even the futility of being sent back day after day to the same crater bed, with the fruits of his previous day's labour ploughed over to be dug out again, didn't deter him. If he worked hard enough he didn't have to think at all, and the complication of everything that had happened since the magnetar could be excluded from his mind.

The regiment known as the Guards was a strong presence on this Rock.

Pirius's principal training officer, Marta, was one of them. Even raw Guard trainees would flow across the Rock's surface as precisely coordinated as components of a machine. What baffled Pirius was the way they always seemed able to keep their kit shining clean, even in the clinging dust. The Guards were an elite, and they knew it, and their superiority began with their obsessive smartness.

Pirius and Cohl weren't in the Guards, however. They were assigned to the Army Service Corps, the lowest of the low.

Their work was to support the front-line troops, and, before they had come here, Pirius had vaguely imagined this might mean they would be safer. As it turned out, in combat the Service Corps had to prepare the ground for advances – which, Pirius learned, often meant going forward *ahead* of the first line of fighting troops. After an action began they would have to help dig and consolidate earthworks, and move back and forth bearing supplies and maintaining comms links. Sometimes, when the electromagnetic environment was particularly ferocious, they would have to run from the front line to the rear and back, bearing messages by hand.

And when the action began its terrible grinding, the Service Corps became field medics and stretcher bearers. Infantry skinsuits were designed to keep you alive as long as possible, but they were primarily fighting armour, and traumatic injuries would be beyond any suit's capacity to stabilise. Pirius was taught how to apply the simple medicine possible through a skinsuit, such as tying off a damaged limb. And he learned how to bundle a body, locked in a rigid suit, on to open-frame stretchers, and to crawl with casualties through the earthworks back to casualty clearing stations.

So as Service Corps they would be exposed to fire just as much as the front-line fighters, if not more so. Not that that gained them any respect from the front-liners, who seemed convinced that the Service Corps had it soft, with the first pick of rations, unlimited benefits and protection from the battle.

There were a few other Navy exiles, like Pirius, and other undesirables in the Service Corps. But most of their number was made up of infantry troopers who had managed to survive one or two actions and grown too old, or perhaps too wounded or shocked, to fight any more. These superannuated misfits felt misunderstood and put-upon. As they worked they would sing their own plaintive song: *We are the ASC / We work all night, we work all day / The more we work, the more we may / It makes no difference* . . . Few of these gloomy veterans were older than twenty.

Eventually they were introduced to more sophisticated surface operations.

The cadets were taught to move in the open. They were organised into platoons of ten, which practised moving together. The basic technique was to advance through lines of trenches towards an enemy position. You scrambled out of one trench, running or crawling across the asteroid dirt, and then hurled yourself into the next. The instructors used drone bots to simulate enemy fire – cadets would be 'killed' by laser spots that made their suits go rigid. The inertial belts were priceless; without them the simplest kick or misstep could send you floating upwards – but of course you also practised how to keep moving forward even if your belt failed. The cadets seemed to enjoy this running around, apparently not imagining how it would be to go through this in combat conditions.

Pirius quickly learned there was more to it than simple trench-hopping. The cadets had to consolidate and reinforce the trenches they found themselves in. And they practised leapfrogging, in which a second line of troops would pass through the first to make a more rapid advance.

It got more complicated still. Platoons of ten apiece were clustered into companies of maybe a hundred warm bodies. They practised manoeuvring as a company, in which one platoon would advance under the covering fire of another, all the while keeping the line intact. The next level up was a battalion, in which a thousand cadets would wash forward in coordinated waves. The instructors would throw unexpected problems in their way, and the cadets learned how to accommodate holes appearing in their lines, or being forced to back up from unexpectedly fortified positions. The cadets did this over and over, until every one of them knew what was expected in any given situation.

These elaborate manoeuvres were all about mutual protection. Each company was covered by those to either side of it, just as each platoon was protected through mutual cover by the fellows down the line – which was why it was so important to keep the line together.

But for an individual trooper, in the end your only real protection was the presence of those around you, in your own platoon. You had to rely on them to watch your back – and if the worst happened, you had to hope that one of *them* would take the hit that might otherwise have taken you out.

The cadets seemed to understand that. If you were stuck in your skinsuit on a Rock falling into Xeelee fire, the great sweeping strategy of the war meant little. You were there to fight for your comrades. Very close bonds formed between the cadets – bonds that were strictly non-Doctrinal, as you weren't really supposed to have loyalties for anything but the greater cause. But the instinct to fight for your comrades seemed as deep as humanity itself. It couldn't be denied – indeed it had to be encouraged, quietly, whatever the Doctrines preached.

Pirius tried not to think about his situation. He knew he wasn't here to think. But there were obvious questions he couldn't help asking. For instance, why use human muscles to dig when you could get machines to do it for you?

He heard a whole series of rationales. Even after millennia of development it was difficult to shield equipment from the blistering radiation environment inside the Mass. Machines were liable to break down – and of course they drew the fire of the Xeelee. Humans were comparatively robust, at least for a while. Then there was the psychological factor: the trenches and foxholes were there to provide cover for the infantry, and nobody trusted a trench dug by a machine as much as one you dug out yourself. It was good for morale, then, to keep digging, digging.

But his pilot's training prompted more questions. Why stick to such a crude strategy? Even using ground troops you could imagine more subtlety. You could coordinate your forces, strike with precision, move on.

He wasn't about to ask such questions of Captain Marta, but, soaking up his training, he could figure out what the answers would be. A Rock offered shelter, so you had to stick to its ground. But in combat a Rock was drenched in firepower – and, even if the Xeelee didn't show up to play, in the hard radiation of the Core. You couldn't rely on communication, coordination in such circumstances; you had to train for a worst case, in which every platoon, maybe every trooper, was cut off from everybody else, save for what she could see of the battlefield around her. In this ultimate war, only the crudest of tactics could be relied on to work.

But, guided by his conversations with This Burden Must Pass, he began to suspect that the truth behind the strategy was ideological. Clinging to humanity was the essence of the Druz Doctrines, the principles that had kept mankind united across twenty thousand years and the span of a Galaxy. So humans had to wage this war, humans had to dig their trenches, and fight and die, not their machines.

Pirius built up a new image of the Front in his head. It was a great shell enclosing the centre of the Galaxy, and it was studded with worldlets like this one, and on every one of them there were human beings, digging and burrowing. They were digging for victory; that was what the instructors told them. And whether or not they ever achieved that victory, Pirius thought, with every spadeful of glistening asteroid dirt the Druz Doctrines and the unity of mankind were reinforced that little bit more.

CHAPTER 14

Two weeks after Pirius Red's first test flight of the Xeelee nightfighter, Nilis set up a briefing for the Minister. It was held on Enceladus, moon of Saturn. Minister Gramm attended with his peculiar Virtual 'advisor' Luru Parz, and Commander Darc and one of his adjutants represented the Navy.

And Nilis began to lecture. Even before this glowering crew, in his typical over-academic way, the Commissary would never just state his conclusions: no, that wasn't his style. He had to establish the facts first; he had to educate his audience.

Since analysing the results of the tests on the Xeelee craft, Nilis said, he had hardened his ideas about the nature and origin of the Xeelee. He tried to talk his way through a very complex series of graphics which supported, he said, his hypothesis about the nature of the Xeelee nightfighter: that it was not just a machine.

'Life on Earth is of course built on oxygen-carbon chemistry. But a wide range of such compounds are possible under chemical law. If you analyse the contents of carbon-compound material scraped from a lifeless comet, you get a broad, smooth distribution like this' – a flat, even curve – 'an indiscriminate melange of many compounds. Whereas if you analyse a scraping of my skin, for instance, a sample from a living being, you get *this*.' A spiky distribution showing a heavy concentration of certain compounds, nothing of others. 'We call this the building-block principle, and it's believed to be a universal feature of life. There is a strong selection towards standard building blocks, you see: living things from Earth use the same handful of key components – amino acids, sugars – over and over, out of all the theoretically possible compounds—'

'A Xeelee nightfighter isn't made of amino acids,' Gramm growled.

'No. But look here.' Nilis showed displays of substructures he had observed in the Xeelee's design, in its condensate hull, even its spacetime-defect wings. The distributions were spiky. 'You see? A characteristic building-block pattern. And that has certain consequences. Of course any life form must have certain features – notably an information store.'

He began to speculate about how a Xeelee genome might be stored. A genotype of an organism was the internal data store that defined that organism's growth and structure; Nilis's own genotype was stored in DNA. The phenotype was the expression of that data, like Nilis's body. Nilis said that extended quantum structures had been discovered in the 'spine' of the craft. So far it had only been possible to hack into the simpler communications loops that controlled the ship's basic operations. But if he was right, somewhere in there was stored the equivalent of Xeelee DNA.

'They may reproduce through some exotic principle, much more sophisticated than our own molecule-splitting. We know they use quantum entanglement to communicate. Perhaps for a Xeelee, giving birth is more like teleportation, making a copy of oneself outside the body.' He imagined what might be possible if human hackers could break into that genotype, how Xeelee technology could be hijacked . . .

His listeners took this in with resentment and impatience. Pirius thought it was remarkable how a genius like Nilis could continually misjudge the mood of his audience. Pirius himself was sanguine. He had become a veteran of incomprehensible technical briefings long before he had left Arches Base, and he knew how to keep up a show of attentiveness while letting his thoughts wander.

Pirius had picked up some gossip from the locals. An ice-coated ball of rock, Enceladus wasn't even Saturn's largest moon – *that* was called Titan. On Titan vast factory ships cruised seas of hydrocarbon slush and processed it into nano-food to feed ever-hungry Earth. Of course these days all this was controlled by the agencies of the Coalition, but Titan had a racy history. Titan had once been the most populous human world beyond the orbit of Earth itself. Even now – so the locals informed him – in the great ports with their ice-carved harbours, where kilometre-long factory ships put in to offload their stores and hundred-metre-high waves lapped like dreams, there were exotic adventures to be had, if you knew where to look.

But Pirius hadn't seen Titan. He was stuck here on Ensh, as the locals called it, which was just another Navy base that could have been anywhere from here to the Prime Radiant itself. Once it wouldn't even have occurred to him to feel restless. But now he felt as if his curiosity had been opened up by his time in Sol system. What else was out there to be experienced – what else might he already have missed, if not for the strange irruption into his life of Pirius Blue? . . .

He tried to focus on the discussion.

Commander Darc was out of his depth. 'Forgive me, Commissary. I'm just a humble tar. Are you saying that the nightfighter is alive? That the Xeelee *are* their ships?'

'I, I—' Nilis stumbled, wiped his face with the back of his hand. He was overworking, Pirius knew, stretching himself thin across Sol system. 'Yes, if you want a short answer. But it isn't as simple as that. I'm saying there is no distinction between the Xeelee and their technology.'

Luru Parz seemed amused by all this. 'But, Commissary, spacetime defects, or condensate – neither seems very promising material to make a phenotype out of. Unlike the carbon-compound molecules of which *you* are made, for instance, there simply isn't much of it about.'

'Quite true.' Nilis smiled at her. 'Most life forms we have encountered have a certain commonality. Space is full of prebiotic chemicals, the carbon-based chemistry that underlies our kind of life – stuff like simple amino acids, ammonia and formaldehyde. This stuff is manufactured in interstellar clouds and rains down on the planets. Even today thousands of tonnes of the stuff falls daily on Earth, for instance. So carbon-water chemistry is really an obvious resource for making life. Of course there is little in common in the detail between humans and, say, Silver Ghosts. But we derive from the same pre-biotic interstellar chemistry; in a deep sense we are indeed cousins.

'But, as you say, Luru Parz, the Xeelee are different. These space-time defects of which they have been baked aren't common at all. Or at least, not now . . . but there was a time in the universe's complicated history when they *were* common. The Xeelee – or their progenitors – must surely have arisen in an earlier age of the universe, an epoch when spacetime defects proliferated. But that era was in the first moments after the singularity. If that's true, the Xeelee have very deep roots in time.'

Gramm made an explosive noise through his plump lips. 'You goad me beyond endurance, Commissary. This is supposed to be a military briefing! Will – you – get – to the *point*?'

Nilis leaned on a desk and glared at Gramm. 'The point, Minister, is that we now may understand why the Xeelee cluster around Chandra, the black hole. They *need* its deep gravity, its wrenching spacetime curvature.'

'Ah.' Luru Parz nodded. 'To them, Chandra is like a last fire in a universe grown cold.'

'But there's more than that,' Nilis said. He started to describe the condensate superstructure of the craft. 'Now, condensate matter was common at a certain stage in the early universe – but a *different* stage from that when the spacetime defects emerged. It was a cosmic age as alien to the first as will our own far future be to us, that age when the stars have died and dark energy dominates the swelling of spacetime . . . But the Xeelee, or their forebears, managed to form a partnership, a symbiosis, with these remote beings. Through that symbiosis they have managed to survive the slow unravelling of the universe – and it persists still, in the fabric of their craft.

'How do we compare, then, with the Xeelee? There are some who argue that there have been ten crucial steps in the evolution of humanity . . .'

The ten began with the development of a DNA-based genetic code, and continued with steps Pirius understood only a little: the exploitation of oxygen to provide free energy, the use of glucose in energy metabolism, the development of photosynthesis, and the incorporation of mitochondria – like miniature power plants – into complex cells. 'The first great triumph of symbiosis,' Nilis said enigmatically. His remaining steps were the formation of a nervous system, the evolution of an eye, the development of an internal skeleton to allow the colonisation of dry land, the evolution of the backboned animals.

'And finally,' said Luru Parz dryly, 'the magnificent emergence of *Homo sap* ourselves.'

Nilis said, 'You might get picky about some of the steps – and alien creatures, of course, would have their *own* set of developmental steps

– but the idea is clear enough. And certainly, for better or worse, humanity has not progressed beyond my step ten.'

'But perhaps in the Xeelee,' said Luru Parz, 'we get a glimpse of what step eleven might be.'

'Yes,' mused Nilis. 'We see extensions of the possibilities of life. A deep merging with technology. And a symbiosis, not just with other denizens of the same biosphere, but with aliens, different biospheres altogether – even with creatures from different ages of the universe, creatures governed by different physical laws. It's actually a remarkable vision,' he said, almost dreamily. 'It's as if the Xeelee are more deeply *embedded* in the universe than we are.'

'Oh, but this is all—' Gramm seemed outraged. 'And is that the message you want me to take back to the Grand Conclave, Commissary? That the Xeelee do not only possess better firepower, processing capability, tactics – they are also, in some sense, biologically *superior*?'

Nilis sighed, the hollows around his eyes deepening. 'Minister, to destroy something you have to understand it. We now know that the Xeelee are far older than we are, that we are dealing with relics of the antiquity of the universe. This battle of ours concerns the past as much as the present, or future.'

That hung in the air for a long moment. Then the meeting continued, even more stormily than before.

CHAPTER 15

On the Moon, Torec spent long days and sleepless nights researching, chairing meetings, forcing face-to-face confrontation with recalcitrant techs, and scouring over every centimetre of her prototype set-up.

Following Nilis's advice, she tried to impose discipline on the project. She forced her warring bands of technicians to agree on the designs for the interfaces between their components, and to work to those designs. And she imposed a series of freeze points beyond which change outside certain boundaries wasn't allowed. The techs grumbled, but they got on with the job. She even suspected they were glad to have her show a bit of toughness, as if this was how they had expected her to behave since the beginning.

But it took three weeks before she was satisfied; three weeks that used up all her remaining time before Gramm's deadline. The next test run would be the last, come what may. It had to work.

This time she was the first on the viewing mound, not the last. Again Nilis's anguished Virtual was here, and Gramm sent a copy of his advisor, the supercilious woman Pila.

But this time Luru Parz showed up too.

Once more the monitor bots floated into their ready positions, and the technicians cleared away from the ungainly prototype. As numerals on a hundred glowing clocks counted down, Luru Parz came to stand beside Torec.

There was an extraordinary stillness about Luru Parz, Torec thought; she was as still as the ancient Moon itself. And she was *dark*. The light was bright, for this was noon of the long lunar day. But

Luru seemed to soak up the light; though her Virtual cast no shadow, she looked oddly like a shadow herself. Torec was given to understand that this Virtual was not an avatar, a semi-sentient copy of an original with whom its memories would be merged after it had fulfilled its function. This Virtual was a mirror of life, which must mean, given the lack of any perceptible time delay, that Luru Parz herself was somewhere within the Earth-Moon system – or else she was linked to the Moon by some FTL channel, which would be hugely expensive.

Luru Parz said to Torec, 'So you have codified Pirius's time-hopping technique.'

'Yes, ma'am.'

'Describe your algorithm.'

Torec took a breath. Despite the way she had hammered away at her techs to get them to talk to her comprehensibly, the theory of the CTC software was still her weakest point. 'We give the system a problem to solve, in the case of our prototype to find a particular protein geometry. And we give it a brute-force way to solve the problem. In the case of protein-folding, we instruct the processor simply to start searching through all possible protein geometries. And we have a *time register*, a special cache that stores a flag if a signal has been received from the future.

'The basic CTC program has three steps. When the processor starts, the first step is to check the time register. If a signal has been received – if the solution to the problem is already in memory – then stop. If not, we go to step two, which says to carry out the calculation by brute force, however long it takes. When the answer is finally derived, we go to step three: go back in time, deliver the solution and mark the time register.'

Luru nodded. 'So the timeline is redrafted. In the first draft timeline, the problem is solved by brute force. In the final version of the timeline, the answer is sent back through time to the moment when the question is posed. So it isn't necessary to run the computation at all.'

'That's correct.'

Luru sighed. 'The joy of time travel paradoxes. You can get the answer to a problem without needing to work it out! But there must be a good deal more to your design. Your closed timelike curves must be pretty short.'

'Actually just milliseconds.'

'Surely you can solve no problem which would take longer to solve than that length of time.'

Torec smiled, her confidence growing. 'No. By breaking a problem down into pieces you can solve anything.' She described how the problem was broken up into a hierarchy of nested subcomponents. At the base level were calculations so trivial they could be handled within the processor's short CTC periods. The answers were passed back in time to become the input for the next run-through, and so on. That way an answer was assembled piece by piece and looped back repeatedly to the zero instant, until the overall problem was resolved. 'The technical challenge is actually decomposing the problem in the first place, and controlling the information flow back up the line,' she said.

Luru laughed, an odd, hollow sound. 'You're computing with multiple time loops, and you think *that's* the only challenge? Ensign, you're a true pragmatist . . . I think it's nearly time.'

Over the glittering, much-patched array of the prototype processor, the bots hovered, utterly motionless against the greater lunar stillness. Behind the prototype the blank Virtual screen hovered, waiting to display the solution.

The last seconds wore away.

And at zero, the screen filled with a molecular diagram. Just like that, with no time elapsed. It was almost anti-climactic, Torec thought.

There was utter silence on the common loops; nobody moved, none of the techs or the observers from the Navy or the Ministry, not even a bot. But on the screen the diagram whirled, as it was ferociously analysed for verification. After ten seconds, the screen turned green, and numerical results scrolled over its surface.

Torec didn't need the details, nor would she have understood them; she just knew what that green colour meant. 'Lethe,' she whispered. 'We did it.'

There was a howling. She turned and saw Commissary Nilis capering barefoot on the surface of the Moon. Some transmission glitch was pixellating his image, and his voice sounded feathery, remote.

But his yell of triumph was echoed by the techs. One of them came sprinting clumsily up the slope to Torec. 'It worked!' A burly girl from Earth, she grabbed Torec and tried to kiss her on the lips. It was typically inappropriate earthworm behaviour, resulting only in a clash of visors, but Torec let it pass.

The bots descended on the prototype complex, checking its physical integrity. But ironically, Torec knew, there should be little for them to find, for as the processor's paradoxical operation had worked, there had been no need for the problem to be brute-force solved and no need even for the little toy ships to chatter back and forth on their FTL hops – in this draft of the timeline anyhow. The curves in time had served their purpose – and so had rendered their own existence unnecessary. It was another peculiar advantage of a time travel computer. If it worked correctly, *it never actually ran at all* – and so it should never wear out. Some of the techs had even debated whether they could get away with the economy of making the processors shoddily, almost at the point of failure – for that failure would never be tested.

The four of them stood in a rough circle: Torec, Luru Parz, Nilis and Pila. Of the four only Torec was physically present, though they all wore skinsuits save the stubbornly uncouth Commissary. The light falling on each of the Virtuals came from different unseen sources, subtly different angles, and that, set against the black sky and shining ground of the Moon, added to Torec's sense of unreality.

Pila said coolly, 'The trial was obviously a success.'

'Thank you,' Nilis said. 'But it's more than that.' He waved a hand, and a crude Virtual diagram appeared before him. It was Pirius's early whiteboard sketch, Torec saw, the asterisk standing for the Prime Radiant and the obstacles surrounding it marked in red – the FTL foreknowledge symbolised by a bar across the approach path, the superior Xeelee computing and defensive ability a circle around the Radiant. Now Nilis snapped his fingers, and that circle around the asterisk turned green. 'Today we have removed one of the three fundamental barriers lying between us and the conquest of the Galaxy. We can out-think the Xeelee, out-manoeuvre their final defences!

'But you understand this prototype is just the beginning, the proof of concept,' he said. 'Much more work will be needed to turn this crude, sprawling prototype design into a battle-hardened unit. Now is the time for a fresh tranche of funding to be released.'

'We at the Ministry do understand,' Pila said, with the faintest condescension. 'That's why I've been authorised to tell you that, with the successful completion of the trial, the project will continue under the auspices of the Navy. The technology is obviously of strategic potential, and funds for its full development will be made available.' She beamed, as if she was handing out gifts.

Torec quietly clenched a fist. She felt vindicated. But Luru Parz stayed silent.

Nilis stepped forward. His face, pocked by resolution flaws, was working as he tried to maintain his smile. 'The Navy? But the CTC processor is just the first step to the greater goal, the strike at the Prime Radiant.'

'Which was only a pipe dream, wasn't it?' Pila said sweetly. 'You still have nothing, not even concepts, for overcoming your remaining obstacles. Commissary, it's time to stop. The Minister feels he has done his duty in backing you this far, on the basis of your previous accomplishments. You've done well! Bask in the glory. Once again you've done your duty for the cause of the Third Expansion, and now your garden needs you.'

Nilis laughed. 'And you'll throw this miracle to the Navy? Who will use it to lose even more battles in ever more ingenious ways – oh, you fools, can't you see what you're doing?'

Pila flinched, and her face closed up. But her Virtual image shuddered.

In a silent explosion of pixels it burst open, and the slim woman was replaced by the massive form of Minister Gramm. He was without a skinsuit, and grease was smeared on his chin. And he was trembling with rage. 'You call me a fool? I am warning you: take the get-out, Commissary. Go home. If you make any more trouble, I will cast you down in the pits of Mercury with this child soldier of yours.'

Nilis trembled too, through anger and fear. But he held his ground.

Luru Parz stepped between the two of them. 'Enough.' Her Virtual form grazed Gramm's, and his belly exploded in a hail of muddy pixels.

Gramm lumbered back. 'Stay out of this, Luru Parz.'

'I will not. You may not be able to see the potential here, Minister, but I can. For the first time in three thousand years we may be glimpsing a way to end the relentless friction of this war – end it before it ends us.'

'My verdict is final,' shouted Gramm, eyes bulging.

'No,' Luru Parz said simply. 'It isn't. The project continues.' She held his gaze.

To Torec's amazement Gramm was the first to back down, a minister of the Coalition somehow beaten by this small, worn-smooth, mysterious woman. Not for the first time Torec longed to know the secret of Luru's power.

Luru turned away. 'There is nothing left to do here but detail. We must move to the next stage. We meet in one week. In person, if you don't mind; these Virtual confrontations are unsatisfactory.'

Torec asked, 'Where?'

'Port Sol,' said Luru Parz. And she allowed her Virtual to break up, the pixels fading from view in the bright light of the late lunar morning.

CHAPTER 16

On Quin Base, after the initial flurry of curiosity died down, Pirius Blue tried to keep his distance from the other cadets. He was too old, too different, too *outside* ever to fit in with these swarming kids.

But, despite his reserve, Pirius became an unlikely favourite of three girls who called themselves Tili One, Tili Two and Tili Three. They were alike in their slight build, their dark colouring and their small toothy faces. They were actually triplets, products of the same ovum. That wasn't terribly uncommon, he learned, if you came from a certain big hatchery on the periphery of this star cluster, where for some reason multiple births were common, 'But it makes sense,' Cohl said with her usual sour humour. 'This *is* the Quintuplet Cluster . . .'

The Tili triplets spent almost all their time together. They always seemed to fix it so they worked together during training exercises, and when they were off duty they stayed even closer. Eating, working on their gear, they were always giggling, talking, their three so-similar heads clustered together. They shared one bunk, and when they slept the three of them tangled up together in a warm heap of limbs and heads. They even made love, in full view of everybody, unembarrassed. But their love-making was gentle, very tender, almost presexual, Pirius thought. Of course this was all inappropriate. Family units, even twins and triplets, weren't supposed to be left together lest the bonds they formed got in the way of loyalty to a wider humanity. But then a lot of what went on here was non-Doctrinal.

Things got complicated when the triplets fixed on Pirius. Apparently they had had some rudiments of flight training, as navigators, before falling foul of the authorities. So they had something in common.

When one of them offered to show Pirius how to repair scuffs on his skinsuit or to clean out the algae beds in his backpack, he accepted with good grace.

They seemed to treat him as a big, clumsy pet. He put up with it. Maybe it was because the Tilis so obviously had each other that he felt a bit more secure with them.

There were a couple of times, though, when they tried to entice him into their crowded bed. As they ran their little fingers over his belly and calves, no offer could have seemed more tempting. But he drew back, again fearing he might somehow lose himself. He was also worried about how *old* the triplets were; like the other cadets they seemed very small, very unformed, very young.

But when one of them came alone to his bed – it may have been Tili Two, or possibly Three – he found it impossible to resist. And when he let himself fall among her skin and lips and soft limbs, he found an immense, consoling relief.

He tried to discuss his feelings with This Burden Must Pass.

'I felt like you once,' Burden said. He was lying on his bunk, propped up on his elbow, bare to the waist, facing Pirius. The usual meaningless clamour of the barracks washed over them. Burden said, 'I was Navy too. At first there is just a torrent of faces here. But after a time, you start to understand.'

'You do?'

'Pirius, you feel these little cadets are somehow different from you, don't you? Not just in experience, in background – something more fundamental. And you know why? *Because it's true.*'

The stock of embryos hatched out of Quin's birthing tanks were developed from the genetic stock of the soldiers themselves. Of course: where else was it to come from? Not only that, the military planners tried to ensure that only *successful* soldiers got to breed. This was meant to be an incentive to make you get through your training, to fight, to survive. There were no families in this world, no parental bonds. But something deep in every human being responded even to the abstract knowledge that something of herself would survive this brief life.

Pirius knew about this, of course; it was the same on Arches. But he had never before thought through the implications.

It was selective breeding. And it had been going on, right across the

Galaxy, long before the war with the Xeelee had come to full fruition. For nearly twenty thousand years mankind had been breeding itself into a race of child soldiers.

'Look at the Tilis,' murmured Burden. 'They could probably cross-breed with anybody in the Galaxy, if they had the chance; we haven't speciated yet. But their bodies are adapted to low gravity, or no gravity at all. *Their* bones don't wash away in a flood of imbalanced fluids, the way our earthworm ancestors' did when they first ventured into space. Their minds have adjusted too; they can think and work in three dimensions. The triplets don't suffer stress from vertigo, or claustrophobia. They are even immune to radiation, relatively.

'There's more. Here on Quin, if you survive combat you breed, but for the genes it's better yet not to wait, not to take that chance. So the cadets become fertile earlier and earlier, until they are producing eggs and sperm long before their bodies are developed enough to fight. Pirius, the Tilis are about sixteen, I think. But they've been fertile since they were ten. Infantry are an extreme case. The attrition rate is horrific; generations are very short here. But the same subtle sculpting has shaped *you*, Pirius. And me. Neither of us is an earth-worm.'

Pirius was shocked. 'Burden, I know *you* don't care about the Doctrines. But why do the officers let this genetic drift go on?'

Burden shook his head. 'You still don't see it? *Because it's useful*, Pirius. If you just remember that one thing, many puzzling things about life here fall into place.'

Burden spoke about himself. The boy called Quero had been born on a base inside yet another Galaxy-centre cluster. He had once flown the greenships: he had been a pilot himself, in fact, and had come through one action.

But all the while his faith had been developing, he said.

The seed of the faith of the Friends of Wigner had come here in legends from old Earth, legends of Michael Poole and the rebellion against the Qax. Its supremely consoling message had quickly taken root among the soldiers of the Galaxy Core. By now you could find Friends right around the Front, around the whole of the centre of the Galaxy.

'I actually grew up with it. I heard kids' stories about Michael Poole and the Ultimate Observer. I didn't take any of it seriously, not really; it was just there in the background. And when I started going through my training and learned that it was officially all taboo, I shut up about it.'

At first none of this had made any difference to Quero's successful career. But as he experienced conflict, he found himself deeply troubled.

'It was seeing death,' he said now, smiling. 'It was bad enough from a greenship blister. It's a lot worse here, on the Rocks. Every death is the termination of a life, of a mind, a unique thread of experience and memory. Maybe death has to come to us all. But like this? I found it hard to accept my place in this unending war.'

Seeking answers, he had turned to the faith of his childhood. He went beyond the simple personalised stories of Michael Poole and other heroes he had grown up with, and he began to re-examine its deeper philosophy for himself. And he had begun to speak out. 'My officers respected Quero, I think. But they had no time for This Burden Must Pass.'

He had been here a while, Pirius gathered. Naturally smart, flexible and courageous, Burden had already survived five combat actions. Once, he said, he had done well enough to be offered a way out, to retrain as an infantry officer. But he would have had to recant his faith, and he had refused, and so he had been cast down yet again.

Pirius asked, 'You don't regret any of it?'

'Why should I?'

'Oh. "This Burden Must Pass." '

'You got it,' Burden said. 'All of this suffering will ultimately be deleted. So what's to regret?'

Cohl had listened to this. She drew Pirius aside. 'And you *believe* all that?'

He was surprised she'd asked. 'Why would he lie about something like that?'

'Then why is it so vague? *Why* was he sent to Quin in the first place – because of his faith? Or because of something that happened on his base, or even during combat?' Her small eyes gleamed. 'See? It's just like his preaching. He talks a lot, but it's all mist and shadows.'

'You don't like him.'

'I don't care enough not to like him. I don't trust him, for sure.'

Pirius turned back to Burden, who had heard none of this. Burden was looking at him with a kind of eagerness, Pirius thought, as if it was important to Burden that he somehow got Pirius's approval.

Sometimes he thought he saw weakness in Burden, somewhere under the surface of composure, command and humour. Weakness and need.

'Burden, you said the officers will tolerate genetic drift if the product is useful. But why do they put up with you?'

'Because I'm useful too.' Burden lay back on his bunk. 'I told you that's the key. Of course I am useful! Why else?'

When he saw his first death on the Rock, Pirius learned the truth of this.

CHAPTER 17

Pirius Red and Torec were reunited at the Berr-linn spaceport. They had been separated for eight weeks. Careless of who was watching them, they wrapped their arms about each other and pressed their mouths together.

'They're mad,' Pirius whispered. 'The earthworms. All of them!'

'I know!' she whispered back, round-eyed.

They stared into each other's eyes, their faces pressed together, their breath mingling, hot. Again Pirius felt that deep surging warmth towards her that he'd started to feel when they first arrived on Earth. It was as if he was whole with her, incomplete when they were apart, as if they were two halves of the same entity. Was this love? How was he supposed to know?

And – did she feel the same way? It looked as if she did, but how were you supposed to tell?

But they had no time to talk about their feelings, no time to recover from their separate adventures, for the very next day they were to be shipped off, at Luru Parz's order, to Port Sol.

To a traveller from the centre of the Galaxy, a jaunt to the Kuiper Belt, only some fifty times as far out as Earth's orbit around the sun, should have seemed trivial. But as the sun dwindled to an intense pinpoint and as Port Sol itself at last swam into view, dark, blood-red, Pirius felt that he was indeed going deep: not just deep in space but deep in time, deep into humanity's murky past.

Nilis's corvette entered a painfully slow orbit. The gravity of a ball of ice a few hundred kilometres across was a mere feather touch. The passengers crowded to the corvette's transparent walls.

Port Sol was an irregular mass, only vaguely spherical, and dimly lit by the distant sun. Pirius saw a crumpled, ruddy surface broken by craters of a ghostly blue-white. Some of these 'craters', though, looked too regular to be natural. And some of them were domed over, illuminated by a soft prickling of artificial light. People still lived here, then. But signs of abandonment overwhelmed the signs of life: shards of collapsed and darkened domes, even buildings that might once have floated above the ice but had now crashed to the ground.

But still – *Port Sol*!

Even to a Navy brat like Pirius, born and raised twenty-eight thousand light years from Earth, the name had resonance. Port Sol was the very rim of Sol system, the place where the legendary engineer Michael Poole had come to build the very first of mankind's starships.

Nilis's excitement seemed as genuine as the ensigns'. Minister Gramm, though, seemed tense, nervous, on the verge of anger. It was evident that Luru Parz had forced him to come out here, and he didn't like it one bit. And Gramm's assistant Pila peered out, analytic and supercilious, apparently as faintly amused by the spectacle of Port Sol as she had been by the Moon.

A flitter slid smoothly up to meet the corvette. It carried a single passenger, a woman dressed in a simple white robe. She had the same look about her as Luru Parz: compact, patient, extraordinarily still, her features small and expressionless. But she was slimmer than Luru, and she seemed somehow more graceful. She said, 'My name is Faya Parz. I am an associate of Luru . . .'

When she announced her name eyebrows were raised. Gramm turned to Pila. 'Well, well,' he said. 'Faya and Luru, Parz and Parz!'

Pila smiled. 'I imagine the Doctrines are stretched rather thin here, Minister.'

This baffled both the ensigns, and Nilis had to explain that under archaic traditions, before the more rational approach instigated by the Commission for Historical Truth, surnames would be shared by members of the same family. It was all thoroughly non-Doctrinal.

The flitter touched down close to one of the illuminated pits in the ice. The party transferred to a ground transport, a sort of car with massive bubble wheels and hooks for traction to save it bouncing out of Port Sol's minuscule gravity well. The car had no inertial adjustment, and as it began to roll along a road roughly cut through the ice, the cabin bobbed up and settled back, over and over, slowly but disconcertingly. Pirius and Torec were charmed by this low tech relic.

Though Gramm and Pila looked politely bored, Nilis was fascinated by the scenery. 'So this Kuiper object is primordial – a relic of the formation of the system,' he said.

'Not quite,' Faya said. 'The reddish colour of the ice is caused by bombardment by cosmic rays.' High-energy particles, relics of energetic events elsewhere in the universe. Over time the surface layers became rich in carbon, dark, and the irradiation mantle became a tough crust. 'Nothing is unmodified by time,' said Faya.

Nilis stood up in the swaying cabin so he could see better. 'But in places impacts have punched through that crust to reveal the ice below. Is that what we're seeing? Those blue pits—'

Faya said, 'Impacts are rare out here, but they do happen, yes. But the feature we are approaching is artificial, a quarry. It was scooped out by engineers to provision a GUTdrive starship. The present-day colonists refer to it as the "Pit of the *Mayflower*", though we don't have archaeological proof that *Mayflower II* was actually launched from here . . .'

In those early days, the starships that had set off from Port Sol had been driven by nothing but water rockets, using ice as reaction mass. They had crawled along much slower than light, their missions lasting generations. With the acquisition of FTL drives, Port Sol was suddenly redundant, its ice no longer necessary. Even as mankind's great galactic adventure had begun in earnest, Port Sol's time was already done. Since then it had orbited out here in the dark, its population dwindling, its name an exotic memory.

But now, it seemed, Port Sol had a new purpose.

An odd flash in the sky caught Pirius's eye: a twinkle, there and gone. He knew that some of the earliest colonies here – from the days even before Michael Poole, very low tech indeed – had relied for their power on nothing more than sunlight, gathered with immense wispy mirrors thousands of kilometres across. Even now nobody knew for sure what was out here. The Kuiper Belt was a vast spherical archipelago, its islands separated from each other by the width of the inner Sol system. In this huge place, perhaps some of those ancient communities survived, following their obsolescent ways, hidden from the turbulent politics of mankind.

His new sense of curiosity strong, Pirius felt a deep thrill to be in this extraordinary place. But stare as he might he didn't glimpse the mirror in the sky again.

The car nuzzled against a small translucent dome set on the edge of the Pit of the *Mayflower*. The dome was cluttered with low, temporary-looking buildings. There was an inertial generator somewhere, and to everybody's relief the gravity in here was no lower than the Moon's, and the walking was easy.

Pirius and Torec were the first out, eager to reach the transparent viewing wall on the dome's far side so they could see the Pit for themselves.

The Pit of the *Mayflower* was a smooth-cut crater a kilometre wide. Despite its size the Pit was itself enclosed by a vast, low dome, around which lesser structures, like this habitable dome, clustered like infants. On the floor of the Pit stood the relics of heavy engineering projects: gantries, platforms of metal, concrete and ice, and immense low-gravity cranes, like vast skeletons. Globe lamps hovered everywhere, casting a yellow-white complex light through the Pit. Nothing moved.

Bustling after the ensigns, Nilis said, 'What a place – a relic of the grandeur, or the folly, of the past. A mine for archaeologists! Ah, but I forget: under the Coalition we are all too busy for archaeology, aren't we, Minister?'

Gramm was waddling at a speed obviously uncomfortable for him, and though the dome's air was cool he was sweating heavily. 'Nilis, we may be far from home. But you are a Commissary and I suggest you comport yourself like one.'

'I am suitably abashed,' Nilis said dryly.

'But you must remember,' Faya Parz said, 'that this is a place of history, not just engineering. Many of those first starships were crewed not by explorers but by refugees.'

Nilis said, 'You're talking about *jasofts*,' he said.

Torec said, 'Jasofts?'

'Or *pharaohs*,' Faya said with a black-toothed smile.

It was an ancient, tangled, difficult story.

Nilis said, 'Before the Qax Occupation, ageing was defeated. The Qax withdrew the anti-agathic treatments and death returned to Earth. But some humans, called jasofts or pharaohs, were rewarded for their work for the Qax with immortality treatments – the Qax's own this time. Made innately conservative by age, selfish and self-centred, utterly dependent on the Qax – well. Those new immortals were ideal collaborators.'

Faya Parz said unemotionally, 'That's judgemental. Some would say the jasofts ameliorated the cruelty of the Qax. Without them the Occupation would have been much more severe. Nothing of human culture might have survived the Qax Extirpation. The species itself might have become extinct.'

Gramm waved his hand. 'Or the jasofts were war criminals. Whatever. It's a debate twenty thousand years old, and will never be resolved. When the Occupation collapsed, the new Coalition hunted down the last jasofts.'

Nilis nodded. 'And so ships like the *Mayflower* were built, and crews of jasofts fled Sol system. Or tried to. We don't know the meaning of the name, by the way: *Mayflower*. Perhaps some archaic pre-Occupation reference . . . In the end, Port Sol itself became one of the last refuges of jasofts in Sol system.'

With an almost soundless footstep, Luru Parz approached them. She said, 'And of course it had to be cleaned out, by the fresh-faced soldiers of the Coalition.'

Gramm snapped, 'Did you bring us here to shock us with this revolting bit of history, Luru Parz?'

'You know why you're here, Minister,' Luru Parz said, and she laughed in his face.

Gramm said nothing. But as he glared at Luru Parz, his eyes burned bright with hatred.

The ostensible purpose of this long trip was a discussion of the future of Nilis's Project Prime Radiant. So Luru Parz led Nilis, Gramm and Pila to a conference room, leaving Pirius and Torec in the charge of Faya Parz.

Faya asked if the ensigns wanted to rest. But they had spent days cooped up on a corvette, and were anxious to see the rest of Port Sol. Faya complied with good grace.

They began a slow circuit of the Pit of the *Mayflower*.

The great domed quarry was surrounded by a ring of satellite domes, each much smaller, with further facilities beyond that. In the unpressurised areas beyond the domes Pirius recognised power plants, landing pads, clusters of sensors, telescopes peering up at the star-ridden sky. No weapons, though; evidently this ancient, enigmatic place was not expected to be a target, for the Xeelee or anybody else.

These were obviously modern facilities. The more ancient landscape of Port Sol – the old starship quarries, the fallen towns, the imploded domes – was tantalisingly hidden beyond a tight horizon.

The domes were mostly occupied by laboratories, study areas and living quarters. But it was a bleak, functional environment. In the labs and living areas there was a total lack of personalisation: no Virtuals, no artwork, no entertainment consoles, not so much as a graffito. There were tight regulations about that sort of thing on Arches Base – across the Druzite Galaxy, personality was officially frowned on as a distraction from duty – but despite their superficial sameness every bunk in every corridor on every level of a Barracks Ball was subtly different, modified to reflect the personality of its owner. Not here, though; the people who manned this place must have extraordinary discipline.

Not that there were many people here at all, as far as the ensigns could see. Once they glimpsed somebody working in a lab, a place of shining metallic equipment and anonymous white boxes. Over-shadowed by immense Virtual schematics of what looked like a DNA molecule, Pirius couldn't even see if it was a man or woman.

'Not many of us are needed,' Faya Parz said. 'There are only twenty-three of us, including Luru Parz. But Luru Parz travels a good deal nowadays.'

Torec shivered. Pirius knew what she was thinking. To a Navy brat, used to the crowds of Barracks Balls, that was a terribly small number, this an awfully remote and isolated place: to think there were no more than twenty-two other humans within billions of kilometres . . .

'The machines do all the work – even most of the analytical work. Humans are here to direct, to set objectives, to provide the final layer of interpretation.'

Torec said, 'Don't you get lonely? How do you live?'

Faya smiled. *You don't understand.* It was a look Pirius had grown used to among the sophisticated population of Earth, but he suspected uneasily that here it might be true.

Faya said, 'We have always been an odd lot, I suppose. An ice moon is a small place, short of resources. There were only ever a few of us, even in the great days. We would travel to other moons for trade, cultural exchange, to find partners – we still do. But there was no room to spare; population numbers always had to be controlled tightly. So marriage and children were matters for the community to decide, not for lovers.' Her voice was wistful, and Pirius wondered what ancient tragedies lay hidden beneath these bland words. 'You know, in the olden days there were floating cities. There was dancing.'

Oddly she sounded as if she remembered such times herself – as if *she* had once danced among these fallen palaces. Faya seemed heavy, static, dark, worn out by time, like a lump of rock from the Moon. It was hard to imagine her ever having been young, ever *dancing*.

Torec asked, 'What do you *do* here?'

Faya said, 'We study dark matter.'

'Why?'

'Because Luru Parz seeks to understand alien tampering with the evolution of Sol system.'

Torec and Pirius dared to share a glance. *They're all mad.*

Pirius knew, in theory, about dark matter. It was an invisible shadow of normal matter, the 'light' matter made of protons and neutrons. The dark stuff interacted with normal matter only through gravity. You couldn't burn it, push it away or harvest it, save with a gravity well. And it was harmless, passing through light matter as if it wasn't there. Pilots and navigators were taught to recognise its presence; sometimes great reefs of the stuff could cause gravitational anomalies that might affect your course.

Aside from that, dark matter was of no consequence. Pirius couldn't see why anybody would study it.

But Faya showed them Virtuals. Sol system had coalesced out of a disc of material that had once stretched much further than the orbit of the furthest planets. Most of the mass of the disc was now locked up in the bodies of the planets, but if you smeared out the planets' masses you got a fairly smooth curve, showing how the mass in the disc had dropped off evenly as distance from the sun increased, just as you'd expect.

'Until you get to Neptune,' Faya said. At the rim of the Kuiper Belt the actual mass distribution plummeted sharply. 'There are many bodies out here, some massive. Pluto is one, Port Sol another . . . But they add up to only about a fifth of Earth's mass. There should have been *thousands* of worldlets the size of Pluto, or larger. Something removed all those planetesimals – and long ago, when Sol system was very young.'

She summarised theories. Perhaps the missing worldlets had been thrown out of their orbits by the migration of a young Neptune through Sol system, as it headed for its final orbit. Perhaps there was another large planet out there in the dark, disturbing the objects' orbits – but no such planet had been found. Or maybe a passing star had stripped the Kuiper cloud of much of its richness. And so on.

Pirius said, 'None of that sounds too convincing.'

Faya Parz said, 'If mankind has learned one thing in the course of its expansion to the stars, it is that the first explanation for any unlikely phenomenon is *life*.'

Luru Parz had come to this place to study the traces of that ancient plunder. Her first theory was that it could have something to do with dark matter. Dark matter was relatively rare in the plane of the Galaxy, and indeed in the heart of Sol system. 'But it is to be found out here,' Faya said, 'where the sun is remote, and baryonic matter is scarce.'

Pirius tried to put this together. 'And you think there is life in the dark matter. Intelligence.'

'Oh, yes.' Faya's eyes were hooded. 'There is six times as much dark matter as baryonic in the universe. Everywhere we look, baryonic matter is infested with life. Why not dark matter? In the past, humans have studied it. We have some of the records. Luru even believes that a conflict between intelligences of dark and light matter is underway – an invisible conflict more fundamental even than our war with the Xeelee. The Qax destroyed much of our heritage, but there are hints in the surviving pre-Occupation records.'

'And this has something to do with the Kuiper Belt's missing mass?'

'We haven't ruled it out. But in the meantime we have found something stranger still.' Faya snapped her fingers. A Virtual image whirled in the air. It was a tetrahedron, Pirius saw, four triangular faces, straight edges. It turned slowly, and elusive golden light glimmered from its faces. But the image was grainy.

'What's this?'

'It's called the Kuiper Anomaly. Obviously an artefact, presumably of alien origin. It was detected in the Kuiper Belt long ago – before humans first left Earth, even. It was the size of a small moon.'

'Was?'

'By the time humans finally mounted a probe to study it, it had disappeared.' She snapped her fingers; the tetrahedron popped and vanished.

Pirius said, 'So perhaps the missing planetesimals were used to manufacture this . . . Anomaly.'

'It's possible. The mass loss looks about right, from what we know of the object's gravitational field. But if so it must have been there a long time, since the formation of the system itself.'

Torec said, 'What was it for?'

'We've no idea.'

'Where did it go? Was it connected to the dark matter?'

Faya smiled. 'We don't know that either. We're here to answer such questions.' She would say no more.

Pirius found it a deeply disturbing thought that some alien intelligence had built such a silent sentinel on the fringe of the system, long before humanity, even as the sun was fitfully flaring to life. In fact he felt resentful that somebody had used that immense resource for their own purposes. Those were *our* ice moons, he thought, knowing he was being illogical.

They completed the circuit of the Pit, coming back to where they had started. They longed to go further – to see more of Michael Poole's heroic engineering, or even find the fabled Forest of Ancestors, where the native life forms in their sessile forms waited out eternity. But they had work to do.

Regretfully, they returned to the conference room. It turned out to be set high on a gantry, overlooking the Pit of the *Mayflower*. It had a startling view of the gantries and cranes that had once built starships.

But nobody in the conference room was interested in the view. They were too busy with a tremendous row.

Luru Parz paced, small, cold, determined.

'In its day, the Coalition served a purpose. We needed a framework, guidance to help us recover from the terrible wasting of the Qax Occupation. But we quickly slipped into an intellectual paralysis. Do you not see that, Minister? Even now we look back over our shoulder at the past, the Occupation, the near-extinction of mankind. The Druz Doctrines are nothing but a rationalisation of that great trauma. And since then, obsessed with history, we have sleepwalked our way into a Galactic war.

'But it can't go on for ever. Nilis sees that. We can't keep up our blockade of the Core indefinitely. Now Nilis offers us a chance to win, to take the Galaxy. I'm not at all surprised that you, Gramm, and your self-serving colleagues are seeking to sabotage his efforts. In fact I'm surprised you have given him as much support as you have. But it's not enough. Gramm, you are going to give Nilis all the backing he needs – all the way to the centre of the Galaxy.'

Gramm sneered. 'Madam, this buffoon *has nothing*. Don't you understand that yet? He is blocked! He has no way to defeat FTL foreknowledge, or to strike at the Prime Radiant itself.'

Faya Parz said, 'Then we must help him. There may be answers.'

Gramm snapped, '*What* answers?'

'Mankind is very old; the past contains many secrets . . . This is a treasure which the Coalition chooses to ignore. We believe that somewhere in this deep heritage we may well discover the key to unlocking the final puzzles.'

Nilis rammed his fist into the palm of his hand. 'You're right. Yes! *That's* where we must go next.'

Pirius said, 'Where?'

Nilis said, 'Why, to Mars. To the Secret Archive of the Coalition.'

Torec whispered to Pirius, 'What Secret Archive? I don't like this talk.'

'Nor me.'

Pila, Gramm's advisor, had been showing increasing irritation. Now she seemed to lose patience. 'Why are we listening to this heretical nonsense? What hold does this woman have over us, Minister?'

Luru Parz smiled. 'Why don't you tell her, Gramm?'

Gramm looked thunderous, but didn't reply.

Luru said evenly, 'Oh, I'm just another of the Coalition's little secrets. Just another Doctrinal violation, tolerated because I am useful. I've had an uneasy, ah, working relationship with Gramm for many years, and his predecessors long before him. Before *that* – well, my life has sometimes been complicated. But things are civilised these days. The Coalition tolerates our research here on Port Sol as long as we share the results. Of course it could destroy us at any time. But on the other hand I could do a great deal of harm to the Coalition.' She opened her mouth wide, showing blackened teeth.

Nilis suddenly seemed to understand. His jaw dropped, and he gulped before he could speak again. 'All this talk of the depths of time . . . Port Sol always was a notorious den of jasoft refugees. And they weren't all cleared out, were they? And you are one of them, Luru Parz. *You are a jasoft.*'

Pila flinched, as if she had been struck; her bland, pretty face curled in disgust, the strongest expression Pirius had ever seen her show. Nilis merely stared, utterly fascinated, his intellect overriding his emotions, as so often.

Pirius was stunned. He stared at Faya, who had conducted them around the Pit. *Was she an ancient too?* She had talked of dancing among the floating palaces of Port Sol – but the ice moon had been all but abandoned for twenty thousand years. Was it possible it wasn't just a dream?

Torec's hand slipped into his. In this cold place, far from home, surrounded by so many gruesome secrets, the touch of warm flesh was comforting.

Pila turned on her superior. She seemed more upset by the violation of orthodoxy than by the cold biological reality of the jasofts. 'Minister, if this is true – why are these monstrosities tolerated?'

Gramm said nothing, his round face crimson.

Luru said, 'Well, I'm useful, you see. *And* I know too much to be dispensed with. Don't I, Gramm?'

'You old witch,' Gramm said tightly.

'Witch? If so, I brought you here to remind you of my spell,' she said, her tone dark.

Gramm glared. But it was clear he had no choice but to give her what she wanted.

When the meeting broke up, Torec approached Luru. She was clearly fascinated.

'But how do you *live*?'

Luru winked at her. 'Most days I sleep a lot.' She put her hands on the ensigns' shoulders; her skin felt warm, soft to Pirius: human, not at all strange. She said, 'You children must be as hungry as I am. We have a lot of work to do. A great mission – a Galaxy to conquer. But first we eat. Come!' And she led them away.

CHAPTER 18

Out on the surface of the Rock, the cadets were learning to advance behind an artillery barrage.

It was another brutally simple, unbelievably ancient tactic. Behind the advancing troops was a bank of monopole cannon, mankind's most effective weapon against Xeelee technology. The guns opened up before the advance began, firing live shells over the heads of the troops. The idea was that the hail of shells would flatten enemy emplacements, and the troops would rush forward and take the positions without a fight. Then the barrage would work its way forward, a curtain of fire always just ahead of the advancing troops, steadily raking out the opposition before the troops even got there. So the theory had always had it.

But in practice Pirius Blue found himself lying in clinging asteroid dust as the barrage flew, so thick it was a curtain of light over his head, and shells of twisted spacetime fell not half a kilometre from him. The shells' pounding seemed to shake the whole asteroid. The sense of physical energy erupting around him was overwhelming, as if all the violence of the Galaxy centre were focused on this one battered old Rock.

The order to advance, actually to run *into* the fire, all but defeated his courage.

The success of this tactic depended on precise timing, coordination between artillery and infantry, and extremely accurate firing by the gunners. But the cannon were only machines, the gunners only human, the infantry were rattled and confused, and in an imperfect universe all were liable to error. The strategy depended a good deal on simple luck.

And, today, his platoon's luck ran out.

*

Pirius actually saw the fatal shell incoming. It was like a meteor, streaking down from the barrage that flew over his head. On the comms loops he heard officers yelling warnings. But for those directly under the path of the shell, no warning could help.

It was the triplets, Pirius saw, recognising their customised uniforms. For a last instant they clung to each other. The shell landed directly over them. There was a soundless flash of light, another giant's footstep, a fountain of dirt.

Pirius ran to the site of the impact. A perfectly pristine crater had been dug into the asteroid.

Tili One had somehow escaped unharmed. Three had lost a hand, but was conscious, though distressed. Of Two there was no sign. Her very substance had been torn apart, Pirius thought, her very atoms dissociated.

Over the heads of the little group, the monopole barrage was dying, as if apologetically.

Marta, Cohl, Burden were all here, standing gravely as the surviving sisters wailed and clung to each other. 'At least it was quick,' Captain Marta said gruffly. 'There can have been no pain.'

One of the Tilis turned on the officer. 'What comfort is *that*? It was a stupid accident.'

Burden stepped forward. He placed a big hand on each of the Tilis' skinsuit helmets. 'It doesn't matter,' he said. 'None of this matters. There will be a better time, a better place, where you will be reunited with your sister, when all of this is wiped clean . . .' And so on. Gradually his words were comforting the girls. They bent their heads to his chest, and he held them as they wept wretchedly.

This was too much for Cohl. She turned on Captain Marta. 'What happened to the Doctrines? If you let him spout words like these, what did she die *for*?'

Marta eyed her coldly, the human half of her reconstructed face as still and expressionless as the metallised side. 'His words are useful,' she said simply.

And so they were, Pirius saw now, just as Burden himself had said, and that was why they were tolerated. It didn't matter whether anybody believed in Michael Poole and the rest or not. Everything here was dedicated to the purposes of the war: even the tolerance of a faith which undermined the war's very justification. Just as long as its adherents were prepared to march off to die.

The Captain snapped, 'Clean up here.' She turned and walked away.

Pirius and the triplets' other friends helped the surviving sisters get back to the barracks. Pirius had never seen anything like their grief.

But there was no time for consolation. The very next day new orders came: Pirius's company was to be thrown into the Front.

For their final preparation Pirius and Cohl were taken to a sick bay.

Here nanomachinery was injected into their eyes. Their retinas werc rebuilt, overlaid with a layer of technology whose purpose was to help their eyes cope with the blinding light of the Galaxy's heart – and perhaps enable them to survive another few seconds. They had both taken many implants before, of course, even deep inside their skulls. But none of them had felt so directly violating.

They endured a night of agonishing pain. Pirius and Cohl and never been lovers, but that night they shared a bunk, weeping in each other's arms.

The next morning, when Pirius looked in a mirror, he saw the silver in his eyes, and his own face reflected back from his pupils. It was as if his very soul had been coated in metal.

TWO

The Qax, alien occupiers of Earth, inflicted the Extirpation on mankind. They churned up the rocks, destroyed the ecology, wrecked our homes, even imposed a new language on us. By these means they tried to destroy our past.

They were right to do so.

The past is a distraction, a source of envy, enmity, bitterness. Only the present matters, for only in the present can we shape the future.

Cut loose the past; it is dead weight.

Let the Extirpation continue. Let it never end.

— Hama Druz

CHAPTER 19

Pirius Red wasn't impressed by Mars.

From low orbit it struck him as a dull, closed-in little world. Aside from the scrapings of ice at the polar caps, its colour was a uniform, burned-out red. Mars was dead, or all but; you could tell that even from space just by looking at its worn craters and soft-edged mountains.

Given this world had been the most Earthlike in Sol system after the home planet itself, it was surprising how little mark humans had made on its surface. There were plenty of ruins, though. Once extensive arcologies had splashed the ancient face of this world with Earth green-blue. But those bubble-colonies had been smashed during the Qax Occupation. The largest of them had been in a region called Cydonia, and from space you could still make out where it had been: the neat circle of the dome's perimeter, the blocky shapes of a few remaining buildings, a tracery of foundations. But the ubiquitous dust had covered it over, washing away lines and colours.

A more striking ruin, in fact, was a massive building put up by the Qax themselves: an exotic matter factory. Its walls were massive and robust, enduring even after twenty thousand years. In the wars that had followed the expulsion of the Qax, the factory ruins had been used as a fortress as human fought human. Pirius sent Virtual images back to Torec to remind her of the similar factory she had explored on the Moon. But Torec was at Saturn, still working on the CTC processor project, out of touch.

Pirius's reaction to Mars seemed to disappoint Nilis. Apparently Mars held a sentimental place in earthworm hearts. Mars was a small world, but it had as much land area as Earth, Nilis said. It had canyons and mountains and huge impact craters – in fact the whole of the northern hemisphere appeared to be one immense basin – and its range of elevations, from the depths of the deepest basins to the heights of the highest mountains, was actually greater than anything on Earth, even if you were to strip away that world's oceans.

Geology was never going to appeal much to a Navy brat. But Pirius was intrigued by Mons Olympus, the tallest mountain in the whole of Sol system – and their destination. For in a grandiose, astonishingly arrogant gesture, the Interim Coalition of Governance had built its Secret Archive into that mightiest of monuments.

The corvette landed at Kahra, the modern capital of Mars. This was a city in the Earth style, a Qax-design Conurbation, a series of domes blown out of the bedrock. But only a few hundred thousand people lived here. In fact there were only a few million on Mars, Pirius learned, less on the whole planet than in a single one of Earth's great cities.

The Martian citizens seemed about as bland and fat as those Pirius had encountered on Earth, though a little taller, a little longer-limbed, perhaps an adaptation to the one-third gravity here. But the officials who processed their arrival stared at Pirius's bright red Navy uniform. Even here, it seemed, his unwelcome fame had spread, which was why Nilis had brought him in the first place. Nilis said conspiratorially, 'You are my battering ram as I smash through layers of officialdom, complacency and sheer obtuse bureaucracy.'

They had a day to wait in the city. Pirius spent some time in fitful exploration.

But even Kahra itself turned out to be something of a fake. During the Occupation the Qax had come to Mars only to destroy its human colonies. They had shipped the surviving settlers back to Earth – where they had almost all died, unable to adapt to a more massive planet's clinging gravity and dense air. Even the exotic matter factory had required only a handful of indentured humans to oversee its automated operation.

So for humans to throw up a Conurbation here, where none had existed before, was an absurdity. There was no Martian Occupation to memorialise; it was an 'empty gesture by earnest coalition politicos eager for advancement', as Nilis put it. This Conurbation didn't even have a number, as did those on Earth; it was known as Kahra, the name of the older city which had been demolished to make way for it, and whose foundations now rested under the dull pink-grey domes.

Kahra, and Mars itself, struck Pirius as an oddly half-hearted place – a Conurbation without a number, a world whose most interesting ruin was alien, a sparse population of unenthusiastic people. The ancient stasis of this world, which had given up on geological processing about the time the first oceans were pooling on Earth, seemed to have sunk into the minds of the settlers. Little controversy from this small dead world trickled up the chain of command to trouble the councils on Earth. There wasn't much news on Mars.

The next morning Pirius left Kahra without regret.

From Kahra it was a short hop to Olympus.

Their flitter landed on an uninteresting, gently sloping plain, featureless save for a massive hatchway set in the ground. Nothing else showed of the Secret Archive above the surface of Mars.

But this was, after all, the highest mountain in Sol system. So Pirius asked permission to spend a few minutes out on the surface. He pulled on his skinsuit, inflated the flitter's blister airlock, and dropped a couple of metres to the Martian ground.

He landed in dust. He broke through a crust of darker, loosely bound material and sank into thicker material beneath that compacted under his weight. Perhaps that crust was an irradiated mantle, like Port Sol. When he took a step he found the going wasn't so difficult, but soon his legs and back were stained by the dust, which was fine and clinging. He remembered Torec's complaints about Moon dust, and how hard that had been to clean off.

The slope was featureless save for a gully a few metres away, cut into the ground. The sky was reddish too, and the sun was a shrunken yellow-brown circle, still rising on this Martian morning. The light of the more remote sun was diluted, and the shadows it cast, though sharp, were not deep. The only motion was near the horizon where a narrow pillar, tracking across the ground, seemed to be shorting between ground and sky. Perhaps it was a dust devil. It was rarefied, feeble compared to the mighty meteorological features he had glimpsed on Earth.

All he could see of the works of mankind were the flitter and the white-painted Archive hatch, set in the ground. And he could see no mountain, no mighty summit or precipitous cliffs.

The air shimmered; a Virtual coalesced. It was Luru Parz, appropriately dressed in a skinsuit of her own.

Pirius felt his heart hammering. He had been unable to come to terms with Luru Parz's revelation that she was effectively immortal, millennia old; it defied his imagination. Standing on this inhuman planet, the most alien thing in his universe was the patient, silent woman before him.

From the flitter the Commissary called, 'Luru Parz. I wasn't expecting you to accompany us.'

'I'm not. Gramm has bent a little, but he won't allow *me* anywhere near the planet, let alone into the Archive. He won't even let me send a Virtual in there. Isn't that petty?' She winked at Pirius, with a kind of gruesome flirtatiousness. 'Still, I thought I should come see you off. What do you think of Mars, ensign?'

'Dusty.'

Luru barked laughter.

Nilis sighed. 'I suppose that sums it up. On Mars there is dust everywhere. It piles up in the craters; it covers these great Tharsis mountains. Even the air is full of it – scattering the light, whipping itself into murky storms . . .'

Luru Parz said, 'And Mars is *old*. The oldest landscapes on Earth would be among the youngest on Mars. But of course even the old can hide a few surprises.' She was still staring at Pirius.

Pirius dropped his gaze, his cheeks hot. But he wasn't much interested in comparative planetology; born in a tube and raised in a box, he had no preconceptions about how planets were supposed to work. 'So where's the big mountain?'

Nilis said, 'Ensign, you're standing on it. Olympus is a shield volcano, seven hundred kilometres across at its base, rising some twenty-five kilometres above the mean level. Its caldera juts out of the atmosphere! But the whole thing's *so* vast it dwarfs human perspectives.'

Luru was watching him again. 'Disappointed, ensign? Everything about Mars seems to disappoint. But before spaceflight, Mars was the only world whose surface was visible from Earth, save for the unchanging Moon. And it was the repository of a million dreams – wasn't it, Commissary? We even dreamed of making Mars like Earth. Of course it's technically possible. Can you see why it was never done?'

Pirius glanced around at the worn landscape, the dust-choked sky. 'Why bother? If you want to make an Earth there are better candidates.'

'Yes,' Nilis said sadly. 'By the time we had the capability to terra-form, we had already found other Earths. Nobody could be bothered with Mars. What an irony! And so Mars was bypassed. This is very ancient stuff, Pirius. But I sometimes wonder if something of those lost dreams still lingers in the thin air of Mars, an ineradicable whiff of disappointment that makes Martians as dull as they are today.'

'We aren't here to dream of the past,' Pirius said.

Luru Parz laughed. 'Well spoken, young soldier! All this talk of pre-Coalition fantasies is of course non-Doctrinal. Let's get on with it.' With a flourish she gestured at the Archive hatch.

The great door began to swing open. The thin air brought only the faintest of sighs to Pirius's ears. A semi-transparent tube snaked out of the hatchway and nuzzled against the hull of the flitter.

'Don't forget your face masks,' Luru Parz said. She snapped her fingers and disappeared into a cloud of scattering pixels.

The woman smiled at them, though the gaze of her pale grey eyes slid away from their faces. 'My name is Maruc. I am an Interface Specialist . . .'

Pirius and Nilis had climbed down a metal-runged ladder into a kind of antechamber, roughly cut from the rock. They faced this Maruc, their mouths and noses hidden by snug semi-sentient masks. It had been made clear that though the air in the Archive was breathable, such masks were to be worn at all times; nobody had explained why to Pirius, but he wasn't in the habit of asking such questions.

Nilis introduced the two of them in his typically boisterous and avuncular way. 'I can't begin to tell you how privileged I feel to be here – *here*, the greatest repository of knowledge in Sol system, why, I dare say, in the human Galaxy!' He clapped Pirius on the back. 'Doesn't it make you fall in love with the Coalition all over again?'

'Yes, sir,' Pirius said neutrally.

Maruc led them out of the anteroom and down some shallow steps into a chamber dug deeper yet into the rock. This vast library, dug into the cooling corpse of Olympus Mons, was evidently a place of low ceilings; Pirius had to duck.

Maruc struck him as odd. She had her head shaven, she wore a standard Commissary-style floor-length black robe, and she was short; both Nilis and Pirius towered over her. The robe he had expected. This Archive had once been an independent organisation, but it had long ago been swallowed up by one of Earth's great Academies, which had in turn been brought under the wing of the all-powerful Commission for Historical Truth. Nilis had set out this long bureaucratic saga for him, not seeming to realise that Pirius was even less interested in the organisational history of the Coalition's agencies than he was in the dusty landscape of Mars.

But Pirius was surprised at Maruc's height, given the general tallness he had noticed in the Martian population. And at first glance he would have said she looked young, only a few years older than himself, perhaps early twenties. But her face was pinched, marked with deep lines on her brow, and her grey eyes, though clear, were sunk in pits of dark-looking flesh. She was a strange mixture of youth and age.

He was staring. When she caught his gaze she hunched in on herself a little.

Pirius looked away, embarrassed. More secrets, he thought wearily.

They passed through a final door and walked into a corridor, a long one; its low arched profile, lit up by floating light globes, receded in both directions until a slow curve took its farther stretches out of sight.

Maruc led them along the passageway. It was punctuated by doors on either side, all identical, none of them labelled. The corridor was evidently very old; the floor was worn and the walls rubbed smooth. The only people he could see were *running*, back and forth along the corridor, off in the dusty distance. Pirius automatically began to count the doors; without that instinctive discipline he would soon have been lost.

One of the doors opened as they passed. A man came out, carrying a stack of data desks. Thin-faced, he was like Maruc in his slight build, but he looked young, with none of Maruc's odd premature ageing. He let them walk ahead and then trailed them a few paces behind, his gaze cast down on the worn floor. This seemed peculiar to Pirius. But Maruc didn't say anything, and Nilis was of course oblivious to everything but the contents of his own head.

One of those corridor runners passed the little party. They had to squeeze back against the wall to let her pass. She wore black, but her robe was cut short to expose bare legs. She ran intently, eyes staring ahead, arms pumping, her long, spidery legs working; her upper chest was high, though her breasts were small, and she seemed to be breathing evenly. She ran on past them without breaking stride, and disappeared down the corridor, following its bend out of sight.

'Remarkable,' Nilis said, watching her go. 'She looks as if she could run all day.'

'Perhaps she could,' Maruc said mildly. 'That is her specialism.'

'Really? Well, well.' Nilis was playing the visiting dignitary, trying to put Maruc at ease, though without much success, Pirius thought.

They walked on. And behind them the strange young man with the data desks still trailed, unremarked.

Maruc opened a door and led them into a room. 'A typical study area,' she said.

Brightly lit by light globes, the room contained desks and cubicles where people and bots, crammed in close together, worked side by side. Most of the scholars worked through flickering Virtual images, but some laboured over data desks. The people were small, neat, their heads shaven like Maruc's. Men and women alike were slim, and it was hard to distinguish between the sexes.

Some of those bare heads looked oddly large to Pirius, their skulls swollen and fragile. It was probably a trick of the light.

The visitors seemed to disturb these scholars. Some of them looked up nervously before cowering into their work, as if trying to hide. Others touched each other, clasping hands, rubbing foreheads or even kissing softly. Not a word was spoken. Pirius could feel the tension in the room until he and the others receded again.

They walked on.

Maruc spoke of how the Archive had been digging its way into Mons Olympus for millennia. In many ways it was an ideal site for a library. Mars was a still, stable world, geologically speaking, and even this, its greatest mountain, had been dead for a billion years. The bulk of Olympus was basaltic rock, and under a surface layer smashed and broken by ancient impacts – in Maruc's peculiar phrase, 'impact gardened' – the rock was porous and friable, quite easy to tunnel into. It grew warmer the deeper you dug, Maruc said, but that wasn't a problem; some of the deepest chambers even used Mars's remnant inner heat as an energy supply. The tremendous shield of rock above was of course a protection from any deliberate aggression, as well as from natural disasters up to a small asteroid strike.

Pirius built up a picture of a great warren burrowed through the vast mound of Olympus, people everywhere, running along corridors and labouring in chambers. After twenty thousand years the Archive must run far, he thought, tens of kilometres, even hundreds: under Sol system's greatest mountain there was always more room.

Maruc stopped at a doorway and opened it to reach another corridor, identical to the first. They walked down this until after a time they turned through another door into yet another passageway, and then they turned again. Pirius kept trying to build up a map in his head, based on the turns they made, the numbers of doors they passed. But all the corridors were identical, and looked the same in either direction, and he began to be unsure which way he was facing.

Besides, the air was thick, increasingly clammy and warm, and despite his face mask he thought he could smell an odd scent – a milkiness, oddly animal. Disconcerted, disoriented, he began to worry that he was getting lost.

But no matter where they went, the little man with the data desks followed them.

They came to another room, full of more scared-looking archivists. Maruc said that some of these had been assigned to assist Nilis.

Only about half the people living here under the mountain were devoted to the data itself. The rest had administrative functions, like Maruc herself, or they were concerned with support work that kept the facility going: there were specialist groups for digging fresh corridors ever deeper into Olympus, others to maintain the flow of air or water, and others to tend the big nano-food banks warmed by Olympus's residual heat.

Data from all across the Galaxy poured into the gigantic holdings here. But after twenty thousand years the new material was a drop in the ocean. These days the bulk of the work was classification – there were whole hierarchies of indices here, Maruc said – and maintenance. There was a constant danger of physical degradation – one function of the rock of Olympus was to shield electronically stored data from damage by cosmic rays – and data items were continually transcribed from one medium to another. With each transcription elaborate checks were made from multiple comparison copies to ensure no errors were introduced.

She said, 'You can see we would have plenty of work to keep us busy even if not a single new item of data ever came in. Because our main task is to fight entropy itself. The Archive is here for the long term.'

'Marvellous, marvellous,' Nilis said.

The community was the result of generations of specialism, she said: you were born to be a librarian, you grew up in cadres of librarians, your seed would go on to produce more librarians, for millennia after millennia. Maruc stood straight, and her eyes shone within their nests of wrinkles. 'We, the community of the Archive, have devoted generations past to this project, and we dedicate future generations too. We are proud of what we do. We believe our project is in the best traditions of the Druz Doctrines.'

'Oh, my eyes, no doubt about that,' said Nilis. He still looked thrilled to be here, Pirius thought, like a glutton let loose in a food store. 'But let me set you a test . . .' He outlined his requirements quickly.

Maruc raised a hand, and within seconds a runner was at her side. This one was a boy, surely younger than Pirius. His long, thin legs and short body made him look ungainly, as if he might topple over. But after sprinting up he wasn't even breathing heavily. Maruc told him what she wanted and he immediately ran off.

Within five minutes, a different runner came to them, accompanying a floating bot. The bot carried a small, battered-looking data desk, just a slab of some shiny black material held invisibly in place, perhaps by an inertial field.

Nilis stood over it, his mouth a round O. 'My eyes, my eyes,' he said.

Maruc smiled. 'I'm afraid we can't let you handle it. Any valid spoken command will be accepted, however.'

The floating data desk was so old that its interface protocols were quite alien. But soon Nilis was speaking to the desk, and his words were translated into a strange, distorted version of standard.

Finally a voice spoke from the desk, a stored recording, a clipped, rather stiff voice speaking the same peculiar dialect.

Nilis's eyes widened further. He said to Pirius, 'Do you know what this is? Do you know know *who* this is speaking?'

'No.'

'Hama Druz himself used this very desk on his return journey from the moon Callisto, where he had gone to hunt jasofts. He used this desk to compose his Doctrines, the very words which have governed our lives ever since. And that voice, cautiously reading out an uncompleted draft – that voice belongs to Hama Druz himself! Listen, listen . . .'

At last, Pirius heard that clipped and over-precise voice say words so familiar that even the antique dialect could not mask them: A brief life burns brightly.'

Nilis said, 'Madam, thank you. I can't tell you – all of mankind's true treasures are here, and you are worthy custodians.'

Maruc observed Nilis's ecstatic reaction with quiet pride.

His face set, Nilis straightened his battered robe. 'But enough indulgence. I have work to do. Madam, if you'll assist me – Pirius?'

'I'll be fine,' Pirius said. 'I'll explore a little more.'

Maruc said, 'I'll assign somebody to guide you.'

'Thank you. I'll wait.'

Eagerly Nilis turned away. Pirius watched Maruc lead him down the corridor.

The second they were out of sight Pirius turned, strode up to the little man who had shadowed them all day, grabbed him by the front of his tunic, and lifted him up until his head rammed against the low ceiling.

'Tell me who you are, and what you want.'

The little man was sweating, trembling, but he forced a grin. He gasped, 'Gladly. If you'll just, you'll just . . .'

Reluctantly Pirius released him. The man dropped to the worn floor of the corridor. He had dropped his data desks; he scrabbled to pick them up. But still he grinned, calculating.

Pirius snapped, 'Well?'

'My name is Tek,' he said. 'I'm a Retrieval Specialist.'

Pirius thought that over. 'A filing clerk.'

'If you want. But we're all specialists here. The lovely Maruc is an Interface Specialist – she interfaces between us and the rest of humanity. Then there are the runners with their long legs, the archivists and indexers with their bubble brains – don't tell me you didn't notice that! Wait until you see the mechanic types who crawl up the big air ducts.' Still clutching his desks, he let one arm trail on the floor and loped about comically.

Pirius had to suppress a laugh.

'All specialists, you see, all of us. But we fit together like the parts of a smoothly running machine.'

'I've never met anybody like you, Tek.'

'Nor I you. But then that's the point – isn't it, sir?'

'What is?' Pirius stepped forward and loomed over the little man until he stopped his capering and stood still.

'Do you think there is *divergence* here? From the human norm. This place is at the heart of the Coalition, *but is it Doctrinal?*'

'What are you saying?'

'Nothing, nothing. Not if you don't *see* it. But look at Maruc, for instance.'

'Maruc?'

'Poor thing. Growing old fast, don't you think? She's only a year older than me, just one year. But she looks a decade older. But you see, she *can't* last long. That's the trouble with being her kind of specialist, an interfacer. You have to know a lot – you have to know *too* much. And so you have to die, and take your poisonous knowledge with you.' His grin widened, nervously.

Pirius understood little of this. 'Maybe *you* know too much,' he said menacingly.

Tek laughed, but Pirius thought he had struck a nerve.

'What do you want, Tek? Why did you follow us?'

'I only want to help you. Whatever you want in here, maybe I can help you find it.' Tek actually winked. 'And in return you can help me.'

Pirius bunched his fists. 'I could kill you in a second.'

'I dare say you could, I dare say. But this is Sol system, sir, not the Front. And here you need different skills. *Subtler* skills.' Tek hugged his desks to his chest and backed away. 'Here comes your escort.'

Pirius glanced over his shoulder, to see another worker approaching.

Tek said, 'If you need me—'

'I won't.'

'– ask a runner. Just ask. And in the meantime be nice to Maruc, even though she's only a drone.'

A drone. That word made Pirius shiver. 'Why should I?'

'Because she's my sister,' Tek laughed again. 'But then, who isn't?' Suddenly he stepped close to Pirius and grabbed his arm. Pirius

171

flinched; Tek's skin was pale, pocked, and his breath was sour. 'Tread carefully, ensign.'

Pirius pulled his arm away.

Breaking into a run, Tek turned a corner and was gone.

Pirius instructed the runner to find him a private room. There he slept until Nilis called for him.

Nilis seemed unhappy. His air of enthusiasm was gone, and his energy had turned into an anxious anger that showed in the fretful set of his face, the way his big hands plucked at his frayed robe. Interface Specialist Maruc trailed behind him, looking uncertain.

'Commissary? What's wrong?'

Nilis was distracted, as if he barely saw Pirius. 'What a place. What a place!' He mopped sweat from his neck. 'You know, in their obsessive toiling, here in this huge subterranean mound of data, the Archivists never throw anything away. And their search engines are remarkably effective. There is so much here, ensign. So many secrets – so much treasure! And all of it buried under the coffin lid of Hama Druz . . .'

'We came here looking for weapons.'

'Weapons?' he said vaguely. 'Ah – yes, of course. Weapons. The Prime Radiant – you needn't look at me like that, ensign; I haven't forgotten our mission!'

'So did you find anything?'

'As a matter of fact I think I did. Ensign, in your base at the Core, did they teach you about "gravastars"?'

They hadn't, but this was what Nilis had turned up in his first hasty search for techniques to counter FTL foreknowledge. And as it turned out, Nilis started to explain, Pirius was going to have to make yet another journey into strangeness, here in Sol system, to track down what Nilis thought he had discovered.

But Nilis stopped and stared at Pirius's arm. 'Ensign, what's that on your sleeve?'

Pirius glanced down. A lozenge shape, glittering brightly, rested on his uniform sleeve; it was no larger than his thumbnail. And it was just where Tek had touched him. Without thinking he clapped his hand over the chip. 'Nothing, sir. Uh, an insect.'

Nilis raised bushy eyebrows. 'An insect? In here? It's possible, I suppose – who's to say? I think our business is done for today.

Tomorrow we will return and start digging properly into this business of the gravastars . . .'

As they were led out of the Archive and back to the golden-brown surface of Mars, Pirius glanced again at the chip. He wasn't disturbed by it so much as by his own reaction. Why had he concealed it from Nilis?

He felt deeply troubled. Perhaps he wasn't such a good soldier after all.

CHAPTER 20

They fell down to Factory Rock.

A dropship was small and basic, just a transparent cylinder big enough for two platoons, twenty infantry, crammed in shoulder to shoulder with their bulky rad-shielded skinsuits and equipment. When Pirius Blue looked out through the ship's curving hull he could see the fleshy bulk of the Spline warship that had brought them here from Quin. His own ship was one of thousands committed to this action. From a dozen orifices in the Spline's hull the dropships poured out in gleaming streams. And when he looked down he could see how the little ships were falling all across the broad face of the target Rock.

The surface of the Rock was covered by a zig-zag lattice of trenches. He was already low enough to see people, tiny figures like toys scurrying clumsily along the trenches or hurling themselves over stretches of open ground. But everywhere points of light sparkled, pink and electric blue, bright on a grey background, and some of those running figures fell, or exploded in soft bursts of crimson. As far as he could see the whole surface of this asteroid was covered by the crawling figures and the sparkling lights. The fire was reaching up to the sky too: a thread of cherry-red light would connect the ground to one of the falling dropships, and it would burst, spilling bodies into space.

And all this in utter silence, broken only by the hiss of air through his suit's systems.

He had known in abstract what to expect. He had seen such Rocks before, from the comfortable cockpit of his high-flying greenship. But he had not imagined this. The scene was even beautiful, he thought.

But there was no more time. The ground flew up at him.

174

*

They had been briefed by Captain Marta.

This was an unusual action, she said, because it was taking place outside the Front.

This Rock – known as Factory Rock – wasn't an assault platform but a human base, a munitions dump and the site of several monopole factories. Monopoles were defects in spacetime, each a nasty little knot with the mass of a trillion protons. They had been manufactured in the early universe during its period of GUT-driven inflation, and now GUT energy was used to churn them out, to a uniform mass and charge, in the vast numbers required by the human war effort. They were useful weapons; they would cut through Xeelee construction material, or even the spacetime-flaw wings of their ships, like steel through flesh.

Factory Rock was an old establishment. It lay in the hinterland beyond the Galaxy centre, a little closer in to the Front than most. In a thousand years of operation, it had had no significant problems save for quagmites, the odd little virus-like critters that were attracted to all GUT engines in factories and ships.

But now the Xeelee had seen a chance to break out of their usual cordon. They had taken this Rock, and had set up well-fortified positions across it. It was a terror tactic. As this Rock went sailing on its own slow orbit behind the human lines, like a rat loose in a barracks, it was causing disruption far out of proportion to its size and direct threat.

So Pirius and his buddies were being dropped to clear the Xeelee emplacements, and if possible to take back the monopole factories.

Captain Marta hadn't tried to hide the fact that these front-line troopers were raw. Some of them had had only days training on their weapons, their laser rifles and starbreaker pistols. But as this target was well behind the main front line, more hardened troops couldn't be spared.

'Remember, all that matters is that one of you gets through to the objective. And you will make that happen. I know you will do your duty.' She smiled, her metallised half-face gleaming. 'The Coalition has invested a lot in each of you, in giving you life, and in your training. Now's the time to make it worthwhile.'

'Yes, *sir*!'

*

The dropship didn't so much land as crash. It just plummeted at the ground, burying its nose in a metre of asteroid dirt.

The hull immediately popped, and the inertial shielding turned off. Following his training, Pirius threw himself out of the ship and into the nearest trench.

The trench was shallow, barely enough to cover him. In fact it was a piece of shit, he thought, surveying it with a now-professional eye; he could dig better in half an hour. But lines of cherry-red light already stitched the air above him, and he pressed himself into the dirt.

The members of his platoon, 57 Platoon, all made it to this crudely dug trench. He saw the corporal, a very young man called Pace, and his sergeant, and Cohl, and the two surviving Tilis in their gaudily customised skinsuits. The Tilis seemed to be functioning, even though it was only three weeks since the death of Two, and Three was still getting used to her prosthetic hand. Many of the troopers were wrestling with their clumsy weapons. But Pirius and Cohl, as Service Corps, were laden with trenching tools, flares, comms posts, med supplies and other non-lethal essentials.

As the enemy fire intensified above them they were all pushing themselves into the broken dirt, their gleaming new weapons already scuffed and coated with dust. He wondered if Burden had made it down safely. His platoon had been scheduled to land some distance away.

Corporal Pace whirled a finger, ordering them to switch their comms to the platoon's dedicated loop. 'Listen up,' he said heavily. 'We're down safe. The line's intact and we're in a strong section of it. We have Guards to the left; and more to the right, further down the line.' That was good. Guards were pains in the ass on the base, but in action Guard units were reassuring to have close, protecting your flank. 'We're about two kilometres from our target factory, which is *that* way.' He pointed. 'In thirty seconds the artillery barrage will start, and in five minutes we'll move. Everybody clear? Good.'

And then, to Pirius's amazement, he snapped his fingers and a Virtual appeared in the air above him, floating over the trench like a multicoloured spectre.

It was a pep talk. A smiling woman's face mouthed words, no doubt uplifting Doctrinal propaganda, that Pirius couldn't hear. They were shown images of field guns, mostly monopole cannons. These were in batteries a couple of kilometres behind Pirius's position, and he knew there were emplacements of more massive siege guns, 'heavies', further back still. The slanting tubes were oddly graceful, Pirius thought, oddly fragile-looking for such powerful weapons. They were lodged on the ground, sacrificing flexibility of deployment for the relative shelter of the asteroid's bulk.

But the first guns were already firing. The heat generated was obvious; the cannon's breeches were red hot, their inertial-control recoil mounts battered and smoking. In the heat the gunners had stripped to the waist, though they wore skinsuit helmets. Sweating, their skinny torsos gleaming red in the glare of their red-hot cannon, they swarmed around the guns like rats. Pirius wondered if Enduring Hope was working in some such inferno.

But if the Virtual was meant to boost the infantry's morale it wasn't working. They were supposed to march safely behind the guns' fire, a tactic in which everything depended on precision and coordination between artillery and infantry. But even in this sanitised image Pirius saw things go wrong, like a recoil mount snapping under the strain.

And the Virtual itself was suddenly stitched through by cherry-red beams. Pace, digging his face into the dirt, shut down the Virtual; it dissipated in a cloud of pixels.

Cohl lifted her head. She was heavily shadowed, but Pirius could see her snarl of contempt. 'At least now we know where the Xeelee emplacements are. The trouble is they know where *we* are.'

And then the artillery barrage started for real.

Pirius felt it before he saw it. The ground's shuddering penetrated the inertial damping of his suit, reaching deep into his belly.

The first shells, piercing electric blue pinpoints, sailed overhead. Each shed energy as it flew, creating a sparkling contrail of exotic particles. He imagined the rows of guns, the lighter cannon and the tremendous 'heavies' behind them, blasting their munitions into the sky, thousands of them along lines that stretched kilometres.

The first shells sailed out of sight, landing somewhere beyond his horizon. He could feel their shuddering impact. Answering fire came from the Xeelee emplacements, he saw. A line of pink-purple beams snaked up as starbreakers sought to shoot down the shells before they had a chance to fall. But more shells followed. Soon there were so many of them that the contrails merged to become a solid glare, and the sky was covered by a curtain of shifting blue. It was a battle of lights in the sky, human blue washing down against defiant Xeelee red.

The violence was immense. It seemed surprising the whole asteroid didn't simply break apart under the strain. He felt fragile, a mote; he knew that one misstep of the mighty beasts treading the ground around him would result in a death so sudden he wouldn't have time to know about it.

Burden was wrong, he thought suddenly. No matter what happened in the future, no matter who or what waited at timelike infinity, nothing could ever erase the blunt reality of this moment. This was *real*, this tortured ground, this outpouring energy. This was life and death – this was the war.

And still that relentless pounding went on, Pirius pressed his face into the dirt, but he couldn't get away from it. It went right through him, working deep into his bones, right into his nerves, until it felt as if he had never known anything else.

Then a piercing whistle filled his ears. It was Pace's command; they were to leave the trench.

Pirius didn't let himself think about it. He blipped his inertial belt. Hauling his pack, a bulky med kit and a comms post, he scrabbled at the dirt with one gloved hand and pulled himself over the lip of the trench.

He floated like a balloon, up into a field of horizontal light beams. All around him other troopers rose; they were all swimming in light.

But the starbreakers cut into them, coming from his left. Bodies burst open and blood spurted into space, instantly freezing. Pirius was falling through a vacuum threaded with fire, an utterly inhuman and lethal environment. It was like a dream, of light and carnage. It seemed impossible for him to survive.

He slammed once more into the asteroid dirt, dragged down by his inertial belt, set to two gravities. Now he was in a shallow bowl, perhaps a crater; it might even have been natural, an ancient impact feature. He was astonished he was still alive.

A body fell heavily on top of him. It was Cohl. Even through the thick layers of her rad-hardened suit he could see how she was breathing hard.

He snapped, 'How many fell?'

'I don't know. Four, five?'

Five dead already, in the first instant.

'It could have been us,' she gasped, wondering. 'It could have been *me*. It was just chance.'

Pirius said, 'Did you see anyone shoot back?'

'No. No, not one.'

They had been trained to expect losses. But the barrage should have cleared the ground before them. It wasn't supposed to be like this.

He thought about the pattern of fire he'd glimpsed. 'The fire came from the left. It came from an emplacement *behind* where the barrage is landing. Something's wrong. The barrage should have cleaned that emplacement out.'

Cohl didn't seem to be listening. She lifted her pack curiously. A hole had been punched clean through it.

'They got the Guards.' That call sounded like one of the Tilis.

'Which unit?' And that was the corporal, Pace; evidently he was still alive.

'To our left. I can see them from here. Every one of them wiped out.'

And now other voices joined in, from Pace's platoon, and another close by. 'To our right, too.' 'We're on our own here.'

It didn't seem possible to Pirius that Guards – arrogant, elite Guards, with their perfect, unmarred uniforms, their trenches as straight and well-defined as geometric exercises, their unshakeable confidence – that *Guards* had fallen so easily.

Pirius tried to think. The barrage hadn't worked, then. Perhaps the timing had gone wrong. Perhaps monopole shells were falling out of place, falling harmlessly far beyond the Xeelee emplacements, maybe even coming down on human troops. The hole in the barrage had allowed at least some Xeelee units to survive, and in those moments when the infantry had burst into the open the enemy had picked targets at will. Now the line was shattered; the survivors were exposed, with no cover to left or right. Everybody knew that an uneven advance was worse than no advance at all, because your flank was exposed.

Pace spoke over the platoon loop. The corporal sounded ragged. 'We have to go on,' he said.

Pirius knew the theory. The 'creeping barrage' ahead of them was a sweeping curtain, continually progressing at about walking pace. The infantry were to follow, coming in right behind it to mop up whatever was left before the Xeelee weaponry had a chance to recover. So they had to move on, or the protection of the barrage would soon leave them behind. But everything was wrong.

'Corporal,' Pirius said. 'We'd be advancing into fire. It would be suicide.'

'Do your duty, Service Corps. On my mark in three.'

Pirius and Cohl exchanged a glance. They had no choice.

Again that ear-splitting whistle sounded.

Pirius roared, 'Shit, shit!' He blipped his inertial field and pulled himself out of the dip.

Again he flew, his armoured chest a few centimetres above the ground, his bulky pack an awkward mass behind him. Around him he glimpsed ten, maybe fifteen others, floating like ghosts above the churned-up dirt. Some of them aimed and fired their weapons as they swam.

But cherry-red light flared immediately, threading more bodies which burst and writhed before they subsided in dream-like micro-gravity slowness back to the ground. One of them was Pace, he saw; the corporal, recognisable by his bright command armband, took a hit even before he got out of the trench.

Pirius hit the dirt again. He was breathing hard, his pack bumping at his back, his faceplate pressed to the dirt. Starbreaker light continued to flare over his head, and detonations in the ground sent dirt flying up all around him. He could feel no pain, and was amazed he still hadn't been hit.

He risked looking up. The barrage still crept forward, smashing its way across the asteroid away from him. Silhouetted before its unearthly light he saw figures moving, troopers trying to work their way from one bit of cover to the next, maybe even trying to advance. But there was no semblance of coordination, and few of them were even firing their weapons. Xeelee starbreakers picked them off with impunity.

He was exposed here; he was on a shallow ridge that actually raised him up above the mean surface. He would last only seconds in this spot.

He saw a line in the ground, a faint shadow a couple of metres ahead. If that was a trench he might live a little longer. If not . . . if not, he had no choice anyhow.

Again he didn't allow himself time to think. *Three, two, one.* He blipped his inertial field, and with a single thrust he threw his body through a shallow arc at the shadow in the dirt. He slammed down at three gravities, hard enough to knock the wind out of his lungs. It was a trench: worn, its lip broken by the scrabbling of gloved hands, but a trench nonetheless. Starbreaker light flared over him, frustrated, a cherry-red lid over this bit of shelter.

But there was something in the bottom of the trench, hard, complicated shapes that shattered and broke under him.

Bodies. The trench was lined with bodies. Pirius could see contorted faces, chests and bellies cut open to reveal internal organs, solid like anatomical models. Their skinsuits sliced open, these fallen troops had frozen where they lay. As Pirius had struggled he had shattered some of the frozen corpses. But there was no horror for him; the cold and the vacuum had sucked out the last of the humanity from these relics.

The trench had been well constructed and was evidently deep. He could see some metres to left and right; the trench zig-zagged so it couldn't be cleaned out by a single sweep of raking fire. And as far as he could see it was filled with those frozen, cut-open corpses, a tangle of rigid limbs and guts and skulls, like a ditch full of smashed statues.

Cohl came sailing in and landed as he had, hard on her belly. Bits of smashed bodies flew high; where they sailed above the lip of the trench starbreaker beams picked them out, vaporising them, as if playing. Cohl thrashed in shock.

Pirius held Cohl's shoulders. 'Take it easy.'

She subsided, breathing hard, eyes wild. She fixed her gaze on his face. 'This is a nightmare.'

'I know.' He glanced around. 'They must be lying six, seven deep. We aren't the first to come this way.'

'We're going to die here, as they did.'

'We're not dead yet.' Pirius took a comms post from his back and thrust it into the trench wall. 'This is Pirius. 57 Platoon. We made it to a trench. There are two of us here. If you can hear this, triangulate on my signal and assemble here.' He let the message repeat, and ducked his head back down into the deeper safety of the trench.

It took only seconds for the first trooper to come plummeting into the trench, heralded by a burst of starbreaker fire. It was a girl, dark and serious, her face contorted with fear; Pirius didn't know her name. She had lost her weapons. And when she saw what she had landed in she thrashed in panic as Cohl had.

In the following thirty seconds four more followed. The two Tili sisters were among them, to Pirius's relief.

And then no more.

Seven of them in the trench, out of twenty in the two platoons who had been dropped here. He looked around at their faces, the faces of these terrified children lost in this terrible place – all of them looking at him.

He felt a weight pressing on his shoulders, as if his inertial field was malfunctioning. Was this what a galactic war had reduced to – him and Cohl in a scratch in the ground with five frightened kids?

He set his comms loop to open, linking him to the whole of the force in this area. Maybe somebody else would hear him, could converge on this place. There was only silence. After a few seconds, it occurred to him to cut out the morale filters.

Immediately he was aware of a roar, like a noisy barracks. The voices merged into a mass, a mob cry, but every so often one of them would bubble to the foreground, and he would hear screaming, muttering, gasping, weeping, calls for help, delirious shouts, even a kind of deranged laughter. It was the sound of the wounded, the sound of thousands of voices calling out together from all over the Rock. They made an unearthly, inhuman sound.

He knew that some of the troopers were listening too. Their faces were round with shock. But even as they listened, in those first few minutes, the cries dwindled and faded away, one by one. If you were wounded in vacuum, with your skinsuit broken, you didn't last long.

And still the bombardment continued, the blinding light overhead matched by the relentless shuddering of the ground. But the shells' immense footfalls marched away into the distance, leaving them far behind.

He risked glimpses out of the trench.

From here, according to his visor displays, they were only about half a kilometre from the target monopole factory. As far as he could see only a single Xeelee emplacement stood between him and the factory; the shells had evidently taken out the rest. The emplacement looked like a small shack of a silver-grey material. It was probably Xeelee construction material, among the toughest substances known: self-renewing, self-repairing, said to be a living entity in itself. Surrounding the central shack were small pillars, each bearing rings that glowed blue.

He let himself slide back into the trench. The others watched him, six pairs of eyes large in the shadows of their visors.

He said, 'We have to try to get to the factory.'

'No,' said one trooper.

'What's your name?'

'Bilin.' He was bulky, but just a boy, despite the massive surface-to-surface weapon he carried on his back. He was scared, and right now Pirius was the focus of his resentment. 'I say we wait for the pick-up.'

There was a murmur of agreement.

'We can't stay here,' Pirius said bluntly.

'We can traverse in the trench—'

'There's no point. We couldn't get any closer to the factory that way. Remember the standing orders. The only pick-up will be at the factory itself. We can't go back. And we can't stay here, in this trench. We've nowhere else to go but forward.' Bilin glared at him, but Pirius stared steadily back. 'Can't you see that? We're not the first here. Look around you. Do you want to die like this?'

The boy dropped his gaze.

Pirius rooted in the grisly bank of frozen body parts beneath him. It didn't take him long to retrieve a laser rifle. He threw it aside. He kept searching until he found a starbreaker gun; this gravity-wave hand-gun, essentially a design stolen from the Xeelee, was far more potent. 'Search the dead,' he snapped. 'If you don't have a weapon, find one. Take anything else you need: water, med-cloaks.'

Cohl went at it with a will. The privates – cadets until yesterday, Pirius reminded himself – were more reluctant; they had been trained to accept death, but nothing in their upbringing had prepared them for this gruesome grave-robbing.

Pirius checked over the starbreaker weapon. It was massive in his hands, reassuring. He'd been given only minimal training in it, but its operation, designed for simplicity and robustness on the battlefield, was obvious. He fired a test shot; pink light snaked out. There was no recoil. The gun anchored itself in spacetime while sending out lased gravity waves that would rip apart anything material.

After a few minutes they were all equipped.

'All right,' said Pirius. 'If you want to live, do as I say.'

He'd expected Bilin to challenge him, and he wasn't disappointed. 'Who appointed you, Service Corps?'

Pirius stared him down. Again Bilin blinked first.

Pirius sketched in the dirt on the side of the trench, showing the Xeelee emplacement and behind it the factory that was their target. 'We have to take out the emplacement. We'll break into two sticks. I'll lead one. Cohl, you take the other. We'll go right, you go left . . .' They would take it in turns, the two parties leapfrogging, alternately covering each other. This routine fieldwork was very familiar to the troopers; they knew how to do it. They started to relax.

He glanced around at their faces, glowing like red moons by the light of the continuing bombardment overhead. Now that somebody was giving them orders again they almost looked confident, he thought. But Pirius couldn't unwind the coiled spring inside himself, not a bit.

He split the seven of them into their two groups. In her group of four Cohl would take the twins, who he wasn't about to separate. Pirius took the troublemaker Bilin with himself, along with the slim, intense-looking girl, the first to have tumbled into the trench, who as far as he remembered hadn't said a word. The two teams moved subtly apart.

Pirius readied his starbreaker. 'We've nothing to gain by waiting. We'll go first. Give us five seconds' cover, then follow.'

'See you on the shuttle,' Cohl said.

The troopers shifted their positions, ready to move again. One boy moved stiffly, staring down at the layer of bodies, obviously reluctant.

Pirius barked, 'What's wrong with you?'

'I don't like treading on their faces.'

Pirius forced himself to yell, 'Never mind their faces! Just do it!'

The kid responded with jerky haste.

Pirius held his hand up. 'On my mark. Five, four—'

Cohl's troop put their heads over the lip of the trench and began firing.

'Three, two.' Pirius snapped off his inertial belt and allowed himself one deep breath. 'One.'

He launched his body out of the trench and into the fire-laced vacuum once more.

The quiet girl fell before she had even got out of the trench, her visor melted open, her face reduced to char. He had never even known her name. But there was no time to reflect, no time to look back, nothing to do but go on.

*

184

Fly, float, scrabble across a hundred metres, less. Fire your weapon if you can, anything to engage the Xeelee guns, and try to ignore the stitching of fire all around you, the way the ground beneath you is constantly raked up by miniature explosions. When you find shelter – a pock-hole in the dirt, a chance heaping – let the inertial belt pull you down as hard as it can. No time to rest. Head above the lip of your cover, start firing again immediately to cover Cohl's crew.

This close to the factory, the ground was littered with bodies, tangled up and frozen, a carpet so deep you sometimes couldn't see the ground at all. Frozen solid, there was no way of knowing how long they might have been there. There was no decomposition here, no smell; it wasn't even a human enough place for that. Pirius wondered how many had died here, how long this desperate battle for a desolate piece of rock had gone on.

Three, four hops, and he was still alive. Their laser beams were invisible save where they passed through kicked-up dust; the star-breakers glowed with their own light.

At last he found himself in a foxhole fifty metres from the emplace-ment. The Xeelee structure was a squat, plain box, unbroken by win-dows. Starbreakers spat from vicious-looking mounts on the roof. Those pale blue rings on their pillars gleamed, set around the structure.

Bilin tumbled after him into the trench, laden by the heavy surface-to-surface weapon.

'Those hoops,' Pirius said. 'We'll take them out.'

'Why?'

'Enemy comms.' It was probably true. The cerulean hoops were another bit of Xeelee technology. They appeared to use spooky quantum-inseparability effects to allow instantaneous communica-tion. No human scientist knew how they worked; you weren't sup-posed to be able to use quantum entanglement to pass meaningful data.

Bilin, now he was in action, had shed his petulance and had un-covered a kind of steely doggedness. He could make a good soldier some day, Pirius thought. He nodded and said, 'Three, two one.'

They lunged over the rim of their foxhole and blasted away at the sky-blue hoops. The emplacement's own starbreaker mounts spat back ferociously, but fire was corning in at the structure from both sides now; the survivors of Cohl's team were mounting a simultane-ous assault.

When the last hoop had exploded, the enemy starbreakers continued to fire, but wildly.

Pirius nudged Bilin. 'Take it out.'

With practised ease Bilin pulled his surface-to-surface over his shoulder, rested it on the asteroid ground, sighted it. When the weapon fired there was no recoil. A bright blue monopole shell shot across the ground, less than a metre above the dirt, tracking a dead straight line.

The shell hit the emplacement. That construction-material wall buckled and broke, like skin bursting. Inside the structure Pirius glimpsed hulking machinery. All the troopers poured their fire through the breach in the wall, until the machines slumped and failed. Still the starbreaker mounts on the roof continued to fire, but they spat erratically, their aim ever more wild.

Bilin stood up and whooped. 'Nice work, Service Corps!'

Pirius snapped, 'Get down, you idiot!'

Bilin grinned, and the out-of-control Xeelee starbreaker severed his head, clean at the neck.

The bombardment curtain was now far away, and Pirius could see no starbreaker light. But still the ground shook, still that deep shuddering worked into his nerves. It took a lot of courage to cross the last bit of open ground to the Xeelee emplacement.

Cohl and her people were already here. They had taken shelter beneath a wall that seemed to have melted and curled over on itself. On the far side of the wall, away from the huddling humans, the ruined alien machines slumped, as if sleeping.

Of Pirius's team, only he had survived, but three of Cohl's team lived, Cohl herself and the two Tilis. So four of the seven who had come to the trench of corpses were left; in the last couple of minutes another three had died.

Cohl had taken a shot to her leg. Her suit had turned rigid and glowed orange as its rudimentary medical facilities tried to stabilise her. There was nothing Pirius could do for her.

Tili One was worse. She had some kind of chest wound. Tili Three cradled her sister's head on her lap, her mouth round with shock. Pirius saw that to be left alone, to lose *both* her sisters, was literally unimaginable for this triplet.

Pirius took his last comms post from his back, stuck it in the ground and set up a repeater signal. He said to Cohl, 'If anybody's left, they'll come here. Make the others wait in the shelter.' Then he stood up, hefting a starbreaker, and peered out of the ruins of the emplacement.

Cohl asked, 'Where are you going?'

'To the factory. It's only two, three hundred metres from here. It's the pick-up point, remember. I'll leave a marker to lead the stretcher crews here.'

Cohl clearly didn't want him to go, but just as clearly she saw the necessity. 'Be careful.'

He crawled out of the ruins of the emplacement, out into the open. He moved cautiously, as he had been taught. He ducked from ridge to crater to trench to foxhole, no more than ten, twenty metres at a time. It was slow going, and exhausting. The condition of his skinsuit got worse quickly; perhaps it was damaged. The air grew increasingly foul, his faceplate so enclosing he felt as if he was choking, and his mouth and throat grew so dry they were painful.

It took him half an hour to cross two hundred metres.

Maybe such caution wasn't necessary; he hadn't seen the glow of a starbreaker since the emplacement mount had finally been shut down. But after what had happened to Bilin he wasn't about to take a chance now.

When he reached the site of the factory, he only knew he was at the right location because his visor displays told him so. There was no factory left: no landing pad, no power plant, no surface tracks, no machinery. Save for a bit of smashed wall jutting at an angle from the dirt, and a line of white dust that might have marked a foundation, there was nothing here but more broken ground. He saw no sign that anybody else had been here recently, none of the thousands he supposed had been dropped with this target as their objective. Perhaps the Xeelee had destroyed it, or perhaps humans had, or perhaps it had been levelled by the barrage. The artillery was meant to spare the factories, which were the objective of the operation; but then the barrage was meant to do many things it had failed to do.

Pirius built a small cairn of bits of rubble, and set a marker on it, with an indication of where the others were sheltering. He felt quite cold, without emotion; perhaps that would come later.

He looked ahead, to the asteroid's horizon. The bombardment still continued, but far away now. The ground was full of bodies, the relics of previous assaults, and where the shells landed the bodies were hurled up by the explosions. The bodies rose up and tumbled in the dust before falling slowly down to the ground again. It was very strange to huddle there with his dry mouth and his stinking skinsuit, watching those bodies going up and down.

He shook himself alert. He made his slow, cautious way back to the ruined emplacement, where Cohl and the others were waiting.

When he got there Tili Three was weeping, utterly inconsolable. Her sister had died in her arms.

CHAPTER 21

The corvette completed its final FTL hop. Suddenly Pluto and Charon hovered before Pirius Red, twin planets that had ballooned out of nothing.

Nilis flinched and threw his hands up. 'My eyes! They might have warned us.'

Pirius had spent his life training for combat in space. He showed no reaction before the soft old Commissary; he was much too proud for that. But he felt it too. After all they were both products of a billion years of common evolution at the bottom of a gravity well, and when whole worlds appeared out of nowhere something deep and ancient inside him quailed.

The twin worlds' forms were visibly distorted from the spherical, for they were *close* to each other. Their separation was only fourteen Pluto diameters; Earth's Moon was by comparison thirty of its parent's diameters away from Earth. It was an authentic double planet. This strange little system was dimly lit by a remote pinpoint sun, and the faintness of the light gave the two worlds a sense of dreaminess, of unreality. But the worlds were strikingly different in hue, with Pluto a blood red, Charon ice blue.

Nilis commented absently on the colours. 'That's to do with a difference in surface composition. Much more water ice on Charon's surface . . . It's a remarkable sight, isn't it, ensign?'

'Yes, sir.' So it was.

They had come here in search of the 'gravastar' technology, hints of which Nilis had dug out of the Archive on Mars. Pirius peered at the double world, wondering what he was going to have to confront here before they got what they wanted.

A Virtual swirled before them, coalescing from a cloud of blocky pixels. It was a short, plump man dressed in the drab costume of a Commissary. His belly was large, his legs short, his shaven head round and smooth. The Virtual image was projected clumsily, and the little man seemed to be floating a few centimetres above the floor.

When he saw Nilis and Pirius, this figure barked a nervous laugh, and small hands fluttered before him. 'Welcome, welcome! Welcome to Pluto-Charon, and our facility. My name is Draq. You must be Commissary Nilis – and are you the ensign from the Front? I've watched all your Virtuals.'

Pirius had seen some of these. They were cartoonish renderings of Pirius Blue's manoeuvres around the magnetar, produced for popular consumption by the Ministry of Public Enlightenment. Pirius didn't recognise much of himself in the lantern-jawed, shaven-headed, Doctrine-spouting caricature that shared his name. 'Don't believe everything you see, sir,' he said. 'And besides, the whole episode has been edited out of the timeline. It won't happen.'

'Oh, but that hardly matters, does it? In the Library of Futures that sort of editing goes on all the time. But I've always thought that *potential* heroism is as admirable as actualized.'

Nilis broke in. 'Draq, you say? You're in charge here?'

Draq blustered. 'Yes and no! There are very few of us curators, you see, Commissary Nilis, and we have been here rather a long time. Things are, well, informal.' His hands fluttered again, and the Virtual drifted until it collided silently with the hull, and pixels flared across his round back. 'You'll have to forgive my excitement. We don't get many visitors.'

'I'm not surprised,' Nilis said dryly, 'since your facility doesn't officially exist.'

Draq pulled a mock-solemn face. 'It is odd, I admit, to be a legal paradox! But the work is fascinating enough to compensate, believe me.'

Pirius felt a tightening of his gut, a subtle shifting of the universe around him as the corvette's drive cut in. Pluto-Charon slid silently across his field of view.

Draq said, 'I have requested your crew to bring you down at our spaceport at Christy. Oh, we're so excited!' He blurred, and crumbled out of existence.

Pirius said, 'Commissary, what kind of place *is* this?'

'Wait and see, ensign. Wait and see.'

The final moments of the descent were unremarkable. Pirius glimpsed a flat, complex landscape, grey-crimson in the light of a swollen moon, but as Christy itself approached the flitter flew over ravines and ridges. Here it looked as if the land had been smashed up with an immense hammer.

'Christy', a very archaic name, turned out to refer to what the corvette's pilots called the 'sub-Charon point' on Pluto. This bit of ground was unique in Sol system. Like Earth's Moon, Charon was tidally locked to its parent and kept the same face to Pluto as it orbited. But, unlike Earth, Pluto was also locked to its twin. Every six days these worlds turned about each other, facing each other constantly. Within Sol's domain, Pluto-Charon was the only significant system in which both partners were tidally locked; they danced like lovers.

And so this place, Christy, was forever suspended directly beneath the looming bulk of the giant moon, and the feeble geological energies of these small worlds had been focused here.

The 'port' was a cluster of translucent domes. There wasn't even a finished pad, just pits in the ice left by the bellies of passing ships. As the corvette settled to the ground, ice crunched softly. Without delay an interface tunnel snaked out of one of the domes and nuzzled against the corvette's hull.

They arrived in a dome that was all but transparent. Charon, suspended directly overhead, was visible through the dome's scuffed surface.

Draq was here in person. As agitated as before, he bustled up, grinning, as Nilis and Pirius approached. Eight more people stood behind him. Some, smoother-faced, might have been female, but they all looked alike to Pirius, round-faced and pot-bellied.

Draq's robes were clearly old, heavily repaired, and he smelled *stale*. 'Welcome, welcome again. We're delighted you have visited us and we're ready to assist you any way we can . . .' As the little man chattered on Pirius wondered how true that was; Draq must be concerned his covert facility had even been *noticed*. His colleagues gathered around the Commissary like infants around a cadre leader. They reminded Pirius of the tiny isolated community on Port Sol:

these characters weren't so far from the sun, but they seemed even odder.

But they weren't paying any attention to Pirius. He walked towards the dome's clear wall, and gazed out at Pluto.

There were clouds above him, wispy cirrus, occluding bone-white stars: they were aerosol clusters, according to Nilis's briefing material, suspended in the atmosphere of nitrogen and methane. The landscape was surprisingly complex, a starlit sculpture of feathery ridges and fine ravines – although perhaps it wouldn't be so interesting away from Christy. Sol was a point of light, low on the horizon, wreathed in the complex strata of a cloud. The inner system was a puddle of light around Sol, an oblique disc small enough for Pirius to cover with his palm. It was strange to think that that unprepossessing blur had contained all of man's history before the first pioneers had risked their lives by venturing out to the rim of Sol system, and beyond.

Charon hung directly over Pirius's head. It was a misty blue disc, six times the size of Luna as seen from Earth. He had been trained for spectacles like this, but he flinched from the sight of a world hanging over him like a light globe. Charon's surface looked pocked. No doubt there was plenty of impact cratering, even here in this misty, spacious place, but many of the gouges he could make out, even with his naked eyes, were deep and quite regular.

'They are quarries.'

He turned. One of Draq's gaggle of followers had come to stand beside him. She was evidently a woman; her face, turned up to the light of Charon, had a certain delicacy about the brow, the cheekbones.

'Quarries?'

'My name is Mara. I work with Draq.' She smiled at him, then looked away. Though she seemed rather awestruck, she evidently didn't share Draq's giggling foolishness. 'Michael Poole himself came here, thousands of years ago. Our most famous visitor – before you, of course! He travelled from Jupiter on a GUTdrive ship, and he and his engineers used Charon ice to make exotic matter—'

'To build a wormhole mouth.'

'Yes. Here Poole completed his cross-system wormhole transit network. When it was done, why, you could travel from Pluto all the way to Mercury almost as easily as you walked through that tunnel from your ship . . . There.' She pointed up towards Charon's limb. Pirius made out a spark of light, no brighter than the remote stars, but it drifted as he watched. 'That's Poole's interface station – or the ruins of it.' The Qax had of course shut down Poole's venerable spacetime engineering, and over the millennia since, most of his interface stations had been broken up, their raw material reused. Not here, though; nobody had bothered to do even that much.

Mara defended her adopted world. 'It's true nobody lives here – nobody but us, that is. The Coalition has tried to establish settlements, but they always fail. There has never been enough to keep people here, no resource you couldn't find on a thousand Kuiper moons, and in more shallow gravity wells at that. But we do have our marvels.'

Pluto's orbit was so elliptical it sailed within the orbit of Neptune. At the closest approach to Sol, the atmosphere expanded to three planetary diameters. Then, when Pluto turned away from Sol and sailed into its two-hundred-year winter, the air snowed down.

Mara described all this lyrically. She seemed eager to have someone new to talk to. Those exiled here called themselves Plutinos, she said. Pirius was drawn by her sense of this remote world, which swam through immense, empty volumes, while slow subtle seasons of ice came and went.

'Ah,' she said now. 'Look up.'

Puzzled, he glanced up at the looming, misty shape of Charon. 'I don't see anything.'

She waved a hand, and the light intensity in their corner of the dome reduced.

As his eyes dark-adapted, more stars came out, peering around Charon's limb, and he made out more detail on the moon's mottled surface. He leaned close to Mara's shoulder to see, and his cheek brushed the coarse cloth of her robe. There was a mustiness about her, but he was not repelled, as he had been by Draq; she was strange, he thought, even eccentric, but oddly likeable. He wondered what her story was, how she had come to be assigned to a covert establishment on this remote world.

She pointed again. 'There – can you see? Look along my arm.'

Suddenly he saw it, stretching between Pluto and its moon. Only dimly visible in Sol's reduced light, a glimmer here, a stretch of arc there, it was nothing like the Bridge that had been erected between

Earth and its Moon – this was finer, more elegant, more organic than that. But it was a line that spanned worlds nevertheless.

Pirius had heard of this. 'It's natural, isn't it?'

'It's spider's web,' she breathed. 'Pluto-Charon is swathed in cobweb.'

Nilis came bustling up. 'One of Sol system's more memorable spectacles,' he said. 'And it is only possible here, where both worlds are locked face to face.' He slapped Pirius on the back, 'But we aren't here to sightsee, ensign! We have work to do.'

Reluctantly they rejoined the rest of the group, who were crowding into a flitter.

The journey was going to be long, Pirius was told; they would be taken right around the curve of the world. He was dismayed that the little craft was already full of these exiled scientists' peculiar odours.

As they took their places, Mara sat beside Pirius. She said, 'You must come back in the spring, when the spiders of Pluto come out to sail between the worlds and build their webbing all over again.'

'Spring? When's that?'

'Oh, about another seventy years . . .'

The flitter lifted smoothly.

They flew silently through the geometry of the double worlds.

Pirius, retreating from the chattering group, spent the journey preparing a long Virtual message to Torec, who was stuck at Saturn, still working on the development of the CTC processor. He fixed a cloak of anti-sound around himself so the Plutinos would not be offended by what he had to say about them.

When the cramped little craft began at last to descend, Charon was long lost beneath the horizon. There was nothing to be seen here, nothing but the fractured, ancient ground. But before the flitter, the ground rose to a ridge. Beyond this, evidently, was what they had come to see.

Draq said, 'We'll walk from here rather than fly. It's best if you come to the facility yourself. There's nothing quite so striking as a purely human experience – don't you think, Commissary?'

Pirius was glad to seal up his skinsuit, which smelled of nothing but him. But the Commissary, as usual, demurred, and insisted that a Virtual projection would do just as well for him.

So Pirius stepped out on to the surface of yet another world. Sol was halfway up the sky, a diamond of light.

He took a few experimental steps. Gravity was only a few per cent of standard. The ice crunched, compressing, but the fractured surface supported his weight. Pluto ice was a rich crimson laced with organic purple. He made out patterns, dimly, in the ice; they were like bas-relief, discs the size of dinner plates with the intricate complexity of snowflakes. The suit's insulation was good, but enough heat leaked to send nitrogen clouds hissing up around his footsteps.

The group began to climb the shallow ridge. There were five of them out on the ice, if you included Nilis. Draq led the way, and Pirius and Nilis followed with two other Plutinos, including Mara, who walked with Pirius. Nilis floated serenely a few centimetres above the ice, barefoot and without so much as a face mask, once more blithely ignoring all Virtual protocols. It was crassly discourteous, Pirius thought, irritated. But the Plutinos were too polite, or too cowed, to mention it.

Where the ground was steeper, the frost covering had slipped away. The 'bedrock' here was water ice, but ice so cold it was hard as granite on Earth and Pirius thought he could feel its chill through the heated soles of his boots. But it wasn't slippery; at Pluto's temperatures even the heat his suit leaked wasn't sufficient to melt the surface.

And when Pirius stepped on to the bare ice, he thought he heard music. He stopped, surprised. The ground throbbed with a bass harmonisation he could feel in his chest. It was as if he heard the frozen planet's beating heart.

Mara smiled. 'Wait and see,' she said.

They reached the shallow breast of the ridge. Pirius saw now that the ridge was one of a line of shallow eroded hills that circled a basin. It was a crater, he realised, but clearly a very ancient one. Though the floor was cracked and tumbled, its unevenness was worn down almost to smoothness. Over perhaps billions of years the remnants of the great scar had sublimated away, the icy hillocks of its rim relaxed to shallowness, and the invisible hail of cosmic rays had battered at the crust, turning it blood red, like the ice of Port Sol.

And Pirius saw what he had been brought to witness. On the floor of this palimpsest of a crater nestled a city.

At first all Pirius could make out was a pale, scattered sparkle, as if stars from the silent sky had fallen down to the ice. Then he realised he was seeing the *reflections* of the stars, returned from silvered forms that nestled on the crater floor.

He tapped his face plate to increase the magnification. The basin was covered by reflective forms, like mercury droplets, glistening on a black velvet landscape. It was a forest of globes and half-globes anchored by cables. Necklaces swooped between the globes, frosted with frozen air. A city, yes, obviously artificial, and presumably the source of the deep harmonics that travelled to him through the ice. But it wasn't a human city, and as the ground throbbed beneath his feet Pirius felt his heart beat faster in response.

Every child in every cadre in every colony across the Galaxy would have recognised this city for what it was, and who must have built it. Every child grew up learning all there was to know about mankind's greatest enemy save the Xeelee – long vanquished, scattered, its worlds invested and occupied, its facilities destroyed, and yet still a figure of legend and nightmare.

Pirius sensed something behind him, something massive. He turned slowly.

He found himself facing a silvered sphere perhaps two metres across. Pirius could see his own reflection, a bipedal figure standing on blood-dark ice, distorted in the sphere's belly, and Sol cast a flaring highlight. The sphere hovered without support above the ice, wafting gently as if in some intangible breeze. Its hide was featureless, save for an equipment belt slung around its equator.

Draq stood alongside the sphere, which loomed over him, and slapped its hide. 'Now, sirs – what do you think of that? Isn't it a magnificent beast?'

It was a Silver Ghost. Pirius wished he had a weapon.

The Commissary, taller and bulkier than any of the Plutinos, drew himself up to his full height. Pirius wondered if he had pumped up his Virtual a little for effect. Nilis seemed coldly furious. 'Curator Draq, I thought Ghosts had been driven to extinction.'

'Evidently not,' Pirius growled. Mara looked at him uneasily.

Draq gazed at the Ghost's hide. 'Look at this stuff! A Ghost's skin is the most reflective material in the known universe – and so the most effective heat trap, of course. But it is actually technological. It contains what we call a Planck-zero layer, a sandwich around a zone where the very constants of physics have been tweaked. And the

Ghosts incorporated that technology into their own biology. Remarkable: at one time every living Ghost went about its business clad in a shell that was effectively part of another universe!'

Mara, standing by the Ghost, actually stroked its hide. Pirius thought her gesture was soft, perhaps meant to be reassuring – reassuring *to the Ghost*.

Pirius's confusion deepened further. 'Commissary, this is a *Silver Ghost*. It shouldn't even exist, let alone be bouncing around on Pluto!'

Draq was intimidated by a Commissary, but evidently not by a kid like Pirius. He even seemed triumphant. 'We've done this to further the goals of the Coalition, ensign. To serve the Third Expansion!'

Nilis turned on him. 'But the boy's right, curator.'

Draq's restless hands, encumbered by his skinsuit gloves, wriggled and pulled at each other. 'But can't you see – that's the sheer *excitement* of the project. The Ghosts were of course wiped out. But perhaps you know that the Ghosts were composite creatures – each of them symbiotic communities, comprising many living beings, some from worlds alien to the Ghosts themselves, and with their technology merged into their structure too. And their technologies were simply too useful. For example, hides like this are grown on controlled farms across the Galaxy. Strange to think that *bits* of what might have been Ghosts are at work, in the service of mankind, right across the Galaxy. If we had been defeated, perhaps the Ghosts would use human leg muscles and livers, hearts and bones in *their* machinery!

'And so when, ah, the decision was made that the Ghosts themselves should be *revived*, under controlled conditions of course, it wasn't hard to reassemble a self-sustaining community. They are quite at home here on Pluto; perhaps you know they came from a chill world, colder than Pluto, and their technology, what we've been able to recover, serves them well.'

'But why?'

'Because Ghosts are a valuable resource.'

Ghosts were . . . strange.

Early in their history their sun had failed, their world had frozen. The universe had betrayed them, literally – and this had taught them that the universe contained design flaws. And so their science turned to fixing those flaws. They ran experimental programmes of quite outrageous ambition. Humans certainly had cause to fear them, before they were crushed.

Draq said, 'Long ago the Coalition councils decided that the Ghosts', ah, *ingenuity* should be revived – put to use as an engine of ideas, a resource for the benefit of mankind. This was done over and over with other races during the Assimilation, you know. Why not the Ghosts?'

Pirius said, 'A resource you had to conceal.'

'Yes! For security – both for humanity's protection from the Ghosts and vice versa. And for deniability, I won't pretend that isn't true. But you're here for the Ghosts, whether you know it or not, Commissary. The gravastar idea is *theirs* . . .'

Mara said coldly, 'This "valuable resource" can talk.'

The Ghost hovered impassively. There was no change in its appearance, yet the grammar of the group changed. Suddenly the Ghost stopped being an object, but became a person, a contributor to the conversation.

Nilis walked up to the silvered hide, his Virtual projection casting a blurred reflection on the Ghost's belly. 'It can talk, can it? I see it has a translator box on that belt.' He stood before the Ghost, hands on hips. 'You! Ghost!'

Mara said, 'There's no need to shout, Commissary.'

Nilis said, 'Do you have a name?'

The Ghost's voice was synthetic, a neutral human-female voice generated by the translator box it carried and transmitted to their receiving gear. 'I am known as the Ambassador to the Heat Sink.'

Nilis seemed startled. He prodded the Ghost's hide, but his Virtual finger slid into the reflective surface, shattering into pixels. 'And do you know the meaning of the name?'

'No,' the Ghost said bluntly. 'I am a reconstruction. A biological echo of my forebears. We have records, but no memory. There can be no true cultural continuity.'

Nilis nodded coldly. 'Despite all our ingenuity, extinction is for ever.'

'Yes,' the Ghost said simply.

Mara's expression was dark. 'What do you think now, ensign?'

Pirius spoke without thinking about it. 'The Ghosts killed millions of us.' He faced the Ghost. 'I'm glad you are conscious. I'm glad you know about the elimination of your kind. I am glad you are suffering.'

The Ghost didn't respond.

Mara's bleak gaze was on Pirius. He had to look away, disturbed by the turmoil inside him.

Nilis seemed fascinated by the Ghost, as his scientist's curiosity overcame his commissary's ideology. 'If you don't know who you are, do you at least know what you want?'

'To serve you,' the Ghost said.

CHAPTER 22

It took ten hours for a dropship to come pick them up from Factory Rock. Pirius Blue and his two wounded charges spent that time huddling in the ruins of the Xeelee emplacement.

When the medical corps orderly clambered out of his little craft, he was surprised to find them. The three of them were the only survivors of two platoons. 'You must be the luckiest man alive,' the orderly said.

'I must be,' said Pirius Blue.

Cohl's injury was obvious; Tili Three was in deep shock. The orderly said he was supposed to separate able-bodied Pirius from Cohl and Tili Three and send them back through different 'processing channels', as he put it. Pirius refused to be parted from his comrades. It boiled down to a stand-off between Pirius and the small, heavy orderly, there on the churned-up surface of the Rock. The orderly caved in, shrugging his shoulders, saying the officers would sort it out later.

So they loaded Cohl and Tili on to the dropship. By now their skinsuits had turned rigid and filled up with a greenish stabilising fluid full of nutrients, anaesthetics and stimulants. You were actually supposed to *breathe* this stuff. Pirius had tried it in training and, no matter what assurances he had got about the glop's oxygen content, it had felt like drowning. But both the wounded were mercifully unconscious; as they were manhandled the dense fluid sloshed around their faces.

The dropship lifted easily. Pirius glanced back at the ruined emplacement, the scarred bit of ground that marked the site of the monopole factory. It was just another battlefield in an unending war of a million battlefields. But it could have been the most important

200

place in his entire life, for he could easily have died here. He knew he would never see it again.

The ride was short, a flea-hop to the nearest clearing station. The dropship skimmed over the ground. The casualties lay like two statues, locked into their rigid suits. The ship had no medical facilities. It couldn't even be pressurised, so the casualties couldn't be taken out of their skinsuits.

The orderly was cheerful; he actually whistled tunelessly as he flew the ship. Pirius shut down his comms loop.

After a couple of minutes more dropships came into sight, other bubbles of light skimming over the asteroid's battered surface, converging from all over the Rock. A crude traffic control system cut in, and Pirius's dropship joined a queue. Soon they were so close to the ship in front Pirius could see its passengers, and their bewildered expressions. Ships streamed the other way, too, dropships heading back out across the Rock to ferry in yet more casualties.

The clearing station had been set up in a wide impact crater. A pressurised dome perhaps a kilometre wide sat in the crater like a huge droplet of water, its skin rippling languidly. It was marked with a tetrahedral sigil, the symbol of free Earth.

The dome was studded with airlocks, to which ships came nuzzling up. Some of them were dropships, others larger boats; there was even a captain's corvette. The ships rose steadily towards a fleet of Spline craft which drifted far above, fleshy, patient moons. Pirius could see movement inside the dome, through its translucent walls: it was a hive of frantic activity. But there was commotion outside as well, and the surface of the Rock around the dome was covered with glistening rows, as if it had been ploughed up, like a big nano-food farm.

Pirius expected his own dropship to dock with one of the dome's ports. He was surprised when the little craft began to descend a few hundred metres short of the dome. It came down on a patch of bare dust, a landing site hastily cordoned off and marked with winking globe lamps.

The hull popped open, and the orderly, still business-like and cheery, asked Pirius to give him a hand with the casualties. They set Cohl and Tili in their rigid suits down on the bare ground.

All around the ship troopers were lying in the dirt, their skinsuits glowing orange or red. This was what Pirius had glimpsed from above, what he had thought looked like the furrows of a ploughed-up nano-food farm. The furrows were rows of wounded, thousands or tens of thousands of them, lying patiently in the dirt waiting for treatment.

'It's always like this,' said the orderly.

Pirius began to see the process. The wounded were brought here from all over the Rock. On arrival they were organised into these rough rows. Close to the dome's walls, tarpaulins had been cast over the dirt, and there were even a few beds. But out here you just had to lie in the asteroid dirt, still locked in your skinsuit, without so much as a blanket beneath you.

Medical officers hurried through the ranks of the newly arrived, peering into each skinsuit, trying to pick out the most severely wounded. Some were marked by a floating Virtual sigil, and the stretcher crews would come out and take prioritised cases into the dome quickly. The whole set-up was like a factory, Pirius thought, a factory for processing broken human flesh.

The orderly glared at Pirius. 'This your first time out?'

'Yes.'

'Rookie, you gave me shit out there by the emplacement. If you're ever in my boat again, be polite. You got that? We all have our jobs to do.' Then, whistling again, he made his way back to his dropship.

Back at Quin Base, the atmosphere was dismal. Casualty lists were posted, simple Virtual displays that hovered in the air. People crowded around, desperately scanning the lists of names and platoon numbers, the smiling images. They chewed their nails, cried, hugged each other for comfort, or wept with relief when they found a loved one who had survived.

Pirius was shocked by this open emotion. There was nothing like the stoicism of a Navy base during an action. It wasn't supposed to *be* like this; you were supposed to give your life gladly, and accept the loss of others.

As Captain Marta had promised, the returned warriors were rewarded with extra food. Pirius opened his own small hamper, left waiting for him on his bunk. The food was sticky stuff, very sweet or salty. It was treat food for children. So few had come back that there was plenty to go round; he could have eaten as much as he liked. But he ate only a little of his portion before giving it away.

Pirius managed to get a message to Enduring Hope with his artillery platoon, telling him Cohl had been injured but was recovering. It occurred to him that he ought to look for the friends of the Tilis and the rest of the platoon. But he didn't know who those friends were – and besides, what would he say? In the end he shied away from the idea, but he felt ashamed, as if he had ducked a responsibility.

That first night there were many empty bunks. The barracks seemed to have been hollowed out. The normal sounds of play and love-making and trivial arguments were replaced by stillness. Once, sleepless, he glimpsed Captain Marta moving through the barracks, her metallised body gleaming, her movements silent and deliberate. She stopped by some of the bunks, but Pirius couldn't hear what she said.

In the days that followed, Pirius learned that the Army had more 'processes' for dealing with the aftermath of such battles.

The day after Pirius's return, a massive reorganisation swept through the barracks. Pirius, Cohl and Tili were to be kept together, but they were assigned to a new platoon, number 85 under the new hierarchy. They were moved to new corners of the barracks. Once Cohl and Tili had returned, the three of them were squashed into a block of bunks with their seven new platoon comrades.

Most of the seven new platoon members were cadets, unblooded, fresh from the training grounds. Reunited cadre siblings greeted each other noisily. The survivors of Factory Rock moved in this new crowd as if they had suddenly grown old, Pirius thought. The energy of the youngsters was infectious, and the mood quickly lifted back to something like the brash noisiness it had been before. Soon it was as if the action on the Rock had never happened, as if it had all been some hideous nightmare.

But in the quietest hours of the night, when the rats sang, you could still hear weeping.

Tili Three was changed. She was nothing like the bright, happy kid who had spent her life in intimacy with her lost sisters; now, left alone, she grew hollow-eyed and gaunt.

Pirius longed to comfort her. But he didn't know how. He told himself that if not for his own actions Tili Three might well have lost her life as well. Why, then, did he feel so unreasonably *guilty*? And how could he feel so anguished about the loss of two privates, when, if you added up all the losses around the Front, ten billion died every year? It made no sense, and yet it hurt even so.

In the end, paralysed by his own grief and uncertainty, he left her alone.

This Burden Must Pass had been on Factory Rock, but his platoon had been far from the main action and had suffered only one casualty, non-lethal. He had been through all this before.

And, just as the dropship orderly had said to Pirius, Burden told him it was always like this. 'They chop up the platoons and push us together, so we're all crowded in just like before. Soon you don't see the big hollow spaces, the rows of empty bunks. You forget. You can't help it.' He spoke around mouthfuls of the treat food.

'It's not the same, though,' Pirius said. 'Not once you've been out there. It can't be.'

'Don't talk about it,' Burden said warningly. 'You're safe in here, in the barracks. It's as if what happens out there isn't real – or isn't unless you talk about it. If you do that, you see, you let it in, all that horror.' His face worked briefly, and Pirius wondered what else he was leaving unsaid.

'I don't understand you, Burden. You've been in the field six times now. *Six times*. If none of this matters, if the Doctrines are a joke to you – why put your life on the line over and over?'

'No matter what I believe, what choice is there? If you go forward, you'll most likely get shot. If you go backwards, if you refuse, you'll be court-martialled and sentenced and shot anyhow. So what are you supposed to do? You go forward, because the only thing you can shoot at in this war is a Xeelee. At least going forward you've a *chance*. That's all there is, really.' That was as much as he would say.

Pirius was mystified by Burden's contradictions. Burden seemed composed, centred. Under his veneer of faith he seemed hard-headed, cynical, and full of a certain gritty wisdom on how Army life was to be survived. He seemed to have strength of faith, and strength of character too, which he'd displayed once again in the most testing arena possible. But sometimes Pirius would catch Burden looking at him or Cohl almost longingly, as if he was desperate to be accepted, like an unpopular cadet in an Arches Barracks Ball.

And Pirius noticed that in this strange time of the action's aftermath Burden was eating compulsively. He devoured as much of the treat rations he could get hold of, and in those first days he always seemed to have food in his mouth. Once Pirius saw him making himself vomit: the ancient system of fingers pushed down the throat.

Burden's mix of strength and weakness was unfathomable.

CHAPTER 23

After five days Pirius Red was still stuck on Pluto.

While Nilis spent time working with the Plutinos, Pirius skulked in the spartan comforts of the corvette with the crew. These two Navy pilots, both women, were called Molo and Huber. They categorically refused to set foot off the ship on to this murky little world. They worked, ate, slept in their compartment. They were interested only in journeys, indifferent to destinations: they were pilots.

They had heard rumours about Project Prime Radiant, though. They thought it was all a waste of time. As far as Pirius could make out, they believed that whatever you came up with the Xeelee would counter it. You were never going to beat the Xeelee, they said. It seemed to be the prevalent attitude, here in Sol system.

Of course there was an immense gulf between the two of them and Pirius. And there was something sexual going on: not uncommon on assignments like this. But at least they were Navy officers. So Pirius shared their bland rations, played their elaborate games of chance and immersed himself, for a while, in the comforting routines of Navy life.

He tried to sort out his feelings.

He told himself he hated the Plutinos for what they had done here. In the four months he had spent in Sol system Pirius had got used to a lot of bizarre ideas. He had seen the wealth of Earth, the strangeness of its people, and the casual, dismissive way the precious Doctrines were regarded here – even what seemed to him the corruption of the likes of Gramm. Perhaps this was too exotic for his simple serving man's imagination. But the sight of a Silver Ghost drifting over the icy ground of a world of Sol system itself, as if it had a right to be there, as if it *owned* it, when by rights it shouldn't even *exist* – it was a challenge to a soldier's deepest instincts, violating everything he had been brought up to value.

No matter how much he thought about it, it didn't get any clearer. And he had nobody to talk it over with. He certainly wasn't about to discuss this with Nilis, who he was starting to think was part of the problem. He wished Torec was here.

At lights out he slept as long as he could. But all too soon the morning came.

On the sixth day there was to be a briefing on the revitalised Ghosts' 'gravastar' technology.

Nilis insisted that Pirius come out of the corvette and join him.

As the two of them followed Draq, Mara and the other Plutinos through the grubby corridors of the compound at Christy, the Commissary was actually humming. For Nilis, Pirius supposed, a day of lectures and earnest academic discussion was a day in paradise.

'We're here to assess this material for its weapons potential, ensign,' Nilis said sternly. 'I suggest you put aside your prejudices and do your duty.'

Prejudices? 'Yes, sir,' Pirius said coldly.

Mara walked beside Pirius, but she ignored him. She hadn't said a word to him since his hostile reaction to the Ghost.

They were led to the most spacious dome of the complex. It was a chilly, cavernous place. Chairs and couches had been set in the middle of the hall, an island of furniture in a sea of empty floor. A relic of a failed colony, its surface tarnished to a golden hue by cosmic rays, this dome was far too big for the small modern population. Ancient bots hovered uncertainly, offering unappetising-looking food and drink.

And Pirius could see a Ghost drifting over the ice outside the dome, obscured by the tint of the aged dome wall. Perhaps it was the one who called itself the Sink Ambassador. He wished with all his heart that it would go away.

Draq climbed a little podium. Self-importantly he began to outline the new idea of a 'gravastar': based on an ancient human theory, developed by a colony of Silver Ghosts here on Pluto-Charon, discovered by Nilis in his hasty trawls of the Olympus Archive, and identified as having the potential to be useful for Project Prime

Radiant. 'Everybody knows what a black hole is,' Draq began. 'But everybody is wrong . . .'

Draq spoke too quickly, made too many weak jokes, and used too many technical phrases Pirius didn't recognise all, such as 'Mazur-Mottola solutions' and 'negative energy density' and 'an interior de Sitter condensate phase matched to an exterior Schwarzschild geometry'. But he had a lot of Virtual schematics, immense displays that filled up much of this huge dome's volume. The special effects were spectacular and entertaining, and Draq, beneath his gaudy creations, gestured like a showman.

A black hole came about if a lump of matter collapsed so far that its surface gravity increased to the point where you would need to travel at lightspeed to escape it. It had happened during the fiery instants after the Big Bang, and could occur nowadays when a giant star imploded. Within its 'event horizon', the surface of no return, still the implosion continued.

Thus the basic geography of a black hole, familiar to every pilot in the Navy. If you fell through the event horizon you could never escape. You would be drawn inexorably into the singularity at the centre, a place where the compression forces had exponentiated to the point where spacetime itself was ripped open. Pirius idly watched gaudy displays of exploding stars, Big Bang compression waves and unlucky smeared-out cartoon pilots.

But now Draq said that the most productive way to think about a black hole was to imagine that the event horizon enclosed a *separate universe*. After all, nothing within the horizon could ever communicate with anything outside. It was as if a gouge had been ripped out of our spacetime and another universe patched into the hole. In fact, he said, with an enthusiastic but unwelcome diversion into equations, that was how you dealt with a black hole mathematically.

Inside a conventional black hole, that new baby universe was doomed to implode for ever into its singularity. But it didn't have to be that way. What if that infant universe *expanded*? After all, that was how the outside universe seemed to behave, and it was possible for gravity to act as a repulsive force: the swelling of the universe itself was being driven by a field of 'dark energy' with exactly that property. Draq said that – theoretically anyhow, under certain conditions – the great violence of the collapse of a massive object could shock a region of spacetime into a new configuration. And if that happened, yes, you certainly could create a new baby universe doomed not to collapse but to expand.

But that expansion was limited. The mass of the collapsing object still drew in matter from the outside world, so there was still an event horizon, the distance of lightspeed escape. But now the horizon was like a stationary shock wave, the place where the infall from the parent universe outside met the expansion of the infant within.

This collision of universes created an 'ultra-relativistic fluid', as Draq called it, like the meniscus on a pond that separated water from air. This exotic stuff was gathered into a shell as thin as a quark, but a spoonful of it would weigh hundreds of tonnes. An unlucky infalling astronaut wouldn't slide smoothly into the lethal interior, as she would if this were a conventional black hole. Instead every particle of her mass would have to give up its gravitational energy at the shock front.

This 'gravastar' was no black hole; it would blaze brightly with the energy of continual destruction. But even so, Draq said, outlining a paradox Pirius didn't begin to understand, the temperature of the shell would only be a billionth of a degree above absolute zero.

Pirius failed to see the point of this. But he enjoyed the Virtual fireworks.

Nilis had become increasingly restless as this went on. At last the Commissary lumbered to his feet. 'Yes, yes, Commissary Draq, this is all very well. But this is nothing but *theory* – and antique theory at that. No such "gravastar" has ever been observed in nature.'

That was true, Draq conceded. The conditions needed to avoid a simple black-hole collapse were unlikely to occur by chance: an imploding object would need to shed a great deal of entropy to make the gravastar state possible, and nobody knew how that might occur in nature.

Nilis demanded, 'Then how do you know the bones of your theory support any meat – eh? And besides, you're describing spherically symmetric solutions of the equations. If I were to find myself inside a gravastar I would be as cut off and trapped, not to mention doomed to incineration by the shock wave, as if I were in a common-or-garden black hole! So, Commissary, what *use* is any of this?'

Draq was clearly nervous, but he fixed his smile like a weapon. 'But that's why we need the Silver Ghosts, Commissary. To go beyond human theory. And to give us experimental verification . . .'

Nilis joined Draq under his imploding Virtuals, and they launched into a complex and convoluted argument, involving asymptotically matched solutions of partial differential equations and other exotica. Pirius had a pilot's basic grasp of mathematics, but this left him cold.

Mara approached him. She had her hands tucked into the sleeves of her robe. She whispered, 'This is a little rich for my blood too. Perhaps we should take a walk.' She wouldn't meet his eyes.

'You don't want to be with me.'

'No, I don't,' Mara said. 'But it's my duty to host you. And it's your duty to understand what we're doing here on Pluto—'

'Don't talk to me about duty.'

'—even if that means you're going to have to confront your feelings about the Silver Ghosts.'

'Why have I got to "confront my feelings"?' he snapped. 'The Ghosts shouldn't be here. That isn't a feeling. It's a fact.'

'What are you scared of?' she asked blandly.

'That's a stupid question.'

She didn't react. 'It probably is. Will you come?'

He sighed. It was her or Draq's partial differential equations. 'All right.'

Suited up, they walked out of the dome. Mara led him perhaps half a kilometre away from the domes of the Christy compound. They didn't speak.

Once more the sharp-grained, ultra-cold frost of Pluto crunched beneath Pirius's feet, and he tried not to be spooked by the immense mass of Charon poised silently above his head.

They crossed a low ridge, perhaps the worn-down rim of another ancient crater, and approached a new structure. It was an open tangle of cables, wiring, small modules; it looked impractical to Pirius, more like a sculpture. But it seemed oddly familiar, and he dug for the memory, left over from some long-ago training session.

Mara spoke at last. 'You understand that the main Ghost reservation, which you saw, is on the far side of the planet. But it was necessary to provide support facilities for the Ghosts who work with us here, at Christy. We decided to take the opportunity to recreate another bit of Ghost technology.'

Then Pirius saw it. 'This is a cruiser,' he breathed. 'A Ghost cruiser.'

Once millions of ships like this had patrolled the Orion Line, the Ghosts' great cordon flung across the face of the Galaxy.

The Ghost ship was kilometres long, big enough to have dwarfed the greenship Pirius's future self would have piloted in the Core. It had nothing like the lines of a human craft. The cruiser was a tangle of silvery rope within which bulky equipment pods were suspended, apparently at random.

And everywhere there were Silver Ghosts, sliding along the silver cables like beads of mercury.

'Of course it's just a mock-up,' Mara said. 'Basically life support. There are no drive units; it can't fly. And no weapons! I always think it looks more like a forest than a ship. But that's what it is, in a sense. The Ghosts are like miniature ecologies themselves, and they turned slices of their ecology into their ships. I've always thought that was a much more *elegant* solution than our own clunky mechanical systems.'

Pirius felt that deep anger welling again. 'Millions of human lives were lost in the defeat of ships like this. And you've built a – a *monument* to our enemy.'

'Yes,' she said testily. 'As you've said before. But don't you think we need to understand what it was we killed?'

He thought he didn't understand her at all. 'Is that why *you're* here? Were you always so curious about Ghosts?'

She hesitated, perhaps wary of giving away too much of herself. 'I suppose so – yes. I've always been a Commissary. I started in the Office of Doctrinal Responsibility: very dry work! I was always blighted by curiosity. Not a good characteristic in the Commission for Historical Truth.' Her smile, behind her visor, was thin. 'Then I found out about this facility, and a number of others, where life forms generally supposed lost during the Assimilation have been preserved – or, as in the case of the Ghosts, revived.'

'*There are others?* . . . Never mind. How did you find out?'

She smiled again. 'The control of the Commission isn't as complete as some like to imagine. Truth finds a way. So I volunteered to come here. The powers that be were surprised, but they processed my application. Pluto is generally a punishment detail, you know. You come here to make amends, to end your career – certainly not to progress it.'

'And was it worth it?'

'Oh, yes, ensign. It was worth it.' She led him around the periphery of the mocked-up cruiser, 'I mean, *look* at this. What's fascinating about the Ghosts to me isn't their technological capabilities but their story: their origin, their account of themselves. You know, the Ghosts call the sky the Heat Sink – the place the heat went.' Since their world had frozen, Mara said, the Ghosts had not been shaped by competitive evolution, as humans had, but by cooperation. 'They are symbiotic creatures. They derive from life forms that huddled into cooperative collectives as their world turned cold. Every aspect of their physical design is about conserving heat, precious heat.

'And they seem to be motivated – not by expansion for its own sake, as we are – but by a desire to understand the fine-tuning of the universe. *Why are we here?* You see, ensign Pirius, there is only a narrow range of physical possibilities within which life of *any* sort is possible. We think the Ghosts were studying this question by pushing at the boundaries – by tinkering with the laws which govern us all.'

'But that made them dangerous.'

'Yes,' Mara said. 'An enemy who can use the laws of physics as a weapon is formidable. But they developed their capabilities, not as some vast weapons programme, but for their own species imperative. Until they ran up against humans, it had nothing to do with *us* . . .'

Pirius sensed movement behind him. A Silver Ghost hovered massively a few metres away, just above the ice surface.

Mara said quickly, 'It's only the Sink Ambassador. It must have followed us. It's probably curious.'

'Curious? You talk as if it's a child.' Pirius saw himself reflected in the Ghost's complacent hide. 'You,' he said. 'You are the Sink Ambassador?'

'That is what I am called.'

'Is she right? That you Ghosts follow your own logic, that you care nothing for humans?'

'I don't know,' the Ghost said. 'I have no reliable data on the past.'

Mara said dryly. 'These new Ghosts won't believe a word we say about their history. Maybe they're right not to.'

'We destroyed you,' Pirius said. 'And we brought you back. Everything about you is in our power.'

'True. But that doesn't alter my perception of you.'

Fists clenched, Pirius stepped up to the Ghost. Suddenly all the complex emotions he had been feeling – his inbred hatred of the Ghosts, his confusion at the reaction of Mara and the others, all that had struck him so overwhelmingly since the day his own future self had docked at Arches – welled up in him. And here was a Silver Ghost, right in front of him. He said on impulse, 'Perhaps Mara is right. Perhaps I must learn about you, as you have learned about humans.'

Mara was disturbed. 'What are you doing, ensign?'

'Remove your hide. Disassemble yourself. *Show me what you are.*'

Mara laid a gloved hand on Pirius's arm. Her eyes were bright with anger. 'I knew I shouldn't have brought you here.'

Pirius shook her off. 'I command this Ghost. *I am human.*'

The Ghost was motionless, save for its usual subtle wafting, and Pirius, shaking with anger, wondered what he would do if the Ghost refused. He remembered his training on how to fight a Ghost. That hide was tough, but if you used all your strength you could get your knife into it, and then you could use the Ghost's own rotation against it and open it up . . .

The Ghost's hide puckered and shallow seams formed, stretching from one pole of the glistening sphere to another, segmenting the surface. The Ghost quivered briefly – then one seam split open. A sheet of crimson fluid gushed out, strikingly like human blood. It had frozen into crystals long before it fell to the Pluto ice.

A Virtual of Nilis coalesced with a snap. 'Stop this.' He stood between Pirius and the Ghost. 'You, Ambassador. Heal yourself.'

The gash in the Ghost's hide closed, leaving only a pale scar. A stark slick of frozen blood showed how much it had lost in those brief moments.

Nilis turned on Pirius. He thundered, 'What were you thinking, ensign? To deal with this I have been forced to leave a meeting I crossed Sol system to attend! Is this really your highest aspiration – the highest achievement of mankind, after twenty thousand long years of interstellar conquest – to use your petty power to cause another sentient creature to destroy itself? *Why?*'

Because it's what I'm trained to do, Pirius thought helplessly. But he flinched from Nilis's furious glare.

'Who is it you're angry with, ensign?' Mara asked. 'The Ghost? Or is the Ghost just a target? Perhaps you are angry about the lies you have been told throughout your life. Now you have been brought to Sol system you see the truth, and you can't handle your rage. But you don't know who to blame.'

'Shut up,' Pirius said.

'Perhaps you would rather have died in combat, without having to deal with such complex truths—'

'*Shut up.*'

Unexpectedly the Ghost spoke. Its translated words were as toneless as ever. 'I gladly obeyed the ensign's command. I am not afraid to die.'

Nilis turned and inspected the Ghost. 'Is that really true?' In an instant, Pirius saw resentfully, he had forgotten Pirius and was taken over once more by his own endless curiosity. 'But what consolation can there be for death? Tell me, Ghost – do you have gods?'

Mara warned, 'All it knows of its culture is what we have taught it. As if the Ghosts studied a human religion, filtered it through their own preconceptions and gave it back to us.'

'Yes, yes,' Nilis said impatiently. 'I understand that. Nevertheless—'

The Ghost said, 'Not gods of the past.'

'No,' said Nilis rapidly. 'Of course not. Human gods were creators. But *your* world betrayed you, didn't it? What creator god would do that?'

'The past is a betrayal. The future is a promise.'

Mara said, 'Commissary, we have tried to study Ghost philosophy. The Ghosts have a different perception of the universe to us, a different story about themselves to tell. Nobody's really sure if concepts like *religion* actually map across to such alien minds.'

'Oh, of course,' Nilis said. 'But I'm of the school that holds that something like religious concepts must arise in any sentient form. Perhaps all mortal creatures, humans or Ghosts, must develop a philosophy to cushion the shock of imminent personal death.'

Mara nodded. 'I'd certainly concede that religious beliefs have survival value – and are likely to play an evolutionary purpose.'

'Yes, yes! Religion provides a rationale for existence in a universe which may otherwise seem chaotic – perhaps an illusory rationale, but a way to cope. And religion has a function as social cement. Cooperation is essential, and religion fuels conformity. Really, religion ought to be a universal . . .'

As this academic talk went on Pirius glared at the wounded Ghost, and he imagined it glared back. Pirius said, 'I don't care what it thinks

214

about gods. I want to know what it thinks of the humans who destroyed its kind.'

Nilis and Mara tensed, but waited for the Ghost's answer.

The Ghost said, 'You are the ones who kill.'

Nilis said quickly, 'Others kill too. The Xeelee kill. *You* kill.'

'Only other kinds. No Ghost would kill another Ghost; it would be a kind of suicide.'

Mara said, 'The Ghosts think human war is insane – not just the war in the Galaxy, all our organised wars. Only humans spend the lives of others of our kind as if they were mere tokens. The Ghosts think nothing is so precious as sentience.'

'Humans aren't killers,' Pirius said. He lifted his hands. 'We didn't choose this war. Before we left Earth humans didn't wage war at all.'

Nilis actually laughed. 'Ah, ensign – another Coalition myth! Don't pay attention to what the political officers tell you. Before spaceflight, despite the lessons of your childhood, Earth was *not* a paradise where humans ruled other creatures in a kind of benevolent despotism; we were *not* noble savages. We have always killed, ensign, always waged war – and as we had no alien enemy to kill in those days, we turned on each other. The proof is in the bloodstained ground of Earth.'

Pirius pointed at the Ghost. 'Commissary, don't you get it? This is why this experiment, this revival of the Ghosts, is so wrong. We're already arguing! Give them a chance and they will worm their destabilising ideas into our minds.'

Nilis was studying him; Pirius had the cold feeling he had become just another fascinating specimen to him. 'Perhaps. But there will be no killing today.'

Mara pointed upwards. 'Look.'

Pirius, stiff in his skinsuit, tilted back and peered up.

The patient bulk of Charon hung suspended over its parent, half-shadowed, a misty form in the light of the pinpoint sun. But now, right at the centre of its face, a spark of light had erupted, blue-white, intense – far brighter than Sol. When Pirius looked away, he saw the new light was casting shadows, knife-sharp.

Nilis clapped his hands with child-like excitement. 'That's the gravastar! What we see is the glow of infalling matter shedding its gravitational energy as it hits the ultra-relativistic wave front. It's really a remarkable technical achievement – the parameters of the controlled implosion of matter needed to create the shock are terribly narrow – stability is difficult to maintain.' He sighed. 'But the Ghosts always were good at this sort of thing.'

Mara said, 'The test is being run on Charon. This is an experimental technology, and the energies involved are immense. There's nobody up there to be hurt. Nobody but a few Ghosts, of course.'

'Remarkable,' Nilis said again, peering up. 'Remarkable.'

That pinpoint of light, reflected, slid over the Ghost's hide now. It was impossible for Pirius to believe that that starlike object, that bit of fire, was in fact far colder even than the ice of Charon itself.

They returned to the dome.

Nilis showed Pirius a summary of the rest of Draq's briefing, and Pirius, his head full of anger, tried to pick his way through the jargon.

He said, 'But, Commissary, I still don't see what use this is. You said yourself that if you got stuck inside a gravastar's horizon you would be as cut off as if you fell into a black hole – and just as dead.'

'Of course. A shock wave in the shape of a closed surface, spherical or not, would be no use to us. But Draq and his team, working with the Ghosts' theoreticians, have come up with another solution.

'Imagine that the shock front is not closed, but open – not a sphere, but a cap. Behind it you have your expanding captive universe, just as before, and where the expansion meets the infall you get your shock wave, the cap. But this toy cosmos isn't symmetrical. At the rear, away from the cap, the curvature flattens, until asymptotically you have a smooth transition to an external solution . . .'

Pirius thought he understood. 'So you have your cap of gravastar horizon,' he said carefully. 'That's lethal; you can't pass through it. And behind it is a zone that is still effectively another universe. But if you approach from the rear, you would move through a smooth bridge from our universe into the captive one—'

'Smooth, yes, save for the detail of a little tidal pull and so forth,' Nilis said.

Pirius wondered how much trouble there would be in that 'detail'.

Nilis beamed. '*Now* do you see the potential, Pirius? Now do you see the application?'

'No,' said Pirius frankly.

'The toy universe is not causally connected to ours. And that means it wouldn't be possible for the Xeelee, or anybody else, to have foreknowledge of what we might hide there – *even in principle* – because, you see, we'll be tucked inside another universe altogether!'

With a triumphant wave, Nilis brought up a Virtual copy of Pirius's old sketch of the assault on the Prime Radiant: the journey in, bedevilled by FTL foreknowledge, the Xeelee ring of fire around the Prime Radiant itself, and then the mysterious Radiant at the heart of it all, sketched as a crude asterisk by Pirius. All of this was in red, but now Nilis snapped his fingers. 'Thanks to Torec's CTC computer, we can out-think the Xeelee when we get there.' That crimson ring around the Radiant turned green. 'With the gravastar technology we should be able to stop foreknowledge leakage.' The inward path became green too. 'Now all we need is a way to strike at the Prime Radiant itself.' Smiling, he said, 'See what you can achieve when you focus on a goal, ensign? See how the obstacles melt away before determination? Now – what would you suggest as a next step?'

Pirius thought quickly. 'A test flight. We need to modify a ship. Equip it with the gravastar shield and CTC processors. See if we can make the thing fly.' He grinned; for a pilot it was quite a prospect.

'Yes, yes. Good!' Nilis slammed his fist into the palm of his hand. '*That* will make those complacent buffoons in the ministries sit up and take notice.'

Mara had listened to this, her gloved hands behind her back. She said now, 'The gravastar is a Ghost technology. No transfer to purely human control would be possible in a short period. *You'll need to take the Ghosts.*'

Even Nilis looked dubious. 'That will be a hard sell to the Grand Conclave.'

'You have no choice.'

Pirius had managed not to think about the Ghosts for a few minutes. Now he felt his fists bunch again. 'I bet the Ghosts intended it this way.'

Nilis said sharply, 'Ensign, you will have to learn to overcome this rage of yours. Even the planning of war is a rational process. Hate is unproductive.'

'Commissary, don't you see? They're doing it again. This is what they are like – the Ghosts – they are devious, sly, always seeking leverage—'

'*Ensign.*' Nilis glared at Pirius, willing him to silence, Mara was studying Pirius, all trace of human warmth vanished.

Pirius, angry, confused and ashamed, longed to be away from this place.

CHAPTER 24

A week later Pirius Red and Torec were reunited at Saturn. They fell into bed.

Pirius buried himself in the noisy pleasure and consolation of sex. She was the centre of his universe, and he had returned to her. He wished he could tell her that, but he didn't know how.

Afterwards he poured out his heart about what had happened on Pluto.

Torec said, 'I can't imagine it.'

But when he described how he had tried to get the Ghost to disassemble itself, she turned away. Even she seemed appalled by his loss of control.

His shame burned deeper – and his fear. They were both changing, both growing, under the dim light of Sol. Maybe that was inevitable, but he was afraid that they were growing apart. He wanted things to stay the same, for them both to be just kids, Barracks Ball squeezes. But that, of course, was impossible. He could see she was maturing, finding her own place here as her achievements started to rack up. But he didn't know the person she was becoming, or if that person would have room for him. Then again he didn't understand himself either – but what he did see of himself, he realised reluctantly, he didn't much like. And if he didn't even like himself much, how could she love him?

But they had little time together. They had a job to do, here at Saturn. They were to devote themselves to work on prototypes and test flights.

Nilis told them the cost of the Project, especially this latest phase, was continually questioned in the remote reaches of Coalition councils, but he was driving it through. 'You can fill Sol system with theories and arguments,' he said. 'But, my eyes, I've learned what makes these politicos tick. Dry-as-Martian-dust bureaucrats they may be, but there's nothing like a bit of live technology to make them sit up and take notice! It's the allure of war, you know, the pornography of destruction and death: that's what motivates them – as long as it is somebody else's death, of course.'

The ensigns had to take Nilis's word for that. But his clarity of purpose as this new phase of his project began was undeniable.

A Navy facility was put at their disposal. It turned out to be a small disused dock in orbit around the bristling fortress world of Saturn, under the overall control of Commander Darc. Once it got underway the development progressed rapidly, because the engineers were keen. Across the Galaxy, combat technology was pretty much static, and the crew, being engineers, enjoyed the challenge of putting together something new.

From the first Virtual sketches of how a standard greenship might be modified, and the first simulations of how such a beast might handle in flight, the two ensigns immersed themselves in the work. Torec applied the crude management techniques she had learned on the Moon, and the complex project ran reasonably smoothly from the start. Pirius felt comparatively at home here among Navy engineers, far removed from such horrors as reincarnated Silver Ghosts.

So Pirius was infuriated when Nilis called him away for yet another new assignment.

Nilis had taken himself off to the heart of Sol system once more, to initiate studies on the nature of the Prime Radiant itself. It was his way; now that the test programme was underway he regarded the gravastar work as 'mere detail', and had switched his attention to the next conceptual phase of his project, the assault on Chandra itself. And he needed Pirius, Nilis said; he wanted one of his 'core team' to be involved in every phase of the project – and Torec's new-found management skills were just too valuable on the test flight work; it was Pirius who could be spared.

And so he summoned Pirius to what he called the 'neutrino telescope' before carelessly leaving Pirius to sort out his own travel. It was maddening – and embarrassing. Pirius had no real idea what neutrinos were, or why or how you would build a telescope to study them, or why Nilis felt neutrinos had anything to do with his project.

But his biggest problem was figuring out where the telescope was.

He asked around the Navy facility. None of the engineers and sailors knew what he was talking about. In the end, Pirius was forced to go to Commander Darc – another loss of face. 'Oh, the carbon mine!' Darc said, laughing. He said the crew he would assign to Pirius would know where they were going.

Pirius spent a last night with Torec. They shared a bunk in a Navy dorm that was big and brightly lit: not as immense as the Barracks Balls of Arches Base, but near enough to feel like home. They talked about inconsequentials – anything but Silver Ghosts or neutrinos, or their own hearts, or other mysteries.

Then Pirius sailed once more into the murky heart of Sol system.

The corvette he took was spartan compared to Nilis's, and the crew, hardened Navy veterans irritated at being given such a chore, ignored Pirius for the whole trip. Pirius ate, slept, exercised. It wasn't so bad; perhaps he was getting used to the strange experience of being alone.

In its final approach the corvette swept around the limb of the planet, approaching from the shadowed side, and the new world opened up into an immense crescent.

Pirius peered out of the transparent hull. The light was dazzling; he was actually inside the orbit of Earth here, and the sun seemed huge. Another new planet, he thought wearily, another slice of strangeness.

But this one really was extraordinary. Under a thick, slightly murky atmosphere, the ground was pure white from pole to equator, and from orbit it looked perfectly smooth, unblemished, like an immense toy. He had never seen a world that looked so *clean*, so pristine. The whole surface even seemed to sparkle, as if it was covered in grains of salt.

The corvette entered low orbit and the planet flattened out into a landscape. The air was tall, all but transparent, without cloud save for streaks of high, icy haze. But Pirius saw contrails and rocket exhausts sparking through the air's pale grey. Once he saw an immense craft duck down from orbit to skim through the upper atmosphere. It was a kind of trawler; air molecules were gathered into a huge electromagnetic scoop, its profile limned by crackling lightning.

This close, though, the geometric perfection of the world was marred by detail. Pirius made out the shapes of mountains, canyons, even craters. But everything was covered by white dust, every edge softened, every profile blurred. Pirius wondered if the white stuff could be water ice, or even carbon dioxide snow, but the sun's heat was surely too intense for that.

Small settlements studded the land. Around these scattered holdings quarries had been neatly cut into the creamy ground, their floors criss-crossed by the tracks of toiling insect-like vehicles. Tiny craft rose into space from small, orange-bright landing pads, carrying off the fruit of the quarries. Many of the buildings were themselves covered with white dust; evidently some of them were ancient.

Pirius asked the Navy crew what the white dust was. Their reply was blunt: 'Chalk', a word that meant nothing to Pirius. But they called this world 'the carbon mine', as Darc had. It was only later that Pirius learned that this 'carbon mine' had once had a name of its own, an ancient name nothing to do with the purposes to which the planet had been put. Once it had been called Venus.

'So, another stop on your grand tour of Sol system, ensign Pirius?'

'It's not by choice, Commissary.'

'Of course. Well, come along, come along . . .' Nilis led the way along bare-walled corridors, padding over floors rutted by long usage.

Nilis was working in an orbital habitat; the corvette had cautiously docked at the heart of a sprawling tangle of modules, walkways and ducts. The habitat was devoted to pure science, it seemed, to the planet's secondary role as a 'neutrino telescope'. And it was *old*: the modules' protective blankets were cratered by micrometeorite impacts, and blackened by millennia of exposure to the hard light of the sun.

Within, the facility was a warren of corridors and small cylindrical chambers. Over a stale human stink there was a lingering smell of ozone, of welding and failing electrical systems. The station had reasonably modern position-keeping boosters, inertial control, life support and other essential systems, but everywhere you looked maintenance bots toiled to keep the place going. The power nowadays came from a couple of GUT modules, but the habitat still sported an antique set of solar-cell wings, its glossy surfaces long since blackened and peeled away.

Nilis said that as a pure science facility, without obvious military potential, this place had always been starved of resource. 'You get used to it,' he said.

He brought Pirius to an observation module. They peered out at the gleaming face of the planet, and Pirius was dazzled. But he could make out the tracery of quarries and roads on the shining surface, and the steady streams of shuttles flowing through the atmosphere.

Nilis said conspiratorially, 'I rather like it here. But it's not a happy place to work. On Pluto, say, you're truly isolated, out in the middle of nowhere. But *here* Earth is close enough to show as a double planet to the naked eye – close enough to touch. Nobody wants to work in a place like this, when home is so temptingly close.'

Pirius ventured, 'Venus is a carbon mine.'

'Yes. Though nobody calls it Venus any more. Nobody but Luru Parz and her kind.'

Pirius knew enough basic planetology to understand that this planet must have been heavily transformed. It was a rocky world not much smaller than Earth, and this close to its parent sun it should have been cloaked with a thick layer of air, a crushing blanket of carbon dioxide and other compounds baked out of the rocks by the sun's relentless heat.

Well, the atmosphere had once been over two hundred kilometres thick, Nilis said; it had massed about a hundred times as much as Earth's, and had exerted a hundred times as much pressure at the surface. The bottom twenty kilometres or so had been like a sluggish ocean, and the rocks beneath had been so hot they had glowed red. That was the planet humans had first visited – and in those days the clouds were so thick that no human eye had ever seen the ground.

'Venus was infuriating. A world so close to Earth, and so similar in broad numbers, but so *different*. For instance there's actually no more carbon dioxide on Venus than on Earth; but on Earth it is locked into the carbonate rocks, like limestone; here it was all hanging lethally in the air. So what do you do?

'In the early Michael Poole days, there were all sorts of schemes for terraforming Venus, for making it like Earth. Perhaps you could seed that thick air with nanobots or engineered life forms, and use the sun's energy to crack the useless carbon dioxide into useful carbon and oxygen. Fine! But there was so *much* air that you'd have finished up with a planet covered in a hundred-metre layer of graphite – and about sixty atmospheres worth of pure oxygen. Any human foolish enough to step out on the surface would have spontaneously combusted!

'So then there were mega-engineering proposals to blast that annoying blanket of air off the planet altogether, with bombs or even asteroid strikes. Happily somebody had a brighter idea.'

It was realised that carbon was actually a vitally useful element – and that the air of Venus contained the largest deposit of carbon in the inner system, larger than that of all the asteroids combined. It would be criminally wasteful to blast it away. So a new scheme was concocted, the planet seeded with a different sort of engineered organism.

'They drifted through the high clouds,' Nilis said, 'little bugs living in acidic water droplets fed by photosynthesis. And they made themselves shells of carbon dioxide – or rather of carbon dioxide polymers, cee-oh-two molecules stuck together in complex lattices.' The nanotech that enabled these engineered bugs to make their shells was based on the technology of an alien species called the Khorte, long Assimilated. 'It was one of the first applications of alien technology inside Sol system,' Nilis said. 'And it worked. When each little critter died its shell was heavy enough to drift down out of the clouds towards the ground, taking with it a gram or two of fixed carbon dioxide.'

Pirius saw the idea. 'The carbon snowed out.'

'Yes. On the ground, as it compressed under its own weight, it melted and amalgamated, and even more complicated polymers were formed. Those who mine the stuff call it *chalk*; something similar forms at the bottoms of Earth's seas.

'It was a very long-term proposition, one of humanity's first mega-projects. But the cost was modest; you only had to pay for the first generation of engineered bugs. The project has now been going on for twenty thousand years – at least that long; it was founded by the ancients, it's believed, in the days even before the Qax Occupation.'

Once Venus's carbon had been locked up in the convenient form of the chalk, it was easily mined and had a myriad possible uses. But, said Nilis, it was only after the first few thousand years of the project that an unexpectedly useful application of Venus's new crust of carbon dioxide polymers was discovered. 'It turned out that some of the structures formed, in the hot, compressed layers of Venus chalk, had very interesting properties indeed.'

Pirius took a guess. 'You're talking about neutrinos.'

'Yes.'

Neutrinos were exotic subatomic particles. Like ghosts they passed through matter, through Pirius's own body, or even the bulk of a world like Venus, barely noticing that anything was in the way. 'And that makes them rather hard to observe,' said Nilis.

Which was where Venus's chalk came in. It was found that some of the more exotic polymers formed at high temperature and pressure in Venus's gathering chalk layers were good at trapping neutrinos – or, rather, traces of their passage.

Neutrinos took part in nuclear reactions: when atomic nuclei fissioned or fused, releasing floods of energy in the process. Nilis said, 'There are two places in nature where such reactions are commonplace. One was in the first few minutes of the formation of the universe itself – the moments of nucleosynthesis, when primordial baryonic particles, protons and neutrons, combined to form the first complex nuclei. The other is in the centre of the stars, which run on fusion power. So, you see, a neutrino telescope can see into the fusing heart of the sun.'

So Venus was given a new role: as a watchtower.

'The ancients believed a deep monitoring of the sun was important – but not for the sun itself. Stars are pretty simple machines, really, much simpler than bacteria, say, and were thoroughly understood long before the first extrasolar planet was visited. No, it wasn't the sun they were interested in but what lay *within* the sun. *Dark matter*,' Nilis said. 'That's what Michael Poole's generation were watching. Dark matter, in the centre of the sun . . .'

As the sun swept through its orbit around the centre of the Galaxy, it encountered dark matter. Almost as ghost-like as neutrinos, much of it simply passed through the sun's bulk. But some interacted with the dense, hot stuff at the centre of the sun, and, losing energy, was trapped. Nilis said, 'It *orbits*, lumps of dark matter orbiting the sun, even within the fusing heart of the star. Remarkable when you think about it.'

It was this strange inner solar system of dark matter, entirely contained within the bulk of the sun, that the Venus facility had been designed to study. The dark-matter particles would annihilate each other, and in doing so released more neutrinos, to be trapped at Venus and analysed.

'I've glanced at the data streams,' Nilis said. 'You can see structure in there: clumps, aggregates – even what looks like purposeful motion. There are some who speculate there is life in there, life forms of dark matter. Why not, I say?'

Pirius was baffled. 'What harm can a trace of dark matter do?'

'I don't know,' said Nilis honestly. 'The ancients obviously feared it, though. I've seen hints in the Archive of much more ambitious projects than this: engineered humans injected into the dark-matter streams in the heart of the sun, and so on.'

And Luru Parz, Pirius thought, who might herself be a survivor of those ancient times, still watched dark matter at the other extreme of Sol system. Here was another deep secret, another ancient fear.

'Commissary, you aren't interested in what's going on in the sun.'

'No. But I am interested in primordial nucleosynthesis.' That was the other source of neutrinos. He was talking about the Big Bang.

As the universe expanded from its initial singularity, Nilis said, physics evolved rapidly. In the first microsecond space was filled with quagma, a swarming magma of quarks, as if the whole universe was a single huge proton. But the universe expanded and cooled, and by the end of the first second most of the quarks had been locked up into baryonic particles, protons and neutrons. For the next few minutes the universe was a ferocious cauldron of nuclear reactions, as evanescent atomic nuclei formed, almost immediately breaking up again, unstable in the ferocious heat. Neutrinos took part in this shatteringly rapid dance.

But then, as the temperature dropped further, simple nuclei like helium suddenly became stable. The universe froze out. Just three minutes after the singularity this flurry of nucleosynthesis was over, and expanding space was filled with hydrogen and helium. There would be no more baking of nuclei until much later in the life of the universe, when the first stars formed.

'And with no more nucleosynthesis,' said Nilis, 'the primordial neutrinos no longer interacted with matter. To them the universe, at three minutes old, was already just about transparent. Those ancient neutrinos still drench space even today. Now, Venus was designed to watch neutrinos from the sun . . .'

'But a neutrino is a neutrino,' Pirius said.

'Yes. And in those primordial neutrinos can be read a story of the earliest moments of the universe. *And it is a story of life*, ensign.'

'Life?'

'Quagmites.'

It had actually been the analysis of the damage suffered by Pirius Blue's greenship, the *Assimilator's Claw*, that had prompted Nilis to come here to Venus, to start thinking about neutrinos.

'It was I who ordered that your ship be subject to a proper forensic examination,' he said. 'After all it had been in close proximity to the Xeelee – not to mention a magnetar! I believed your ship might carry traces of its adventures from which we might learn more. And so I wanted it to be given more than a cursory glance in an Engineering Guild repair shop.'

What Nilis's scientists had discovered had not, in the event, been about the Xeelee at all, or even the magnetar. It was quagmites.

Nilis said, 'Have you really never wondered what quagmites actually *are*? And how they come to be so attracted to GUT energies?'

'No,' Pirius said honestly. To pilots quagmites were just an odd kind of virus which gave you trouble if you used a GUTdrive anywhere in the Central Star Mass. Since GUTdrives were essentially an obsolete technology, carried as backup in case more effective sublight drive systems failed, nobody ever gave quagmites much thought.

'Yes, yes, I understand your point of view,' Nilis said. 'You aren't even interested in the fact that these things are so obviously *alive*, are you?'

Pirius shrugged. Life in itself wasn't very interesting; as mankind had moved across the face of the Galaxy, life had been discovered everywhere.

'Pirius, when its GUTdrive lit up the *Claw* was peppered by small but dense projectiles.' He clapped his hands, and produced a Virtual image of the greenship. A translucent cutaway, it was laced through by a complex tracery of shining straight lines. 'You were shot up, as if you had flown through a hail of bullets. The particles were bits of quagma, and they left tracks like vapour trails in the matter they passed through. The scars cut through everything – the hull, the equipment, even the bodies of you and your crew. But those greenships are tough little vessels; your systems took a lot of damage, but there was enough redundancy to see you through.'

'We're used to quagmites, I suppose,' Pirius said. 'We design around them.'

'But look,' Nilis said, and he traced the lines with his fingers. 'Look here, and here . . . Can't you see, even in this simple summary image? These lines weren't inflicted at random. *There are patterns here*, pilot! And where there are patterns there is information.

'Every aspect of the lines seems to contain data: their positions in three dimensions, the timing with which they were inflicted, the nature of the projectiles which caused them. There's really a remarkable amount of information, here in these scars – a whole library full, I suspect. Not that I have come anywhere near extracting more than a fraction of it yet. It seems a coarse way to leave a message, like signing one's name with bullets sprayed at a wall. But you can't deny it's effective!

'You must see the significance of this discovery. The quagmites were attracted to your GUTdrive energy, yes; they appear to feed off it. But they weren't attacking you. *They were trying to communicate with you*. And in those two facts, I believe, lies the answer to the mystery of the quagmites' nature.

'The quagmites are alive, Pirius. They are creatures of this universe, just as we are. But the stuff of which they are made isn't so common now. Do you see? Once again we have to confront universal history. For the quagmites – like the Xeelee! – are survivors of a much earlier age . . .'

He spoke of those moments before nucleosynthesis, just a microsecond or so after the singularity, when the universe was a soup of quarks, a quagma. The quagmites had swarmed through a quagma broth, fighting and loving and dying. But the quagma cooled. Their life-sustaining fluid congealed into cold protons and neutrons, and then further into atomic nuclei. They were thinking beings, but there was nothing they could do about the end of their world.

'They found a way to survive the great cosmic transition, the congealing of their life stuff.' His rheumy eyes were vague, as he considered prospects invisible to Pirius. 'I wonder what they see when they look at us. To them we are cold, dead things, made of dead stuff. All they see is the occasional bright spark of our GUTdrives. And when they do, they come to feed, and to talk to us.'

'Not to us,' Pirius said, 'To our ships.'

'Ha!' Nilis slapped his thigh. 'Of course, of course. I have to say this is not entirely an original insight. Quagmites have been studied before. The lessons are still there, I found, but buried deep in our Archives. Sometimes I wonder how much we have forgotten, how little we retain – and the older our culture grows the more wisdom we lose. What a desolating thought!'

Pirius tried to bring him back to the point. 'Commissary, I don't see what this has to do with the Project.'

'Well, nor do I,' Nilis said cheerfully. 'Which is why we have to find out! You see, I deduced from the captured nightfighter that *the Xeelee too* are relics of an earlier cosmic epoch, earlier even than the quagmites. Surely it isn't a coincidence that we find them both swarming around Chandra!' Nilis rubbed his face, smoothing out his jowly flesh, 'Clearly there is a pattern, which we must understand. That is why I have been seeking ways to study the early universe, like this neutrino telescope. And I must continue to study, to gather data, to learn . . . But if any of this is correct, there is the question of *why*.'

'Why what?'

Nilis waved a hand vaguely. 'Why should the universe be so fecund? Why should it be that at every stage it is be filled with life, with burgeoning complexity? It surely didn't *have* to be so.' He leaned closer and spoke conspiratorially. 'The ancients did a lot of thinking about this, you know. You can imagine a universe that would *not* support life, at any stage. Of course in that case nobody would be around to observe it. There were some philosophers who speculated that our universe's fecundity *is no accident*. Perhaps it was designed in, somehow, or at least nurtured. Perhaps the universe itself is an immense artefact, a technological womb of spacetime! But these ideas were suppressed, like so much else, when the Coalition's grip tightened. For a mankind traumatised by near-extinction at the hands of the Qax, the idea that such powers might exist was simply too challenging. So the ancient work was buried – but not destroyed.'

Pirius knew by now that Nilis had a habit of letting his research run away, far beyond any practical use. 'But what do we *do*?'

Nilis grimaced. 'All this is very indirect, based on long chains of deductions. We need to get closer to the target. I would like, somehow, to make some direct observations of Chandra itself. But I fear that to do that I must return to the centre of the Galaxy – or at least a part of me.'

Pirius didn't know what he meant. 'But, Commissary – what am *I* doing here?'

'The staff here will continue to work on my quagmite analysis. I want you to work with them. You have been trained in the behaviour and properties of the quagmites. These habitat-dwellers are a bit theoretical; perhaps you will give their thinking some meat! And,' he said more hesitantly, 'I thought you might appreciate a little quiet time to reflect.'

Pirius nodded. 'Oh. So this is a punishment for Pluto.'

'Not a punishment, not at all. I just want you to, umm, work your way through the issues that caused your breakdown.'

'Breakdown?' Pirius was indignant. 'What are you, a psych officer? . . . Sorry.'

'It's all right,' Nilis said evenly. 'What do *you* think was going through your head, out there on the ice?'

Pirius tried to find the words. 'It was just – out in a place like Arches, you grow up in a Rock. It's your whole world. You train, you fight, you die. And that's it. It's the same for everybody. It doesn't even occur to you that other things are possible. You never question *why* your life is the way it is. The Doctrines are just in the background, as unquestioned as – as—'

'As the Rock under your feet.'

'Yes.'

'And then you come to Earth,' Nilis said gently.

'And then you come to Earth. And suddenly you question everything.'

'The trouble is not the state of the Galaxy, you know, not even Earth.'

'Then what?'

'The trouble is you, Pirius. You're growing, and it isn't comfortable. All your life you have been conditioned, by agencies with an expertise millennia old. Since I plucked you out of Arches, you have been confronted by experiences which contradicted that conditioning. Now, because you're no fool, you're going one step further. You're starting to understand that you *have* been conditioned. Isn't that true?'

'I suppose so,' Pirius said miserably.

'And you will discover the real Pirius – *if* there's anything of him inside that conditioned shell.'

'And then what?'

'And then,' Nilis said, 'you're going to have to decide what it is *you* want to fight for. Of course this is my fault. I never anticipated how hard it would be for you, and Torec. But we are so different, Pirius! I live on Earth – which is after all where humans evolved. Whereas you grew up in a sort of bottle. I respond to the rhythms of the turning Earth, you to a clock. To me the day starts with dawn; to you it is reveille. There are birds in my world, birds and flowers, nothing but rats in yours. Even our language is different: I have my feet on the ground, but my ideas are sometimes blue-sky – but such metaphors mean nothing to you! And you don't have a lover, you have a *squeeze* . . . I never foresaw how unhappy it would make you.'

'Maybe you should have,' Pirius said harshly.

Nilis drew back. 'But I had higher goals. As for Venus, my instructions stand.'

He turned away and peered out at the mined surface of an engineered Venus. 'You know, carbon has always been the basis of human molecular nanotechnology. Defect-free engineered diamond is much stronger and harder than any metal could ever be. Right across the Galaxy our tools, the walls of our homes, the battleships and corvettes of our fleets, even the implants in our bodies, are made of diamond and nanotubes, carbon molecules that once drifted in Venus's thick clouds. And it has been that way for *twenty thousand years*. Like Earth, this single world has exported its very substance to sustain a galactic civilisation. And, like Earth . . .' He let the sentence tail away.

Pirius said, 'Like Earth, it is becoming exhausted.' It must be true, he thought. He could see it just by looking out of the window. The air was still thick, but it must be only a trace of the dense air ocean of former times. 'But Venus was always dead.'

'Actually, no . . .'

In its early years Venus had been warm and wet, not unlike Earth – although, thanks to a peculiar history of collisions during its formation, it spun slowly on its axis. Like Earth, Venus had quickly spawned life forms based on carbon, sulphur, nitrogen, water; and on a world where the 'day' was longer than the year, a complex and unique climate and biota established itself.

Nilis said, 'When the climate failed and the ground turned red hot, survivors found places in the clouds – living inside water droplets, little rods and filaments breeding fast enough for generations to pass before the droplets broke up. Soon the lost ground wasn't even a biochemical memory. They learned to specialise; there was plenty of sulphuric acid floating around up there, so a sulphur-based metabo-

231

lism was the thing to have. And that was what the first human explorers found. It was a whole cloud-borne biota, lacking any multi-celled animals, but in some ways as exotic and complex as anything on Earth or Mars. But Venus's carbon was just too valuable.'

'And the native life?'

'I'm told there is a petri dish or two to be found in the museums.' The shadow-free glare of Venus emptied his face of expression, and Pirius couldn't be sure of the Commissary's opinion of this ancient xenocide.

CHAPTER 25

On Quin Base, a month after Factory Rock, training started again.

At first it was mindless fitness exercises. After that came elementary surface operations: trench work, moving over open ground, the new platoons learning to operate together. Just like old times, Pirius Blue thought.

Things had changed for him, though. Now that Pirius was a veteran, even though he was only a buck private and Army Service Corps at that, he was expected to share his experience with his platoon-full of black-pupilled newbies. So he took the lead in the exercises, and showed them how to dig into the asteroid ground without getting electrostatically charged dirt over their faceplates.

Having some responsibility again felt good, he supposed. But most of all Pirius relished the fitness work, even the meaningless pounding around Marta's famous punishment crater. He ran and ran, until his difficult thoughts dissolved into a fatigue-poison blur.

One night he came back from the surface through the usual route of airlocks and suit stations, and limped his way to his bunk. He was stiff and sore, and wanted nothing but to sleep off the day's work.

But the bunks around him were empty. Even Tili was missing – even Cohl.

Pirius lay down and massaged an aching shoulder. He peered up into the shadows. His new eyes changed the way he saw the world, even a mundane scene like this, if only at the fringes. You saw new colours, to which the cadets gave names like *sharp violet* and *bloody red*. And you made out new details. He could see the hot breath rising from his own mouth, curling knots of turbulence that rose up and splashed languidly on the bunk above him. Pointlessly beautiful.

Where was everybody? Well, what did he care? But curiosity got the better of him. Besides, he felt oddly lonely; after months in this crowded barracks, he was getting addicted to company.

He rolled out of his bunk.

Barefoot, he padded down the barracks' centre aisle. The place was quieter than usual, with hardly anybody about, the general horseplay, fighting, flirting and sex subdued. But he heard a single clear voice, speaking softly and steadily.

He turned a corner and came upon a crowd.

This Burden Must Pass was standing on an upturned locker, hands spread wide, smiling. Before him privates and cadets sat on the floor, or crowded together on bunks, squashed up against each other with the casual intimacy of familiarity. There were perhaps fifty of them here gathered around Burden.

Pirius sat down on the floor at the back, folding his legs under him. The cadets wriggled to make room, but he still ended up with warm bodies pressed against either side. Glancing around, he saw Tili Three and Cohl. Burden noticed him, and Pirius thought he acknowledged him with a wink. But Burden didn't break his smooth flow.

Burden was talking about his religion, the creed of the Friends.

'Entropy,' he said. 'Think of it that way. You start out with a hundred in a company. A hundred move out of some dismal trench. Ten die straight away, another ten are hit and injured. So eighty go on to the next earthwork. And then it's over again, lads, and ten more fall, ten more are wounded . . . On it goes. It's entropy, everything slowly wearing down, lives being rubbed out. It's relentless.' He smacked one fist into another. 'But entropy is everywhere. From the moment we're born to the moment we die we depend for our lives on machines. Entropy works on them too; they wear out. If we just accepted that, the air machines and water machines and food machines would fail, one by one, and we would be dead in a few days. But we don't accept it. Everything wears out. So what? *You fix it.*'

The cadets' smooth young faces, so alike when you saw them all together, were like clusters of little antennae turned towards Burden, metallised eyes shining. Tili's face, still young, was lined by grief. But as Burden talked Pirius saw those lines fading, her eyes clearing. She even smiled at Burden's poor jokes. Burden might be talking a lot of garbage, but it was clearly comforting garbage, comforting in a way that no words of Pirius could have been. He wondered, though, how Burden was feeling inside, as he absorbed the pain of these damaged children.

And it was certainly non-Doctrinal.

Burden spoke on. '*We* won't last much longer. None of us will. But our children will survive, and our children's children, an unending chain of blood and strength that will go on for ever, go on to the end of time. And at the end, at timelike infinity, where all the world lines of all the particles and all the stars in the whole universe, all the people who ever lived, when all of it comes together, our descendants will meet – no, they will *become* – the Ultimate Observer. And the final observation will be made, the final thoughts shaped in the ultimate mind. And everything will be cleansed.' He waved a hand. 'All of this, all our suffering and grief, will pass – for *it will never have happened.* The universe is just another balky machine. Any one of you could fix a busted air cleanser or biopack. Some day, we'll fix the universe itself!'

Tili Three spoke up. 'But Michael Poole didn't wait for timelike infinity.'

'No.' Burden smiled. 'Michael Poole went into the future. He sacrificed himself to save his children, *our* children. He is with the Ultimate Observer – is, was, always will be . . .'

The listeners asked more soft-ball questions. But Cohl asked a tougher one. 'How do you *know*? Are we supposed to accept this on faith?'

Burden wasn't perturbed. 'Of course not. Past and future aren't fixed; history can be changed – in fact it changes all the time. You know that, Cohl. *You* lived through an action that got deleted from the timeline. So you know that contingency is real. It's not much of a leap of faith to imagine that some day somebody will make a purposeful change – an intelligent change – and wipe away all our tears.'

Cohl's expression was complex. She kept up her mask of scepticism. But *she wanted to believe,* Pirius realised with a shock; even Cohl, once an ultra-orthodox Druzite. She might have her suspicions about the man, but she was listening to his words and seemed to want to accept Burden's strange and comforting faith.

A small Virtual drifted before Pirius's eyes: it was Captain Marta's face. 'Come to my office, private. We need to talk.'

With a mixture of regret and relief, Pirius slipped away from the little congregation. Nobody seemed to notice.

Marta's office was unglamorous. It was just a partitioned-off corner of the barracks, the furniture no more than a bunk and a table where data desks were untidily heaped. The only luxury seemed to be a coffee machine. But in one corner there was a kind of cubicle, like a shower, with walls pocked with interface sockets. Pirius wondered if this equipment had something to do with Marta's complex injuries.

Marta waved him to a chair. Pirius could hear the whirr of motors as she sat down opposite him. 'Sorry to drag you off from Quero's lecture.' She eyed him. 'And you can lower those eyebrows, private. Of course we know about Burden and his proselytising.'

'Burden's talk comforts them,' he said.

'Of course it does. That's why it's so successful in the first place, I suppose. And why we turn a blind eye.' She sipped her coffee, and Pirius saw that the metallic surface of her face extended through her lips to the roof of her mouth. 'We allow them to stay in their cadre groups, or even their families if we have to, because it gives them something to fight for. And Burden's waffle about the end of time comforts them when they fall. The ideologues at the centre disapprove, of course, but out here we have a war to wage.'

Pirius wondered how to put his own doubts about Burden into words – or even if he should. 'I don't get Burden,' he admitted. 'He is his own man. In combat he fights as hard as anybody—'

'Harder than most,' said Marta laconically.

'And he's not afraid of being ostracised for his faith. But sometimes he seems – weak.'

Marta eyed him. 'Burden has depths. And a past which he's apparently not prepared to share with you. But, you know what? It doesn't bother me. If Burden took a hit tomorrow, all his emotional complexity would disappear with him. In the meantime, he can think what he likes, *feel* what he likes, as long as he does such an effective job. As long as our soldiers fight, who cares what goes on in their heads?'

Pirius was silent.

'You're judging me, private,' Marta said more heavily.

'I'm having trouble with your contempt for us. Sir.'

She nodded, apparently not offended. 'Not contempt. But I have to manage you from birth to death, and send you into war. Not contempt, no. Distance, I suppose. This is the nature of command.'

'If you're so tolerant about the Friends, why did you give Tuta such a hard time when we got here?'

'Tuta? . . . Oh. Enduring Hope. That had nothing to do with religion. Surely you see that. I was trying to knock a cadet into shape. That's my job,' she said neutrally. 'So what do you think about the Factory Rock action now?'

'It was a screw-up,' he said vehemently.

'You think so?'

'Of course it was. The barrage was mistimed and off-target. Our line was broken before we even left the trench. Our flanks were exposed and we walked into fire. We didn't have a chance.'

'I can see you're a perfectionist, Pirius,' she said dryly. 'There are always mistakes in war. But the important thing is that *we won*, despite the mistakes. We took back Factory Rock. You have to have the right perspective.'

'Perspective? Sir, I was the only survivor, of two platoons, to reach that monopole factory.'

'It doesn't matter how many fall as long as one gets through. I told you that in the briefing. We plan for wastage. The losses were a little high this time, perhaps, but most of those who fell were wet behind the ears. The Coalition hadn't invested much in them. They were *cheap*. Of course, Pirius, nobody would have got through, or still less got back, if not for the way you took the initiative.'

'I was just trying to stay alive.'

'Believe me, even that's beyond the capabilities of most of your comrades out there.'

'Sir—'

'Tell me about the Tilis. How does what happened to them make you feel?'

He struggled to find the right words. 'I was close to my crews in the greenships. You have to be if you're to work together. But this time—'

'This time you weren't flying around in the antiseptic comfort of a greenship; you were down in the dirt with the blood and the death.'

'I saw her sisters die, and I've seen Tili Three grieve. And it's not worth it. Even if we win the Galaxy.'

'The cost of a single life is too high.' She seemed to suppress a sigh. 'And so you don't want to hear me talk about the cost of a private's training. For you, right now, it isn't about economics, is it, Pirius? Being one in a trillion doesn't reduce the significance of that one person you know. War doesn't scale that way.'

He said hesitantly, 'So you feel like this?'

'No. But I know how *you* feel.' She gazed directly at him. 'This is a stage you have to go through, private.'

He said, 'I don't want to stop feeling like this, sir.'

'Tough. If you're smart enough for responsibility, you're smart enough to understand the situation we're all in, and the choices we have to make.'

He thought that through. 'Responsibility? Sir, are you offering me some kind of command?'

'You proved yourself out on that Rock, private. You may be a wetback reject, and your service record is a piece of shit. You'll always be Service Corps. But you could make corporal.'

'I don't want it,' he said immediately.

'What you want has very little to do with it. Anyhow it's academic.'

He couldn't follow her. 'It is?'

'Somebody has been asking for you. I believe you've met Commissary Nilis?'

CHAPTER 26

One minute left. Torec wriggled in her seat, trying to find a comfortable position among the equipment boxes that had been bolted into this greenship's little cabin.

Commander Darc had made it clear he didn't approve of countdowns. Torec's cockpit, and the displays of the test controllers on Enceladus, were full of clocks, and you could follow the timings; there was no need for melodrama, said Darc. But Torec had always had an instinct for the flow of time, and she couldn't help the voice in her head calling out each second with uncanny precision: *Fifty-five, fifty-four, fifty-three . . .*

It was the first full-scale, all-up test flight of a ship modified with Project Prime Radiant's new technologies. And with every second her tension wound up further.

She looked out of the blister, directly ahead of the ship, where the misty bulk of Saturn drifted. Enceladus was a pale crescent to her starboard side. The space around her was cluttered with sparks, the observation drones and manned ships assigned to monitor this latest test. It was strange to think that among the watching Navy crews, staff officers and academics was a Silver Ghost. More ominously, in there somewhere were rescue craft waiting to haul her and her crew out of a wreck.

And directly ahead of her, a silhouette against the face of Saturn, was a night-dark delta wing. It was the Xeelee nightfighter, captured by Pirius Blue and hauled here to the heart of Sol system itself.

The nightfighter drifted, brooding, dark on dark. It made everybody nervous. The plan was that the Xeelee would briefly be returned to autonomous functioning; the fly was Torec's sparring partner in this test flight. The nightfighter was disarmed, of course, and its workings were riddled with cut-outs and dead man's switches. Even so that fly was surrounded by a shell of Navy ships. But using the Xeelee was the only way to simulate something like genuine battle conditions.

But whatever the Xeelee did wouldn't matter if Torec failed.

If all went well, ships like this might one day sail triumphantly against the Prime Radiant itself. But for now this long-suffering greenship was nothing but a mess.

The greenship was the standard design, with the stout central body and the three arms supporting its crew blisters. It was an intrinsically graceful configuration, stabilised centuries ago and scrupulously maintained ever since by the Guild of Engineers, the most powerful of the Coalition's technical agencies. But on this ship those clean lines had been spoiled by extra modules, attached so hastily they hadn't even been painted. It was all prototype equipment, of course. The CTC gear had come down in size an awful lot since the first proof-of-concept rigs on the Moon, but the CTC module was still a great egg-shaped pod that made the greenship look as if it was about to pup. The hull even showed scarring where the CTC had exploded in the middle of a static trial, two of its internal FTL drones losing their way and colliding.

Even her Virtual instruments had been cluttered up with additional displays. The whole thing was crudely programmed and liable to instability. And then there were the extra boxes, like a beefed-up inertial generator, and hard-wired units designed to run the gravastar shield itself. All this gear had been crammed into a blister which barely had room for the pilot who had to occupy it. It was *not* reassuring.

Forty-one, forty . . .

At least her crew, sealed in their cabins, looked calm enough. They were both Navy veterans, both nearly twice her age. Emet, the navigator, was a tall, haughty man whose service had been confined to Sol system itself. But the engineer, Brea, was more approachable. She had seen action in the clear-out of a cluster of Coalescent warrens: human worlds gone bad, relics of the ancient Second Expansion in one of the Galaxy's halo clusters.

Both Brea and Emet had been suspicious of Torec, this kid put in command of them. But the three of them worked well together as a crew, and as they had come through the stop-start misadventures, hold-ups and downright disasters of the testing programme they had, Torec thought, learned mutual respect. Brea had actually asked Torec to share her bunk in their Enceladus dorm the night before. Torec preferred hetero, and she missed Pirius. But she had accepted out of politeness.

Ten. Nine . . .

She snapped her full attention to her instruments. For once every indicator was green, the ancient colour of readiness. She could hear a chattering in her communicator loops, a thousand voices talking. As she had been trained, she took deep breaths and let the adrenalin kick lock her into full awareness of where she was, who she was, and what she was about to do.

Five. Four. A last glance at her crew, an acknowledging wave from Brea. The sublight drive was warming up, and despite her beefed-up inertial protection she could feel the mighty energies of the gravastar shield generators gathering, like a slow, deep growl.

One. The ship jolted forward, its sublight drive kicking in—

She called, 'Go, go!'

Nearby ships blurred, turning to streaks of light that exploded past her view and away. Directly ahead, Saturn itself loomed, becoming larger every second. And at the centre of her view, a spider in the heart of its web, the Xeelee waited for her.

'Sublight nominal,' yelled Emet.

Maybe, Torec thought, but she could feel how sluggish the laden ship was, how poor its balance had become.

'Grav coming on line,' engineer Brea reported, 'in ten, nine . . .'

Red lights flared around the periphery of her vision – too much information to absorb in detail – bad news she didn't want to know.

'Three, two,' Brea called. 'Go for grav?'

She ignored the alarms. 'Do it.'

'*Zero.*'

The sublight drive cut out – but the ship's acceleration increased, and Saturn blurred and streaked, as if her view of it was being stirred by a spoon. The grav shield was working. The muddled vision ahead was a mark of the shield's operation; the passage of light itself was being distorted by the spacetime wave gathering before her. It was a wonderful, remarkable thought: a new universe really was opening up ahead of her, a universe projected from the clumsy pods and modules bolted to her ship, and the expansion of that universe was drawing in the ship itself.

And now a harsher light gathered, as if burning through mist. It quickly formed a searing disc two, three, four times the apparent size of Saturn. This was the shock front, the place where a spacetime wave was breaking. The light came from the infall of matter to that front, mass-energy lost in an instant.

The chattering voices cut off. She could only hear her crew, and her own breath rasping in her throat.

'Shock formed!' Brea yelled. Emet whooped.

At this moment Torec was alone with her crew in a spacetime bubble snipped out of the cosmos – the three of them, alone in a universe they had made. But the day wasn't won yet.

'Is it stable?' No reply. 'Engineer, *is it stable*?'

'Negative,' Brea said sadly.

There was a last moment of calm.

Then the disc swelled, rarefied, became a mesh of blue-white threads – and burst. The shock wave slammed into the plummeting greenship. It was a searing pulse of gravitational energy condensing into high-energy radiation and sleeting particles. The ship was smashed in an instant.

Torec's blister hurled itself away. Tumbling, she saw the hull crushed like a toy, its bolted-on modules rupturing and drifting free. The three arms were reduced to truncated stumps. She could see nothing of her crew. The nightfighter glided smoothly over to the site of the wreckage, and, unchallenged, fired a token pink-grey beam into the dissipating cloud – a harmless marker, but the symbolism was not lost on Torec.

Then her pod flooded with foam that froze her limbs to immobility, and she was trapped in darkness.

The sick bays on Enceladus were like Navy sick bays everywhere. They did their job, but they were bare and cold, the staff unsmiling: it was a place where you got repaired, not a place where you could expect to be comfortable. Torec was keen to get out of here, but it was going to take another day before the bones of her broken arm knit well enough.

Navigator Emet had already gone. He had come out of the blow-up with barely a scratch, but as soon as he had been discharged he had requested a transfer to another assignment.

Brea hadn't come out of the smash at all.

After six hours, Darc and Nilis came to visit her.

Pirius was still on Venus. Nilis said he had told Pirius what had happened.

A Virtual replay of the last moments of the run cycled in the air over Torec's bed, over and over. Torec was forced to watch her own blister, the interior milky with foam, shoot out of the expanding debris cloud that used to be a greenship.

Darc growled, 'Look at that Xeelee. You know, Commissary, I'm prepared to believe it *is* alive. You can see the contempt.'

Nilis was pacing, barefoot. He was over-stressed, and extremely distressed by what had happened. 'Oh, my eyes, my eyes,' he kept saying.

Torec suppressed a sigh. 'Sir, Brea died doing her duty.'

'But if not for me she wouldn't have been put in harm's way in the first place.'

Darc said thunderously, 'Commissary, with respect, that's maudlin nonsense. Brea was a soldier. *Soldiers die*, sir, by putting themselves in harm's way, as you call it. It's a question of statistics; that's how you have to look at it.'

Nilis turned on him, eyes rimmed red, clearly furious. 'And is that supposed to comfort me?'

Darc's expression didn't change. 'If you want comfort, know that she died doing her duty.'

Nilis snorted and resumed his pacing. 'Well, if we're not allowed to complete the test programme, she will have died for nothing.'

Darc laughed. 'You aren't going to trap me that way, Commissary, I'm not convinced that throwing away more time and money, and more lives, on this programme is justified. I've seen no sign that you're coming close to solving these instability problems with the grav shield.'

Torec knew the situation was delicate. Darc's power was all

negative. He couldn't approve the continuation of the test programme off his own bat – but he could get it shut down. And she was scared that after a failure that embarrassed him as much as anybody else, he was ready to use that power. She said brightly, 'We still have another ship. It's already being prepared.'

'That means nothing,' Darc said. 'Ensign, engineers work on engines unless they're stopped by force; you know that. It doesn't mean I'll be approving another run.'

Nilis glared. 'For you to shut us down now, after just one run, would be criminally irresponsible, Commander!'

Darc was very still, sitting in his chair, not moving a muscle. But Torec could hear the menace in his voice. 'I know you're under stress. But I won't have you say that about me. I've been under pressure to terminate this programme since the first poor results came in. In fact, Commissary, I've been championing you, keeping you alive.'

Nilis wasn't intimidated. 'Oh, have you? Or are you looking out for yourself, Commander? Seeking whatever advantage you can gain from the project, while always keeping your backside covered, in the grand Navy tradition!'

Torec saw Darc's hands close on the arms of his chair, his knuckles whiten.

To her relief, before they came to blows, there was a soft chime and a small Virtual window opened up before her. It revealed a shining sphere. She gaped.

'I have a visitor,' she said.

When Darc saw the Ghost's image, he snarled, 'Send it away. I won't have that monstrosity in a naval facility.'

Enough, Torec thought. 'It's my visitor,' she said. 'Not *yours*, sir, with respect.'

Darc shot her a glance, but he knew she was right; by ancient Navy tradition sick-bay patients had a few temporary privileges. But he waved a hand at the Virtual of the test run, dispersing it – as if, Torec thought, the Silver Ghosts assigned to the project hadn't seen the whole thing live and first-hand anyhow.

The Ghost's bulk was barely able to pass through the door. It hovered beside Torec's bed, massive, drifting slightly, the glaring lamps of the room casting highlights from its hide.

She shivered, as if the Ghost's immense mass was sucking the warmth out of the air. She pulled her med-cloak a little higher, and the semi-sentient wrap snuggled more tightly into place. A Silver Ghost, a bedside visitor in a Navy hospital, come to see *her* . . .

Nilis's characteristic curiosity cut in. He stood before the Ghost, hands on hips, rheumy eyes alive with interest. 'So,' said Nilis. He held out a liver-spotted hand, as if to stroke the Ghost's surface; but he thought better of it and pulled back, curling his fingers. 'Which one are you?'

'I am the one you call the Ambassador to the Heat Sink.' The Ghost's chill contralto voice seemed heavily artificial in this small sick-bay room. 'We met on Pluto.'

'Of course we did. I should have guessed it was you. But how would I know if you were lying, if you're a different Ghost entirely? Hah!'

The Ghost didn't respond. Darc, still as a statue, was almost as unreadable.

Nilis went on, 'And what are you doing here?'

'It's come to see *me*, Commissary,' Torec said gently.

Nilis made a mock bow.

Torec plucked up her courage and faced the Ghost. She could see herself in its hide, a distorted image of a head and shoulders, clutching her med-blanket. 'Maybe that's what's so scary about you,' she said aloud.

The Ghost said, 'I do not understand.'

'That every time I look at a Ghost, I see myself.'

The Ghost rolled slowly, slight imperfections on its surface marking its movements. 'Identity is a complex concept which does not translate well across cultures.'

Torec said, 'Why have you come to see me, Sink Ambassador?'

'Because your project is failing,' it said.

Nilis nodded. 'Yes, yes. We are battling the instability of your gravastar shield, it can't be denied.'

Darc snorted. 'And it's a fundamental flaw. The spherically symmetric solution of the equations – a complete gravastar, a shell surrounding a ball-shaped pocket universe – would be stable. Your half-and-half solution, a spherical cap preceding a pocket universe that matches to ours asymptotically, is analytically complete but is *not* stable.' He gave a thin-lipped grin. 'Oh, don't look so shocked, Commissary. Even Navy grunts know a little math. The problem is simple: instability. You have your pilot balancing a ten-metre pole on the palm of her hand; she can run as fast as she likes, but sooner or later she will fall.'

The Ghost said, 'But we have a solution.'

Nilis and Darc both turned to face the Ghost, startled.

Torec smiled. 'So that's why you've come. You weren't concerned about my health at all.'

The Ghost seemed to think that over. 'No offence.'

Nilis gaped. 'Did a Silver Ghost just make a *joke*?'

Darc said sternly, 'You say you have a solution. Describe it.'

The Ambassador rolled, and Virtual images scrolled in the air. Torec recognised a map of the phase space of a system. It was a schematic diagram of the possible states of the gravastar shield. It looked like a slice of a rolling landscape, with valleys, peaks and plains, and it was marked with contours that showed regions of chaos and stability, attractors and poles.

'The trick,' said the Ghost, 'is to use the instability, not to fight it. You are trying to emulate the stability of the strongest attractor, which is the spherically-symmetric solution here.' A point on the map winked red. 'So you allow the shield to form at low velocities, or even when the projector is stationary. You find an equilibrium, but it is not stable. Then when you try to fly, the smallest instability disrupts the solution. Your running child trips on a pebble, Commander, and the pole is dropped.'

Nilis laughed out loud. 'You have spent a long time studying human idioms.'

'We have little else to do,' the Ghost said.

'So,' Darc growled, 'what do you suggest instead?'

'It would be better to operate the projector when it is being carried at close to lightspeed.'

Nilis frowned. He walked up to the image and poked his finger into its shining innards. 'But that would bring us up to this region.' It was the complex border between order and chaos. 'The shield would be no more than metastable.'

'But solutions in this part of the phase space, on the edge of chaos, would be responsive to small adjustments.'

'Ah.' Nilis nodded. 'Which would make the shield more manageable, because it would respond more sensitively; we could control out the instabilities before a catastrophic disruption.'

Darc was visibly unhappy. '*How* rapidly would we have to react?' He brought up a Virtual of his own, ran some quick calculations. 'There,' he said in triumph. 'Look at that! Your metastable shield will flap like a sheet in a breeze. There's no way we could react quickly enough to respond to it.'

'Of course you could,' the Ambassador said. 'You have arbitrarily high processing speeds available on your ship. Your CTC-processor technology—'

Darc shot to his feet and stalked up to the Ghost, fists clenched. 'Is that the game? How do you even *know* about that? If you think I am going to let you anywhere *near* the CTC system—'

Nilis said, 'Commander, please. We're simply discussing possibilities.'

Darc remained standing, glaring at the Ghost. 'Why are you doing this? Humans destroyed your kind. Why would you help your conquerors?'

'Curiosity,' the Ghost said.

'And nothing else?' Darc asked heavily.

'Nothing. You recreated us at a whim. You could destroy us as easily. We have no hope.'

Darc's eyes narrowed with suspicion, but he stayed silent.

Nilis was still thinking over the idea. 'This would actually simplify the overall design, of course . . . You don't seem happy, ensign.'

Torec said, 'I'm a pilot, sir. No pilot likes giving up control.'

'Hmm. I can sympathise with that. And of course this sort of active control system isn't without risks. You would go into battle behind an intrinsically unstable system. If the CTC failed, you would die immediately.'

'But we all die one day, Commissary.'

He embarrassed her by allowing his eyes to fill up. 'Lethe, this laconic courage – I'm sorry! I can't get used to it.'

The Ghost said, 'You have one more test ship.'

'One more chance,' Nilis said. 'The modifications would be straightforward.' He stared at Darc.

Darc held his stubborn stance for a moment, then seemed to give in. 'All right. Lethe take this whole plagued project! But what are we to do for a crew?'

Torec sat up straight. 'I'm willing to give it another go, sir.'

Nilis said, 'I'd expect nothing less. But we must make this crucial trial work. I would suggest that the ensign's ideal crewmates are in this room.'

Darc stared at him, then at the Ghost, which rolled silently. 'You have got to be joking.'

But he wasn't.

CHAPTER 27

'The Central Star Mass,' Nilis said. 'Isn't that what you call it, Pirius Blue? *The Mass* – what a mundane name for a place where you can find ten million stars in a space a few light years across – a volume in which, at the Galactic vicinity of Sol, you would on average find *one*. How marvellous, that we feeble humans should have come so far!'

He had called Pirius Blue to the small quarters he had been allocated in Quin's Officer Country. His face shining with enthusiasm, his long robe as scuffed and threadbare as ever, he bumbled around the room, setting out his data desks on the low table. The Commissary was just as Pirius remembered from the trial, though he seemed older, rather more careworn. But Nilis hadn't been prepared for Pirius's new eyes; at first sight he had recoiled, his shock comical.

This wasn't the real Commissary, of course. Nilis was too busy with his mysterious projects in Sol system to come all the way to the centre again in person. This was only a Virtual.

Nilis was still struggling to get political support for his schemes. He said he had forced his way into Quin Base on a pretext. He had managed to persuade his bosses at the Commission for Historical Truth that it was time somebody took a fresh look at the deviant religions sprouting here in the Core. But quizzing This Burden Must Pass about the nature of the Ultimate Observer was not Nilis's true goal.

'Let me get this straight,' Pirius said. 'Sir,' he added.

Nilis waved that away. 'Please, please. We know each other too well for formality!'

But he was talking about a different Pirius, Blue thought, indeed a different Nilis. 'You want to send a scouting mission inside the Front – into the Cavity. You want to fly to Chandra itself.'

'Or as close as we can get to it, yes.'

Nilis talked rapidly about the project he was devising out at Sol's lonely orbit – aided, in part, by Pirius's own younger self, his FTL twin Pirius Red. Pirius Blue had heard nothing of this before, and he was stunned by Project Prime Radiant's scope and ambition.

'But if we are to strike successfully we have to know more about Chandra itself,' Nilis said. 'Even after three thousand years of war here at the Galaxy's heart, we still know woefully little.'

And that, he said, was where Pirius Blue came in.

'You want me to fly the mission.'

'To scope it out, define, it, choose a crew . . . Yes! You will be the commander, Pirius Blue. It will be an historic flight.'

'Historic? Suicidal.'

Nilis said gravely, 'Suicidal? Not necessarily. There are many myths about this war, Pirius Blue. We are locked into ways of thinking, ways of fighting. After three thousand years of stasis we have talked ourselves into believing that taking the war to the Xeelee is reckless, even suicidal, as you say. But we're only talking about a scouting mission! And how do you *know* it would be suicidal? Do you know how long it is since a mission of this type was actually studied? I've looked high and low and I can't find one – a long time indeed! – even though the information is of such obvious value. But everybody *knows* it's impossible. And of course, I am reluctantly coming to see, there are plenty in high places with a vested interest in the war *not* being concluded . . .'

'Sir?'

'Never mind. Anyhow as commander it would be your duty to make the mission survivable, wouldn't it?'

Pirius was full of doubt. Everything Nilis said sounded reasonable – and exciting. But it also conflicted with his training, everything he had been brought up to believe.

Nilis said, a little exasperated, 'Look – I would not *order* you to do this. Yes, there are obvious dangers; yes, you might not survive – and, yes, I am asking you to have faith in me, in a fat old fool from Earth. But the mission is, quite simply, vitally necessary. *We must know more.*' He watched Pirius's face with a kind of wistful longing. 'Oh, Pirius, this is such a strange encounter. I feel I know you so well! Look at you now, the way you hold your head when you listen to me, your seriousness, your focus on your duty, even the play of the light in your eyes. You're so familiar. And yet it's Pirius Red I've come to know, and *you* don't know me at all, save for your brief encounter with a bumbling old fool at your hearing! It's so strange, so strange. Sometimes I think that by hurling ourselves around the Galaxy faster than the speed of light we are pushing our humanity too far.'

Pirius suddenly saw a new element in his relationship with the Commissary – or at least his FTL twin's. This old man was *fond* of him, Pirius thought with a queasy horror. His unwelcome twin, Pirius Red, had allowed this ridiculous old man to form some kind of sentimental bond with him. Surely it wasn't sexual. But he knew Nilis had a 'family background'. Perhaps it was as a father might feel for a son, an uncle for a nephew, or some similarly unhealthy atavistic tie. What a mess, he thought.

Nilis's Virtual was of the highest quality. In the jargon, it was an avatar.

The avatar's job was to live out this chapter of Nilis's life on the original's behalf as fully as was possible. The avatar was a fully sentient copy of the real Nilis, with identical memories up to the moment when this copy had first been generated. Here in Quin Base Virtual Nilis couldn't touch anything, of course; those data desks on the table were as fake as he was. But while here, for authenticity of experience, he would have to live according to human routines. He would eat his Virtual food, sleep, even eliminate his unreal waste. He could even smell, he said, and he declared that Quin Base stank of something called 'boiled cabbage'. And when his visit was done, his records would be sent back to Earth, where they would be integrated into Nilis's own memory.

Nilis had wanted to take home as rich an experience as he could, the better to shape his subsequent decision-making. But he would always have the odd feeling that he had lived out these ten days twice, once in his garden on Earth, and once here at the Galaxy's crowded heart.

Pirius tried to concentrate on the mission. He could see its value. 'But – why me? I haven't even flown since the magnetar.'

'Because I know you.' His big watery eyes were still fixed on Pirius. 'Because we've already proven we can work well together.'

'You're still talking about my twin.'

'But your twin *is* you – he has all your talent, all your potential – save only that in *you* that potential has begun to be realised. And besides,' he said with disarming honesty, 'how many front-line pilots do I actually know? Oh, come, Pirius! You know, in your shoes *I* would be galvanised by curiosity. We may be skirting a deep scientific mystery here, Pirius, something that could tell us a great deal about the nature of our universe, and our place in it.'

Pirius could hardly deny that. But when he thought about leaving here, about leaving Tili Three and Burden and the others, he felt deeply uneasy. He already felt guilty at having survived on Factory Rock where so many had fallen; how could he justify walking out on them now?

Nilis leaned forward, made to touch Pirius's shoulder, remembered it was impossible. 'Pirius, you're hesitating, and I don't know why. You're wasted here!' he said. 'All these drone kids, their endless digging, digging. You're meant for better things, pilot.'

Pirius stood up. 'And every one of those *drone kids*,' he said, 'is better than you, Commissary.' Nilis said nothing more, and Pirius left the room.

Pirius Blue talked it over with Cohl.

'The whole thing's insane,' he said. In three thousand years, there had of course been many scouting missions beyond the Front and into the Cavity, deep into the nest. That complex place, crowded with stellar marvels as well as the greatest concentration of Xeelee fire-power in the Galaxy, was known to every pilot as a death trap. 'We'd be throwing our lives away.'

'We . . . ?'

He sighed. 'If I have to do this, I'd want you with me. But it's academic, because nobody's going anywhere.'

'Because it's insane?'

'Correct.'

'Well,' she said, 'not necessarily.' She was lying on her bunk, her hands locked behind her head; she seemed undisturbed by the usual barracks clamour around her. In fact she had something of Nilis's remoteness. But then, Pirius thought with loyal exasperation, Cohl was a navigator, and most navigators were halfway to double domes anyhow.

'What do you mean?'

'Maybe it could be done. There's a lot of junk in there, you know, in the Cavity. Astrophysical junk. Plenty of places to hide.' She rolled over. They had no data desks here, no fancy Virtual-generation facilities, and so she started sketching with a wet finger in the dirt on the floor. 'Suppose you went in this way . . .'

The Cavity was a rough sphere some fifteen light years across at the centre of the Mass, bounded by the great static shock of the Front. It was called a 'Cavity' because it was blown clear of hot gas and dust by Chandra and the other objects at the very centre. But it was far from empty, in fact crowded with exotic objects. As well as a million glowering stars, there was the Baby Spiral, three dazzling lanes of infalling gas and dust. And the Baby, like everything else in the Cavity, was centred on the Prime Radiant itself: Chandra, the super-massive black hole, utterly immovable, the pivot around which the immense machinery of the inner Galaxy turned.

Cohl said: 'There are lots of ways in. You could track one of Baby's arms, for instance. Even so you'd have to take some kind of cover.'

'Cover?'

'Other ships. Rocks, even.' She glanced at him. 'Not everybody is going to get through; you have to take enough companions with you to make sure that *somebody* makes it. It's a question of statistics, Pirius.' She rubbed her chin. 'Of course the navigation would be tricky. You're talking about finding your way through all that astrophysics *and* keeping a small flotilla together . . .'

He saw she was losing herself in the technicality of planning such an ambitious jaunt. But technicalities were not uppermost in his own mind.

After a while she noticed his silence. 'You're not happy about this, are you?'

'Am I supposed to be?'

She said, 'It won't make any difference, you know. To *them*. Whatever we do.'

'To who?'

'To the dead ones.'

Pirius looked at her. 'I thought it was only me who had thoughts like that.'

'You ought to talk about it more. You'll just have to make up your own mind about the mission, Pirius. But I'll follow you, whatever you decide.'

He was moved. 'Thank you.'

She shrugged. 'What's to thank? Without you the Xeelee would have fried me already – *twice*. And as for the guilt, maybe you should go talk to This Burden Must Pass. He's always full of philosophical crap, if that's what you need.'

That made him laugh, but it seemed like a good idea. But when he went to find Burden, Nilis had got there before him.

Virtual Nilis, reluctantly fulfilling the nominal purpose for his projection here at Quin, was interviewing Burden in his small office.

Pirius wasn't the only visitor. Perhaps a dozen cadets and privates had gathered outside the office's partition walls. They sat on bunks, or storage boxes, or just on the floor, and they stared into the room with steady longing.

Nilis seemed relieved to close the door on them. 'They're coming in relays,' he whispered, shocked.

'That's military training for you,' Burden said dryly. He was sitting at ease in one of the office's small upright chairs. Unlike the Commissary he seemed quite relaxed.

Nilis whispered, 'I don't know what they want.'

Pirius grunted. 'That's obvious. They're here because they think you're going to take Burden away.'

Nilis, bustling clumsily around the room, flapped his hands. 'I'm here to analyse, not to condemn. Even Commissaries are pragmatic, you know; if this quasi-faith helps the youngsters out there keep to their duties we're quite willing to turn a blind eye. But we do have to be sure things don't go *too* far. Of course, by showing such devotion to their, ah, spiritual leader, those cadets are actually making it *more* likely, not less, that sanctions will have to be applied.'

Burden said, 'Commissary, maybe you should go out there and talk to them about it. They're the ones who are affected by my "sermonising", after all.'

'Oh, I don't think that would be appropriate – no, no, not at all.'

Pirius thought that was an excuse. How could the Commissary possibly do a proper analysis of Burden's faith if he didn't talk to those actually affected? Nilis seemed afraid, he thought: afraid of Quin, or of the people in it, which was why he clung to this little room.

Pirius sat down on the room's only other chair. Nilis, with nowhere to sit, flapped and fluffed a little more; then, with a sigh, he snapped his fingers to conjure up a Virtual couch. 'Not really supposed to be doing magic tricks, you know,' he said apologetically. 'Against the rules of an avatar!'

Pirius asked, 'So, Commissary, has he converted you to a belief in the Ultimate Observer?'

'How comforting it would be if he had,' said Nilis, a little wistfully. 'But I know too much! Religions have long been a theoretical interest of mine, which is how I was able to wangle this assignment – and intellectually is the only way I can respond, you see.

'That's not to say there isn't some merit in this new faith. Consider the Friends' beliefs. A Friend worships her descendants, who she believes will far surpass her in power and glory. That's not such an irrational belief, and guides behaviour in an unselfish way, as any worthwhile religion should. The old legend of Michael Poole has entered the mix too. Like some earlier messiahs, Poole is supposed to have given his life for the future of mankind. Of course that's an example always to be admired. Quero's faith is crude and somewhat shapeless, but it does have some moral weight. And it is interesting, academically, for its novel setting . . .'

Most human religions, said Nilis, had originated on Earth. Once carried to the stars, they had mutated, adapted, split and merged, but they had generally retained the same core elements.

'A religion born on Earth will have archetypes derived from planetary living – where the sun must rise and set, where seasons come and go, where living things die but are renewed, without the intervention of humans but dependent on the cycles of the world. So you find a worship of the sun, and of water, often sublimated into blood; you find a fascination with the figures of mother and child, and with the seed which, once planted in the ground, endures the winter and lives again. Many religions feature messiahs who defeat death itself, who die but are born again: the ultimate sublimation of the seed.

'But *here*,' he said, 'you have a religion which has emerged, quite spontaneously, among a spacegoing people. So new archetypes must be found. Entropy, for instance: to survive in an artificial biosphere one must labour constantly against decay. You can't rely on the world to fix itself, you see; there are no renewing seasonal cycles here.

'And then there is contingency. Back on Earth, FTL foreknowledge is understood – it is an essential strategic tool – but it doesn't affect *people*, which made the arrival of your FTL twin, Pirius, something of a nine-day wonder. Out here, though, everyone knows that the past is as uncertain as the future, because you *see* the future change all the time, as those ships come limping home from battles that haven't happened yet. It happened to you, Pirius! Here the notion that all of this suffering may be washed away by a history change is an easy one to sell.'

Pirius said, 'You make it sound almost reasonable, Commissary.'

'Well, so it is! Religions will always emerge, even in a place as emotionally sterile as this; and religions will naturally exploit elements in their environments. It would be fascinating to see how this new faith develops in the future.'

'But you don't seem to have anything to say about why the cadets *need* Burden's teaching in the first place.'

Nilis folded his fingers over his ample virtual belly. 'Soldiers have always been superstitious,' he pronounced. 'Something to do with a need to take control of one's destiny in a dangerous and out-of-control environment. And the ordinary troops have always championed the Druz Doctrines. We have come so far from home.' He flexed his fingers before his face, almost curiously. 'We still have the bodies of plains apes, you know. But nothing else of our native ecology has survived: nothing but us and our stomach bacteria and the rats and lice and fleas . . . Now we have come to a place so lethal we have to dig into bits of rock to survive. There is nothing left of our origins but *us* – and all that holds us together is our beliefs. Lose them and we will become shapeless, flow like hot metal.

'I think the ordinary soldier intuits something of that, and has clung to the Doctrines as a result. But the Doctrines are too severe – inhuman, lacking hope. If you were going to devise a consoling religion you wouldn't start with *them*. Druz would not even have us commemorate the dead!'

Burden said, 'And hope is what I give the cadets.'

Nilis nodded vigorously. 'Oh, I see that.'

'Then why,' Burden said evenly, 'won't you talk to them?'

Nilis was immediately nervous again. 'Oh, I couldn't possibly – it isn't necessary—'

Burden stood smoothly, crossed to the door and opened it. The disciples who had gathered outside filed in immediately, a dozen or so of them, their small faces solemn. They stared at Nilis, who was probably, Pirius thought, the most exotic creature they had even seen.

Tili Three walked boldly up to him. She ought to be more wary of a Commissary, Pirius thought. But there was none of the dread antique grandeur of the Commission for Historical Truth about Nilis. Tili reached out to touch Nilis's robe. Nilis gaped at her silvered prosthetic hand. Her fingers passed through the hem of his robe, scattering pixels like insects. He actually backed up against the wall, his big hands fluttering defensively before his chest. It was hard not to feel sorry for him.

Burden said, 'Why are you afraid?'

'They are so young,' Nilis said. 'So young – just children—'

'Children who have seen their comrades die,' Pirius said.

'I'm not afraid of them but of *me*,' Nilis said. He made to pat Tili's head, but when his palm brushed her hair it broke up into a spray of multicoloured pixels. The little firework display made the cadets laugh, and Pirius saw tears well in Nilis's foolish old eyes. 'You see? I knew I wouldn't be able to bear this, to come to one of these terrible nurseries – even Arches Base was like an academy compared to this – *they are so young*! And, my eyes, I can't save them all – I can't save any of them.'

Pirius Blue said, 'Perhaps we can, Commissary.'

Nilis whispered hoarsely, 'At any rate we must try.'

CHAPTER 28

In Saturn's orbit, the modifications to the last test greenship took a week of hard work.

It may have been conceptually simplifying to hook up the grav generator to the CTC, as Nilis had suggested, but grumbling Navy engineers, trying to marry together two literally alien technologies, were quick to point out the gap between concept and actuality. At least the delay gave Torec a chance to recover from the last run.

And then, suddenly, here she was, strapped into the cockpit of a greenship once more, with the cold, dark spaces of Sol system stretching around her. This second ship's blister seemed to be filled with as much clutter as before, and she had to squirm to get comfortable. It wasn't indulgence; when you flew the last thing you needed was to be distracted by a cloth fold up your ass.

Those sparkling monitor ships were all around her, and she could hear the subdued chatter on her comms loop, just as it was before. Saturn was ahead of her – but this time it was visible only as a pinpoint, not a disc, and her tame Xeelee wasn't visible at all, save in the sensors. The target area was much further away. In the first step of the new mission profile the greenship would be pushed close to lightspeed by its conventional sub light drive; a drawback of the new manoeuvre was that it needed much more room to work.

When she glanced at her crewmates in the other blisters of the greenship it wasn't two hardened Navy tars she saw but, to her right in the navigator's seat, the stolid form of Commander Darc – and to her left a new enlarged blister held the massive form of a Silver Ghost. It looked as if the cabin had been filled with mercury. It was scarcely believable that she, a mere ensign, was sitting here in control of such a craft, with such a strange crew, but here she was. As the last seconds ticked away, and the clock in her head counted down, she shivered with anticipation.

She polled her crew one last time. 'Ambassador. Ready?'

'All my systems are nominal,' the Ghost's translated voice said. 'Commander—'

'Don't waste time with useless chit-chat, ensign,' Darc snapped.

'No, sir,' she said.

Once more she felt the throbbing of the gravastar generators, deep in her bones. *Three, two, one.*

The ship jolted forward.

'Sublight nominal,' Darc called.

'Ambassador?'

'The shield generators are ready.'

'All right. Commander, push us to ninety per cent light.'

'On your order.'

A deep breath. 'Do it.'

The surge was all but intangible. But as they went relativistic the speckling of stars before her turned blue and swam closer, like disturbed fish.

Darc called, 'Ten seconds to Saturn.'

A random thought passed through her mind. If this Ghost wanted to carry out some sabotage – to destroy this test ship, to kill a Navy commander – it was in a perfect position to do it. *Too late to climb out now, Torec.*

'Shield on my mark,' she called.

'Ready,' said the Silver Ghost.

Three. Two. One.

The blueshifted stars swam again.

Torec didn't even know if the trial had been successful until she brought the greenship back to Enceladus. At least this one hadn't blown up.

The base medical officer tried to bring the crew in for checks, but neither she nor Darc was willing to take time out for so much as a shower. Hot, stiff, sweating after hours in their cramped blisters, they ran down ice-walled corridors to the briefing room where Nilis waited for them. They were trailed by the silent Ghost, with its escort of heavily armed Guardians.

In the briefing room a Virtual representation of the greenship, reconstructed from the records of a dozen monitor drones, was a toy hanging in the air, two metres long. She watched as it went to ninety per cent light, and the gravastar shield opened up. The shield was beautiful, Torec thought, a banner of shining, sparkling light, pure white, like some living thing. And behind it she saw only stars. The ship she was riding had been cut out of the universe, and existed once more in a cosmos of its own.

Nilis said, 'You created a perfect spherical cap, subtending an angle of around forty degrees. Congratulations, ensign. I wonder if any human has visited not one but *two* new universes before. Perhaps you have set a record . . .'

'I'm just glad it worked.'

He grunted. 'As pragmatic as ever! Well, so it did; the Ambassador's strategy of surfing at the edge of chaos was tricky to manage, but very effective – as you can see.'

Darc said, 'Coming up on the Xeelee encounter.'

The view shifted to a static image of the nightfighter. It orbited Saturn, penned in by a swarm of watchful drones. The gravastar cap was a missile that plunged at the Xeelee out of the left side of the image.

Nilis snapped his fingers, and in slow motion the incoming grav cap was reduced to a crawl. 'See how the Xeelee is reacting,' Nilis said. '*Here* it deploys its sublight drive.' Night-dark wings swept before the clouds of Saturn, quite beautiful. 'It knows the gravastar cap is coming, of course, but it knows nothing of what it is concealing.' The fly flickered out of the image, which changed to a long shot centred on a shrunken Saturn. Now the Xeelee fly was a black dart that plunged at the cap, flickering, making rapid, short FTL jumps.

Darc said, 'That's a classic Tolman manoeuvre. It's trying to send images of the encounter to its own past.'

'Yes. But it's impossible. It's looking into a region that isn't causally connected to the universe it inhabits; all the world lines terminate on that cap.'

The cap dissolved suddenly, turning into a thing of wisps and shards that quickly dissipated. The grav shield gone, the greenship dropped back into its parent universe. And it tore at the Xeelee, monopole cannon firing. The nightfighter tried to evade, but the greenship, controlled by its paradoxical CTC processor, was too fast; it seemed to anticipate every move. A hail of monopoles ripped through the Xeelee's spacetime wings.

The watching audience cheered – even Torec, who had been there; she couldn't help it. The nightfighter went limp, deactivated by its human masters, and its escorting ships closed in to return it to its pen.

Nilis closed his fist, and the Virtual died. Without its light and colour the briefing room seemed empty.

'We did it,' Torec breathed.

Nilis stayed composed, apparently already thinking ahead to the next step. 'It appears so. I've sent the records to the relevant Grand Conclave committees, with Commander Darc's agreement. Now we must wait for approval to move to the next stage.'

'Yes. But we did it. Commissary, we did it!' Whooping, she ran to him, grabbed his arms and began to jump up and down. After a moment he gave up his pretence of solemnity; barefoot, his scuffed robe flapping, he joined her in jumping around the room.

The Ghost hung silently in the air, and Darc watched it thoughtfully.

Torec had naively imagined that the successful test flight would have been enough to have convinced the brass to give Nilis's project the go-ahead. All they needed now was to find a weapon that could strike at the Prime Radiant when they got there.

But days went by as they waited for a response from the oversight committees.

And when it came, it was a shutdown. Though the committee members recognised the technical achievements of Nilis and his people – and the promising new technologies would be thoroughly evaluated for applications by the Navy and other forces, et cetera, et cetera – the case for continuing with Nilis's Project Prime Radiant remained unproven, and no more funds would be released for it. Torec couldn't believe it. Another success had brought nothing but another canning.

Even Commander Darc seemed sympathetic. 'You know I'm no supporter of your project,' he said to Nilis. 'But I do admit that your research has been yielding fruit. You always made too many enemies, however, Nilis. And now they've caught up with you.'

But Nilis was suffused with a determined grimness that belied his shabby exterior. 'It's not over yet,' he said, and he stalked off.

CHAPTER 29

Pirius Red was startled to receive a call from Luru Parz. The Virtual image was so good he couldn't tell if it was a direct broadcast or a copy.

She said simply, 'I want you to get me into Mons Olympus, ensign.'

The call came early in the morning. He was still aboard the Venus orbital habitat. He finger-combed tousled hair, and tried to pull his tunic straight. The Virtual just stared at him, humourless. He said, 'I'll make a call to the Commissary—'

'I didn't call Nilis. I called you. Every agency that knows of my existence, especially the Commission for Historical Truth, has banned me from such facilities as the Archive. I doubt if even Nilis could buck that. I'm asking for *your* help, ensign.'

Such a breakdown in anything even remotely resembling a chain of command was deeply disturbing to Pirius. 'I don't know how I can even get to Mars. Or how to get you into the Archive.'

She smiled. 'Spread your wings.'

He stared at her. Was it possible she knew somehow of the chip the peculiar Archive Retrieval Specialist Tek had pressed on to his sleeve? He wished he had got rid of that thing the moment he found it – but he'd chosen not to, he reminded himself, and had kept it for two months since.

'Luru Parz, why do you want to do this?'

She nodded, watching him. 'A *why* question. No good soldier ever asks *why*. But you do, Pirius! Gramm and his cronies continue to block Nilis's progress. I intend to force them to act. Ensign, our beloved Coalition is a mountain of lies and hypocrisy. Surely you know that by now. That doesn't bother me personally; it probably has to be that way to survive. But the threat of exposure is my leverage – and *that's* why I need to get into the Archive.' Her eyes narrowed and she leaned forward. 'Am I frightening you?'

'You always frighten me.'

She laughed, showing her blackened teeth. 'How sane you are! But you understand I am working towards the same goal as Nilis, don't you? A goal which you can't help but instinctively embrace, despite your lifetime of conditioning.'

He made a decision. 'I'll help you.'

'Of course you will,' she said dismissively. 'I'll meet you in Kahra.' The Virtual broke up and dissipated.

In the event Luru Parz was right. It proved remarkably easy for Pirius to organise this strange trip back to Olympus.

He needed the Commissary's approval to use his corvette. But Nilis, at Saturn, was still preoccupied with details of the gravastar shield tests, as well as his ongoing studies of the first moments of the universe, and some mysterious business he was conducting in the Core, and continuing battles with Gramm and the Coalition bureaucracy, and, and . . . When Pirius called he waved his Virtual hand vaguely. 'Just get on with it, Pirius.'

As for getting into the Archive, there was Tek's chip. It wasn't hard to work out its interface. The clerk's smudgy Virtual image directed Pirius to a port on Olympus – not the one he had visited before, another of the thousand or so that studded the mountain's mighty flank.

So he had no excuse not to do as Luru Parz asked, despite his dread at the very thought of her.

The journey to Mars was uneventful. Pirius travelled alone, save for the corvette's crew; he gambled his way through the interplanetary journey.

As she had promised, Luru Parz met him at Kahra. After an overnight stay they boarded a flitter for the final hop to Olympus.

They landed at coordinates Pirius had extracted from Tek's chip. When the flitter settled to the ground the situation – the gentle slope, the dust-soaked sky, the washed-out-red-brown colours, the hatch set in the ground – seemed exactly the same as his last visit.

Tek kept them waiting.

Luru Parz was calm. 'We have to give him time. Remember he is working covertly in there. Believe me, it's a difficult environment in which to act independently.' Pirius didn't know what she meant.

He was restless, anxious. The flitter was little more than a bubble a couple of metres across. Its hull was so transparent it would have been invisible save for a thin layer of Martian dust. And Pirius was stuck inside it with an immortal.

They sat opposite each other, so close in the tiny flitter that their knees almost touched. Even in person Luru had that dark, still quality, as if light fell differently on her. He could *smell* her, a faint dusty tang, like the smoky smell of the dead leaves that littered corners of Nilis's unruly garden.

She was studying him. 'Do I horrify you, ensign? I am a living embodiment of everything you have been brought up to despise. Every breath I take is illegal.'

'It isn't that.'

Her eyes narrowed. 'No, it isn't, is it? I suppose you've been in Sol system long enough to be able to perceive shades of grey. Then what?'

'You're the strangest human being I have ever met.'

She nodded. 'If indeed I am still human. After all, as Hama Druz himself understood, human beings aren't meant to last twenty thousand years.'

It was the first time he had heard the actual number; it shocked him. 'It is unimaginable.'

'Of course it is. It is a monstrous time, a time that should frame the rise and fall of a species, not a single life. But the alternative to living is always worse.'

She had been born during the last days of the Qax Occupation. While no older than Pirius she had been forced to make a compromise: to accept the gift of immortality in return for becoming a collaborator. 'I thought it was the right thing to do, to help preserve mankind. It would have been easier to refuse.'

When the Qax fell, the jasofts, undying collaborators, were hunted down. Many of them fled, on starships launched from Port Sol and by other routes. But the nascent Coalition soon discovered much of the information and experience they needed to run Earth was locked up in the heads of the jasofts. 'They could never admit what they were doing,' Luru said. 'But they were forced to turn to us. And that mixture of secrecy and power gave us opportunities.'

But time flowed by relentlessly, mayfly generations came and went and still Luru Parz did not die. She continued to build her power base, and to watch the slow working-out of historical forces.

'Every few generations there would be a fresh surge of orthodoxy,' she said dryly. 'Some new grouping in the Commission for Historical Truth would decide we ancient monsters should be got rid of once and for all.' She found places to hide, and spent much of her life out of sight. 'But I survived. It got harder for us as the Coalition strengthened, of course. But the Coalition's very stability was good for us. If you live a long time in a stable economic and political system it's not hard to accumulate wealth and power, over and over. It's a change of regime you fear.'

Having been born with mankind under the heel of a conqueror, she had lived through the whole of the stunning Third Expansion, which had seen humans sweep across the Galaxy. And in this manner, twenty thousand years had worn away.

Pirius said, 'I can't imagine how it feels to be you.'

She sighed. 'The scientists used to say that the human brain can accommodate only perhaps a thousand years' experience. It isn't as simple as that. Of course we edit our memories, all the time. We construct stories; otherwise we could not survive in a chaotic, merciless universe that cares nothing for *us*. If I think back to the past, yes, perhaps I can retrieve a fragment of a story I have lived. But I live on, and on, and on, and if I look back now I can't be sure if I am visiting a memory, or a memory of a memory . . . Sometimes it seems that everything that went before today was nothing but a dream. But then I will touch the surface of a Conurbation wall, or I will smell a spice that was once popular in Port Sol, and my mind will be flooded with places, faces, voices – not as if it were yesterday, but as if it were *today*.'

Her eyes now were clear, bright, behind lenses of water. 'And do you know what? I *regret*. I regret what is lost, people and places long vanished. Of course it is absurd. There isn't room in the universe for them all, if they had lived. And besides I *chose* to leave them behind. But I regret even so. Isn't that foolish?'

She leaned forward; that smoky scent intensified. 'Let me tell you something. You think I have banished death. Not so. *I live with death.* Faces like yours flash before me, and then crumble and vanish. How can I care about you? You are just one of a torrent, all of you winnowed by death.'

265

'And so you work to stay alive.'

'What else is there? But I have come to see that though I will outlive *you*, it's very unlikely I could outlive humanity: if I am to survive, I need the infrastructure of mankind. And that is why I have come out of hiding. I'm not doing it for mankind, ensign, or for the Coalition, or for Nilis, and certainly not for Hama Druz and his dreary preaching. I'm doing it for myself.'

Pirius sat back. 'I wonder how much of this is true. Perhaps this is all a fantastic story you tell to baffle the credulous.'

She smiled, unperturbed. 'Well, that's possible.'

'But your power is real enough. I've seen it. And, whatever you are, the goal is all that matters.'

She clapped her small hands. 'There – I knew you were a pragmatist!'

The hatch in the flank of Olympus opened at last. A wormlike tube slid out and nuzzled against the flitter's hull.

As they prepared to enter the Archive, Pirius thought of her stories of the lost starships, immense multiple-generation arks that had fled from Port Sol, most of them never to be heard from again. Perhaps they were still out there, arks of immortals driving on into the dark. He felt an intense stab of curiosity. After twenty thousand years, what would have become of them? He supposed he would never know.

He focused on the moment.

As on his first visit, Luru insisted they both wear their skinsuit helmets.

Once again Pirius found himself in a maze of tunnels and chambers. It looked much the same as where he had entered before. But in this section the hovering light globes were sparse, as if it was less used.

And here was Tek, small, compact, stooped, cringing. Once more he carried a set of data desks clutched to his chest as if for reassurance. 'I knew you would return, ensign.' But then he made out Luru Parz, and Tek flinched back. 'Who are *you*?'

'Never mind that. Take us to the breeding chambers, whatever you call them here.'

Pirius had no idea what she meant.

He sensed Tek understood. But the specialist said, 'I don't know what you're talking about.' He huddled over his data desks. He was actually shaking, Pirius saw; whatever he had hoped to achieve by bringing Pirius back here, he hadn't expected this.

Luru Parz stepped up to him. 'So you're a clerk, are you?'

'Yes, I—'

'Then what are you doing out here, away from all the other clerks?' She snatched the data desks out of his grasp. 'What do these contain?'

'I don't know,' he said.

Pirius touched her arm. 'Luru Parz, he's only a clerk.'

'He's not even that. Are you, Tek?' She hurled the desks on to the rocky floor, where they smashed. Tek whimpered, covering his face with his hands. Luru Parz laughed. 'Oh, don't worry, ensign. Those desks contained nothing of any value to anybody – anybody but him, that is. Tek, they were fakes – like you – weren't they, *clerk*?'

Pirius said, 'What do you mean, "fakes"?'

'He's a parasite. He mimics the workers here. He runs around with data desks, he sleeps in their dormitory rooms, he eats their food. It's a common pattern in communities like this. The genuine clerks are busy with their own tasks – and here you aren't supposed to ask questions anyhow. So Tek gets away with it. He's just like a genuine clerk. Except that you don't do anything useful, do you, Tek? And where did you come from, I wonder? Kahra, was it? And what forced you to hide here in Olympus?'

'You don't know anything about me.'

Luru Parz said, 'You snivelling creature, I don't care enough about you to destroy you – but I will, unless you cooperate with me. So what's it to be? *Where are the breeding chambers?*'

Tek shot Pirius a glance of pure hatred, apparently at the ensign's betrayal. But he replied, 'You mean the Chambers of Fecundity.'

Luru Parz laughed again. 'That's better. Now – a *clerk* wouldn't know the way to such a place, because she wouldn't need to know. But *you* know, don't you, Tek?'

'Yes.'

She sighed theatrically. 'At last. Move. Now.'

His mouth working, Tek led them along the corridor.

Pirius said, 'I don't get any of this.'

'You'll see.'

Tek brought them to a door, as anonymous as the rest. When he waved his hand, it slid open silently.

The corridor beyond was packed with people. Pirius quailed. But

Luru Parz grabbed his hand and shoved Tek forward, and the three of them pushed their way in.

Pirius was taller than almost everybody here, and he looked down on a river of heads, round faces, slim shapeless bodies. As they joined the crush, he was forced to shuffle forward with small steps, through tight-packed bodies that smelled overwhelmingly sour, milky – he wondered if his mask had an option to shut out the smell as well as to filter the air. There were no lanes, no fixed pattern, but the crowd, squeezed between the worn walls of the corridor, seemed to organise itself into streams. He couldn't tell if the people around him were male or female, or even if they were adults; their slim, sexless forms and round faces were like prepubescent children. But they all wore plain Commission-style robes, and they all seemed to have somewhere to go, an assignment to fulfil.

He was *touched*, all the time, as slim bodies pressed against his; he felt the pressure of shoulders against his arms, bellies in the small of his back, fingers stroking his hands, hips, upper legs, his ears, his face mask – he brushed those curious probings away. Around him everybody else was in constant contact. He even saw lips touching, soft kisses exchanged. There was nothing sexual about any of this, not even the kissing.

The constant shuffling went on, off into the distance as far as Pirius could see. Light globes floated over the rustling mass. And nobody spoke. Oddly it took him some moments to notice that. But, though not a word was exchanged, there was a constant sibilant sigh all around him. It was the sound of breathing, he realised, the breathing and the rustling clothes of thousands of people – thousands in this one corridor alone, burrowed under the mountain.

And *they were all alike* – all with the same pale, oval faces, the same wispy grey eyes. That was the strangest thing of all. Was it possible that they were all somehow related? It was a disgusting thought, a base animal notion.

He spoke to Luru Parz. 'I had no idea it was like this. Our visit before—'

'You were only shown the outer layers.' They were both whispering. 'Where the Interface Specialists work: the acceptable face of the Archive. Everybody – I mean, every decision-maker in the Coalition –

knows the truth of this place, that *this* is what lies beneath. But the smooth-browed interfacers allow them to ignore that fact, perhaps even to believe it doesn't exist at all.'

'How many people are there here, under this mountain?'

'Nobody knows – *they* certainly don't. But they've been here for twenty thousand years, remember, from not long after the time of Hama Druz himself, burrowing away. This is our greatest mountain. I doubt they've exhausted it yet.'

If every corridor across Olympus was like this, then surely the Archive must house *billions*. He tried to imagine the vast machinery that must be required to keep them alive and functioning: continents covered by nano-food machines, rivers and lakes of sewage to be processed. But what was the purpose of the effort, all these teeming lives?

They walked on. As they pushed on deeper into the mountain, it seemed to Pirius that the character of the crowd was slowly changing. It was hard to be sure – there were so many faces, all so similar, it was hard to focus on any – but the people pressing around him looked smaller, smoother-faced, younger than those he had first encountered. But they seemed more agitated too. They recoiled from him, their blank, pretty faces tense with a baffled suspicion.

Pirius said, 'We are disturbing them.'

'Of course we are,' Luru Parz muttered. 'We're outsiders. We're like an infection penetrating a body. The Archive is reacting to us. It's going to get worse.'

They came to a junction of corridors. Crowds poured into the centre, which was filled with a single teeming, heaving mass of bodies. Somehow individuals found their way through the crush, for as many people poured out of the junction and into the surrounding corridors as entered it. Above their heads a broad tunnel cut straight up. Its wall looked smooth save for metal rungs pushed into its surface. Perhaps it was a ventilation shaft, Pirius thought.

As they stood there, alarm spread quickly. The mob in the plaza became more disorderly, a tense, heaving mass from which scared glances were cast at Pirius and the others.

Pirius said, 'We can't get through this.'

'We have to,' Luru Parz said. She kept hold of Tek's arm, ensuring he couldn't get away. Then she put her shoulders down and shoved her way into the mass of the crowd.

Pirius followed, flinching from every soft contact. People quailed away from him, but there always seemed to be more, and every step was a battle.

'But *how* is the alarm spreading? I haven't heard any of them speak a single word, not since we came through that first door.'

'Ah, but they don't need words,' she said. 'They've long gone beyond that. Perhaps all that kissing has something to do with it. Or maybe it's something in the air. That's why you're wearing that facemask, Pirius!'

Communication through scent or taste? 'It doesn't sound human.'

'Whatever. Just keep your mask sealed . . . Look up.'

They had reached the centre of the plaza now, and were directly underneath the ventilation duct. Things moved over the lower walls. These creatures had skinny, spindly bodies and enormously long limbs. Their hands and feet were huge and they clung to the vertical walls as if they were fitted with sucker pads. They looked like spiders, Pirius thought. But they each had just four limbs, two arms and two legs and they wore orange jackets and belts stuffed with tools. They were working on systems behind opened panels in the walls. One of them turned to look down at Pirius. Despite the uncertain light the spider-thing's face was distinct: round, pale, with dark hair and smoky grey eyes, a human face.

They came at last to another door. Tek, battered by the crush of the crowd, cowered nervously.

'Twenty thousand years is a *long time*,' Luru Parz said to Pirius. 'The human species has only been around a few multiples of that. It is time enough.'

Pirius asked, 'Time enough for what?'

For answer, Luru opened the door.

The chamber was huge. The light from the few floating globes was low and Pirius's view was impressionistic, of a domed roof, a vast floor inset with pools of some milky fluid through which languid creatures swam. Like everywhere else in the complex the room was crowded. There must have been several thousand people visible in that one glance. Pirius marvelled to think that all of this was concealed under the immense basaltic pile of Mons Olympus.

He took a step into the room. The air was thick with steam, which his semi-sentient mask battled to keep from condensing on his faceplate.

Luru Parz placed a hand on his arm, 'Don't crack your visor in here, of all places,' she said. *Don't.'*

The people here were as small, rounded, uniform as they were everywhere else. As he walked forward they scuttled out of his way, but the sea of people closed behind him, and they hurried back and forth on their tasks. They seemed to be women – or rather girls; they were even younger here than in the rest of the complex. They carried bits of food, jugs of water, clothes, what looked like medical equipment. It was like a vast, low-technology hospital, he thought.

He paused by one of the pools. It was no more than waist deep, and filled with a milky, thick fluid that rippled with low-gravity languor. Women floated in this stuff, barely moving. They were naked, and droplets of the milky stuff clung to their smooth skin.

And they were pregnant, mountainously so.

But they were all ages, from very young girls whose thin limbs and small frames looked barely able to support the weight of their bellies, to much older women whose faces bore more wrinkles than Luru Parz's. Attendants, female, moved between the women, wading in the waist-deep milk. They stroked the faces and limbs of the pregnant ones and caressed their bellies.

'The breeders,' Luru Parz said grimly. 'It's always like this at the heart of the warrens. Breeding chambers like this are the most sacred places in the complex, the most precious to the drones. See how alarmed they are. But they won't harm us.'

Pirius was struggling to make sense of this. 'And this is where the Archive is controlled from?'

'No,' she said, sounding exasperated, 'Do you still not see, ensign? *Nobody controls the Archive.* These mothers are its most important single element, I suppose. But even they, perpetually pregnant, don't control anything, not even their own lives . . .'

At last Pirius understood what this was; he had been trained to recognise such things.

The Archive was not a human society at all. It was a Coalescence. It was a hive.

In the beginning it really had been just an Archive, a project to store the records of the Coalition's great works: nothing more sinister than that.

But its tunnels had quickly spread into the welcoming bulk of

Olympus. Very soon there was nobody left with a firm grasp of the Archive's overall geography. And, with sections of the Archive soon hundreds of kilometres from each other – several days' transit time through these cramped corridors – it was impossible for anybody to exert proper central control.

It was soon obvious, too, that that didn't matter. People were here to serve the Archive – to record information, to classify, analyse, store, preserve it; that was all. You might not know what *everybody* was doing across the unmapped expanse of the library, but you always knew what the next guy was doing, and that was usually enough. Somehow things got done, even if nobody was sure how.

Then times of trouble came to Sol system.

For long periods the Archive was left isolated. The corridors of Olympus were always crowded. No matter how fast new tunnels were dug, no matter how the great nano-food banks were extended, the population seemed to grow faster. And people were stuck in here, of course; if any of the librarians and clerks stepped out on Mars's surface unprotected, they would be dead in seconds.

There was a period of complicated politics, as factions of librarians fought each other over the basic resources that kept them alive. Strange bureaucratic kingdoms emerged at the heart of Olympus, like the ancient water empires of Earth's Middle East, grabbing a monopoly on vital substances in order to wield power. But none of these 'air empires' proved very enduring.

At last another social solution was found. Nobody planned it: it simply emerged. But once it was established, it proved remarkably stable. In the end, it was all a question of blood ties.

Despite the Coalition's best efforts to establish birthing tanks, age-group cadres and the rest of the homogenising social apparatus it deployed elsewhere across the Galaxy, in the dark heart of Olympus, out of sight, families had always prospered. But now some of these clerkish matriarchs shifted their loyalties. The matriarchs began to produce more children of their own. They exerted pressure on their daughters not to have kids themselves but to stay at home and help their mothers produce more brothers and sisters. It made sense, on a social level. These close ties kept the families united, and prevented ruinous squabbles over limited resources.

And then the genes cut in. Organisms were after all only vehicles that genes used to ride to the next generation. If you remained childless yourself, the only way you could pass on your genes was indirectly, through the fraction you shared with your siblings. So, in these cramped, stifling conditions, as the daughters of librarians gave up their own chances to have babies in order to support more sisters from the loins of their fecund mothers, the genes were satisfied.

It worked. The resource wars stopped. A handful of families grew spectacularly fast, spreading and merging until at last the Archive was dominated by a single broad gene pool. Just five thousand years after the Olympus ground had first been broken, almost everybody in the Archive looked remarkably similar.

The population swelled, united and organised by the peculiar new genetic politics. And there was plenty of time for adaptation.

The peculiar society that had developed in the Archive was an ancient and stable form. *Nobody* was in control. People didn't follow orders, but responded to what others did around them. This was local interaction, as the social analysts called it, reinforced by positive feedback, people reacting to their neighbours and evoking reactions in turn. And that was enough for things to get done. Food and other resources flowed back and forth through the warren of tunnels, the vital systems like air circulation were maintained, and even the nominal purpose of the Archive, the storage of data, was fulfilled – all without central direction. It was as if the Archive was a single composite organism with billions of faces.

And that organism was bound together by genetic ties, the ties of family.

'Beyond Sol system, other Coalescences have been discovered,' Luru Parz said. 'Relics of the earlier Expansions. But all warrens are essentially the same. I think it's a flaw in our mental processing. Anywhere the living is marginal, where people are crowded in on each other and it pays to stay home with your mother rather than strike out on your own, out pops the eusocial solution, over and over. I sometimes wonder where the *first* Coalescence emerged: perhaps even before spaceflight, on Earth itself.

'Of course the hives are terribly non Doctrinal. Are these women *human* as you are? No. They have evolved to serve a purpose for the Coalescence. And there are many specialists. You've seen them your-self: the long-legged mechanic types, the runners, the archivists with their deep, roomy brains. Specialists, you see, adapted to serve par-ticular purposes, the better to serve the community as a whole – but all diverging from the human norm. Officially, everywhere they are found the Coalition cleans out Coalescences—'

'But not here,' Pirius said. 'They left this one to develop, *here*, on Earth's sister planet. On *Mars*.' And they gave it mankind's treasure, he thought, the Archive of its past.

He probed at his feelings. He found no anger. He felt only numb. Perhaps he had experienced too much, seen too much. But this was even worse than finding a nest of Silver Ghosts in Sol system. To allow humans to diverge like this, here at the very heart of Sol system – it went against the basics of Hama Druz's teachings.

Luru seemed to sense his discomfort. 'Nobody meant it to be like this, ensign. And when it did happen it was simply too *useful* to discard, no matter what the Druz Doctrines had to say. In the end, the powerful folk who run the Coalition are pragmatists. Like you.'

It was a relief to Pirius when a corpulent Virtual of Minister Gramm gathered in the air, shadowed by a nervous, barefoot Nilis. He and Luru Parz had been tracked down.

Nilis grasped the situation much more quickly than Pirius. He didn't have to fake his anger and repugnance.

But Gramm was lordly, defiant. 'So now you know about Olympus. Do you think I will apologise for it to the likes of you?

'Listen to me. This Archive is essential to the continuance of the great projects of the Coalition. We humans are poor at the archival of information, you know. Paper records rot in a few thousand years at most. Digitally archived data survives better, so long as it is regularly transferred from store to store. But even such data stores are subject to slow corruption, for instance from radiation. The half-life of our data is only ten thousand years. But all our efforts are dwarfed by what is achieved in the natural world. DNA far outdoes tablets of clay or stone. Some of our genes are a billion years old – the deep ancient ones, shared across the great domains of life – and over the generations genetic information has been copied more than twenty *billion* times, with an error rate of less than one in a trillion.'

He sighed. 'We are fighting a war on scales of space and time that defy our humanity. We need to *remember* better by an order of magnitude if we are to sustain ourselves as a galactic power. And so we have this place. This Archive is already ancient. Its generations of clerk-drones live for nothing but to copy bits of data, meaningless to them, from one store to another. Perhaps the hive will one day be able to emulate the copying fidelity of the genes – who knows? It's certainly a goal that no other human social form could possibly deliver. Commissary, like it or not, hives are good libraries!'

Nilis shouted, 'And for that grandiose goal you will tolerate this deviance in the heart of Sol system? Your hypocrisy is galling!' His raised voice disturbed the swimming mothers; they drifted across their pools, away from him.

'You always did think small, Nilis,' Gramm said dismissively. 'In a way it's rather elegant to turn one of our fundamental human flaws into a source of strength, don't you think? And speaking of corruption and deviance, you' – he challenged Luru Parz – 'what is it you want here, you old witch?'

'I told you I knew where the bodies were buried,' she said levelly. 'Gramm, once again you're stalling over funding Nilis's projects. That will stop.'

Gramm growled, 'You have threatened me before. Do you really think exposing this hive-mountain will bring down the Coalition?'

'No,' she said, unperturbed. 'But it will show you I'm serious. There are far worse secrets in Sol system than *this*, Minister Gramm, as you know better than I do. And now you are going to help me find a weapon. Nilis needs something to strike at the Prime Radiant. I think I know where to find one.'

Nilis looked interested. 'Where?'

'In the past, of course. But locked away, in an archive buried even deeper than this one.'

Gramm glared at her, his mouth working. But Pirius saw that Luru Parz had beaten him again.

Nilis was staring at her. 'Madam, you are a nest of mysteries. But this deeper archive – where is it?'

She said, 'Callisto.'

The name meant nothing to Pirius. But Nilis blanched.

The strange stand-off lasted a few more minutes, until blue-helmeted Guardians in fully armoured skinsuits broke into the chamber to escort them all away.

As they left, Pirius drew Luru Parz aside. 'There's something I still don't understand. Why did Tek give me that contact chip in the first place? What did *he* want?'

She sighed. 'He was just probing, seeking an opportunity. It's the way a Coalescence works.'

Pirius shook his head. 'That doesn't make sense. Why would Tek act on behalf of the Coalescence? He is a parasite.'

'*But he's part of the hive too*. Don't you see that? It's just that he doesn't know it. None of them does!' She plucked his sleeve. 'Come on, ensign, let's get out of here. Even through my mask the stink of this place is making me feel ill.'

They hurried after the Guardians, making for the cool, empty surface of Mars.

Behind them, the Coalescent mothers swam in their milky pools, and naked, round-shouldered attendants scurried anxiously.

CHAPTER 30

Pirius Blue had almost forgotten how it was to sit in a greenship cockpit.

It was like being suspended in open space, with nothing between you and the sky. And this Galaxy-centre sky was full of stars, a clustering of globes that receded to infinity. Many of them were bright blue youngsters, but others glowered red, resentfully old before their time. There was a great sense of motion about the barrage of stars, a sense of immense dynamism – and in truth these crowded stars were flying rapidly through this lethal space, though their motion was only visible on timescales of years, too slow for mayfly humans to perceive.

Huddled in a corner of Pirius's greenship cockpit, Virtual Nilis looked faintly absurd in his skinsuit, Virtual-tailored to fit his ample girth. He said, wondering, 'So many stars, giant, violent stars, far more massive than Earth's sun, crowded so close they slide past like light globes lining a roadway . . . It is as bright as a tropical sky! There is an old paradox. Once it was believed that the universe is infinite and uniform, everywhere full of stars. But that cannot be so, you see, for then whichever direction you looked your eye would meet a star, and the whole sky would shine as bright as the surface of the sun. Perhaps that paradoxical sky would look something like *this*.'

'It's a beautiful sight, Commissary,' Pirius Blue said. 'But remember, in this place, every star is a fortress.'

That shut him up, to Pirius's relief. Pirius had work to do; the mission clock was counting down. He blipped the greenship's attitude controllers, tiny inertial generators fixed to each of the three nacelles and to the main body.

Before him, the spangling of crowded Galaxy-centre stars shifted. He made out seven sparks against that background, the emerald lights of the seven greenships that were going to accompany him and his crew into the unknown depths of the Cavity.

'Systems seem nominal,' he reported.

Enduring Hope called from his engineer's position: 'Sure, genius, like you can *feel* the ship's degrees of freedom just by sitting there. In fact I fixed the inertial control before you started playing.'

'I knew I could rely on you, Hope.'

Now Cohl chipped in, 'Do you want to give me some warning before you start throwing this tub around the sky? I'm trying to get the nav systems calibrated. I know that's merely a detail to you two heroes, but I'm sentimentally attached to knowing where I am.'

'It's all yours, navigator . . .'

Virtual Nilis was wide-eyed. 'Pirius – you must be glad to see your crew again. Back in their rightful habitat, so to speak. But is it always like this?'

'Oh, no,' Pirius said. 'I think we're a little subdued today.'

But it had been good when the three of them had been reunited, down on Quin: Cohl with the limp that had been her souvenir from Factory Rock, and Enduring Hope, back from his artillery brigade. Hope, amazingly, had lost weight. It turned out to be tough physical work on those monopole-cannon battalions, and after months of it Hope had never looked fitter.

And it had certainly been a joy when the three of them had first boarded a ship again, which they had quickly dubbed the *Assimilator's Other Claw*. It wasn't much of a combat ship, as it was laden with a massive sensor pod that spoiled the sleek lines of its main body. And it could never be the same as their first ship, of course. But it was a ship nevertheless – their ship. They had marked their skinsuits with sigils that recalled the first *Claw*, and Pirius Blue felt an extraordinary surge of joy to be back in a greenship blister.

Nilis was watching him with his characteristic mixture of pride and longing, 'I suppose the banter is a social lubricant. But I'm surprised you get anything done. Well, I'm privileged to be here. To see *this*. It's so different. You know, we humans aren't designed to function in such an environment. On Earth you are on a plain, so it seems, a few kilometres wide, with clouds a few kilometres up. In the sky everything is so remote it looks two-dimensional – even the Moon. There is

278

no *depth*. The scale is kilometres or infinity, with a gap in between. Here, though, you have stars scattered through the depth of the sky – space is filled up – and you get a sense of immensity, of perspective that's impossible on Earth.'

Pirius shrugged. 'Does it matter?'

'Oh, I think so.' He peered at Pirius curiously. 'To comprehend a sky like this, the very structure of your sensorium, your mind, must differ from mine, Pirius Blue. Genetically we could be identical. But our *minds* are so different we might as well belong to alien species.'

This was uncomfortably heretical to Pirius. Everybody was essentially the same; that was the Doctrine's decree. If Nilis wanted to believe he was some kind of divergent, that was up to him. 'I'm just trying to do my job, Commissary.'

'I know.' Nilis sighed. 'And my gabbling is getting in the way! Thank you again for hosting me.'

Hosting: there was something else Pirius didn't want to think about too hard. As the whole purpose of the mission was to take Nilis through the Cavity, it had been decreed that the safest place to lodge him was with Pirius – that is, *in* him. All flight crew had implants of various kinds studded through their nervous systems, serving as trackers, backup comms systems, medical controls, systems interfaces. It had been trivial to download Virtual Nilis into Pirius's head. Trivial, but not welcome. But it had been orders.

Nilis held up his hands. 'I know you're uncomfortable. I'm here to observe, not to interfere. I won't get in your way.'

Before accepting the download Pirius had insisted on an off-switch. 'No,' he said vehemently. 'You won't.'

A peremptory voice called over the common loop. 'This is Dray. Shut up and listen.'

The babble on the loop immediately dried up. Pirius glanced at the array of seven ships around him. Dray's was one of a pair directly ahead, the tip of the loose wedge formation. Commodore Dray was a formidable, muscular woman, her head shaven bare, and the leader of this expeditionary force.

She said now, 'Here are your idents. I am Wedge Leader . . .' She ran through the other crews, numbering them in sequence, one side then the other, so that Dray, in Wedge Zero, led a line of even-numbered ships, and Wedge One led a line of odd numbers. Pirius in the *Other Claw* was Wedge Seven.

'And here are the rules,' said Dray. 'One. I am in command, and none of you is going to so much as fart without my permission. I'm talking to you, Pirius. I've seen your record. If it was up to me you would still be digging graves on a Rock. But it wasn't up to me, so here you are, and if there are any stupid stunts on this trip I'll shoot you out of the sky myself.'

Pirius had no doubt she meant it. 'Sir.'

'Rule two. We are going to fulfil our objectives. Rule three. We are eight ships going in, and we will be eight coming out, subject only to rules one and two.'

A chorus of voices replied, 'Understood.'

'Now, I had imagined you had all seen the briefing, but perhaps not. I also assumed you were experienced crews, but this formation is so slack I must be wrong about that too. Form up, damn it! I'm looking at you, Wedge Three.'

'Sir.'

The seven lights slid subtly across the sky, and Pirius blipped his sublight drive to tweak his own position.

'We're a minute from our first FTL jump, and we're going to hop in formation. The first hop will be the most difficult . . .'

That was true, for this tiny formation was about to leap right into the heart of the Galaxy.

'When we get through that it's plain sailing,' Dray said. 'And even if it isn't it will be fun. Nearly time. Good luck, everyone.' Another quick chorus of acknowledgement. 'Five, four, three . . .'

The Galaxy's inner structure was nested around the ferocious mass at the very centre.

Within the broad plane of the spiral arms was set the Core. That immense shining bulge itself contained a denser kernel, the Central Star Mass: millions of stars crowded into a few tens of light years.

Immense streams of molecular gases poured inwards through the Mass – but a few light years out from the centre they collided with a ferocious solar wind blowing out of the very centre. That solar wind created the Cavity, a hole in the heart of the Galaxy surrounded by a stationary shock front of infalling gas, the Circumnuclear Ring. At the Circumnuclear Ring, the human expansion through the Galaxy had stalled; the soldiers who fought and died there called it the Front. The Cavity had its own marvels: the Baby Spiral, a miniature Galaxy contained wholly within those few scraped-clear light years, and deeper still the dense, fast moving astrophysics around the central black hole itself.

Dray and his little flotilla of greenships planned a bold FTL jump of no less than five light years, which would take them right through the Front and into the Cavity. They were going to make this leap in the relativistic turbulence of the Galaxy centre, whose violence, even as far out as this, reached up into the higher dimensions on which FTL technology depended. And they were going to do it in formation.

That, anyhow, was the plan.

When the jump came the sky was suddenly so bright it was as if it had exploded.

Dray was calling: 'Two and Four! Wedge Two and Four, report!'

Pirius ignored everything and checked his ship's systems. The Cavity was a lethal environment, saturated with radiation and laced with massive particles fleeing at close to the speed of light. But the *Other Claw* had survived the FTL jump, and was protecting her crew.

When he was satisfied he looked up.

Suddenly he was sitting on the edge of the Cavity, actually inside the central space contained within the Front. Through a blizzard of stars he could clearly see the Baby Spiral. The convoy had emerged from its jump close to the terminus of the spiral arm called East, where it lost its coherence and merged into the mush of the Circumnuclear Ring. From Pirius's point of view East was a tunnel of infant stars and crimson-glowing gas that wound deeper into the Cavity. It was like looking into the guts of an immense machine, he thought, a machine of gas and dust and stars. All of this was tinged with blueshift, for he was already flying further inward; the *Other Claw* had emerged from the hop with a velocity a high fraction of lightspeed, a vector arrowed straight at the heart of the Galaxy.

Against this astounding background, Pirius had eyes only for the green sparks arrayed around him. The array was noticeably more ragged than it had been before the jump – and seven had been reduced to six, he saw now.

'Two, Four!'

'Four here,' came a reply. 'We lost Two. The FTL shift brought him too close – I was lucky to pull away myself.'

Nilis gasped. 'We lost a crew? So suddenly?'

Pirius said grimly, 'You can see what kind of cauldron we're in. FTL jumps aren't too precise at the best of times.'

'To die in a place like this.' Nilis had lowered his hands now, and the complex light swam in his eyes. 'And are we already moving?'

Cohl called dryly, 'The law of conservation of momentum isn't particularly relevant if you pass through an FTL hop, Commissary. If you tweak the hop you can emerge with any three-space momentum you want. As my instructors used to say, in operations like this physics is just a tool kit.'

'Remarkable, remarkable.'

'Let's go to formation B,' Dray called. 'Close up.'

The green lights slid around the sky; once more Dray was at the tip of the wedge, and the other ships, including Pirius's, formed its flanks.

Dray ran through the procedures that lay ahead. 'One light-day jumps. We wait one tenth of a second at each emergence; we set our formation; we jump again. Everybody clear?'

'Sir.'

'On my mark. Three, two.'

With a gut-twisting lurch the *Assimilator's Other Claw* leapt across another thirty billion kilometres, across a space that could have held *three* copies of all of Sol system out to Pluto side by side, a monumental leap completed too rapidly for Pirius's mind even to be aware of the transition before it was done.

And then the ship did it again. And again. Virtual Nilis moaned and buried his head in his hands.

It was an uncomfortable, juddering progress, a series of flickering lurches, ten every second. The miniature spiral arm was a tunnel, a few light days wide, that stretched out ahead of the ships, leading them towards the still more exotic mysteries of the very centre. But the surviving ships around Pirius pushed on, glowing bright defiant green, their neat wedge formation a challenge to the chaos of the cosmos.

Virtual Nilis sat up and dared look around, plucking at the threadbare sleeve of his robe. His eyes were wide, and the Virtual generators artfully reflected Galaxy-centre light in them. 'So much structure, so precisely delineated. Do you realise, even now we know virtually nothing about the details of this place – not the geography, but the *why* of it. Why should this extraordinary toy spiral exist at all?

And why three arms, why not one or five or twenty? Is it really a coherent structure or just some chance assemblage, gone in a million years? We have been so busy using this place as a war zone we have forgotten to ask such questions.'

As Pirius laboured at his instruments, Nilis talked on and on, about other galaxies where the central black holes weren't sleeping giants like *this* one but voracious monsters that seemed to be actively eating their way through the gaseous corpses of their hapless hosts; and he spoke of galaxies racked by great spasms of star formation, tremendous eruptions of energy that spanned hundreds of light years.

'We rationalise these things away with our physics, coming up with one theory after another. But we know that life's thoughtless actions have shaped the evolution of matter, even on astrophysjcal scales. So how can we tell what is natural? *We* have been waging war here for millennia. But there is evidence that the Xeelee have been fighting here much longer, tremendous ancient wars against a much more formidable foe. And what would be the consequence? Perhaps everything we see is a relic of an ancient battleground, like the trench-furrowed surface of a Rock, worked and reworked by conflict until nothing is left of the original . . .' He seemed to come to himself. 'I'm talking a lot.'

'Yes, you are,' Pirius said tensely. 'I should have left you back at the base.'

Nilis laughed, though his face stayed expressionless. 'I'll try to—'

'Flies! My altitude fifty degrees, azimuth forty . . .'

Pirius quickly converted that to his own point of view, and peered out of his blister. He couldn't see the nightfighters. But in his sensor view, there they were, resolutely night-dark specks in this cathedral of light.

'Remarkable,' Nilis said. 'This is a three-dimensional battlefield, with no common attitude. You use spherical coordinates, and you are able to translate from one position to another in your head—'

'Shut up, Commissary.'

Somebody called, 'I count five, six, seven.'

Cohl said, 'All nightfighters, I think.'

Enduring Hope called, 'I'm surprised they took so long.'

'No,' said Dray grimly. '*We* surprised *them*. Pattern alpha.'

The seven greenships turned with the precision of a single machine, and Pirius felt a stab of pride.

Now the Xeelee were dead ahead. The greenships continued to plough towards them.

'Sublight,' Dray called. 'Half lightspeed.'

The greenships cut their FTL drives. The *Assimilator's Other Claw* dropped back into three-dimensional spacetime with a velocity of half the speed of light, arrowed straight at the Xeelee. The enemy was now just light minutes away, no more remote than Earth was from its sun. The greenships were closing so fast that the background, the Spiral's boiling clouds of gas and dust, was tinged faintly blue.

As the nightfighters neared, Pirius could see how they swarmed, flying over, under, around each other, rapid movements whose pattern was impossible to follow, like the flies that had earned them their barracks-room nickname. Their movements were almost like a dance, Pirius thought; smooth, graceful, even beautiful. But not human.

And they were close, terribly close. Pirius thought he saw the first tentative cherry-red flicker of a starbreaker beam.

'Break on my mark,' Dray said. 'Three, two, one—'

The wedge formation dissolved. Three of the greenships peeled away, suddenly making a dash for it back along the great roadway of the spiral arm. The rest, including Dray and Pirius's ship, closed up tighter. Only the four of them now, four green sparks in this dazzling Galaxy-centre light storm, four against the dense pack of Xeelee flies dead ahead.

Nilis murmured, 'I don't understand—'

'Shut up,' said Pirius.

For a time – a moment, a heartbeat – the Xeelee held their position, and Pirius thought the subterfuge wasn't going to work. And if not he was a dead man.

But then the Xeelee broke. Moving as one they tore after the three departing ships.

Pirius whooped, flooded with relief and exultation. There were answering cries from the other ships. 'Lethe, it worked!'

Dray briefly shut down the loop, so that only her voice sounded. 'Let's keep the partying for later,' she said dryly. 'Formation C. You know the drill.'

The *Other Claw* banked and turned.

Nilis gripped the edge of his Virtual seat. 'Oh, my eyes,' he whispered, evidently more upset by a bit of aerobatics than by a head-on approach to a pack of Xeelee fighters.

The four ships soon settled down into a new simplified wedge. Dray ordered them to sound off once in position: Three, Four, Seven called in. Pirius in Seven trailed Dray, the leader; Three flew alongside Dray, trailed by Four.

Nilis spoke up again. 'We flew at the Xeelee. Why didn't they repel us?'

'They thought we were a diversion,' Pirius said. 'That the others, One, Five, Six, were the ones with the real mission – whatever they imagine it to be. The Xeelee made a quick decision, chased the others. But they were wrong.'

'Ah. Those others, One, Five Six – *they* were the diversion. Clever! Perhaps we are better liars than the Xeelee. What does that say of us? . . . But of course it would only work if the Xeelee didn't know of it in advance.'

'We were flying anti-Tolman patterns.' Patterns intended to disrupt the abilities of the enemy to send signals back into their own past. 'It's all part of the game. It's a gamble, though; you can never be sure what you'll come up against.'

'But it worked,' Nilis said. 'An ingenious bluff!'

Pirius saw a flaring of light up around azimuth forty degrees, a green nova. Somebody up there was fighting and dying, all for the sake of an 'ingenious bluff'.

Dray had seen the same lights. She called gruffly, 'Let's make it count.'

'Yes, sir.'

'On my mark. Three, two, one.'

That juddering light-day hopping began again, and once more the stars swam past Pirius as he hurtled along the glowing lanes of dust.

CHAPTER 31

Exerting her new power, Luru Parz brought Nilis and his little retinue to Jupiter. A week after the confrontation under Olympus, it was clear that she was the driver of events.

Pirius Red knew nothing about the 'Archive' to which he was being brought. Even Nilis, normally so loquacious, would say nothing. But Pirius's psych training cut in: it was a waste of energy to worry about the unknown.

Besides, here was Jupiter. And Pirius thought that of all the ancient strangeness he had seen in Sol system, Jupiter was the most extraordinary.

The sun appeared the tiniest of discs from Jupiter, five times as far as Earth from the central light. When Pirius held up his hand it cast sharp, straight shadows, shadows of infinity, and he felt no warmth.

And through this reduced light swam Jupiter and its moons.

Once it had been a mighty planet, the mightiest in Sol system in fact, more massive even than Saturn. But an ancient conflict had resulted in the deliberate injection of miniature black holes into the planet's metallic-hydrogen heart. Whatever the intention of that extraordinary act, the result was inevitable. It had taken fifteen thousand years, but at last the implosion of Jupiter into the knot of spacetime at its core had been completed.

Once Jupiter had had a retinue of many moons, four of them large enough to be considered worlds in their own right. In the final disaster, as gravitational energy pulsed through the system, the moons had scattered like frightened birds. Three of those giant satellites had been destroyed, leaving Jupiter with a spectacular ring of ice and dust. But even now bits of moon were steadily falling into the maw of the black hole, and their compression as they were dragged into the event horizon made the central object shine like a star.

One large moon had survived, to follow a swooping elliptical orbit around its parent, and that was Luru Parz's destination now. The moon, she said, was called Callisto.

Pirius watched Callisto's approach. It was a ball of white, quite featureless to the naked eye, lacking even impact craters as far as he could see. But it was surrounded by a deep, diffuse cloud of drones. Some of them swam close to the corvette. They were fists of metal and carbon that glistened with weapons.

Nilis said, 'A deep defence system. Even Earth itself doesn't have such aggressive guardians.'

'And very old,' Luru Parz said. Even she seemed tense as the corvette descended through the cloud. 'This cordon was first erected during the lifetime of Hama Druz himself – following Druz's own visit here, in fact.'

'I didn't know Druz had come here,' Pirius said. He actually knew very little about the moral founder of the Third Expansion.

'Oh, yes,' Luru said. 'And what he found here shocked him into the insights that led him to formulate the famous Doctrines – and to order Callisto to be cordoned off. This little moon is a key site in the history of mankind. Twenty thousand years have worn away since then, *and* the whole set-up has been subject to the implosion of a black hole a few light seconds away. Some of these old drones may be a little cranky. They have been instructed to recognise us. But—'

'How ironic,' Nilis said grimly, 'if we were to be thwarted by a malfunctioning antique robot.'

'There are many in the Coalition councils who wouldn't shed a tear to see the back of me – or you, Commissary.'

The ship continued to descend. The icescape of Callisto flattened out to a frozen ground streaked with colour, pale purple and pink; perhaps the ice was laced with organic compounds. It was smooth as far as Pirius could see, smooth all the way to the horizon. But a shallow pit was dug into the ice, and at the centre of the pit there was a settlement of some kind, a handful of buildings and landing pads.

Luru Parz said, 'Once Callisto was just a moon, you know. It was peppered with impact craters, like every other moon – not like *this*. At this site there was a major crater called Valhalla – I don't know what the name means – and in the time of Michael Poole there were extensive ice-mining projects. But it all changed after Hama Druz's visit.'

Pirius said, 'What happened to the craters?'

'What do you think?'

He thought it over. 'The surface looks as if it melted. What could melt a moon?'

'It was *moved*,' said Luru Parz, watching him. 'In the process the surface shook itself to pieces.'

'Moved . . .' Pirius knew of no technology which could achieve such a thing.

Nilis prompted, 'And the reason we are here?'

'This was the last refuge of many jasofts,' Luru Parz whispered. 'And here is stored their oldest knowledge. But it will take a sacrifice to retrieve it.' She wouldn't look him in the eyes, and Nilis looked away.

Pirius still had no idea what they wanted of him. Despite his training, dread gathered in his belly.

The corvette passed through the last line of the drones and began its final approach.

Pirius descended into the deep core of Callisto.

He rode an elevator with Nilis, Luru Parz, a servant bot and a taciturn Navy guard. They passed down a shaft cut into the ice, its walls worn smooth. Pirius touched the walls; the ice was slick, cold, lubricated by a layer of liquid water. Beneath a surface patina of dust and grime he saw that the ice had a structure, a lacy purple marbling, receding into meaningless complexity. More strangeness, he thought.

It was cold, surely not much above freezing, and their breath fogged air that stank, stale. The elevator, a simple inertial-control platform, was itself an antique, and as it descended it shuddered and bucked disconcertingly. He felt as if he was being dragged down into the strata of time that overlaid every world in this dense, ancient system.

They arrived in a chamber cut deep in the heart of Callisto. Only the handful of floating globes which had followed them down the shaft cast any light, and the party huddled, as if nervous of what might lurk in the dark.

Pirius stepped off the platform. The chamber was a rough cube maybe twice Pirius's height, crudely hollowed out. It might almost have been a natural formation, save for notches in the floor and a regular pattern of holes in the wall. The only piece of equipment he could see was a kind of door frame, set purposelessly in the middle of the floor.

Luru Parz walked over the ice. 'Once this was a mine. Nothing more sinister than that. But when I was last here the mine had long been shut down. Chambers like this, and the tunnels and shafts that linked them, had been pressurised and occupied. There was equipment here.' She pointed to notches in the floor. 'That was a kind of bed, I remember.'

Pirius had been expecting something like Mons Olympus, he supposed, some kind of library with bots and toiling archivists, Coalescent or not. 'There's nothing here,' he said. 'Was this the library?'

'This never was a library,' Luru Parz said. 'This was a laboratory.'

'Then where?'

'Through there.' She pointed to the door that led nowhere.

There was a moment of stiff silence, as Pirius looked from one to the other. He said, 'I think you ought to tell me what's going on.'

Nilis stared at him, agonised. Then, his arms tucked into his sleeves, he padded to the bot. The bot's carapace opened to reveal a tray of drinks that steamed in the cold. Nilis picked one up, cradling it in his hands. 'Lethe, I need this. What a tomb of a place!'

Luru Parz watched this with contempt. 'A man called Reth Cana worked here, ensign. Long ago. Ostensibly he came to look for life . . .'

Before humans came, nothing much had happened to this moon since it accreted from the greater cloud that had formed the Jupiter system. The inner moons – Io, Europa, Ganymede – had been heated by tidal pumping from Jupiter. Europa, under a crust of ice, had a liquid ocean; Io was driven by that perennial squeezing to spectacular volcanism. But Callisto had been born too far from her huge parent for any of that gravitational succour. Here the only heat was a relic of primordial radioactivity; there had been no geology, no volcanism, no hidden ocean.

Nevertheless, Reth Cana had succeeded in his quest.

They were cryptoendoliths, Luru said, bacteria-like forms living hidden lives within the dirty ice of Callisto. They survived in rivulets of water, kept liquid by the heat of relic radioactivity, and they fed off the traces of organic matter locked into the ice at the time of the moon's formation.

Luru Parz said, 'The biochemistry here is a matter of carbon-carbon chains and water – like Earth's, but not precisely so. Energy flows thin here, and replication is very slow, spanning thousands of years. The cryptoendoliths themselves weren't so interesting – except for one thing.'

Reth had believed there were pathways of chemical and electrical communication, etched into the ice and rock, tracks for great slow thoughts that pulsed through the substance of Callisto. Locked into their ice moon, there had been few routes of development open to the cryptoendoliths. But, as always, life complexified and sought new spaces to colonise. 'The cryptoendoliths couldn't move up or down, forward or back. So they stepped *sideways* . . .'

Nilis asked coldly, 'Was Reth Cana an immortal, Luru?'

'A pharaoh, yes. But not a jasoft, not a collaborator. He was a refugee, in fact; he came here fleeing the Qax and waited out the Occupation. Of course as soon as the Occupation was lifted, he became a refugee once more, hiding from the Coalition and its ideologies. He returned here to escape. And he helped others do likewise.'

Pirius said, 'What do you mean, these bugs grew sideways?'

'I mean,' said Luru Parz, 'that these remarkable little creatures found a way to penetrate another universe. And not just any old universe. Ensign, do you know what is meant by configuration space?'

'Imagine there is no time. Imagine there is no space . . .' In the still cold of Callisto, as she described extraordinary ideas, Luru's voice was a dry rustle.

'Take a snapshot of the universe. You have a static shape, a cloud of particles each frozen in flight at some point in space.' A snapping of fingers. 'Do it again. There. There. There. Each moment, each juggling of the particles, gives you a new configuration.

'Imagine *all* those snapshots, all the possible configurations the particles of the universe can take. In any one configuration you could list the particles' positions. The set of numbers you derive would correspond to a single point on a mighty multi-dimensional graph. The totality of that graph would be a map of *all* the possible states our universe could take up. Do you see? And that map is configuration space.'

'Like a phase space map.'

'Like a phase space map, yes. But of the whole universe. Now imagine putting a grain of dust on each point of the map. Each grain would correspond to a single point in time, a snapshot. This is *reality dust*, a dust of the Nows. Reality dust contains all the arrangements of matter there could ever . . .'

Slowly, as Luru explained and Nilis tried to clarify, Pirius began to understand.

Configuration space was not Pirius's world, not his universe. It was a map, yes, a sort of timeless map of his own world and all its possibilities, a higher realm. And yet, according to Luru Parz, it was a universe in itself, a place you could *go*, in a sense. And it was filled with reality dust. Every grain of sand there represented an instant in his own universe, a way for the particles of his universe, atoms and people and stars, to line themselves up.

But this was a static picture. What about time? What about causality?

If you lined up reality dust grains in a row you would get a history, of a sort, Luru Parz said. But it might not make sense as a history; nothing like causality might emerge, just a jumble of disconnected snapshots one after another. But the sand grains attracted each other. If they came from neighbouring points in the greater configuration space, the graph of all possible instants, the moments they mapped must resemble each other. And so the grains lined up in chains, each line of grains representing a series of instants which, if you watched them one after another, would give you the illusion of movement, the illusion of time passing – perhaps, if the grains were similar enough, even the illusion of causality.

Something like that.

And configuration space, he slowly understood, was where Luru Parz wanted to send Pirius.

It was beyond his imagination. 'You want me to go into a *map*? How is that possible?'

Luru said, 'Reth Cana discovered that, constrained in this space and time, the endoliths found a way into configuration space – and Reth Cana found a way for humans to follow. He could download a human consciousness into this abstract realm.'

'I can see the appeal of that for pharaohs,' Nilis said with dark humour. 'An abstract, static, Platonic realm – a place of morbid contemplation, a consolation for ageless pharaohs as they sought to justify the way they administered the suffering of their fellow creatures.'

Luru Parz smiled thinly. 'Of course it is a realm beyond our experience. So Reth constructed metaphors, a kind of interface to make its features accessible to human minds. There is an island – a beach. You'll see a mountain, Pirius, and a sea. The mountain is *order*, and at its peak is that special dust grain that represents the initial singularity: the Big Bang, the unique event when all the universe's particles overlaid each other.'

Pirius said, 'And the sea?'

'The sea is the opposite. The sea is disorder – maximal entropy – the ocean of meaninglessness to which everything washes, in the end.'

Pirius stood before the doorway, set up in the abandoned laboratory of Reth Cana. It looked as if it led nowhere. In fact, Luru Parz was saying, it led to a different realm of reality altogether. 'And if I walk through this door—'

'You will split in two,' Luru said, '*You* will still be here, walking out the other side. But a copy of you will be made.'

'Like a Virtual.'

'Yes. It will feel like you, have your memories. But it will not *be* you.'

'And this copy will be in configuration space.'

'Yes.'

'But *why* must I go there?'

'Because that is the place the pharaohs went. The pharaohs flocked there from all over Sol system and beyond,' Luru Parz said. 'Their knowledge – some of it preserved from long before the Qax Occupation – went with them too. Configuration space is a black library – the final library – and it contains much we have lost.'

Nilis said, 'You chose not to follow these undying refugees into configuration space, Luru Parz.'

Her face was blank. 'Unfinished business,' she said.

Pirius said, 'And this lost knowledge is what you want me to bring back.'

'Yes. The ancients had considerable powers. Don't forget it was human action that turned Jupiter into a black hole. Perhaps they even knew how to land punches on the supermassive monster at the centre of the Galaxy.'

He understood. 'You want me to find a weapon in there. A weapon to strike at Chandra, in this hideous old library of yours.'

'Yes . . . But there's a catch.'

'A catch?'

'Once in there, the refugees didn't stay human for long. Which is somewhat inconvenient. Try to hold on to yourself, ensign. Your identity. And *stay away from the sea*.'

Pirius peered at the portal. 'Will I be able to come back? I mean, uh, *he* – the Virtual copy.'

Nilis strode up to him and took his shoulders. Pirius had never seen Nilis look so grave. 'Pirius, I have taken you far from your home, your duty. I have asked you to face many extraordinary situations – and many dangers. But this is by far the most difficult thing I have ever asked you to do.'

Pirius said slowly, 'I can't come back.'

Luru Parz laughed. 'But it doesn't matter. Sentient or not, it will only be a copy, like a Virtual. And it won't last long. It has to be you, ensign.' She smiled, showing her blackened teeth. 'You're the only suitable resource we've got. I'm worn smooth with time, Nilis here is too aged . . . Only you have the strength to endure this.'

Pirius looked at the frame. He felt numbed, not even afraid; perhaps his imagination was exhausted. He shrugged. 'There are already two copies of me running around the Galaxy. I suppose I'm used to being split in half. When shall we do this?'

Luru Parz said, 'The equipment is ready.'

Nilis gaped. '*Now?* Just like that?'

'Why delay?' She stepped close to Pirius, so close he could smell her musty odour through the chill tang of the ice. 'Do it, Pirius. Step through and it will be over. Don't think about it. Just step through . . .' She was grotesquely seductive. He felt oddly compelled to obey. It was as if he had a gun in his hand, pointed to his head; no matter how rational he was there was always a trace of a compulsion to pull the trigger – and that self-destructive compulsion was what Luru Parz was working on now. 'Do it,' she whispered, like a voice in his own head.

Nilis said, 'Oh, but this is so— I wish I could spare you this ordeal!'

'It will only be a copy,' Luru said. 'Not you. What does a copy matter?'

Enough. Pirius turned away from Nilis. Luru Parz was right. If he had to do this—

He stepped into the frame. There was a flare of light, electric blue, blinding him. He pushed forward further, into the light.

He staggered. Gravity clutched at him, stronger than the ice moon's wispy pull, as if inertial shielding had failed. The ground under his feet felt soft, dusty, like asteroid regolith.

The blue glare faded. He stood stock still, and blinked until he could see.

He was standing on sand, bits of eroded rock. He felt the gravity stress his bones, pull at his internal organs.

He was here, then, in configuration space. He felt like himself. But *he* was the copy, projected into this strange realm, while another Pirius, the original, was back on the ice moon.

He struggled with fear. Callisto was only seconds in his past, and yet he could never go back. He somehow hadn't imagined his impulsive action ending up like this – or hadn't let himself imagine it, as Luru Parz had surely calculated when she talked him into this. And he didn't want to die.

'Lucked out,' he said to himself.

He looked around. The sky above him was open – no roof, no dome. But he was used to that by now. The light was bright, but diffuse, shadowless, without a single source, without a sun.

A mountain loomed over the horizon, a pale cone made misty by distance. The ground sloped gently towards a sea that lapped softly. But the sea was black, like a sea of hydrocarbons, as if this was Titan. He looked the other way and saw a tangle of some kind of vegetation. He dug the words out of his memory. *Ocean. Land.* This was a *beach*, then, an interface between land and the open ocean; he was on a beach.

None of this was real, of course. All of these props, the beach, the ocean, were a rendering of a more profound reality into terms he could grasp. Metaphors, drawn from the human world. But not *his* world. This was an abstraction to suit a different mind, a mind that had grown up on Earth. This would have been a strange place to a Navy brat even if he hadn't got here by such a strange route.

But he had a mission. He was here to find a weapon that could strike at a galactic-centre supermassive black hole. That was something to focus on. And maybe after that he could find some way to survive after all.

He turned and trudged up the beach, towards the vegetation. It was difficult walking on the sand, which gave with every step.

The wall of vegetation that fringed the beach was thick, apparently impenetrable. He didn't know much about plants, save what he had seen in Nilis's garden. But then this tangled bank was not a true forest; the plants that grew here were not 'trees'. The trunk-like shapes he saw, crowded with waxy, grey-green leaves, were each composed of dozens of rope-like vines tangled up together.

When he looked down he saw that the vines spread out into the dirt at the base of the vegetation. They did not dig into the ground like roots, though. Instead they spread over the surface, bifurcating further – until, he saw now, they blended into structures in the sand itself, at last dissipating altogether in a scattering of grains. It was a gathering of structure, he thought, rising from the sand, melding into these apparently living things.

Luru Parz had told him none of this had anything to do with biology but, somehow, with causality, with chains of consequences gathering in significance . . .

He was never going back.

Suddenly the truth of it hit him, blinding him to the place in which he found himself. He probed for a sense of loss, of abandonment, found only numbness. He tried to think of other times, other places: the ancient ice mine on Callisto, and the deeper past beyond that, the worldlets of Arches Base, the dorms, the soft warmth of Torec. It took an effort, as if the brief moments he had been here were expanding to fill his life.

After all, he remembered, *he* was a mere representation of somebody else. He wasn't real, and that lost life had never been his. His fear faded.

Luru had warned he might lose himself in here. Maybe losing his fear was the first stage of that. Real or not, he had his duty; *that* was real enough.

Something rustled, deep inside the tangle of grey-green. He looked up, startled. Two eyes peered back at him – human eyes? But another rustle, a shake of the leaves as if a wind had passed, and they were gone.

He plunged into the vegetation. 'Wait,' he cried. 'Wait!' He had to rip aside the tangle of vines by main force, and even so was barely able to move forward.

There was a face before him. Two bright eyes, peering from green shadow. He froze, shocked. At first he could make no sense of it. He saw eyes, nose, a mouth. But the proportions seemed wrong – the eyes too close, the mouth too wide. Then it *shifted*, as if one face were melding into another, or a Virtual image were failing. But the eyes were steady, that gaze locked on his. Was it possible this was the relic of some jasoft, come here to flee from the Coalition?

And was this a glimpse of his own fate?

'Help me,' he said. It came out as a whisper, and he tried again. 'Help me . . .'

Humanity is in peril. We need to strike at the Prime Radiant of the Xeelee. We need a way to harm a supermassive black hole.

It seemed absurd. What could such things matter here? What was a war, even, in a place where a handful of sand grains held a million possible instants? What indeed was life or death? And yet he remembered his duty; he tried to speak to that monstrous, shifting face. 'If there is anything left of the human in you, you must answer—'

A fist slammed into his face, with impossible force. He felt his nose crunch under the impact. And something was forced into his mouth, hard enough to tear the muscles of his cheeks.

The blow hurled him backwards, out of the forest, his hunched body ripping through the tangle of causality. He landed on the beach, sprawled in reality dust. And his hand was burning, as if he had dipped it in fire. The pain distracted him even from the ache of his shattered face, the bitterness of the stuff in his mouth. The black ocean was lapping close to him, much further up the beach than before. Tides, he thought. Second-hand gravitational effects working on open bodies of liquid. Bits of facts from his training, from a life that was lost.

He held up his arm. His hand was *gone*, the stump neatly filmed over with pink flesh, as if the hand had never been. The black stuff wasn't water. It must have burned off his hand like the strongest acid. Neat it might be, but the pain was agonising.

Causality, he thought. Entropy. That's what Luru said the sea means. I am being eaten by a sea of entropy, dissolved into disorder.

He forced himself to roll over, away from the ocean. Pain lanced up his arm.

The stuff in his mouth shifted, blocking his breathing. He could suffocate lying here. Or the blow itself might turn out to be lethal. There were ways to kill people like that, he remembered; you rammed your face into your opponent's nose, to push a shard of bone into the brain.

He was going to die here. But he was just a Virtual – not Pirius, not Pirius Red or Pirius Blue. He was Pirius Grey, he thought, Pirius the shadow. His death didn't matter.

His mouth worked. Perhaps he could spit the crud out from his mouth. But some instinct made him bite into it. A thick, acidic fluid spurted into his mouth. He bit again, and forced himself to swallow.

Perhaps he had succeeded. He had come seeking answers, and he had been given a cruel feeding. But what had he expected, a textbook? Some philosophers said that humans shouldn't dream of contact with the Xeelee; their warmaking was the only possible contact. And perhaps this revolting mouthful *was* the solution he had been sent for.

He tried to think of his name again. It was fading, fading like a dream in the moments after waking. Grey, grey.

Pain striped along his left hand side. He cried out. The black ocean had washed a little further up the beach. He tried to scramble away.

Deep inside Callisto, Pirius stepped into the door frame. There was a fiare of light, electric blue, blinding. He pushed further forward, into the light.

On the far side of the portal he felt a hard, cold surface under his feet. Ice?

The blue glare faded. He stood stock still, and blinked until he could see.

Suddenly his heart was hammering. He was still in the chamber, on Callisto, standing on the other side of the portal. *He* was Pirius, not the copy; he would have to leave that other to do his duty for him. 'Lucked out,' he said.

'My eyes,' said Nilis. 'Oh, my boy, what a terrible thing . . .'

Luru Parz said, '*Look.*'

Pirius turned. A Virtual projection hovered over the service bot, a complex, fast-shifting display, elusive, dense. Even the Navy guard was staring.

Pirius asked, 'What is it?'

'Data,' said Luru Parz. 'From configuration space. Coming back through the portal.'

'I think it worked,' Nilis said. 'You found something, Pirius!'

Luru Parz growled, 'Now all we have to do is figure out what it is.'

CHAPTER 32

The flight approached the terminus of East Arm.

The three main arms of the Baby Spiral, three fat streams of infalling gas, came to a junction, melding into a massive knot of turbulence. Pirius Blue could see it ahead, a tangle of glowing gas filaments. He knew that just on the other side of that central knot of gas lay the brooding mass of Chandra itself, and the powerful alien presences that infested it. No human crew had ever got so close, and lived.

The silence on the *Claw*'s crew loop was telling. He remembered the words of his first flight instructor. 'You pretty kids are all so smart. You have to be smart to fly a greenship. But in combat there's only one thing worse than being smart. And that's being imaginative . . .'

Pirius knew he ought to come up with something inspirational to say. But he didn't understand how he felt himself. Not fear: he seemed to be finding a kind of acceptance. He recalled fragments of conversations with This Burden Must Pass, where that proselyte of the Friends of Wigner had mused about how it would be to reach the end of time and approach the Ultimate Observer, to approach a god. Perhaps it would be like this, the calm of being utterly insignificant.

Then the Xeelee attacked.

'Azimuth eighty! Azimuth eighty!' That was Four screaming, off to Pirius's starboard.

Pirius glared around the sky. This time he saw the nightfighters just as the instruments blared their warnings. They were a ball of swarming ships, black as night, coming at him from out of the shining clouds. Starbreaker beams spat ahead of them, a curtain of fire. The nightfighters were beautiful, he thought, lethally beautiful. In this turbulent, violent place, the Xeelee looked like they had been born here.

No time for that.

Dray shouted, 'Pattern delta!'

'Locking in,' Cohl snapped.

Pirius threw the *Other Claw* on to its new trajectory. The Galaxy centre whirled around him, the merging lanes of gas spilling about his head.

Again the little convoy split, this time into two pairs. It was a copy of their first feint. This time Three and Four peeled off and went shooting away to Pirius's port side, haring into the shining corridor of the Arm, as if trying to escape back to the Front. Meanwhile Wedge Leader and Wedge Seven, Dray and Pirius, went straight for the Xeelee, their weapons already firing.

Again there was a heartbeat of delay, as if the Xeelee were trying to decide what was happening. But this time they didn't follow the decoy; this time they came straight on at Dray and Pirius.

Cohl said, 'Lethe. They knew.'

'I don't understand,' Nilis said.

'They didn't fall for the bait,' Pirius said. 'We were meant to look like a rearguard. The Xeelee were supposed to chase after the others. But they didn't.'

'Your navigator said, "They knew".'

'FTL foreknowledge,' Pirius said. 'You can always tell when it cuts in. Suddenly they know what you're going to do before *you* do.'

'They may know,' Dray said forcefully. 'But that doesn't mean they can stop us. Pirius, you're less than a hundred light days from Chandra. Make a single jump. Get in there, do what you have to do, get out.'

Cohl said, 'It's impossible.'

Pirius glanced at his instruments. This was the core of the Galaxy, full of immense masses throwing themselves around, spacetime churned to a foam. He took a breath. 'Yes, it's impossible. But we're going to do it anyway.'

He was aware of Nilis tensing beside him, his pale fingers gripping the edge of his seat. Virtual Nilis was an authentic, fully sentient re-creation; perhaps death was as dark a prospect for such a creature as for a full human.

That knot of Xeelee were approaching; ten more seconds and their weapons would find their range.

'Commodore—'

'You're on your own, Pirius. For those who have fallen!'

Abruptly Dray's ship threw itself at the Xeelee, monopole shells spraying. Pirius saw the formation of the nightfighters momentarily waver; as she passed through them Dray made their wings rustle. But soon the Xeelee were closing over that brave green spark.

'Another gone,' Nilis said.

But she had bought a little time. 'Cohl—'

'Laid in.'

'Do it.'

In the instant of transition Pirius could *feel* the instability of Galaxy-centre spacetime; the jump felt like a kick to the base of the spine.

Violent blue light flooded the cabin. With warning Virtuals flickering all around him, Pirius gazed out of the blister.

To his left was a bank of stars, hot, blue-white. There were pairs, and triples and quadruples, stars close enough to distort each other; he saw one loose giant being torn to wispy shreds by a hard blue-white companion. There was much loose gas too, great glowing clouds of it, here and there scarred by nova blisters. This was shown on his maps as IRS 16, a cluster of young stars nucleating out of the rich gas and dust that poured in along the arms of the Baby Spiral. In this environment these bright young stars, huge and fast-lived, were like babies born in a furnace.

Stars to his port side, then. And to his starboard, something much more strange.

He saw more stars – but some of these stars had tails, like comets. They swarmed like fireflies around a central patch of brightness, a background glow of shifting, elusive light. It was like a solar system, he thought, with that central spark in place of a sun, and those trapped stars orbiting it like planets. The whole of this intricate, compact mechanism was cradled by one of the arms of the Baby Spiral – West Arm, opposite the one he had followed in; it looked like a jewelled toy set on a blanket of gold. But great chunks had been torn out of the arm, and blobs of glowing gas sailed away, dispersing slowly. Everything here was jammed together by ferocious gravity, and this was a terribly crowded place, crowded with huge, rushing masses that anywhere else would have been separated by light years. This was the very heart of the Galaxy, the immediate environs of Chandra itself. But the black hole was invisible, somewhere at the heart of that flock of captured, doomed stars.

All this in a glance.

Pirius focused on his ship. The *Other Claw* had come out of her FTL jump with a velocity vector which had taken it through a sharp left turn and sent it screaming through the narrow gap between the IRS 16 star cluster and Chandra. As they fled, data on Chandra was pouring into the ship's stores through Nilis's sensor pod, he saw. This was what they had come here for: they were fulfilling the mission objectives. But they didn't have long. All around this cluttered panorama black flecks flew like bits of soot: the Xeelee, disturbed, were rising to drive out the intruder.

Nilis breathed, 'My eyes – that I should live to see such a thing! You know, those stars won't last long here. But their intense solar wind sweeps this Cavity clear of gas and dust. And when it hits Chandra—'

Cohl said, 'The Xeelee are closing, Pirius.' She downloaded tactical Virtuals to Pirius's station, so the pilot could see what she saw.

More Xeelee had come out of nowhere. Suddenly they were surrounded, trapped.

Pirius cursed. Another misjudgement. He snapped, 'Options.'

'Pray,' said Hope morbidly.

Cohl had nothing to say.

Pirius tried to think. The plan had always been to fly through the gap between the star nursery and the central Chandra system itself, get through to the relatively flat space beyond, and then make another massive jump back to East Arm, their route home. But they hadn't banked on being alone, with no cover and with forewarned Xeelee rising. It was unlikely that they could survive another FTL jump all the way out, not from here.

But, unexpectedly, Nilis had an idea.

The Commissary sounded dry, calm, as if he had moved beyond fear. 'Make for IRS 7.'

Pirius quickly called up another map. IRS 7 was a star lost in the Cavity: it was a red giant, and it trailed an immense comet-like tail. 'It's only half a light year away.'

'Lethe,' said Hope, 'its tail is longer than that. What use is it to us?'

'A place to hide,' said Nilis. 'And we could make it in a single, short FTL jump . . . Couldn't we, pilot?'

'Too risky,' Cohl said.

'Every jump in this environment carries risks. A short jump is more survivable.'

'It will be no use, even if we live through the hop,' Cohl said. 'The Xeelee are on to us. FTL foreknowledge.'

'Then we throw them off,' Nilis said.

'I'm amazed how calm you are, Commissary,' Pirius said.

'We can discuss my personality later. I suggest we get on with it.'

A wand of starbreaker light waved through space, above Pirius's head. The nightfighters were finding their range; one touch of that pretty light and his life would be over. No more time for debate.

He waved his hand at his Virtual displays. 'We need to make the hop anti-Tolman, if we can. Come on, Cohl, work with me.'

Nilis said, 'A lot of people have died to get us this far. We have to get through, complete our mission.'

'We don't need to be told, Commissary. Navigator?'

'I have a tactical solution. It's a botch.'

'Lay it in. On my mark. Three, two—'

In the last second the *Other Claw* shuddered. And then Chandra's shining astrophysical architecture vanished.

They came out tumbling. Pirius fought to stabilise the ship.

Nilis peered out curiously. They were immersed in a uniform crimson glow that utterly lacked detail, as if they had hopped into the interior of an immense light globe.

Pirius snapped, 'Engineer. Report.'

Enduring Hope called, 'We were hit half a second before the hop. Bad luck . . . The weapons bay took it.' He laughed. 'I don't think we hit a single Xeelee. But the weapons bay soaked up the energy of that shot, and saved us.'

'Other systems?'

'The sensor pod is intact,' Nilis said. 'We didn't lose any data. And now we're in the tail of IRS 7?'

'I think so.'

The 'tail' was the remnant of the outer layers of the hapless red giant, blasted away by the ferocious stellar wind generated by the blue star cluster at the centre, Pirius said, 'We aimed for the root, where the tail meets the surviving envelope.'

'So we're actually *inside* the body of a star . . . Good piloting.'

'We're still alive. So, yes, it was good enough.'

'And the Xeelee?'

'No sign that they are on to us yet.' Pirius glanced at his displays. 'I'll wait a couple of minutes. Then we'll work our way along the tail, a series of short hops. And once we're out of there, if we're lucky—'

Nilis nodded. Pirius studied him cautiously. Still he seemed remarkably calm, and Pirius thought his face seemed smoother, as if lacking some character, some detail. 'Commissary, are you all right?'

Nilis smiled at him. 'As perceptive as ever! . . . I could never pass this on to him, you know.'

'Who?'

'Nilis – ah, Nilis Prime. My original. He must get the data, of course, and my analytical impressions. But I think I should keep back the rest. The *emotions*. I've already begun the process of deletion.'

'You're a Virtual. It's against your programming to edit yourself.'

Nilis shook his head. 'You can't hand out sentience without enabling choice.' His smile faded. 'It feels – odd, though. To be closing down sections of my mind. Like a partial suicide. But it's necessary. He wouldn't go on, you see, with the Project, if he *knew*.'

'Knew what? The fear?'

'Oh, not that. Fear is trivial. Pirius, at most only three of our eight ships will make it home. No, not fear: the horror of seeing those around you die, and die for your ideas. Nilis has never really confronted this, you know, sitting in his garden on Earth, immersed in his studies. And he won't be strong enough. I know, because *I'm* not. But he must go on; he has to complete Project Prime Radiant, for all our sakes.'

'Commissary—'

'*I'm* all right. I've already cut it out of myself, you see.' Nilis lifted his Virtual face, red giant light casting subtly shifting shadows from the lines of his expressionless face. 'Shall we go home?'

CHAPTER 33

Nilis stayed at Saturn, studying the material Pirius had retrieved from configuration space, which appeared to be a spec for a weapon system. But, apparently plagued by guilt, he sent Pirius Red back to Earth, ordering him to rest up. Pirius didn't like the idea, but he didn't protest.

The rest cure didn't work out, though. Pirius Red was alone again, alone in Nilis's apartment, aside from a few bots.

Of course here he was on Earth itself, surrounded by a vast population, a population of billions: a greater crowd than any other human world, save only the pathological Coalescent communities. Somehow that made it worse than in the Venus habitat.

He tried walking in the Conurbation's teeming corridors and parks. He even dug out one of the Commissary's old robes so he wouldn't stand out from the crowd so much. But he had nothing in common with these chattering, confident swarms with their rich, intricate social lives, their baffling business, their soft hands and unmarked faces. They were so remote from everything he had known from his origins in the Core that he may as well have been from a separate species.

And even if he could stand the openness out of doors, even if he could tolerate the people, he was still *on Earth*. Every time the sun went down, the sky glowed bright in the lights of the Conurbations, and beyond the glow strode the immense, arrogant engineering of the Bridge to the Moon around which interplanetary traffic crawled constantly. It was like being trapped in some vast machine.

So his days were troubled. And when he lay alone in the dark, his thoughts were drawn back to Callisto, over and over.

He didn't understand it. Why should he feel so disturbed? All he had done was walk through a doorway. *He* was the Pirius who had walked out unharmed; it was not *him* who had been mapped to a new level of reality, with no hope of return, to be leached of his humanity. He despised himself for his weakness.

But if he *didn't* think about Callisto, images of the hive in Olympus came into his mind – or of the strange immortal, Luru Parz – or, worst of all, the Silver Ghosts on Pluto, and the shameful, helpless way he had reacted, like a machine. He felt as if his mind was becoming like Callisto, ancient and battered. And he feared that, if he looked too hard, he would find deep inside it the kind of strangeness Luru Parz had uncovered in that ice moon.

Perhaps Nilis had been right that he needed a break. But Nilis had not been able to see that being on Earth, alone, was precisely the wrong kind of rest cure for a Navy brat. He longed for Torec, his only point of familiarity in this strange solar system. But she was out at Saturn. He was able to speak to her. Nilis even let him use expensive inseparability channels so there was no time delay. But it wasn't the same. He needed to be touched, held.

And anyhow even Torec seemed cold.

After forty-eight sleepless hours he called Nilis. He begged to be brought out to Saturn and put back to work.

Pirius arrived in time for a test firing of what Nilis called the 'Callisto weapon'.

He was brought to Nilis's corvette, which the Commissary was using as his work base. The interior was cluttered, with data desks strewn on the floor, bots of all sizes tumbling through the air and Virtuals obscuring every view. Nilis was here, with Commander Darc, Torec and various assistants. In this noisy mess it was impossible to see how any work got done. Nilis and Darc seemed to be working closely, but their arguments crackled like lightning.

Pirius spotted Torec, peering out at the test rig. He made straight for her. He hadn't seen her for weeks, since before Venus. She acknowledged him with a nod, but turned away. He stood awkwardly, arms suddenly heavy, longing to touch her. He just didn't understand.

He pulled himself together. He stood with her and looked out of the hull.

Orbiting far from Saturn's patient golden face, the test rig was a set of twenty GUTdrive engines, mounted in a loose spherical framework perhaps fifty metres across. Technicians and bots crawled over it. It had been put together in a few days, and it didn't look much like anything, let alone a weapon for striking at the most formidable fortress in the Galaxy.

But a few kilometres away the captive Xeelee ship waited, surrounded by its usual cordon of watchful guardian drones; today, once again, the nightfighter was the test target. Spinning slowly, surrounded by its attendant cloud of bots and techs, the test rig looked about as much a threat to the patient Xeelee as a spitball.

He said, 'It looks like shit.'

Even that didn't force a smile from Torec. 'Actually we've come a long way in a few days. But we're as under-funded as ever. We need GUTdrive generators, but all Nilis was able to get hold of are those dinged-up decommissioned relics. You can see the scars where they have been cut out of wrecks.'

'Darc and Nilis are at each other's throats.'

'That's just their way. Darc is keen, once he forgets that he disapproves of the whole thing. He likes getting his hands dirty – especially on something new like this. He's OK.'

Pirius looked covertly at her so-familiar profile, the finely carved chin, the upturned nose, the lines of her face softened by golden-brown Saturn light. 'And you've kept busy.'

She shrugged. 'It's not so bad right now. When, if, we get through this proof-of-concept stage I'll be involved in developing the flight hardware. You too, I guess.'

His need to touch her was an ache. 'Torec, listen. I—'

She held up a hand, silencing him. A green light flared beyond the hull.

The techs and bots backed away from the rig, leaving only a few drones for close-in monitoring. Pirius watched Torec silently counting down, tracking the clock in her head as she always did: *Three. Two. One.*

The rig quivered. Waves of distortion, easily visible, spread out from each of the GUTdrive generators, as if they were pebbles thrown in a pool.

GUTdrive engines worked by allowing a fragment of compressed mass-energy to expand, releasing energy through the decay of a unified superforce. In this configuration, rather than using that energy to drive a spacecraft, the engines were each supposed to create a spherical wave of distorted spacetime. The engines had been positioned so that the ripples moved inwards, into the rig.

As the waves converged, blue-white light flared, dazzling. The flash dissipated immediately – but now a concentrated knot of distortion was travelling along the axis of the rig. Shifting, oscillating, the distortion made the stars blur as it travelled. It was like an immense drop of water, Pirius thought. As it burst from the rig the knot broke open struts, and sent the scavenged GUTdrive engines flying – and it was aimed straight at the nightfighter.

But before it had travelled more than a few hundred metres the ball of distortion swelled up, burst silently and dissipated.

There was a rustle of movement in the corvette, a collective sigh of disappointment.

Darc clapped Nilis on the back. 'Scratch another run. Never mind, Commissary. We're not done yet.'

'Indeed not.'

Torec said to Pirius, 'Timing is everything. The implosion in the centre is what we're trying to design. If the amplitude is large enough you get nonlinearity – a shock wave, its profile distorting as it travels, what the techs call a "classical scalar wave". I think we've got the amplitudes right, but not the timing. If the waves don't converge right at the centre, they just pass through each other harmlessly.'

Pirius said, 'And if the timing *is* right – what's supposed to happen?'

Torec stared at him, the first time she'd looked at him directly since he had got here. 'You were on Callisto, and you don't know?'

Pirius said helplessly, 'I just did my job there.'

'This is a design from the Occupation era. *It's a black hole cannon*, Pirius.' She smiled faintly. 'Can you believe that? We're making a cannon to fire black holes at the Xeelee. And you know what else? It was designed by Friends. Friends, just like Enduring Hope!'

Pirius, stunned, stared at the battered test rig. The techs and drones were already going back to work.

Nilis asked Pirius to spend some time with him.

They sat together in Nilis's cabin. It was clear to Pirius that the Commissary wanted something. But Nilis was still guilty about how Pirius had been 'used' on Callisto, and he seemed to want to make it up to him by talking to him.

He said his 'Callisto weapon' did indeed date from the time of the Qax Occupation. Pirius was amazed that the Friends of Wigner, in his day an illegal fringe cult out on Arches, had roots that deep.

Back then the Friends had been a group of rebels on Earth. During the early phase of the Occupation the control of the Qax had been relatively light – and remarkably enough the Friends had been able to assemble a whole spacecraft, equipped with black hole cannons, under the noses of Earth's occupiers.

The Friends had known that a wormhole bridge to the deeper past was soon to be opened; spanning fifteen centuries, this audacious stunt had been set up by none other than Michael Poole. When the bridge opened, the Friends hurled themselves and their ship into the past. Ignoring the humans of Poole's time they had set to work preparing their battery of black holes – but their purpose was not to use their cannons as weapons. Their target was Jupiter. In the guts of the gas giant these grenades of twisted spacetime would collide and merge, each collision sending out pulses of gravitational waves. By programming this sequence, the Friends hoped to shape the collapse of Jupiter, and so sculpt the final black hole that would result.

'So that was what happened to Jupiter,' Pirius said.

'Yes. Quite a monument!'

'But if they could make black hole cannons, if they could go back in time, why not just fly out to the Qax home world and wipe them out?'

Nilis smiled. 'Spoken like a true pragmatist! But the Friends' objective was more philosophical . . .'

The first Friends of Wigner had taken their name from an ancient philosopher who had pondered the mysteries of quantum physics. Beneath the world perceived by humans was a scaffolding of uncertainty. Quantum functions pervaded space, each a description of the probability governing a particle or system, and it was only when an observation was made that a particle could be pinned down to a particular place, or to a definite speed.

'But this ancient philosopher, Wigner, took that logic a step further,' Nilis said. 'Any observer is *herself* a quantum object – everything is, we all are – and therefore herself subject to quantum uncertainty. You need a *second* observer to make her real, and thence to make her observation real. If Wigner is the first observer, his friend is the second.'

Pirius thought that over. 'But what about the friend's quantum function? That isn't made definite until a third observer makes an observation of *her*.'

'You have it,' said Nilis approvingly. 'And then you need a fourth, and a fifth.'

Pirius's head was swimming with infinities. 'But no matter how many observers you have, how many friends of Wigner you line up, you always need one more. So *nothing* can be real.'

'This was called the paradox of Wigner's friends,' Nilis said. 'But the Friends believed they had a resolution.'

The chains of unresolved quantum states will build on and on, growing like flowers, extending into the future. At last the great chains of quantum functions would finally merge at the last boundary of the universe, at timelike infinity.

'And there, argued the Friends, will reside the Ultimate Observer, the last sentient being of all. All quantum functions, all world lines, *must* terminate in the Observer – for otherwise, she would not be the last. The Observer will make a single climactic Observation—'

'And the chains of observations will collapse.'

'History will be made real at last, but only at its very end.'

Pirius said, 'But I don't see how this was going to help the Friends get rid of the Qax.'

The Friends had come to believe that the Ultimate Observer might not be a passive eye, but that this final being might have a choice: that she might be able to exert an influence on how the chains of quantum functions were collapsed, on *which* cosmic history out of the many possible was selected.

'And if a being has such power,' Nilis said, 'perhaps she can be lobbied. And that was what the Friends intended to do. They were going to send the Ultimate Observer a message.'

'How? With Jupiter?'

'Singularities themselves have structure, you know . . . The singularity at the heart of the Jupiter black hole was to be shaped, and loaded with information. It would be a plea to the Ultimate Observer. The Friends wanted the Observer to select her chosen history to favour humanity – in particular, to pick out a causal line that would *not* include the Qax Occupation.'

Pirius thought that over, and laughed, wondering. 'That's astonishing.'

Nilis said, 'It's a terribly nihilistic philosophy – don't you think? Just like their modern intellectual descendants, the Friends actually seem to have believed that they, their memories, their whole lives would be wiped out of existence when the Ultimate Observer makes her choice and some optimal timeline is plucked out of the quantum tangle. The Friends were not just escaping the Qax, ensign. Perhaps they were escaping from themselves.'

Pirius wasn't convinced. He thought of Enduring Hope, back in the Core. If you were stuck in the middle of an endless war, the notion of an end-of-time arbiter who would one day delete all the pain from the world was a comforting idea.

But he had believed it was myth. He hadn't known that this airy nonsense about a cleansing at the end of the universe might actually have some physics in it. It was a spooky thought.

'Of course their scheme was over-complicated, and it didn't work,' Nilis said. The Friends didn't even manage to make their black hole properly, let alone send their plea to the end of time. They managed to destroy Jupiter, though.'

The Qax responded to the treachery of the Friends with devastating force. No longer would their rule be light; no longer could human cultural artefacts be used to camouflage rebellion. The Extirpation began: human history would be deleted, human minds wiped clean, even the fossils in the ground would be pulverised. The Qax intended that humans would never pose a threat to the Qax again. They came close to succeeding.

The Friends' black hole technology was suppressed. And after the Occupation, when the Coalition came to power, such ancient horrors were suppressed again. But a handful of pharaohs kept the old knowledge alive, tucked away where even the long arm of the Commission for Historical Truth could not find it. The pharaohs had always known a day would came when it would be needed again.

They fell silent.

'I have a new assignment for you,' Nilis said hesitantly. 'You might find it sticky.'

'Sticky?'

'I need you to think about Pirius Blue.'

Pirius hadn't thought about his temporal twin for days. 'Why?'

It turned out that Blue had been having adventures of his own. Astonishingly, he had flown a ship deep into the Cavity, to scout the Prime Radiant itself.

'I'm trying to build up a picture of Chandra – its nature, its surrounds,' Nilis said earnestly. 'I have the material I discovered in the Olympus Archive, the data from the neutrino telescope, and now Blue's first-hand experience. I need to put it all together – to assemble a theoretical model of our objective. I was there, you know,' he said with a sort of modest pride. 'In the Cavity. I sent in an avatar to ride with Pirius Blue. I like to think I acquitted myself well enough! But even that experience isn't enough. I need to know what Blue himself perceived.'

Pirius nodded slowly. 'So why don't you talk to him?'

'It is a question of nuances,' Nilis said. He reached out his big hands towards Pirius. 'I'm not sure I understand *you*, you see. We discussed this before. Our backgrounds are so different! Of course nobody knows Pirius Blue as well as you do. Nobody will be able to understand his words, his body language – what remains *un*said – as well as you. This is *very* important. Listen to your time brother, Pirius Red; listen to his feelings . . .'

Pirius took the assignment.

For the rest of the day he sat in Nilis's musty cabin watching Virtual recordings of Pirius Blue, more battered, more weary, even *older*, as he described his extraordinary jaunt into the Core.

Pirius Red still felt a lingering resentment at this stranger from the future who had sent him into involuntary exile. But mostly, Red felt envy: envy for a man who had once more had the opportunity to carry out his duty in the most testing of circumstances, and envy for the companionship of his crew. Watching this scratchy Virtual report, Pirius Red felt shut out, denied.

At the end of the day, Torec and Pirius retired to their room on the corvette. They didn't speak.

Pirius stripped off his uniform and allowed it to slither into the closet. He got into the bed turned his face to the wall and closed his eyes, hoping for sleep. At least he wasn't on Earth; at least he was back in space, and he could hear the comforting sigh of cycled air, feel the thrumming of the corvette's drive.

He was surprised when Torec slid into his bunk.

He turned to face her. Her face was so close he could feel her breath on his cheek. Her eyes, dimly visible in the low light, were closed, her mouth tight shut.

He put his hand on her arm. He felt firm flesh and muscle. He whispered, 'Things aren't the same.'

He could feel her roll on to her back. 'The trouble is, Pirius, things have changed for me. While you've been away, I've been *useful*.'

He knew that was true. There had been her work on the CTC processor, the test flights of the modified greenships, even this early work on the black hole cannon. He remembered her confusion when they had first been brought to Sol system, when she hadn't even wanted to get out of bed.

She said, 'I know it's chance that I'm here at all. It could have been anybody.' She shifted again. 'Look, Pirius, I might have been brought here for you. But now I've found my own place. That's what I'm trying to say. You can't come swarming back and expect things to be as they were before.'

'I don't think I ever did expect that,' he said.

'Then what?'

He shrugged. 'I need you.'

She snorted. 'Yeah. For sex.'

'Not just that.' He hesitated to say the word, knowing it sounded soft. 'Company.'

She laughed. 'What are you, a Coalescent drone? Life isn't about company, Pirius. It's about doing your job. '

Defensively he said, 'Yes. But maybe we can help each other to be more effective. Have you thought of that?'

'What help do *you* need? It wasn't even you who was sent into that weird other-place on Callisto.'

'It was a copy of me who went off and died, to spare me having to do it. Just as Pirius Blue is a copy of me, who saw friends die in action, who went back into the Core again – and because *he* lived through that, *I* won't have to. All these copies of me, taken away to die. And I'm left standing here.'

'This talk is stupid.'

He whispered, 'Or perhaps I'm not real. Pirius Blue could have died out there, at the magnetar. What if he did die? What if I'm his ghost? Or perhaps I'm existing in somebody else's memories, or dreams. Perhaps Pirius Blue dreamed of Earth before he died, and everything I think is happening to me is happening inside his mind, in the last fraction of a second before the starbreaker hits—'

'And maybe you've got your pointy head so far up your own ass it's coming out the other end.' She pinched his kidney, hard enough to make him yelp. 'Is that real enough for you?'

Before she could do it again he rolled over and grabbed her. Laughing, they wrestled. He finished up above her, with his hands locking her arms above her head. Her face was a pool of soft shadows beneath him; she looked very young.

He said, 'You're tougher than me. You always were. But don't you feel – dislocated?'

'Well, a little. But you tell anybody back on Arches I said so I'll kick your butt.'

Hesitantly, he bent down and kissed her, very softly, just brushing her lips. At first she was cold, unresponsive. Then she opened her mouth, and he felt the tip of her tongue on his teeth.

Once again the test rig was readied for a fresh shot at the patient Xeelee nightfighter.

It had been decided to try hooking up the CTC processor to the control systems of the test rig's GUTdrive engines. It was possible that the CTC's greater processing speed would permit the refinement of the control of the spacetime wavefronts sufficiently to get the result the designers wanted. Commander Darc railed at the foolishness of hooking up one experimental technology to another, but the CTC had already proven itself in the control of the grav shield. And as Nilis said, 'Compared to the rest of this lash-up, CTC is a mature technology.'

The work proceeded fast. Torec had as much experience as anybody with CTC systems, and so she had been drawn back into the heart of the project. Pirius was left stranded on the observation deck of the corvette, watching the techs work at the modified rig. It was easy to spot Torec with her bright red team leader's armbands over her skinsuit.

Nilis stood with him. He waved a hand in the air, and brought up Pirius's old Virtual sketch of the Project. The path to the Prime Radiant and the Xeelee barricade around it were green, the asterisk that represented the Radiant itself was glowing red. 'What do you think, ensign? Is today the day when we will find a weapon to strike at the Prime Radiant itself?'

Pirius was embarrassed by the hubristic sketch. 'I hope so, sir.'

Torec's voice sounded softly in Pirius's ear. 'Are you watching? Three. Two. One.' Pirius pressed his face to the hull.

Again he saw flexing spacetime permeate the crude rig of struts and GUTdrive engines, again those waves of distortion washed into the heart of the rig. But the distortions seemed stronger to Pirius this time, their crowding propagation somehow more urgent.

Purple-white light flared at the centre of the rig, a glaring pinpoint. The framework itself pulsed and flexed, and struts snapped. But the frame held, and that central pinpoint cast shadows over its complex structure. The pinpoint of light was a black hole. It was about as massive as a Conurbation dome, crushed into a space the size of an electron, glowing through Hawking evaporation at a temperature measured in teradegrees. It was working, then: he held his breath.

For a second the black hole waited at the heart of the rig. The framework pulsed and cracked.

And then the dazzling spark leapt straight out of the frame and hurled itself in a dead straight line across space to the Xeelee. When it hit, the nightfighter seemed to fold over on itself, as if crushed by a vast fist.

For a long moment, nothing moved: the observers, Saturn's broad disc, the crumpled Xeelee ship, the broken rig. Then, in Pirius's monitors, remote cheering started.

Nilis said, 'My eyes. I think we've done it.' He snapped his fingers. On Pirius's diagram, the crimson asterisk turned bright green.

CHAPTER 34

Conurbation 11729!

It was a city known only by the number given to it by alien conquerors, but it was a number known throughout the Galaxy. This place had been the base of Hama Druz himself, twenty thousand years before. Ever since, it had been the beating heart of a human Galaxy.

And it was here that Nilis and his team came to confront the mighty power that had ruled all mankind since Druz's day, the Interim Coalition of Governance, seeking its blessing to establish a new Navy squadron and to equip it with upgraded ships, with CTC processors and gravastar shields and black hole cannons – seeking its blessing to take Project Prime Radiant to the centre of the Galaxy itself.

From the air the city looked almost ordinary, just another of the Qax's inhuman clusterings of domes of blown rock. But the ancient blisters glittered with windows and balconies, the city was covered with a shining spider's web of walkways and monorails, and steady streams of traffic, both intra-atmospheric and from space, washed through the ports that ringed the central dome cluster. The old Qax architecture was still the foundation of everything, but the sense of power here was palpable, even compared to the rest of Earth – power, and wealth.

The flitter landed at a small pad outside the largest of the domes. It carried only Nilis and his two ensigns, in their best dress uniforms. But even so blue-helmeted Guardians insisted on coming on board the ship and subjecting each of them to whole-body searches that lasted long minutes. This massive dome housed the principal headquarters of some of the Coalition's most powerful ministries and agencies, and there were plenty of enemies of the Coalition who would wish to do harm here, given a chance – not just alien foe, but human rebels. Back in Arches Base such a thing would have seemed no more than a theoretical possibility, but this was Earth. The ensigns submitted silently.

At last they were released, and Nilis led them into the dome itself.

The tremendous enclosed space was flooded with light, and spectacular buildings soared in contemptuous defiance of the laws of physics. There were arches and T-shapes and inverted cones, their frames studded with inertial controllers and anti-gravity generators; some of them even floated. People hurried across the floor in streams, or along walkways that threaded through the air between the build-ings. There was a hubbub of noise, a constant shouting; it was the sound of merged human voices, a million of them in this one dome alone.

And above it all the grey Qax shell loomed, a rocky sky. Beneath its grand curvature light globes clustered like stars. Some of the floating buildings nuzzled against the shell of the dome itself; perhaps they had penthouses built through the dome, to reach the sky.

Pirius reached for Torec's hand, and they clung to each other. It was a city designed for giants, not mere humans like themselves.

Nilis hurried, barefoot as ever, his arms full of data desks. 'We mustn't be late. Mustn't be late! All Luru Parz's morally dubious arm-twisting has won us is a hearing before Minister Gramm and his sub-committee. It has to go well today, this latest war of words, or all our technological achievements will count for nothing.'

At last Nilis brought them to a doorway. It was itself huge, but was a mere detail at the base of the building above it. This, said Nilis, was a centre of the Grand Conclave itself, the Coalition's supreme body.

In the foyer they were subjected to yet more searches, by yet more Guardians. Nilis wasn't allowed to take any equipment beyond here, and he had to download his data from his bots and data desks into copies provided by the Guardians. He had been prepared for this, but he fretted at the continuing delays.

When they were released they hurried across the foyer to a narrow, silver-walled elevator shaft. In this expensive machine there was no sense of acceleration; Pirius had no idea how high they climbed – or perhaps descended.

The doors slid back to reveal a conference room. Nilis hurried

forward, muttering apologies for his lateness. Pirius and Torec followed more slowly, eyes wide.

They were in another vast chamber, a rectangular box eight or ten
metres high and maybe a hundred metres deep. There must have
been hundreds of people in this one room. It was dominated by a
table, a single vast piece of furniture large enough to seat fifty. Every
seat was occupied, with the portly figure of Minister Gramm at the
head of the table and his advisor Pila beside him. Behind those at the
table itself were more rows of chairs; the attendees seemed to have
brought teams of advisors, in some cases stacked three or four rows
deep. Bots hovered, drifting over the gleaming tabletop, serving drinks
and topping up bowls of food.

It wasn't the size of the gathering that startled Pirius, though,
but the décor. The shining tabletop was deep brown, and obviously
grained. It was that strange substance called *wood*. Panels of the stuff
covered the walls, and even the ceiling. Pirius had never seen wood
before he had come to Sol system. Evidently, somewhere on Earth
trees still grew and gave up their strange flesh to rooms like this; it was
harder to imagine a more powerful statement of wealth.

But the ensigns were dawdling, staring. Heads were beginning to
turn, sophisticated mouths turning up with mocking smiles. Nilis
frantically beckoned them. Shamed, Pirius and Torec hurried to the
Commissary.

Commander Darc was already here. Sitting bolt upright, evidently
uncomfortable, he ignored the ensigns. The three of them were Nilis's
only 'advisors', and rows of empty seats stretched behind them. But
then who else could Nilis have brought? Luru Parz the jasoft? A
Coalescent Archivist from Mars? A *Silver Ghost*? The marginal nature
of Nilis's project and his motley crew of misfits, aliens and illegals had
never been more apparent than now, as it faced its greatest political
test.

Nilis sorted through his data desks. He said to the ensigns, 'I will
make the presentation today. You shouldn't have to talk.'

Pirius said fervently, 'Good.'

'As far as I'm concerned you two are here to make a point with your
very presence. *You* are what this war is about. You may be asked
questions; there's nothing I can do about that. If so, confer with me or
Commander Darc before answering. That's quite acceptable in terms
of the etiquette of meetings like this.'

Torec whispered, 'I thought we were only presenting to Minister Gramm.'

Nilis sighed. 'I'm afraid life here at the centre of the Coalition is a little more complicated than that, child.'

Gramm, as Minister of Economic Warfare, served on something called the War Cabinet. Under the chairmanship of a Grand Conclave member called the Plenipotentiary for Total War, this subcommittee was dedicated to the prosecution of the Xeelee war in all its aspects. Now Gramm had been appointed head of the inter-agency committee which had been given the responsibility of overseeing Nilis's Project Prime Radiant.

'But most of the great agencies have representatives on our oversight committee,' Nilis said cynically, 'as they do on most initiatives that might affect their interests. Around this table there are ambassadors from the Army and Navy, the Guardians, the Ministry of Psychological Warfare who do their best to out-guess the Xeelee, with no notable success, and some of the specialist guilds like the Communicators and Engineers and Navigators, and the Surveyors of Revenues and the Auditor General's Office. Even the Benefactors are here! – though I don't see what our greenships have to do with their free hospitals and dole handouts. And of course there are representatives of the many arms of the Commission for Historical Truth. Gramm, as chair of the committee, has a lot of sway. But any decision is a collective one.'

Darc grunted. 'It's amazing the Coalition doesn't collapse under its own bureaucracy. And look at all those black robes!' Glancing around the table, Pirius saw that the few martial uniforms, like Darc's, were far outnumbered by the glum robes of Commissaries; they seemed to swarm through the big room, a black-clothed plague. Darc said, 'We are at war. But we seem to divert an awful lot of our energies to policing our own ideological drift.'

Nilis said sternly, 'This is politics, Commander.'

'Hmmph. Give me combat any day!'

Minister Gramm hammered on the tabletop with a gavel – a wooden hammer on a wooden table, a remarkably archaic gesture. The susurrus of conversation around the table died. Without preliminaries Gramm called on Nilis to make his opening remarks.

Nilis lumbered to his feet, a smile fixed on his lined face. His voice was forceful. But Pirius could see the beads of sweat on his neck.

*

319

Formally speaking, this was just another stage in the decision-making process: the mandate actually to go to war with this new weapon would not be given today. All this committee was being asked to approve was to release a further tranche of funding – granted a much bigger tranche, as Nilis was asking to establish a new Navy squadron equipped with his new technology at the centre of the Galaxy. But still Pirius knew it was the most important decision point in the project's uncertain progress so far.

The Commissary quickly sketched the objectives of Project Prime Radiant. He set out his familiar argument that striking at the Prime Radiant, a target 'logically upstream' of the many secondary targets in the Core, would if not finish the war then at least shorten it. He described the problems to be overcome if that ultimate target was to be hit, and set out his three proposals for doing so: the use of grava-star shielding to defeat the Xeelee's ability to see the strike force coming before it even set off; the revolutionary CTC processors to outmanoeuvre the Xeelee's last line of defences; and the black hole cannon to strike at Chandra itself. All this was illustrated with Virtual displays, technical summaries, maps of the war zone and bits of imagery from the project's work so far.

Pirius thought he spoke well, uncharacteristically avoiding excessively technical language. And Nilis included plenty of spectacular action images, such as shots of Pirius Blue's jaunt to Chandra, the captive Xeelee ship being baffled by the grav shield and finally yielding to the black hole cannonade. For armchair generals, he always said, there was nothing so impressive as a bit of footage of actual hardware.

He drew it together in a simple graphic summary – more sophisticated than Pirius's old asterisk diagram, but not much. Then he sat down, visibly trembling, and mopped his brow. 'Now for the hard part,' he whispered.

Gramm said there would be a recess before detailed questioning began. But he opened the floor for first reactions.

A Commissary raised a finger. With a head like a skull and paper-thin flesh stretched tight over angular bones, he was one of the oldest people Pirius had ever seen – aside from Luru Parz, of course – older than anyone was *supposed* to get, according to the Doctrines. He seemed to be so prominent in this company he didn't feel the need to introduce himself.

Pirius was shocked when the very first question was directed at him, not Nilis.

'I'd like to ask our hero ensign what he thinks of this.' The old man's voice was soft as a whisper. 'Would he be willing to fly this lash-up into the Xeelee nest?'

Pirius glanced at Nilis and Darc; Nilis shrugged.

Pirius stood. Every face turned to him, the hard expressions of military commanders, the softer curiosity of the swarming black-robed Commissaries, 'Sir, I would say—'

'What, what? Speak up!' A ripple of laughter passed around the room.

Pirius cleared his throat. 'Sir, this technology is unproven in battle. That's obviously true. But we are proposing many more proving stages before it is deployed. It will require courage to take such a new weapon into battle. I have no doubt that many will give their lives trying. But try we will.'

Nilis gently patted Pirius's back.

The old Commissary nodded. 'All right, ensign. One thing we are not short of is the courage of our soldiers. But this melange of ancient and possibly illegal technologies – how can it work? Put it this way. If this was such a bright idea, why didn't somebody think of it long ago?'

Pirius knew he should consult Nilis before replying. But he had heard such comments many times since becoming involved with Nilis's project, even from military personnel. He said forcefully, 'Sir, what's behind your question is: if this is a good idea, *why didn't the Xeelee have it first?*' There was an ominous silence. 'I think some people believe that if it didn't come from the Xeelee it can't be any good – that Xeelee technology must be better than ours, simply because it is Xeelee. But if we think like that it's a recipe for defeat.' The old Commissary's mouth was round with shock. *What am I saying?* . . . 'With due respect, sir,' he gabbled, and sat down hastily.

Gramm was glaring across the table at him. 'Commissary Nilis, I suspect your pet soldier has already lost your case for you – or won it In any case we must go through the motions. Two-hour recess.' He slammed his gavel on the table.

On the way out, Pirius was the target of amused stares. But Nilis, furious, wouldn't even look at him.

*

When the committee reconvened, the grilling was ferocious.

The points raised by the military agencies, Pirius thought, were mostly fair. The representatives of the Green Army and the Navy asked detailed technical questions. Nilis was able to field most of these, others he passed to Darc and the ensigns. When a question came his way Pirius made sure he referred to Nilis and Darc first – not that the Commissary would have given him any choice. Torec answered more than Pirius, and did so well, Pirius thought enviously – calmly, with no visible sign of nerves, and yet with a control and discipline that Pirius himself had so obviously lacked.

Towards the end of this session, though, with the military representatives still dominating the proceedings, the questioning took a direction that puzzled Pirius. Points were raised about how the technologies could be applied on other battlefields than the very centre. There was a great deal of manoeuvring, too, about how each military force would place representatives in the project.

When the meeting broke again, Nilis snorted, 'What a distraction! It's been a tactic of my opponents all along, to divert my discoveries to lesser targets – to waste this unique possibility.'

Pirius frowned. 'But the commanders are just doing their jobs, aren't they, Commissary? They have to think through the options.'

Commander Darc shook his head. 'What is going on in this room is politics, remember. The Navy and the Green Army, to name but two, have been at each other's throats since they were founded. And the individuals around this table all have their own career strategies, their own rivalries and ambitions. Now they are manoeuvring, you see. If our technology is promising, they each want to get hold of it for themselves to further their own careers. If our Core assault does go ahead, and it happens to go well, they will want to take the credit. Conversely, if it goes wrong, as I suspect most of those here believe is likely, they don't want to be blamed.'

Torec was angry. 'Maybe it would be better if we put our effort into fighting the Xeelee rather than each other.'

Darc laughed, not particularly unkindly. 'Of course there will be honest doubts, too. I tell you, Commissary, there are many serving officers who don't like your project just for the *feel* of it. This fiddling with physics: it's more like a Ghost project than anything humanity would devise. It has their glistening sheen all over it . . . That might be our biggest obstacle of all.'

In the next session the many representatives of the Commission for Historical Truth took over, and the lines of questioning drifted away from the military justification of the project and into realms of philosophy, ideology and legalism.

The sinister Office of Doctrinal Responsibility, as the Commission's ideological police force, had agents throughout the Galaxy and assigned to every front-line unit: even Arches Base had its political officers, or 'Doctrine cops', as the troops called them. They were widely mocked, but their power was feared. And now the Doctrine cops on this committee dug into the question of the legality of what Nilis had been up to.

It was of course impossible for the Commissary to deny that he had been assisted by a jasoft, or that he had called on a post-human colony on Mars, or that his gravastar hadn't been developed by humans at all. But he was able to fend off their probing. It was not him, he pointed out, who had allowed Luru Parz to survive, or let a Coalescence to develop under Mons Olympus, or revived a colony of the long-extinct Silver Ghosts. These developments happened long before he was born, presumably with the full knowledge and even cooperation of the Commission.

'And why did all this happen? Because these divergences are *useful*. They may be non-Doctrinal but they are valuable resources, and those who allowed such developments, far wiser than I, knew that it is sometimes necessary to compromise the purity of one's ideology. If we were to lose the war all our ideology would count for nothing anyhow. I am merely following in the footsteps of my wiser forebears.'

This mixture of flattery and blame-shifting seemed effective, and he deflected them further with a bit of philosophy. Was knowledge morally neutral? If a fact came from a dubious source, was its utility to be overridden by its ethically compromised origin? If so, who was to be the arbiter of what was 'clean' science and what was not?

By the time the Doctrine cops gave up, Nilis was sweating again. He had been on shaky ground. After all it was one of Nilis's 'pragmatically useful resources', Luru Parz, who, by threatening to expose the existence of other 'morally compromised facilities', had forced this committee to consider Nilis's requests in the first place.

But now the Office of Cultural Rehabilitation waded in. This department of the Commission was a sister to the ancient Assimilation programme, which had been tasked with absorbing the resources of conquered alien races for the benefit of mankind's projects. Rehabilitation had the mission, still in fact ongoing, of seeking out relics of older waves of human colonisation. These pre-Third Expansion pockets of humanity, having been seeded before the establishment of the Coalition, were of course non-Doctrinal by definition. Many had even lapsed into eusociality, becoming Coalescences. But all of them had to be brought into the fold, their populations re-educated. The ultimate goal of Rehabilitation was to ensure that every human in the Galaxy was assigned to the single goal of the great war.

Now, it seemed to Pirius, Rehabilitation officers were expressing concern about Nilis's project, not in case it failed, but if it *succeeded*. Would it actually be moral to end this war? The entire human economy of the Galaxy was devoted to the war: if it ever ended, the resulting dislocation would be huge. And without the war's unifying discipline, how could central control be maintained? There would be riots; there would be starvation; whole worlds would break away from the light of the Coalition and fall into an anarchic darkness.

One dry academic even suggested that a true reading of Hama Druz's writings showed that that ancient sage had been arguing, not for the conquest of the Galaxy, but for the continual cleansing of unending conflict. The war had to go on, until a perfect killing machine had been forged from imperfect mankind. Of course victory was the ultimate goal, but a victory *too soon* could imperil that great project of the unity of a purified species . . .

Torec and Pirius were amazed. But since they had come to Sol system, it wasn't the first time they had heard people actually argue *against* victory.

Pirius thought he could see what was really going on here, beneath the dry academic discussions. These ancient agencies weren't concerned for the myriad people in their care; they were only concerned about their own survival. If the war went away, he thought with a strange thrill, any justification for the continuance of the Coalition itself, and its Galaxy full of ideological cops, would vanish. And then what?

Perhaps he was growing cynical.

The session overran its allotted time. At last Gramm banged his gavel, and ordered the committee to reconvene in the morning.

While they had talked the planet had spun on its axis, taking Conurbation 11729 and its busy inhabitants into its shadow

Nilis's party was assigned quarters on a residential floor of the huge building. The room given to Torec and Pirius seemed impossibly luxurious. After a while they stripped blankets off the too-soft beds, making themselves a nest on the floor.

But a bot called, sent by Nilis. It contained some technical updates Gramm had requested, and Pirius, as Nilis's representative, was to accompany the bot to the Minister's office. Reluctantly Pirius allowed his uniform to slither back into place over his body.

The bot led the way through a maze of carpeted corridors to the Minister's office.

Pirius had been expecting opulence. The room was richer than anything he had seen at Arches Base, of course – and a lot richer than Nilis's apartment, for instance. The carpet on the floor was a thick pile, and even the walls were covered by some kind of heavily textured paper.

But the room was windowless: that was significant, as Pirius had learned that the most prized rooms in any Conurbation-dome building had window views. And this was a working room. The only furniture was a desk, a small conference table and chairs – and a couch, upholstered with maroon fabric and laden with cushions, on which rested the great bulk of the Minister of Economic Warfare himself.

Gramm had kicked his shoes off and loosened his robe. Lying there, his stomach had spread out like a sack of mercury, and his jowly face was slack and tired. A table floated at Gramm's right hand; Pirius could smell spicy food. Bots and small Virtual displays hovered around Gramm's head, and voices whispered, constantly updating the Minister on whatever was happening in the corners of his complex world. Gramm's fat hand dug into the plates, but he never so much as glanced at what he was pushing into his mouth. Pirius had never seen the Minister look so deflated, so exhausted.

It seemed to take the Minister a long time to notice the ensign standing to attention at the door. He snapped, 'Oh, come in, boy, come in. I won't bite. Not *you*, anyhow.'

Pirius stepped forward, 'Sir, I've come to deliver—'

'A message, I know, from your ragged-robed master. Well, you've done it.' He looked away and continued to eat.

Pirius waited awkwardly. He was becoming used to these non-military types with their ignorance of protocol, but he was reluctant to move until he was dismissed. Maybe he'd be left standing here all night.

At length Gramm noticed him. 'You still here? . . . I suppose it's been a difficult day for you. Must all be very strange.' He guffawed. 'Though it was a delicious moment when you told that pompous old fool Kolo Yehn that he had an inferiority complex about the Xeelee. Hah! I'll have to make sure *that's* highlighted in the minutes.'

Pirius felt colour rise in his cheeks. 'I was only speaking my mind. Sir.'

Gramm eyed him, chewing. 'Lethe, you're a spirited one. Look, ensign, I can imagine what you think of me.' He brushed crumbs from his vast belly. 'I can see myself through your eyes.'

'I have no personal opinions, sir.'

'Oh, garbage. But what you perhaps don't see – look here. Do you know what my job is?'

'You're Minister of—'

'That's my *role*. My function is to prosecute this damn war. I take the strategic goals of the Coalition as a whole and turn them into operational goals. Maybe you've seen today that given the infighting that goes on at every level, even at the highest reaches of the Coalition, those strategic goals aren't always clear. But that's the principle.

'Now, all the time I am bombarded.' He waved a hand, and the bots and Virtuals around his couch swarmed like insects. 'I have whole teams of experts, advisors, lobby groups, all battling for my ear, even within my own Ministry. And then, of course, there are the other agencies beyond Economic Warfare to be dealt with – negotiated with, beaten back, soothed. And all of this against the background of the war.' He sighed and pushed more food into his mouth. 'The war, the damn war. It's more than just a theatre for heroic exploits by boy heroes like you, ensign. You know, you're lucky, out there in the Core. All you have to think about is your comrades, your ship, your own hide. *I* have to think of the bigger picture – of *all* the millions of little Piriuses running around and hunting for glory.'

He propped himself up on his elbow. 'And here's that bigger picture. We've beaten back the Xeelee. We've pushed them out of the disc of the Galaxy. It's been an epochal achievement. But they still lurk in the Galaxy's Core. We have them bottled up there – but the cost of that containment is huge. We have turned the whole Galaxy into a machine, a single vast machine dedicated to a single goal: to keeping the Xeelee trapped. It's dreadful, it's costly – it's working. But I have to be parsimonious with my resources.

'Now, whether you see it or not – and no matter what that old monster Luru Parz says – we've been responsible with your project so far. We've tried to apply resources sensibly, commensurate with the successes you've actually achieved, bit by bit as the concept has been proved. But now we're being asked to take a much greater leap of faith. You might think a couple of dozen greenships isn't much in a war that spans a Galaxy. You might think you're under excessive scrutiny – that you're being opposed, arbitrarily, through the mechanism of the funding. Perhaps some do have such a motive. But for me it's not like that. We're stretched thin, ensign, thinner than you might understand. Even a single ship, lost unnecessarily, might make the difference, might cause it all to unravel. That's the great fear – and Nilis's is only one of a hundred, a thousand such requests I have to deal with right now. Do you see what you're asking me to risk, if we commit to Nilis's madcap jaunt?'

'You fear that if we draw resources away, the Front could collapse.'

'Yes. And if the Xeelee *were* to punch out of there, we'd be lost; they would surely never allow us to establish a position of dominance again. Nilis isn't unique, you know. Especially in the Commission there are many corners, lots of bits of unaccounted-for funding – plenty of places for the likes of Nilis to dream their dreams.'

'Nilis is more than a dreamer.'

'Well, perhaps. But, as I say, he isn't unique. It doesn't take a genius to perceive that our glorious war effort has stalled, that it is an exercise in monstrous waste. At any moment there must be dozens of Nilises running around with bright ideas for shortening or ending the war.' He rubbed his greasy jowl. 'And maybe once a generation you will have a true Nilis, a plan so well-thought-out, so convincing, that you believe it might, just might, work.'

'Once a generation?'

'It's in the records. No doubt Nilis himself is aware of many of them.'

'But since the war began, there have been a *lot* of generations.'

Gramm laughed. 'Quite so. And a lot of bright ideas. Some of them probably bore passing resemblances to Nilis's scheme.'

'So what happened to them?'

'They were blocked. By people like me.' He shifted and stared at Pirius. 'Look at it from my point of view. Now, I know that to win the war we're going to have to take a risk. But the question is *which* risk? Is Nilis's idea the one—'

'Or should you wait until a smarter idea comes along?'

Gramm's eyes narrowed. 'You do have qualities, ensign; I can see why Nilis plucked you out of the mire. You see, the easiest thing for me to do would be to pass on this project of yours – not even to turn it down; just to stall. I won't be in this office for ever. Let my successor make the difficult decisions, if she dares. This war has lasted three thousand years. The battle is not mine. I am merely a custodian. How could I bear it if the crucial failure came on *my* watch? . . . But I fear deferral isn't an option for me.'

'Sir? Why not?'

'Because we're losing.'

The vast Galaxy-wide operation, held together by the rigid ideology and the ruthless policies of the Coalition, was containing the Xeelee. But mankind really was stretched to the limit. And, bit by bit, entropy was taking its toll.

'You can forget about this theoretical Commissary nonsense of a perpetual war, of forging a perfect mankind in its cold fire. The machine isn't that perfect, believe me. We won't fall tomorrow, or the day after. I don't know when it will come – probably not even in my time. But come it will.' He stared at the ensign again, and Pirius saw despair in his deep-sunk eyes. 'Now do you see why I'm listening to Nilis?'

'Yes, sir.'

'I know Nilis understands this history, and he's learned from it. He's played the bureaucratic game with surprising skill, you know. But now we're beyond games, and coming to the crunch decision. Can you promise me that your mentor's lunatic scheme is going to work?'

'No, sir.'

'No. How easy it would be if you could!'

Pirius thought he understood. This man, so alien to anything in Pirius's background, was conscientiously trying to make an impossible decision, a decision that could save or doom mankind, one of a hundred such decisions that faced him daily against a background of half-truths, hope, promises and lies. 'We both have our duty, sir. As you implied, perhaps mine is easier.'

Gramm rubbed his eyes with fleshy fingers. 'Lethe, ensign, that pompous old fool Kolo Yehn was right. Whatever we're running out of, at least there's no shortage of courage. Get out of here.' He waved his hand. 'Go, before I have to throw you out.'

Pirius reported this conversation to Nilis. He didn't anticipate the Commissary's reaction.

'You see what this means.' Nilis was whispering, wide-eyed, his hands locked together in a white-knuckled grip.

'Sir?'

'Gramm is going to say yes – he's going to back us. Of course he has to get the decision from his committee. But if *he* backs it, it will be hard for any of them not to follow along. We're going to the Core, ensign. We're going to have our squadron.' Nilis padded around his room, plucking at his fingers.

Pirius shook his head. 'Then why aren't you leaping with joy, Commissary?'

'Because they've called my bluff,' he said rapidly. He seemed terrified. 'While I was pushing against a locked door it was easy to be bold. But now the door has swung open, and I have to deliver on my promises.' He turned to Pirius. 'Oh, my eyes, my eyes! What have I done? Pirius, what have I done?'

THREE

Genetically, morphologically, I am indistinguishable from an inhabitant of Earth of the long dark ages that preceded space-flight.

I rejoice. For that changelessness is what makes me human.

Let others tinker with their genotypes and phenotypes, let them speciate and bifurcate, merge and blend. We unmodified humans are a primordial force who will sweep them all aside.

It must be this way. It will avail us nothing if we win a Galaxy and lose ourselves.

— Hama Druz

CHAPTER 35

There was no place. There was no time. A human observer would have recognized nothing here: no mass, energy, or force. There was only a rolling, random froth whose fragmented geometry constantly changed. Even causality was a foolish dream.

The orderly spacetime with which humans were familiar was suffused with vacuum energy, out of which virtual particles, electrons and quarks would fizz into existence and then scatter or annihilate, their brief walks upon the stage governed by quantum uncertainty. In this extraordinary place whole *universes* bubbled out of the froth, to expand and dissipate, or to collapse in a despairing flare.

This chaotic cavalcade of possibilities, this place of non-being where whole universes clustered in reefs of foamy spindrift, was suffused by a light beyond light. But even in this cauldron of strangeness there was life. Even here there was mind.

Call them monads.

This would be the label given them by Commissary Nilis, when he deduced their existence. But the name had much deeper roots.

In the seventeenth century the German mathematician Gottfried Leibniz had imagined that reality was constructed from pseudo-objects which owed their existence solely to their relation to each other. In his idea of the 'monad' Leibniz had intuited something of the truth of the creatures who infested this domain. They existed, they communicated, they enjoyed a richness of experience and community. And yet 'they' didn't exist in themselves; it was only their relationships to each other that defined their own abstract entities.

No other form of life was possible in this fractured place.

Long ago they had attended the birth of a universe.

It had come from a similar cauldron of realities, a single bubble plucked out of the spindrift. As the baby universe had expanded and cooled, the monads had remained with it. Immanent in the new cosmos, they suffused it, surrounded it. Time to them was not as experienced by the universe's swarming inhabitants; their perception was like the reality dust of configuration space, perhaps.

But once its reality had congealed, once the supracosmic froth had cooled, the monads were forced into dormancy. Wrapped up in protective knots of spacetime, they dreamed away the long history of their universe, with all its empires and wars, its tragedies and triumphs. It had been the usual story – and yet it was a unique story, for no two universes were ever quite the same. And something of this long saga would always be stored in the monads' dreaming.

The universe aged, as all things must; within, time grew impossibly long and space stretched impossibly thin. At last the fabric of the universe sighed and broke – and a bubble of a higher reality spontaneously emerged, a recurrence of the no-place where time and distance had no meaning. Just as the universe had once been spawned from chaos, so this droplet of chaos was now born from the failing stuff of the universe. Everything was cyclic.

And in this bubble, where the freezing of spacetime was undone, the monads awoke again; in their supracosmic froth, they were once more briefly alive.

The monads considered the bubbling foam around them.

They dug into a reef of spindrift, selected a tangle of possibilities, picked out one evanescent cosmic jewel. *This one* – yes. They closed around it, as if warmed by its glow of potentialities.

And, embedding themselves in its structure, they prepared to shape it. The monads enriched the seedling universe with ineffable qualities whose existence few of its inhabitants would even guess at.

The new universe, for all its beauty, was featureless, symmetrical – but unstable, like a sword standing on its point. Even the monads could not control how that primordial symmetry would be broken, which destiny, of an uncountable number of possibilities, would be selected.

Which was, of course, the joy of it.

For the inhabitants of this new cosmos it began with a singularity: a moment when time began, when space was born. But for the monads, as their chaotic ur-reality froze out once more into a rigid smoothness, the singularity was an end: for them, the story was already over. Encased in orderly, frozen spacetime, they would slumber through the long ages until this universe in turn grew old and spawned new fragments of chaos, and they could wake again.

But all that lay far in the future.

There was a breathless instant. The sword toppled. Time flowed, like water gushing from a tap.

History began.

CHAPTER 36

So Pirius Red and Torec, having completed a circuit across the face of the Galaxy that had taken them all the way to Earth, returned at last to where they had started.

The flight through the complicated geometry of Arches Base lifted Pirius's heart. Past the asteroids that wheeled like fists, he made out the burning sky of the Core, the giant stars and light-year-long filaments of glowing gas, the endless explosion of astrophysics beyond. Compared to the cold clockwork emptiness of Sol system, out on the Galaxy's dead fringe where you couldn't even *see* the Core, this crowded, dangerous sky teemed with life and energy.

'Lethe, it's good to be home,' he said with feeling.

When they disembarked Captain Seath herself greeted them. She allowed the Commissary to pump her hand, and nodded curtly to Pirius and Torec. But Pirius read the expression on her reconstructed face. Whatever they had achieved in Sol system, they would always be two jumped-up ensigns to *her*. It was almost reassuring.

Seath told them that the accommodation for the new 'squadron' that was being formed to carry out Nilis's 'project' – she pronounced those words with unmistakable disdain – wasn't ready yet. So Nilis was offered a room in Officer Country, while Pirius and Torec were taken to a Barracks Ball.

They walked into the big central space of bunks and lavatories. They hadn't been assigned to this Barracks Ball before. It stank, of course, as all barracks did, of piss and sweat, food and disinfectant, but it didn't smell familiar. And among the ranks of faces that peered at them, with curiosity, apathy or hostility, there was nobody they knew.

They were assigned bunks a couple of blocks apart. Torec stroked Pirius's back, and made her way to her own bunk. Pirius unpacked his few personal effects and stripped out of his gaudy dress uniform, which made him feel a little better.

But he did this surrounded by staring faces. It wasn't just the curiosity of cadets confronted by a stranger. They gazed at him as if he had two heads. They said nothing to him, and he had nothing to say to them. They snubbed him when he went to get food. Even when he lay down in the dark he sensed the strangers around him watching him, assessing him – excluding him.

They looked so *young*, he thought, their faces blank, like desks empty of data. They were like children. And what was happening to him was childish, as the factions and cliques of the barracks combined to bully a new victim. It was just as Nilis had said: they might look like adults, and they would have to fight and die for mankind. But they were not long out of childhood, and every now and again it showed.

Childish it might be, but the pressure was extraordinary.

He clambered out of bed, made his way to Torec's bunk and crawled in beside her. They lay nested together, his belly against her back.

'We said we wouldn't do this,' she whispered. 'We have to fit in.'

'I couldn't stand it any more,' he replied. 'Don't throw me out.'

After a time she turned over and kissed his forehead.

In many ways she was the stronger one. But he sensed that she was as glad he was there as he was to be there. They clung to each other, innocent as children themselves, until they fell asleep.

The next morning Captain Seath led them to a flitter. The little ship slid out of port and threaded its cautious way through the crowded sky.

Seath asked coolly, 'Sleep well?'

'No, sir,' Pirius said honestly.

Torec said, 'Captain, I don't understand. Why does everybody hate us?'

'I don't imagine they hate you.'

Pirius said, 'We're the same as we were before.'

Seath eyed him, 'No,' she said, 'you're not. You've done extraordinary things. *You've seen Earth*, ensign. Even I can't begin to imagine it. And you've been close to power, closer than anybody here, closer than me, closer even than the base commanders. You have changed. And you can't change back.'

'There's no place for us on Earth,' Pirius said.

Seath laughed. 'There's no place for you here.'

'Where, then?' Torec asked.

'Why, nowhere.' She shrugged. 'It's not your fault. It's the way of things. The only people who understand you are each other – and each other is all you will ever have. You'll just have to get on with it.'

As she said that, Pirius felt Torec moving subtly away from him. He sensed a return of her old resentment: they had come all the way back to Arches, and she *still* couldn't get away from him.

The base for Nilis's pet squadron was just another Rock among the hurtling asteroids of Arches. Known only as Rock 492, it was a kilometre-wide lump of debris. On its battered surface was a cluster of buildings of bubble-blown asteroid rock, and a few broad pits that had once been landing pads and dry docks. But all this was long abandoned.

They had to climb out of the flitter in their skinsuits.

The buildings, long stripped of anything usable, were so old their surviving walls were pocked with micrometeorite craters, and a thin silt of dust had gathered around the bases of their walls. Some of their domes had cracked open altogether.

Only one of the buildings was airtight to regulation standard. When they clambered inside, through a temporary airlock hastily patched into a hole in the wall, they found themselves in a cavernous hollow. Bots crawled over the floor and roof, patching up defects. But even the bots looked old and worn out, and the engineers who supervised them weren't much better. There was no gravity in here – or rather, only the microgravity of the asteroid, just a feather touch – and the light, cast by a few hovering globes, was misty, the air a shining silver-grey.

Pirius cracked his faceplate and took a deep breath. The air was stale, so lacking in oxygen his chest ached, and it stank of oil and metal, and of the burning smell of raw asteroid dust, oxidising busily. As the irritating dust got to work on his sinuses he started to sneeze.

'Lethe,' he said. 'Is this it?'

'Nothing works but the inertial deflectors,' Torec said. That had to be true, or else the whole Rock, plummeting through the complicated geometry of Arches, would have been a hazard. She sighed. 'Don't they realise we are trying to save the Galaxy? How are we supposed to do that if the toilets don't work?'

But there was nothing to be done about the strange internal politics of Arches, the Navy, the Coalition, and humankind in general. So they got to work.

For the next few days they wrestled with ancient air and water cyclers, balky nano-food systems, and hovering light globes that wouldn't stay still. Even the machines didn't seem to like them: they resisted being fixed, and developed faults and quirks that simply seemed perverse. Their social life didn't get any better either. If they had been outsiders in the Barracks Ball they were definitely not wanted here, by engineers who clearly believed they had better things to do than labour over a lump of shit like Rock 492.

But in another way it was fun, Pirius thought. Getting immersed in the guts of a broken pump or a clogged air filter system was dirty, hard work, but it was a job that was finite and understandable and something you could *finish*, unlike the diffuse politicking of Earth.

The systems came online one by one. As they heard the labouring of air pumps, and felt the shuddering of water pumping through the pipes, the place started to seem alive. And because they had worked so hard over it, Pirius and Torec thought of it as *theirs*. Before he had gone to Earth the only homes Pirius had ever known had been one Barracks Ball after another. Now Rock 492 was starting to feel like home – though he and Torec only dared discuss such thoroughly non-Doctrinal matters in whispers, and they would never have mentioned it to Captain Seath.

The ensigns were summoned to regular meetings with Nilis.

These were always held in the Commissary's room in Officer Country. Even though he had assimilated the experiences of his avatar Virtual who had ridden with Pirius Blue through the Cavity, Nilis seemed as scared of Arches' daunting sky as when he had first come here, and he tended to hide in his room. But he had quickly made this faceless little cabin his own, spreading his clutter of data desks, clothes and other bric-a-brac over every surface, and filling the air with clustering Virtuals. Torec said he made every place he stayed into a nest, as rats made nests. Pirius thought a little wistfully of what it must mean to have a real home, and to miss it, as Nilis clearly missed his.

Torec complained about the state of Rock 492. But Nilis said there was nothing he could do about it for now. They would have to wait for a meeting he had scheduled with Marshal Kimmer, the senior Navy officer on the base. After this 'showdown', as Nilis called it, he was sure their requests would be properly met as the oversight committee had mandated.

Pirius wasn't so sure. He knew that officers like Marshal Kimmer tended to regard their bases as their private domains. He wouldn't take kindly to what he would surely see as interference from out-of-touch bureaucrats on far-off Earth, no matter what their formal authority.

Nilis had continued to analyse the data he had gathered on Chandra, the monstrous, enigmatic black hole at the centre of the Galaxy, and hypothesised on its nature and what the Xeelee were doing with it.

He knew now that the Xeelee used Chandra to make nightfighters. Somehow, Nilis had deduced from remote images, they peeled space-time-defect wings and other structures out of the distorted environment of the black hole. That much had long been suspected by Navy intelligence. But Nilis said he suspected the Xeelee had a more profound use for the black hole.

It was all to do with computing. There were fundamental limits to computing power, he said. The processing speed and memory of any computer were limited by the energy available to it.

He picked up a data desk and waved it around in the air. 'This is a sophisticated gadget, the end result of twenty-five thousand years of technological progress. But what does it weigh – around a kilogram? From the point of view of the gadget's purpose, which is computation, almost all of this mass is wasted. Merely a framework. This desk would be able to achieve a lot more if *all* of its mass-energy were devoted to computing. In the form of photons, say, this kilogram of stuff could process at the rate of ten to power fifty-one operations per second. That's a million billion billion billion *billion* . . .' Similarly, the memory capacity of a computer depended on how many distinguishable states its system could take. If Nilis's inert kilogram were converted to a litre of light, the capacity would become some ten thousand billion billion billion bits.

'In fact, our most advanced computers have a design something like this,' he said. 'Perhaps you know it. At the core of the "nervous system" of a greenship is a vat of radiant energy, much of it gamma-ray photons, but some of it more exotic higher-energy particles. Energy is bled off from the ship's GUT generator, to keep the photon soup at around a billion degrees. Information is stored in the positions and trajectories of the photons, and is processed by collisions between the particles. To read it you open up a hole in the side of the box and let some of the light out.'

There were limitations with such a design, because the rate at which information could be extracted, limited by lightspeed, was much less than the computer's storage capacity. 'You only get a glimpse of what's going on in there,' said Nilis. 'So our best computers are massively parallel, with subsections working virtually independently.' The input-output rate could be increased if the computer were made smaller, because it took less time for information to be moved around. But as the size was reduced the energy density would increase. 'You encounter more and more exotic high-energy particles,' said Nilis, 'until you pass the point at which you can control them. Gamma-ray processing is the limit of our technological capabilities right now. But of course that's not the *physical* limit. If you keep crushing down your computer, keep increasing its density, you finish up with—'

'A black hole,' said Torec.

'Yes.' He beamed, and plucked at a thread dangling from the sleeve of his battered robe. 'And then the physics becomes simple again.'

Pirius began to see it. 'And Chandra is a black hole – the biggest in the Galaxy.'

'Exactly,' Nilis whispered. 'I thought the Xeelee were using Chandra to power their central computing facility. Now I believe that the Xeelee are using *Chandra itself*, a black hole with the mass of millions of suns, as a computer. The audacity!'

Torec asked, 'How can you use a black hole as a computer?'

Nilis said that information could be 'fed' to a black hole computer during the hole's formation, or by infalling matter later. 'The data would be stored on the hole's event horizon in the form of impressed strings.'

Pirius was becoming baffled. 'Strings?'

All of reality could be looked on as an expression of vibrating strings. Invisibly small, these loops and knots shimmered and sang, and their vibration modes, the 'notes' they sounded, were the particles of the universe humans could discern. Pirius took in little of this, but he liked the idea that the universe was a kind of symphony of invisible strings in harmony.

'A black hole's event horizon is a terminus to our universe, though,' Nilis said. 'Strings can't extend beyond it. So they become embedded in the surface – like wet hair plastered over your head. The strings bear information about how the hole was formed, and how it grew.' To get at the information you had to let the hole evaporate, as all black holes did, by emitting a dribble of 'Hawking radiation'. The smaller the hole the more rapidly it evaporated.

'You won't be surprised that the Silver Ghosts once dabbled with this kind of technology,' Nilis said ruefully. 'They created microscopic black holes, with information and processing instructions encoded in the formative collapse. Small enough holes evaporate very quickly – they explode, in fact. The computation's output is encoded in the radiation they emit in the process. You can solve some spectacularly hard problems that way.' He sniffed. 'The Ghosts did get it to work. But each micro-hole computer was a one-off; you could only run one program, because it blew itself up in the process! Even the Ghosts couldn't find a way to make the technology practical.'

'And,' Torec prompted, 'this is what the Xeelee are doing?'

'Yes. But *they* don't restrict themselves to mere microscopic holes.'

He showed them data extracted from Pirius Blue's jaunt into the Cavity. They still had no good close-up images of Chandra, but somehow the Xeelee were controlling the inflow of matter to the event horizon. And through that control they were 'programming' the monstrous black hole. They allowed the Planck-scale dynamics of the event horizon to process the input information, and were 'reading' the results by analysing the Hawking radiation the black hole gave off.

'At least that's what I think they are doing,' Nilis said. 'There is still a great deal we don't know about black holes. For instance there must be structure in the deep interior, close to the singularity. There the strings and membranes that underlie subatomic particles must be torn and stretched, perhaps reaching dimensions comparable to the black hole itself. Can this "fuzzball" be used for computing purposes? I don't know – I can't rule it out. Or perhaps the Xeelee work on some other principle entirely . . .

'It's remarkable,' he breathed. 'A black hole is a convergence of information and physics, a junction in the structure of our universe. And the Xeelee are using this miracle as a tactical computer!' He grinned. 'No wonder they were able to fend us off so easily. But now, thanks to your CTC computer, we've changed the rules – eh, ensigns? Even a black hole computer can't beat *that*.

'But I don't think I've got to the bottom of it yet.'

'Of what, sir?'

'Of Chandra.'

His proximity to the Galaxy's centre had inspired him to start a whole new line of research, he said. He would go to the Navy's archives for tactical material from three thousand years' worth of scouting missions, and perhaps even hunt out scientific data from more innocent times, when Chandra had been thought to be a mere astrophysical marvel, not a military target. 'In the quagmites and the Xeelee we have already found two layers of life, from quite different cosmic epochs – and a third, if you include us! I'm beginning to wonder what else is there in Chandra's nested layers, waiting to be uncovered. Perhaps there is more life to be found in there, still more ancient and strange, perhaps permeating the singularity itself.

'We understand so little,' he said, 'even now. If you look back at the theories of the ancients you can see how they groped for understanding. Their physics made them capable of recognising a black hole, say, and describing its broad features. But their science gave them no real understanding of what it *is*. Some of what we are capable of today would have seemed impossible to the ancients, as if we were defying the laws of physics themselves! But you have to wonder how incomplete our own precious theories may be.'

Pirius kept his face blank. With Torec's hand curled warmly in his own, he daydreamed of other things.

After a week Nilis set up his 'showdown' with Marshal Kimmer in a conference room in Officer Country. Pirius and Torec were summoned to attend.

The Marshal was thin as a blade and impossibly tall, so tall that outside Officer's Country he had to stoop or else his bald head would have scraped the ceiling. His cheekbones were so sharp they looked as if they would cut through his flesh, and his mouth was invisibly small. But he had space-hardened eyes implanted in his face, tokens of the battlefield. They masked Kimmer's expression completely, as was perhaps their intention.

The Marshal didn't so much as acknowledge Pirius's presence, as if the ensign didn't even exist. But officially, Pirius supposed, given his future crime, he didn't.

Nilis opened with a bumbling presentation on the latest incarnation of his Project Prime Radiant, and how it would be carried out. The operational details were starting to be refined, through work with Darc, Torec, Pirius and others. Nilis described how a squadron of modified greenships would sail into the Cavity behind a single, carefully selected Rock, known as Orion Rock, which would be used for cover.

Commander Darc sat alongside Nilis. Pila was here, Minister Gramm's aide and now his representative at the Core. She sat silently, obviously not wanting to be here; she seemed to regard the base, the Core, and the whole messy business of the war with utter disdain. And here were Pirius and Torec, sitting awkwardly at the table, hoping nobody would notice them.

Marshal Kimmer sat motionless and expressionless through the presentation. He had brought various aides who sat behind him, whispering to each other.

At last Nilis finished, to everyone's relief, including his own. He dispersed his last Virtual image with a wave of his hand and sat down, mopping sweat from his brow with his robe's grimy sleeve. 'Marshal, the floor is yours.'

The Marshal remained silent for long heartbeats, his expression thunderous. Pirius didn't dare so much as breathe.

When the Marshal did speak his voice was so soft Pirius could barely hear it. 'Let me see if I've got this straight. You want twenty greenships.'

'A full squadron of ten, yes, plus reserve craft, and others for development and training—'.

'*Twenty ships*. And it's not just the ships you want. There's the crew as well, plus backups. And the ground crew. *And* all the facilities that will be required to modify these ships with your gadgets, and to train up the crews in their use. You want me to draw away these resources from the front line for this wild scheme of striking at Chandra itself. Is that what you're asking me?'

'Marshal—'

'Next, your tactical plan. You will sail into the Cavity behind a Rock. Fine, but not just any Rock. You want Orion Rock itself? Commissary, we have been developing stratagems based on Orion for *a thousand years*.' His voice was rising steadily. 'And you want to throw away all that work, all that preparation, on *this*?'

Nilis was sweating harder. 'Marshal, *this* could win the war.'

Kimmer stood grandly, and his aides scuttled to their feet. 'Every few years we have to put up with one or other of you gadgeteers or armchair strategists who imagine you know how this war should be fought, better than those who have served the Coalition over three thousand years. You may have fooled them on Earth, Commissary. But this is the Front. And you don't fool me.' He made to stalk out of the room.

Pirius glanced at Torec. He had anticipated Kimmer's reaction, but even so he felt numb despair. There was none of the brute wisdom he had sensed in Minister Gramm in Kimmer. Gramm was a flawed man, but he had a deep, troubled sense of a responsibility for the conduct of the war. In Kimmer there was nothing but resistance to a challenge to his own power. Pirius could hardly believe that they had come all this way, achieved so much, only to be faced by yet another block.

Unexpectedly, Commander Darc spoke up. 'Wait, Marshal.'

Kimmer turned, his expression cold. 'Did you speak, Commander?'

'Sir, you're my superior officer, I apologise for speaking out of turn. But I have to point out you're wrong. The Commissary isn't asking you for anything. The Grand Conclave has issued an executive order, and the Commissary is merely passing on its instructions. We have to give Nilis what he needs to do the job.'

Kimmer hissed, 'This fat earthworm has fooled you as he fooled the Conclave, Commander.'

'No doubt you're right, sir. But in the meantime we have our orders.'

Kimmer glared at his aides, who confirmed in whispers that Darc was right. Kimmer's mouth worked. Pirius knew he would make the Commander pay for what he had said.

'All right, Commissary. As the Commander says, I have my orders. Until I've had time to appeal against the executive mandate, you and your stooges can have what you want.' He stabbed a finger at Nilis. 'But I do have discretion on how I carry out those orders. I won't take any usable resources away from our vital struggle. You'll have your ships. But they will not come from the line: you can have the superannuated, the battle-damaged, the patched-up wrecks. And I won't let you waste the lives of my best crews either. Do you understand?'

Nilis nodded his head. 'Quite clearly.'

'Oh, Nilis – one more thing. If you mean to use Orion Rock you'll have to be quick about it. It will be in position in ten weeks.'

Nilis gasped. '*Ten weeks?* Oh, Marshal, but this is — we can't be ready—'

Darc put his soft hand on Nilis's shoulder. 'It's all right, Commissary. Ten weeks it is, sir.'

Kimmer seemed still more infuriated. He stalked out of the room, followed by his chattering aides.

The Commissary was trembling. 'I thought I had blown the whole thing,' he said hoarsely. 'My stumbling and rumbling, like a buffoon – how can I deal with a marshal if I can't hold myself together for five minutes?'

'You did fine, sir,' Pirius said awkwardly.

Pila elaborately stifled a yawn. 'It was a lot of nonsense anyhow.'

Torec was puzzled. 'Ma'am?'

'Oh, come on, ensign, even you aren't that naïve. Kimmer knows the chain of command as well as any of us. We saw nothing here but the ingrained resistance of a man who can accept no new way of doing things, even if it might resolve the deadlock of this war. And he especially can't take advice from an outsider like *you*, Nilis. Kimmer had no choice but to comply, and he knew it. This was all just posturing.'

Nilis said, 'Pretty formidable posturing, though!'

Pirius was troubled. 'But still, if what the Marshal said comes to pass – if we're only going to get lousy equipment and useless crew—'

'We'll make it work,' Nilis said. 'Why, you've already got Rock 492 up and running, haven't you?'

Pirius shook his head. 'Fixing a broken air cycler is one thing. Putting together a squadron is another.'

Darc glanced at Nilis. 'Ah, but the most important element of any squadron is its leader. Isn't that right, Commissary?'

'Oh, without a doubt, Commander. And how lucky we are to have found the right officer for the job!' Nilis clapped his hand on Pirius's shoulder and beamed.

Pirius turned cold inside.

Torec's mouth dropped open. 'Him? You are *joking*. Sir.'

'Thanks,' Pirius said to Torec.

Nilis said, 'You've already been a hero once, Pirius, in another timeline. Now you have to do it again.'

'But sir, I can't command. I'm not even commissioned.'

Darc grinned. 'You are now.'

'But – *ten weeks*?'

Darc shrugged. 'That's the hand we've been dealt; we make it or we don't.'

Nilis was watching Pirius. 'Of course you have to make up your own mind, Pirius. Do you remember the conversation we had at Venus?'

'Yes, sir.'

'So tell me – where has your self-analysis got to now?'

Torec said, 'I don't know what he's talking about.'

Pirius said, 'He's asking me if I have found anything to fight for.' He faced Nilis. 'There's only one goal worth dying for,' he said.

'Yes?'

'And that's victory – an end to this war. And then we will have to find out what humans are *supposed* to do with their time.'

Nilis nodded, apparently not trusting himself to speak.

'Oh, how noble you all are.' Pila shook her elegant head. 'The preening of you military types never ceases to astound me.'

Darc ignored her. 'So what do you say, Squadron Leader?'

'Where do I start, sir?'

Darc murmured, 'Well, that's up to you. But first I rather think you'll need to find your crews.'

It was a relief to be able to get back to Rock 492.

At first Pirius and Torec had had to live in their skinsuits, relying on their backpacks for warmth, food, water, even air when the dust got too bad. Before the lavatories had started working they had to relieve themselves in their suits, and every couple of days went out to a flitter to dump their waste. But as the systems recovered they had begun to sleep with their faceplates open, and at last, as the air slowly became fresh and warm, they abandoned the skinsuits altogether. The filters couldn't do much about the suspended asteroid dust, and they both suffered irritated sinuses.

That night after the meeting with Kimmer, they slept as usual huddled together in a corner of the bubble dome, their skinsuited bodies pressed together under a blanket. The touch of microgravity was so gentle they all but hovered over the floor, drifting like soap bubbles. In the quietest hour, the inertial adjusters suddenly came on line. As a full gravity grabbed them they ended up in a tangle of limbs, laughing. The floor was suddenly full of ridges and knobs – they would need a mattress tomorrow, Pirius told himself – and they felt the new, uneven gravity field pull at their internal organs.

The Rock too adjusted to its new state. Like most asteroids, 492 wasn't a solid mass but a loose aggregate of dust and boulders. As the inertial machines in its core did their work, 492's components scraped and ground against each other as they sought to find a more compact equilibrium, Pirius could hear the deep groaning of the asteroid, a rumbling that shivered through his own bones, as if they were lying on the carcass of some huge uncomfortable animal.

In the morning, they found their faces and hands were covered with a silvery patina: it was the asteroid dust, which had at last settled out of its suspension in the air.

CHAPTER 37

The balancing sword tipped and fell. The primordial simplicity of the new universe was lost. From the broken symmetry of a once-unified physics, two forces emerged: gravity, and a force humans would call the GUTforce – 'GUT' for Grand Unified Theory, a combination of electromagnetic and nuclear forces. The separating-out of the forces was a phase change, like water freezing to ice, and it released energy that immediately fed the expansion of the seedling universe.

Gravity's fist immediately clenched, crushing knots of energy and matter into black holes. It was in the black holes' paradoxical hearts that the sleeping monads huddled. But the black holes were embedded in a new, unfolding spacetime: three dimensions of space and one of time, an orderly structure that congealed quickly out of the primitive chaos.

Yet there were flaws. The freezing-out had begun spontaneously in many different places, like ice crystals growing on a cold window. Where the crystals met and merged discontinuities formed. Because the spacetime was three-dimensional, these defects were born in two dimensions, as planes and sheets – or one dimension, as lines of concentrated energy scribbled across spacetime's spreading face – or no dimensions at all, simple points.

Suddenly the universe was filled with these defects; it was a box stuffed with ribbons and strings and buttons.

And the defects were not inert. Propagating wildly, they collided, combined and interacted. A migrating point defect could trace out a line; a shifting line could trace out a plane; where two planes crossed a line was formed, to make more planes and lines. Feedback loops of creation and destruction were quickly established, in a kind of space-time chemistry. There was a time of wild scribbling.

Most of these sketches died as quickly as they were formed. But as the networks of interactions grew in complexity, another kind of phase shift was reached, a threshold beyond which certain closed loops of interactions emerged – loops which promoted the growth of other structures like themselves. This was *autocatalysis*, the tendency for a structure emerging from a richly connected network to en-courage the growth of itself, or copies of itself. And some of these loops happened to be stable, immune to small perturbations. This was *homeostasis*, stability through feedback.

Thus, through autocatalysis and homeostasis working on the flaws of the young spacetime, an increasingly complex hierarchy of self-sustaining structures emerged. All these tangled knots were machines, fundamentally, heat engines feeding off the flow of energy through the universe. And the black holes, drifting through this churning soup, provided additional points of structure, seeds around which the little cycling structures could concentrate. In the new possibilities opened up by closeness, still more complex aggregates grew: simple machines gathered into cooperative 'cells', and the cells gathered into colonial 'organisms' and ultimately multicelled 'creatures . . .'

It was, of course, life. All this had emerged from nothing.

In this universe it would always be this way: structures spontane-ously complexified, and stability emerged from fundamental prop-erties of the networks – any networks, even such exotica as networks of intersecting spacetime defects. Order emerging for free: it was wonderful. But it need not have been this way.

Deep in the pinprick gravity wells of the primordial black holes, the feeding began.

CHAPTER 38

When Squadron Leader Pirius Red went back to the barracks, with his new officer's epaulettes stitched to his uniform, he walked into a silent storm of resentment and contempt. After a few minutes he ducked into a lavatory block and ripped his epaulettes off his shoulders.

The new squadron leader spent twenty-four hours paralysed by uncertainty and indecision. He had no real idea where to start.

Nilis called Pirius to his cluttered room in Officer Country.

When he got there, the Commissary, irritated and distracted, was working at a low table piled with data desks while abstract Virtuals swirled around him like birds. He seemed to be pursuing his studies of Chandra. There was nowhere to sit but on Nilis's blanket-strewn, unmade bed. There was a faint smell of damp and mustiness – it was the smell of Nilis, Pirius thought with exasperated fondness, a smell of feet and armpits, the smell of a gardener.

Pila was here, to Pirius's surprise. Minister Gramm's assistant, slender and elegant, looked somehow insulated from Nilis's clutter. Her skin shone with a cold beauty, and her robe of purple-stitched black fell in precise folds around her slim, sexless body. She didn't acknowledge Pirius at all.

Nilis clapped his hands, and his Virtuals crumpled up and disappeared. 'Fascinating, fascinating. I am studying Chandra's central singularity now, what we can tell of it through the external features of the event horizon and the surrounding spacetime. Even there, deep in the heart of the black hole, there is structure . . . That thing at the centre of the Galaxy, you know, is like an onion; just when you've peeled away one layer, well, my eyes, all you find is another layer underneath, another layer of astrophysics and life and meaning – quite remarkable – I wonder if we'll ever get to the bottom of it.'

Pirius didn't know what an onion was, and couldn't comment. But he could see Nilis was restless. 'You seem unhappy, Commissary.'

Nilis said ruefully, 'Perceptive as ever, Pirius! But it's true. I am frustrated, I thought I would make fast progress with this work here at Arches, now I am so close to the object of my study. But suddenly it has become much *more* difficult. I'm being denied access to records. When I do track down an archive I find it's been emptied or moved – I'm even short on processing power to analyse it!' He shook his head. 'I try not to be paranoid, any more than any citizen of our wonderful Coalition has a right to be. In Sol system I was given assistance with my studies. Now it feels as if I am being impeded at every step! But if it's purposeful, what I don't see is *why* – and who is trying to block me.'

Pila said with her usual cold sarcasm, 'I wouldn't want to keep you from your absorbing work, Commissary. But you called us here.'

'Quite so, quite so.' He took a sip from some tepid drink that had been standing so long on the table it had dust on its surface. 'Let's get on, then. I wondered how the new squadron is doing. What are your priorities, Pirius?'

That was easy. 'We have to assemble the hardware and the crews. Then we will run two parallel programmes: technical development, to get the new equipment fitted to the ships and make them combat-worthy, and training, to get the crews ready to fly the mission.'

'Good, good; nobody would argue with that. But time is short. What actual *progress* have you made?'

'I'm proud to have been given this commission, sir . . .'

The Commissary's sharp, moist eyes were on him, and Nilis clearly noticed the patches where Pirius had ripped off his epaulettes. 'You haven't actually got anywhere – have you, Squadron Leader?'

'He is over-promoted,' Pila said coldly.

'No,' Nilis said. 'This is a battlefield promotion. Needs must, madam. Pirius is right for the job, I'm convinced of it. I've seen his work in two different timelines! But where he lacks experience, we must find ways to help him.'

Pila looked at him suspiciously. 'Which is where I come in, is it? I think you'd better get to the point, Commissary.'

Nilis turned to Pirius. 'Pilot, have you selected your adjutant yet? Every squadron leader needs one.'

Pirius felt even more out of his depth, 'I'm not even sure what an adjutant does, sir.'

Nilis laughed. 'Of course not. Which is why your choice is particularly important. Your adjutant is your key member of staff. She is your personal assistant, if you like. She is responsible for the day-to-day running of your squadron, leaving you to concentrate on the flying. She drafts your orders, filters demands on your time, and ensures you get the resources you need, everything from GUTdrive parts to ration packs. You see? Now, have you any thoughts?'

Pirius shrugged. 'Torec, perhaps—'

Nilis said gently, 'Torec is a fine woman, a warrior, and a close companion. But she doesn't have the skills – the political, the administrative – that you're going to need now.'

Pirius suddenly saw where this was going.

Pila's face was extraordinary; Pirius would never have imagined that so much anger and contempt could be expressed with such stillness. She said, 'Are you joking, Commissary? *Me*?'

'Joking? Not at all,' Nilis said breezily. 'Think about it for a moment. The job won't be so terribly different from what you do for Gramm. You undoubtedly have the administrative skills. And with your, umm, strong personality you will cut like a blade through the buffoonery and obstructionism of the various turf warriors here at the base. You could even pull levers at the Ministry of Economic Warfare if you have to. Besides, as one of the party who came with me from Earth you understand the nature of our unique project better than anybody at Arches.

'And,' he said with a dismissive wave, 'it needn't interfere with your primary duty, which is spying for Minister Gramm. You can do that just as effectively while getting on with some worthwhile work as well.'

Colour spotted Pila's cheeks, but she still hadn't moved a muscle. 'You wouldn't dare say that if Gramm was here.'

'Oh, he already knows! I discussed the idea with him before broaching it with you. He's quite agreeable. I think he finds the idea of you having to cope with front-line soldiery quite amusing.' He folded his hands in his lap, and looked from one to the other.

Pirius took that as his cue. He stood up. 'I think we're done here.'

'So we are, pilot,' Nilis said genially.

'Madam, welcome aboard—'

'Don't even talk to me, you twisted little freak!' In the windows of her pale eyes he saw the contempt of this earthworm for the soldiers who fought and died to protect her.

But Pirius held his nerve. 'Working together is going to be interesting. But I think the Commissary is right. And we only have ten weeks. There's an empty room down the corridor. Maybe we should start right now.'

Pila stood stock still, and Pirius wondered what even the Commissary could do about it if she refused to cooperate. But with a last murderous glance at Nilis, she stalked out.

Nilis was immersed in his Virtuals before Pirius had even left the room. But he called, 'Oh, Pirius. Get those epaulettes sewn back on. That doesn't look good – not good at all.'

Reluctant or not, Pila was remarkably efficient. Within forty-eight hours she had secured Pirius a small office of his own – small, plain, with hardly any facilities, but a room in Officer Country nonetheless. And she had already pulled various bureaucratic levers effectively enough to line up candidates for the squadron.

The first of them was a woman, a former pilot called Jees.

Long before Jees reached his office Pirius could hear the whirr of exoskeletal supports as she clumped down the corridor. When she came in, he was shocked. Her lower body had been sliced away on a line that ran from her ribs on her right hand side to her pelvis on her left, and the flesh and bone and blood replaced by a cold mass of silvery prostheses. When she sat down the chair creaked at her inhuman weight.

But her hair, cut short, was a bright blonde, and her skin was unlined. She was even beautiful. She could have been no more than his own age. But her eyes were dull.

She told him her history. She had been involved in two actions. She had survived the first, but had been caught by a starbreaker in the second. She had been lucky to live at all, of course. Most of her squadron, cut apart, hadn't. She told this story unemotionally, lacing it with dates and reference numbers that meant nothing to Pirius. 'If you get back to base they fix you up. The medics.' A half-smile crossed her face. 'As long as there's a piece of you left they can replace what's missing.'

It was impossible to feel pity for her; she was too damaged for that.

'Your current assignment is ground crew.'

'Yes, sir.'

'You really think you can fly again?'

'I volunteered,' she said. 'I'm a pilot, not a mechanic. You've seen my evaluation. My reflexes and coordination and all the rest are as good as they were. Augmented, some of them are better, in fact. But—'

'You know that's not what I'm asking.'

Pila watched Jees, coldly evaluating.

Jees tapped her head with a metallic finger. 'Everything that counts about me is still here. And what I am is a pilot. I want to get back out there and prove it.'

Pirius nodded, thanked her and let her go.

Pila waved her hand, and a box in a Virtual checklist turned from red to green. 'It's obvious. We take her.'

'We do?'

Pila shrugged elegantly. 'She's a volunteer, one of the few we've had. She can handle the mission technically. Her nerve isn't broken, according to the psychologists. In fact she's powerfully motivated; she has a grudge against the Xeelee, and who can blame her? But we aren't going to find many like her, Pirius.'

From the beginning Pila had complained bitterly about the pool of available candidates. 'The superannuated and the criminal,' she said. 'That's all that's being made available to us. Crew who are useless anywhere else, and so won't impede Marshal Kimmer's own grand goals. And there are precious few of *them* . . .'

The fact was, in this war walking wounded were rare. Day after day the fragile greenships flew into Xeelee fire like moths into flames. If anything went wrong your chances of surviving were slim: death worked efficiently here.

Even 'criminals' were hard to find. Penal units were handed the worst, the most dangerous assignments, and if you happened to survive an action you were thrown back out again. Life expectancy was not long, the turnover rapid. But then if you fell out with a Doctrine cop you had demonstrated some incorrigible character flaw – and, deemed beyond hope of rehabilitation, you were eminently disposable.

But Pila had quickly found that even these battle-damaged antiques and failed renegades were hoarded, like every other resource, by jealous, empire-building local commanders. Pirius decided he was going to have to visit a penal detail to try to drum up volunteers. And that meant he would have to go to Quintuplet Base, where he knew at least one incorrigible rebel was still stationed – himself.

When he told her his decision Pila grinned, her eyes quite without humour. 'For the first time I am glad I have been forced into this assignment. I will enjoy watching you confronting your own unresolved issues, Pirius.'

But he was able to put that aside for a while, as he had a much more agreeable chore to complete first.

A week after Pirius's promotion, the first test flights of greenships modified to Nilis's full design were scheduled. Flexing his squadron leader's muscles, Pirius decided to take the very first flight himself.

So he found himself sitting in a greenship's pilot blister, with Torec as engineer and the intimidating presence of Commander Darc as navigator. Before the great dislocation of Blue's irruption into his life Pirius Red had actually completed his pilot training, but he had never flown in action. It was a huge relief to be aboard a greenship again, back where he belonged.

He checked over his ship. The greenship sat on its launch cradle on the tightly curving surface of Rock 492. The feather-light gravity of the dock touched the ship gently, and Pirius could see that the rails of the cradle had barely made a groove in the loose surface dust.

Light as a soap bubble it might be, but it was an ungainly beast even so. It was a superannuated fighter, one of just five begrudgingly donated so far by Marshal Kimmer and his staff. And it had been in the wars. The central body was scarred and much patched – and you could clearly see where the nacelle bearing the pilot's pod had once been sliced clean through. This ship had been sent out again and again, until it was too battered to be worth fixing up: too worn out, in fact, for any use except Nilis's complicated project.

This beat-up old bird would have been ugly enough if it had been left as nature and the Guild of Engineers intended. But Nilis had made things worse with his 'enhancements'. Not one but *two* of Nilis's patent black hole cannons had been fixed to its flanks, along with a bulky pod where the exotic ammunition for these weapons was stored. The whole thing was swathed in a tangle of cables and wires and tubing. The ruining of the greenship's classic streamlined finish didn't matter, of course, since a greenship never flew in an atmosphere. What did matter was how the massive pods attached to the main body affected the ship's dynamic stability.

The greenship was a mess, no two ways about it. Pirius thought the ironic name Darc had given it was apt: *Earthworm*. This poor ship looked as capable of swooping gracefully through space as fat old Nilis himself.

But still this was the bird Pirius was going to fly today. And as he and his crew worked through their final preparations, he felt his heart beat that bit faster.

Then, with a soft command, he powered up his control systems. Much of the display was standard, concerned with handling the ship in its normal modes under the FTL drive or the sublight drives, after his years of training as familiar to Pirius as his own skin. Most of these displays were Virtual: only life support controls were hardwired, so they wouldn't pop out of existence no matter what hit the ship. But now Nilis's additions booted up. Designed in haste and patched in hurriedly, they overlapped each other as they competed for space, crumbling into flaring, angry-looking crimson pixels.

Torec was grumbling about this. 'Lethe,' she said. 'It's just as it was back in Sol system. You'd think they would have ironed this out by now.'

Commander Darc said, 'We're all under pressure, engineer.'

Despite Torec's complaints, one by one the ship's systems came up. When most of the flags shone green with 'go', Pirius snapped, 'Engineer?'

'It's as good as it's going to get,' Torec said gloomily.

'Then let's get on with it.'

Pirius grasped a joystick and pulled it back steadily. He could feel the ship around him coming to life: the thrumming of the GUT-energy power plant, the subtle surges of the sublight drive. But as the ship lifted off the dirt he could feel an unwelcome wallowing as the ship laboured to cope with its additional mass. The inertial shielding seemed to be hiccupping too. He wasn't surprised when an array of indicators turned red.

As they hovered over the dirt, his crew laboured to put things right. 'The problem's the power plant,' Torec called. 'The weapons systems have been patched into it. There's enough juice to go around, in theory, but the problem is balancing the demands. Greenship power plants aren't used to being treated like this.'

'Work on it, engineer,' Pirius said. 'That's what these trial flights are about, to show up the glitches and fix them.'

'Well spoken, Squadron Leader,' Darc said dryly. 'But you might want to look at your handling. That extra mass has screwed our moments of inertia.'

Pirius said, 'The nav systems have been upgraded to cope with the changes.'

'Well, the patches don't seem to be working. The central sentient thinks it's stuck in one sick ship.' Darc laughed. 'It isn't so wrong.'

'We'll deal with it,' Pirius said grimly.

The crew continued to work until they had got the blizzard of red lights down to a sprinkling. Then, when he thought he could risk it, Pirius lifted the ship away from the Rock. The ascent was smooth enough.

Pirius glanced down at the receding asteroid. He could see the shallow pit from which they had lifted. Standing around it, in defiance of all safety rules, was a loose circle of skinsuited techs. These complex trials, as Nilis's team tried desperately to turn their prototypes and sketches into a working operational concept, had drawn a lot of cynicism from these world-weary techs, especially the Engineers' Guild types: these observers were here, he knew, not to watch a successful trial but to see a cocky pilot screw up, crash and burn. His determination surged. It wouldn't happen today.

Darc sensed what he was thinking. 'Give them a show, pilot.'

Pirius grinned, and clenched his fists around his controls. The *Earth-worm* hurled itself into the sky, straight up. The sublight jaunt, peaking at around half the speed of light, lasted only a fraction of a second, but Pirius glimpsed blueshift staining the crowded stars above him.

When it was over Rock 492 had gone, snatched away from his view. And the target Rock was dead ahead, exactly where it was supposed to be.

He felt a surge of triumph. 'Still alive — Oh, *Lethe*.' He was encased in red lights once more.

'We need to stabilise the systems,' Torec warned.

Pirius sighed. 'I hear you, engineer,' Once again the crew went to work, nursing their deformed steed; gradually the red constellations were replaced by an uncertain green.

The target, only a couple of hundred kilometres away, was another asteroid, a bit of debris probably older than Earth. This Rock had been used for target practice by crews from Arches for generations. It was impossible to tell if the immense craters that pocked its surface were relics of the asteroid's violent birth or had been inflicted by trigger-happy trainees.

'Look at that thing,' Darc said. 'Looks as if it has been cracked in two.'

Pirius said, 'Let's see if we can't crack it again. Engineer, how are the weapons?'

Two threads of cherry-red light speared out from the pods on the *Earth worm*'s main body and lanced into the battered hide of the target Rock.

'Nothing wrong with the starbreakers,' Torec said.

'Then let's try the black hole cannon.'

'My displays are green,' said Torec. 'Most of the time anyhow.'

'Your course is laid in, pilot,' Darc called from his navigator's seat.

Pirius settled himself in his seat, smoothing out creases in his skinsuit. He stared at the Rock, trying to visualise his flight.

Nilis had explained his latest tactics carefully. The microscopic black holes fired by the cannon had been enough to destroy a Xeelee nightfighter, but they would be pinpricks against a Galaxy-centre black hole and the living structures that fed off it – unless, Nilis had determined, *two* holes could be fired off together, If the holes could be made to collide correctly they would emit much of their mass-energy in a shaped pulse of gravitational waves – and Pirius had seen, in the wreckage of Jupiter, how much damage that could do. If such a bomb were set off at the event horizon of Chandra, the great black hole would flex and ripple, 'like a rat shaking off fleas', as Nilis had said.

But such a feat required huge accuracy. The greenships were going to have to fly around the black hole at an altitude of precisely a hundred kilometres above the event horizon: 'precisely' meaning not more than ten metres out. Such a jaunt through the twisted space around a massive black hole was going to be 'fun', in Darc's words, and the resistance of the Xeelee was going to make it more fun still. If they couldn't achieve that degree of accuracy the mission was a waste of time.

So today's test was crucial. If Pirius couldn't hit a dumb piece of rock, then Chandra was out of reach.

As the systems stabilised, the crew grew quiet. They would have to work together tightly during this manoeuvre. As pilot Pirius would direct the line, navigator Darc was to check the accuracy of their trajectory, while engineer Torec worked the weapons. But the closest approach, during which they would have to fire the cannon, would happen in just a fraction of a second.

Darc said, 'Pilot? I think we're as ready as we'll ever be.'

'Roger that. Engineer?'

'Do it.'

Pirius took his controls. The ship quivered, poised. 'Now or never,' he said. He closed his fists.

The Rock flew at him, exploding to a battered wall that seemed about to swat the greenship out of space. At the last moment the asteroid swivelled, dropped beneath his prow and turned into a lumpy landscape. Closest approach – but as the black hole cannon fired, it was as if the ship had taken a punch to the guts and red lights flared everywhere.

And then his blister flooded with impact foam, and he was cut off, embedded in a rigid casing in the dark. It was over, as suddenly as that.

Frustration raging, he screamed, 'Tactical display!' A working sensor projected a tiny Virtual image on to the inner surface of his faceplate.

The cannon had actually fired, and dotted yellow lines, neatly sketched, helpfully showed the track of the black hole projectiles. They missed each other, and passed harmlessly through the loose bulk of the target Rock, which sailed on, ancient and serene. And at the moment of closest approach the ship had exploded. Three crew blisters came flying out of an expanding cloud of debris.

Only nine weeks left, he thought helplessly. Nine weeks.

CHAPTER 39

The universe inhabited by the spacetime-defect fauna was quite unlike that of humans. There was no light, for instance, for the electromagnetic force which governed light's propagation had yet to decouple from the GUT superforce. But the spacetime-flaw creatures, huddled around their black holes, could 'see' by the deep glow of the gravity waves that criss-crossed the growing cosmos.

To them, of course, it had always been this way; to them the sky was beautiful.

The basis of all life in this age was the chemistry of spacetime defects, an interconnected geometric churning of points and lines and planes. Most life forms were built up of 'cells', tightly interconnected and very stable. But more complex creatures, built from aggregates of these cells, were not quite so stable. They were capable of variation, one generation to the next.

And where there is variation, selection can operate.

On some of the black hole 'worlds', fantastic ecologies developed: there were birds with wings of spacetime, and spiders with arms of cosmic string, even fish that swam deep in the twisted hearts of the black holes. 'Plants' passively fed on energy flows, like the twisting of space at the event horizons of the black holes, and 'animals', exploiters, fed on those synthesisers in turn – and other predators fed on *them*. Everywhere there was coevolution, as species adapted together in conflict or cooperation: 'plants' and 'animals', 'flowers' and 'insects', parasites and hosts, predators and prey. Some of this – the duets of synthesisers and exploiters, for instance – had echoes in the ecologies with which humans were familiar. But there were forms like nothing in human experience.

The creatures of one black hole 'world' differed from the inhabitants of another as much as humans would differ from, say, Silver Ghosts. But just as humans and Ghosts were both creatures of baryonic matter who emerged on rocky planets, so the inhabitants of this age, dominated by its own dense physics, had certain features in common.

All life forms must reproduce. Every parent must store information, a genotype, to pass on to its offspring. From this data is constructed a phenotype, the child's physical expression of that information – its 'body'.

In this crowded young universe the most obvious way to transmit such information was through extended quantum structures. Quantum mechanics allowed for the long-range correlation of particles: once particles had been in contact, they were never truly separated, and would always share information.

Infants were budded, unformed, from parents. But each child was born without a genotype. It was unformed, a blank canvas. A mother would read off her own genotype, and send it to her newborn daughter – by touch, by gravity waves. In the process, depending on the species, the mother's data might be mixed with that of other 'parents'.

But there was a catch. This was a quantum process. The uncertainty principle dictated that it was impossible to clone quantum information: it could be swapped around, but not copied. For the daughter to be born, the mother's genotype had to be destroyed. Every birth required a death.

To human eyes this would seem tragic; but humans worked on different assumptions. To the spacetime fauna, life was rich and wonderful, and the interlinking of birth and death the most wonderful thing of all.

As consciousness arose, the first songs ever sung centred on the exquisite beauty of necrogenesis.

CHAPTER 40

The senior representative of the Guild of Engineers at Arches Base was called Eliun. He arrived for the review of the failed test flight with two aides. The review was held in a shabby conference room deep in Arches' Officer Country. Eliun immediately made his way to the head of the table and sat comfortably, hands folded over his belly.

Nilis bustled among his data desks and Virtuals, his movements edgy and nervous. The scratch crew of the lost *Earthworm* were here, Pirius, Torec and Darc. All had survived the ordeal intact, save for Commander Darc whose broken wrist was encased in bright orange med fabric.

Pila took her place beside Pirius. Even after working closely with her Pirius couldn't read the expression on her beautiful, pinched face. Perhaps she thought that with this latest failure this embarrassing and awkward project would be terminated at last, and she could return to the comforts of Earth and her slow, complicated ascent through the ranks of the Coalition civil service.

And, in one corner of the room, a Silver Ghost hovered, a sensor pack strapped to its equatorial line. It was the Ambassador to the Heat Sink. Two blue-helmeted Guardians, who had been assigned to it since Sol system, stood at its side, weapons ever ready. Nobody commented, as if having a Ghost here at a Core base was an everyday event. But the Navy guards posted at the door couldn't help but stare.

The Guild-master was sleek, only a little plump, and his skin glistened as if he treated it with unguent. He wore a peculiar outfit covered with pockets, insignia, and little readout displays. It turned out to be a stylised skinsuit of a very archaic design. This commemorated a time when the Engineers had always been the first on the scene in case of some disaster. Those days were long gone, though, and Pirius Red learned that Eliun's suit wasn't even functional.

Though he was a master engineer, Eliun didn't seem at all perturbed to be summoned to a review of a catastrophic engineering failure. But Pirius knew Eliun need defer to nobody here. The Engineers were independent of the Navy and the Green Army, and in particular of Training and Discipline Command, the powerful inter-service grouping that ran this base. In fact the Engineers were independent all the way to the top, to the Grand Conclave of the Coalition itself. And in the comfortable form of Eliun, Project Prime Radiant had found yet another institutional opponent.

Darc glowered at Eliun with undisguised hostility, and even Nilis seemed coldly angry. The atmosphere was tense, and Pirius suspected uneasily they were in for some fireworks.

He was restless himself. Since the test flight two more days had worn away, two days of no progress towards the goal.

Nilis called the meeting briskly to order. 'You know why we're here.' He clapped his hands to call up a plethora of Virtual displays – far too much information, Pirius thought; it was typical of Nilis. 'Let's start with the basics.'

Once again the doomed *Earthworm* slid past the patient face of the target. Once again it blew apart, three fragile crew blisters careening out of the wreckage only just ahead of the main fireball. Pirius winced from embarrassment at having lost a ship, and at the uncomfortable memory of the break-up itself. Two days later he was still chipping bits of solidified impact foam off his skinsuit.

Nilis ran the failure again and again, at one-thousandth speed, then one ten-thousandth, then slower still. 'You can see that the black hole cannon did fire successfully,' he said. 'But the structural failure occurred at that moment of firing.' He nodded to Torec, the ship's engineer.

Torec walked through key moments in Nilis's Virtuals, picking out freeze-frame images and referring the audience to bits of technical detail. 'Firing the black hole shells places the greatest stress on the ship's systems as a whole.' To provide a stable platform when the cannon fired, the greenship's inertial adjusters had to keep the ship anchored in spacetime. But the recoil of these spacetime bullets put far more strain on the adjusters than they had been designed for. 'Remember each shell has the mass of a small mountain. The energy drain is huge, the momentum recoil enormous. And unless the structural balance is *exactly* right, you get a failure. As in this case.'

She spoke well, Pirius thought with a mixture of envy and nostalgia. She had grown so much. The mixed-up cadet who had been press-ganged into flying with him to Earth a few months ago could never have made such a presentation.

Eliun spoke for the first time. 'Show me the point of failure.' His voice was like the man, oily, unperturbed.

Torec ran through a series of stop-motion images of the greenship at the moment of its terminal catastrophe, magnified so heavily they broke up into crowding cubical pixels. She showed the first instants of failure, using two bright red laser-pointer beams which intersected on the ship's Virtual image. The point they picked out was a flare of light, right at the junction of the cannon pod with the main hull. In that first moment the failure looked harmless, but the ship hadn't held together for another half-second. Skewered neatly by the criss-crossing beams, the point in space and time when the *Earthworm* had died was unambiguous.

Pirius knew that all this was irrelevant, to some extent. For him the greatest failures of the test flight had been navigation and accuracy. Even if they could overcome the problem of the damn ship blowing itself up in the moment of firing, to get the one hundredth of one per cent accuracy of positioning Nilis was demanding, the navigational control of the ships was going to have to be improved by an order of magnitude.

Idly Pirius glanced over his shoulder at the source of the laser pointers. They came from light globes that drifted at the back of the room. The beams' location of the failure point on the Virtual had been precise to well within the size of a pixel on that much-magnified image. An idea hovered at the back of his mind, elusive. He tried to relax his thinking . . .

'—Pirius.'

Nilis was calling his name. Commander Darc was glaring at him.

'Sir, I'm sorry. I was just thinking that—'

'Yes, yes,' said Nilis impatiently. 'I asked if you as pilot had anything to add to Torec's expert presentation.'

'No. I'm sorry,' Pirius said.

Nilis harrumphed. Now he turned to Commander Darc, as the *Earthworm*'s navigator.

Darc had clearly been waiting for this moment. His strong face blank and threatening, he turned on Eliun, who had been looking faintly bored. 'I have no report, Guild-master. Only a question.'

'Go ahead, Commander.'

'You've seen the report. You saw the summary before you walked into the room. How will you help us resolve this issue of structural integrity?'

Eliun spread his fingers on the table. 'I'm sure your analysis, if sufficiently deep, will—'

'Our analysis,' Darc cut in. '*Ours*. But the Commissary's project is a scratch operation that has been running on a shoestring for a matter of weeks. Whereas you have been running greenships for millennia.' He leaned forward and glared. 'I would like to know, Guild-master, why the Engineers have obstructed this project from the day Nilis came here.'

That unexpected shot got through Eliun's defences; for an instant shock creased his face. But he said with quiet control, 'Commander, I'll enjoy speaking to your seniors about your future career path.'

Nilis bustled forward, his own agitation obvious, a vein showing in his forehead. This was the crux of the meeting, Pirius saw. Nilis said, 'Well, that's your privilege, Guild-master. But before we descend into personal attacks, shall we examine the issue? You see, faced with our cruel timescale, we've been struggling not only against a shortage of resources and antiquated test craft, but against – how shall I put it? – *secrecy*.

'After the prototype work in Sol system, we're now trying to integrate our new systems into a greenship's design. But as the Commander implies we've been given *nothing* by your people on the craft's technical aspects. Surely you have blueprints, records, practical experience you could offer us? And then there is the GUT engine itself. Again we've been given no documentation. Remember, we're trying to use it to run black hole cannon! As we've tried to work our way through its antiquated interfaces, we've felt more like archaeologists than engineers. My eyes, you *must* have the technical knowledge we're straggling to retrieve here! You've been running ships of more or less this design for, what – three thousand years?'

'A little longer,' Eliun said smoothly, 'And not of "more or less" this design, Commissary – *exactly* this design.'

Darc eyed him. 'Three thousand years of stasis. And you're proud of that, are you?'

'It's clear that you misunderstand our objectives. Our mission is not innovation but preservation . . .'

The Guild of Engineers was an ancient agency. It had grown out of a loose band of refugees from the Qax Occupation, who had spent centuries stranded in space. When the Qax were thrown out they had come home, their antique technology carefully preserved. In the internecine struggles that had developed during the establishment of the Interim Coalition, mankind's first post-Occupation government, the Engineers, with their ancient bits of technological sorcery and their proud record of resistance to the Qax, had been well-placed to grab some power for themselves. And they had kept their place at the highest levels of the Coalition ever since.

'But you're not *engineers*,' Darc said contemptuously. 'Not if you resist innovation. You're museum-keepers.'

Eliun said, 'Commander, our technologies reached their plateaux of perfection millennia ago. There can be no innovation that does not worsen what we have. We Engineers preserve the wisdom of ages—'

'You pore over your ancient, unchanging designs, polished with use—'

'—and we standardise. Have you thought about that? Commander, your pilots fly greenships of *identical* design from one end of this Galaxy of ours to the other. Think of the cost savings, the economies of scale!'

Nilis was as angry as Pirius had ever seen him. 'But your perfect designs and your standardised parts lists are not winning the war, Guild-master! And – yes, I'll say it now – in your obstructionism you seem bent on ensuring that this project, which might hasten the war's end, never gets a chance to fly.'

Pirius laid a hand on Nilis's threadbare sleeve. 'Commissary, take it easy.'

Nilis shook him off. 'If there's one thing I can't bear, Pirius, it is the hoarding of knowledge as power. There's too much of that on Earth – too much! And I won't have it here.'

Eliun said coldly, 'And I won't take lectures in duty from rogue Commissaries and junior naval officers.'

'Then we are at an impasse. I suggest we adjourn this meeting until I've heard from Earth.' Nilis turned to Pila. 'Adjutant, would you please open a channel to Minister Gramm's office, on Earth? I think we must appeal to the Minister, and through him to the Plenipotentiary for Total War and the Grand Conclave itself, where I hope this issue will be resolved.'

Eliun laughed in his face. 'Commissary, don't you understand? *The Engineers have seats on the Conclave too.*'

'We will see,' said Nilis darkly, and he stalked from the room.

Pirius felt oddly calm. He had sat through too many meetings like this. And he had been distracted from these fireworks by his vague thoughts about intersecting laser light. As the meeting broke up, he tapped Darc and Torec on the shoulders. 'Listen. I have an idea . . .'

As they left the room they passed the Silver Ghost, which hadn't moved or said a word during the interrupted meeting. Pirius wondered what emotions swirled beneath that glistening, featureless hide.

On the way, Pirius called ahead for a sim room to be set up.

Only a few minutes after ducking out of Nilis's adjourned meeting, the three of them were once more sitting in their crew blisters, at the end of the outstretched limbs of the *Earthworm*. The Virtual simulation around them was faultless, although the target Rock looked a little too shiny to be true.

As they waited for the sim to finish booting up, Darc growled, 'This is bringing back unhappy memories. Whatever you're planning, Pirius, I hope it's worth it.'

Pirius said hesitantly, 'Commander – can I speak freely?'

Darc laughed.

'The way you took on the Guild-master. I was surprised.'

'Did you enjoy watching me blow my career?'

'No, sir.'

'Not that there's much left to blow,' Darc said. 'Marshal Kimmer will see to that, once this project is over.'

Pirius said frankly, 'When we started this, I'd never have thought you would come out fighting for the Commissary like that. With respect, sir.'

Darc grunted. 'I don't much like Nilis. I think he's an irresponsible idiot, and his project is almost bound to fail. *Almost.* But in that "almost" is a universe of possibility. If there's a chance we can win the war with it, we have to resource the project until the point at which it fails. That's our clear duty. And I never imagined the kind of crass reaction and ass-covering conservatism that we have come up against, over and over. I've seen a side of our politics I don't like, pilot, even inside the military.'

Torec said, 'I suppose we have all come on a long journey.'

Darc said, 'But if either of you repeat any of this to Nilis I'll rip off your heads with my bare hands. Do you understand me?'

'Received and understood,' Pirius said.

With a soft chime the sim signalled it was ready to run.

Darc said, 'It's time you explained what we're doing here, Pirius.'

'I want to try an idea,' Pirius said. 'It came to me when Torec used those laser pointers in the meeting.'

She sounded baffled, 'Lasers?'

'Bear with me. We'll run through our approach to the rock. Everything will be exactly as before. I've downloaded Torec's structural analyses of the failure—'

'So we'll fall apart, like before.'

'Maybe. But this time, Torec, I want you to fire the starbreakers as we go in.'

'What's the use?' she asked. 'They will only scratch the Rock's surface. And if the cannon fails—'

'Just do it. But, Torec, *I want you to cross the beams . . .*'

They both grasped the idea very quickly. It took only minutes to programme new instructions into their weapons and guidance systems.

Once again Pirius took the controls; once again the ship swooped along its invisible attack arc towards the Rock. They ran the whole thing in real time, and, thanks to the simulator's precise reproduction, the ship's handling felt as clumsy as it had before.

But this time around, one second before the closest approach to the Rock, the starbreakers lit up. They swivelled and crossed at a point exactly a hundred kilometres below the ship's position. So the *Earthworm* sailed in on its target through the sim's imaginary space with an immense, slim triangle of cherry-red light dangling beneath it.

When the ship passed the rock, the crossed starbreakers dug deep into its impact-chewed surface. Dust fountained up: that point of intersection was lost in the rock's interior layers. Too low, then. But the guidance system, slaved to the starbreakers, jolted the ship upwards until the crossing point was touching the Rock's surface, just stroking it, leaving little more than a furrow of churned-up regolith.

All this in the second of closest approach.

When the black hole cannon fired the projectiles sailed down the lines of the starbreakers and collided with each other at the point of their intersection, precisely one hundred kilometres below the ship.

The simulation software wasn't up to modelling the collision of two point black holes, or to show realistically the detonation of an asteroid. But the ship, suffering the same structural failures as before, blew up pretty convincingly. The Virtuals melted away, leaving Pirius, Darc and Torec sitting side by side in a room walled with blank blue light.

Torec said, 'So we're going to use starbreakers as an altimeter. You think big when you want to, Pirius, don't you?'

Darc brought up a re-run of the last moments. They had to see it with their own eyes before they believed it.

'I think it worked,' Pirius said.

Darc growled, 'Pilot, you are learning understatement from that fat Commissary.'

Pirius allowed himself one second of self-congratulation. Then he stood up, pushing away the restraints of his couch. 'We've a lot to do,' he said. 'We'll need to see what we can do about improving the accuracy of the starbreaker mounts. They weren't intended for pinpoint work like this. And we'll have to slave the guidance properly to the starbreakers.'

'Yes,' Torec said, and she added with feeling: 'I'd also like to find a way to fire these damn cannon without killing myself.'

Nilis came bustling into the sim room. 'Here you are!' he cried. He was cockahoop. He grabbed Pirius by the shoulders and shook him; for Nilis this was a remarkably physical display. 'My boy – my boy!'

Darc said dryly, 'I take it the Grand Conclave endorsed your stance, Commissary.'

'In every particular. That polished oaf Eliun and his cronies have been ordered to cooperate with us, or else simply hand over their data to my technicians. The Conclave have backed me. They backed *me*! I have to pinch myself to believe it. Can you see what this means historically? The logjam at the top of human government is finally breaking up . . . Is the madness that has gripped us for so long at last falling away? And I couldn't have done it without you, Commander!'

'Don't push it, Commissary,' warned Darc.

Pirius thought this over. He was starting to get a sense of the drama unfolding around this strange project. Today a power centre as old as the Coalition itself had suffered a historic reversal. However this mission turned out, nothing would be left the same: twenty thousand years of history really were coming to an end here. And, in a sense, it was because of him.

With one finger Torec gently closed his mouth, which was gaping open. 'So we beat another bureaucrat,' she said. 'Now all we've got to do is dive-bomb a black hole.'

'Yes. How soon can we set up a fresh test flight?'

'Tomorrow,' said Darc. 'And then we're going to have to think about a training programme – how to fly this thing in anger . . . Always assuming you can find the crew to fly.'

'We aren't going to get bored, sir,' Pirius said.

Darc laughed.

They made their way out of the sim room, talking, planning.

CHAPTER 41

As the young universe unfolded, some of the spacetime-chemistry races developed high technologies. They ventured from their home 'worlds', and came into contact with each other. Strange empires were spun across galaxies of black holes. Terrible wars were fought.

Out of the debris of war, the survivors groped their way to a culture that was, if not unified, at least peaceable. A multispecies federation established itself. Under its benevolent guidance new merged cultures propagated, new symbiotic ecologies arose. The endless enrichment of life continued. The inhabitants of this golden time even studied their own origins in the brief moments of the singularity. They speculated about what might have triggered that mighty detonation, and whether any conscious intent might have lain behind it.

Time stretched and history deepened.

It was when the universe was very old indeed – ten billion times as old as it had been at the moment of the breaking of its primordial symmetry – that disaster struck.

Light itself did not yet exist, and yet lightspeed was embedded in this universe.

At any given moment only a finite time had passed since the singularity, and an object travelling at lightspeed could have traversed only part of the span of the cosmos. Domains limited by lightspeed travel were the effective 'universes' of their inhabitants, for the cosmos was too young for any signal to have been received from beyond their boundaries. But as the universe aged, so signals propagated further – and domains which had been separated since the first instant, domains which could have had no effect on each other before, were able to come into contact.

And as they overlapped, life forms crossed from one domain into another.

For the federation, the creatures which suddenly came hurtling out of infinity were the stuff of nightmare. These invaders came from a place where the laws of physics were subtly different: the symmetry-breaking which had split gravity from the GUT super-force had occurred differently in different domains, for they had not been in causal contact at the time. That difference drove a divergence of culture, of values. The federation valued its hard-won prosperity, peace and the slow accumulation of knowledge. The invaders, following their own peculiar imperatives, were intent only on destruction, and fuelling their own continuing expansion. It was like an invasion from a parallel universe. Rapprochement was impossible.

The invaders came from all around the federation's lightspeed horizon. Reluctantly the federation sought to defend itself, but a habit of peace had been cultivated for too long; everywhere the federation fell back. It seemed extinction was inevitable.

But one individual found a dreadful alternative.

Just as the cosmos had gone through a phase change when gravity had separated from the GUTforce, so more phase changes were possible. The GUTforce itself could be induced to dissociate further. The energy released would be catastrophic, unstoppable, universal – but, crucially, it would feed a new burst of universal expansion.

The homelands of the invaders would be pushed back beyond the lightspeed horizon.

But much of the federation would be scattered too. And, worse, a universe governed by a new combination of physical forces would not be the same as that in which the spacetime creatures had evolved. It would be unknowable, perhaps unsurvivable.

It was a terrible dilemma. Even the federation was unwilling to accept the responsibility to remake the universe itself. But the invaders encroached, growing more ravenous, more destructive as they approached the federation's rich and ancient heart. In the end there was only one choice.

A switch was thrown.

*

A wall of devastation burned at lightspeed across the cosmos. In its wake the very laws of physics changed; everything it touched was transformed.

The invaders were devastated.

The primordial black holes survived – and, by huddling close to them, so did some representatives of the federation.

But the federation's scientists had not anticipated how long this great surge of growth would continue. With the domain war long won, the mighty cosmic expansion continued, at rates unparalleled in the universe's history. Ultimately, it would last *sixty times* the age of the universe at its inception, and it would expand the federation's corner of spacetime by a trillion times a trillion times a trillion times a *trillion*. Human scientists, detecting the traces of this burst of 'inflation', the single worst catastrophe in the universe's long history, would always wonder what had triggered it. Few ever guessed it was the outcome of a runaway accident triggered by war.

As the epochal storm continued the survivors of the federation huddled, folding their wings of spacetime flaws over themselves. When the gale at last passed, the survivors emerged into a new, chill cosmos. So much time had passed that they had changed utterly, and forgotten who they were, where they had come from. But they were heirs of a universe grown impossibly huge – a universe all of ten centimetres across.

CHAPTER 42

Quin Base shocked Pirius Red.

He was dismayed by the cramped corridors and heaped-up bunks of the barracks, the crowding, the stink of shit and urine and semen, the metallic odours of failing life-support systems. The people swarmed through their cavernous lairs, feeding and sleeping, shouting and wrestling and rutting. The only difference he could see between privates and cadets was the gleaming metallised pupils of the 'veterans'. He thought their silvery stares made them seem inhuman, like huge, lithe rats, perhaps.

If he had been faced with hostility in the barracks back at Arches, here he was regarded with undisguised loathing. In fact the station commander, a stern prosthetic-wearer called Captain Marta, insisted he and Pila were accompanied by guards wherever they went.

Pila, oddly, didn't seem disturbed by this squalor. 'What did you expect? Pirius, you are a pilot; you are relatively skilled and intelligent, and in battle you would be expected to show individual initiative. The conditions of your upbringing and training reflect that. These cadets are animals to be thrown on to some dismal Rock to dig and fight and die. This is a war of economics, remember. How much do you think it is *worth* spending on their brief, wretched lives?'

Pirius wondered if she was wearing nose filters.

'You just don't fit in,' said Enduring Hope.

'Thanks,' said Pirius dryly.

Hope and Pirius Red faced each other across the small room in Quin's cramped Officer Country that had been commandeered for Pirius's use. This engineer, who had flown with Pirius Blue aboard the

Assimilator's Claw in a different destiny, was one of the first candidates selected by Pila. Pirius Red had only met Hope before across the courtroom during the hearing on the magnetar episode.

Hope seemed to regard Red as an inferior version of Blue. It was deeply disconcerting to be known so well by somebody Pirius had never properly met before – known, and judged, and found wanting.

'You don't belong here,' Hope said. 'Your adjutant doesn't either, but she looks like an earthworm, and you can see she doesn't care.'

'How perceptive,' murmured Pila.

'You, though – you're neither one thing nor the other. You're not an earthworm, but you walk around like one. You want us to accept you, to take you back. Everyone can see it in your face. You're *needy*. But you can't come back. You're polluted.'

'Maybe,' Pirius said tightly. 'But I had no choice about what happened to me.'

Hope shrugged. 'Doesn't change the fact.'

'And whatever you think about me, I have a job to do. I want you to help me do it.' He outlined the assignment he wanted Hope to take. On Rock 492, Hope would be in overall charge of the ground crews. He knew Hope had been assigned to artillery batteries here on Quin, and he imagined Hope, a born engineer, would be attracted by the idea of getting back to working on ships.

But Hope said, 'Why me? There are plenty of other engineers stranded on this Rock.'

Pirius shrugged, 'I – I mean, Pirius Blue – once selected you for his crew. I have to trust my own judgement.' He forced a smile at his own weak joke. 'And remember, our duty isn't to do what we want—'

Hope leaned forward, suddenly angry. 'Don't patronise me with creche slogans, you desk jockey. I know all about duty.'

'I'm sorry. Look, Hope, I won't have you assigned if you don't want it. I want to work with you, not against you.'

Enduring Hope stood up. 'I'll do it if Pirius does it. I mean,' he said caustically, 'the real Pirius.'

Pirius Red faced other problems when he interviewed other candidates.

He was brought a young woman called Tili, who, it was said, had shown intuitive promise as a navigator before she had been banished to this dismal place for some irrelevant misdemeanour. Her condition shocked him. She had been wounded in action, and though her physical injuries were healed her eyes were wide and filled with an inchoate pain. He got off to a bad start when she wouldn't even respond to her name. It seemed she had been one of a set of triplets; but since the other two had been killed she had insisted on being known only by her 'family' number, Three.

She wouldn't volunteer for his squadron, but she would follow orders, she said. 'But it makes no difference whatever we do.'

'Of course it does—'

'No. Ask This Burden Must Pass.'

'Who?'

She shrugged, and sat apathetically until he released her.

After similar experiences with other cadets, as Burden's name came up repeatedly, Pirius realised that to penetrate the strange, deviant culture of this base he was going to have to meet this front-line prophet.

And, as he had always known, he was going to have to confront his own future self.

This Burden Must Pass – or Quero, as Pila insisted on calling him – didn't fit into this colony of child soldiers. He was too tall, too old, too experienced. He sat in Pirius's commandeered office with a relaxed calm, and yet somehow dominated the room. He was centred, that was the word; he made Pirius feel young, unformed.

Pirius said, 'You're a good flyer. Your training record is clear about that.'

'Thank you.'

'And you're good at keeping yourself alive, I'd want you in my squadron for those qualities alone.'

Burden nodded. But as he took in the notion that Pirius was offering him a flight post he avoided Pirius's gaze, oddly, 'Whatever you say.'

Pirius delivered his standard line. 'I'm reluctant to draft you. I want volunteers, if I can get them; the mission is going to be tough enough as it is without reluctant conscripts.'

'You're wise.'

'But the point is,' Pirius said, 'there are many others here on Quin who won't consider coming with me unless *you* are there. I don't understand the hold you have over them.'

'I suppose I give them hope,' Burden said.

'It's this philosophy of yours, isn't it? You're a Wignerian. You believe that all of this' – he waved a hand – 'will be wiped out when—'

'When we reach timelike infinity,' said Pila coldly. She regarded Burden with undisguised loathing. For all her cynicism, she was a strict Druzite and Burden's nonconformity shocked her. 'You're only here because you're an opinion former.' She waved manicured fingers. 'Out there, in that pit you call a barracks.'

'I don't want to form anyone's opinion. I'm only myself.'

'Garbage,' Pila said. 'I'm astonished the commanders here tolerate your deviance. I wouldn't, for a second.'

'You'll get used to it. And after all it doesn't matter. This burden must pass,' Burden said, and he grinned.

'In any case,' she said, 'it doesn't make any difference if you join us or not. Because whatever we do, all of this will be erased anyhow, won't it? And so what's the point of getting out of your bunk?'

'There is always a point,' Burden said mildly. 'All the worldlines contribute to the whole, in some sense beyond our understanding. And of course there are always the people around you. You must care for them, as they care for you. I do believe in timelike infinity, in the final convergence—'

Pirius nodded. 'But we have a duty to behave as if it's not so. As *this* is the only chance we get.'

Burden eyed him, 'You understand. You and I – I mean, Pirius Blue – have had long discussions about these points. You're deeper than you look, Pirius Red.'

'Thanks,' Pirius said. 'Look, I'm not interested in your endorsement for myself. But it seems I need it to get my job done. Will you fly with me?'

Now the moment of commitment had come, and Pirius, watching Burden closely, thought he saw a flash of fear in his eyes. There were depths to this strange man, he realized. 'You can refuse if you want,' he said, groping for understanding.

But the instant had passed, and Burden's smiling control returned. 'I think you know I will accept.'

Pila snorted her disgust. But she turned another box in her checklist from red to green.

As Burden made to leave, he turned back. 'One more thing.'

'Yes?'

'There have been rumours.'

'Rumours?'

'That you brought a Silver Ghost with you from Earth. A live Ghost.'

Pirius glanced at Pila, who rolled her eyes; they had had little cooperation from the Quin commanders over security. He said, 'I can't comment on that. And I don't understand your interest anyhow.'

'It doesn't matter,' said Burden.

Pirius sensed it actually mattered a great deal. There was much he didn't understand about Burden, he thought – perhaps a lot Burden didn't even understand about himself.

But there was no time to think about it now, because he had to face a still more difficult interview.

Pirius Blue was arrogant, cocky.

His face, of course, was Pirius Red's own. But Red was shocked by how old he had become, even compared to his memory from the trial seven months ago, as if far more than a couple of years now separated them. And the infantry-standard silvered discs that replaced his pupils were eerie, glinting.

'Let me get this straight,' Blue said. 'You want me to fly in your kiddie squadron. You want *me* to report to *you*.'

Red worked hard to keep his temper under control. 'It isn't unprecedented.' That was true; he had had Pila look out the records. 'There have been many instances of temporal twins serving together.'

'Yes, but not with one under the command of another.'

'What's wrong with that?'

'I'm *you*,' said Blue. 'Or rather, I'm what you wish you were. I'm the older, wiser, more experienced, better-looking *you*.' He actually leered at Pila, trying to put her off. Red felt obscurely proud of the contemptuous loathing she projected back.

In his brief few days as a squadron leader, Red had begun to learn the elements of command. Now he summoned all that up. 'Get this straight,' he snapped, and Blue looked surprised at his tone. 'I don't like this situation any more than you do. But I'm stuck with it. I've got a mission, I've got my duty, and I intend to perform it.'

'Don't lecture me, you – you—'

'What?' Pirius stood up and leaned over the table. '*What?* What do you think I am? I'm not your clone. I'm not a cadre sibling, or a brother, or even a twin, I'm not some failed copy of you. *I'm you.* Maybe you resent my existence. But believe me, I resent yours far more. I'm here,' he said. 'So are you. Get over it.'

Blue shook his head. 'If you're drafting me—'

'I've drafted nobody. I'm looking for volunteers.' That seemed to surprise Blue. 'I know you can do the job,' Red said. 'Because I know myself that well.'

'So you want me to volunteer.'

'No. I want more than that. I want you to support me.'

'Why? To make you feel good?'

'No. Because you'll bring with you good people, like Enduring Hope and Cohl.'

'I'll think about it.'

'Crap. Tell me now, or walk away.'

Blue, staring boldly at him, shook his head. 'You speak to me that way. But you've no idea what I've seen here. None at all.'

'Give me an answer.'

The silence stretched. Pila sat silently, evidently fascinated, as the two halves of Pirius, locked together by fate and mutual loathing, faced each other down.

Eventually Pirius Blue agreed. Pirius Red always knew he would, though the two of them would fight all the way to Chandra. After all, that was what he would have done himself.

As Blue turned to go, Red stopped him. 'We're going to have to learn to get along. We'll always have seventeen years of our lives in common.'

'So what?' Blue snapped. 'That's the past.'

'Aren't you going to ask about her?'

Blue's back stiffened. 'Who?'

'*Torec.* Come on, Blue. We need to talk it over.'

Blue shrugged. 'There's nothing to talk about. She's your Torec. Mine is – lost in a timeline that's never going to exist. You get used to it.' And he walked out.

CHAPTER 43

The monstrous swelling of the age of inflation was over.

The universe continued to expand, more sedately than before, but relentlessly. Still phase changes occurred, as the merged forces broke up further, and with each loss of symmetry more energy was injected into the expansion.

The release of the electromagnetic force from its prison of symmetry was particularly spectacular, for suddenly it was possible for light to exist. The universe lit up in a tremendous flash – and space filled immediately with a bath of searing radiation. So energetically dense was this first exuberant glow that it continually coalesced into specks of matter – quarks and anti-quarks, electrons and positrons – that would almost as rapidly annihilate each other. There were no atoms yet, though, no molecules. Indeed, temperatures were too high for the quarks to combine into anything as sedate as a proton.

The primordial black holes, surviving from the age of spacetime chemistry, again provided some structure in this seething chaos; passing through the glowing soup they would gather clusters of quarks or anti-quarks. Though the quarks themselves continually melted away, the structure of these clusters persisted; and in those structures were encoded information. Interactions became complex. Networks and loops of reactions formed, some were reinforced by feedback loops.

Certain consequences inevitably followed. For this universe it was already an old story – but it was a new generation of life.

But this was a universe of division. For every particle of matter created there was an antimatter twin. If they met they would mutually annihilate immediately. It was only chance local concentrations of matter – or antimatter – that enabled any structures to form at all.

In these intertwined worlds of matter and antimatter, parallel societies formed. Never able to touch, able to watch each other only from afar, they nevertheless made contact, exchanging information and images, science and art, reciprocally influencing each other at every stage. Mirror-image cultures evolved, each seeking to ape the achievements of the unreachable other. There were wars too, but these were always so devastating for both sides that mutual deterrence became the only possible option. Even a few impossible, unrequitable parity-spanning love affairs were thrown up.

The fundamental division of the world was seen as essentially tragic, and inspired many stories.

The various matter species, meanwhile, were not the only inhabitants of this ferocious age. They shared their radiation bath with much more ancient life forms. To the survivors of the spacetime-chemistry federation this age of an endless radiation storm was cold, chill, empty, the spacetime defects which characterised their kind scattered and stretched to infinity. But survive they had. Slowly they moved out of their arks and sought new ways to live.

CHAPTER 44

In the end it took a whole week before Pirius had assembled his team of thirty, including himself and Torec, to serve as primary crew, and nine more as backups. But now here were only seven weeks left before Kimmer's deadline, and serious work on training and development hadn't even begun.

Pirius brought his recruits, from Quin and elsewhere, back to Rock 492. Even that was a budget operation; he and Pila had to scrounge spare spaces on scheduled transport ships.

On the journey back from Quin, he couldn't avoid his other self. But whenever they passed each other, their tense silence was chill. Everybody stared, fascinated.

Once back at 492, Red called Burden and Pirius Blue to the office he had had Pila set up. They stood side by side, at attention, but somehow Blue made his insolence show.

'I need two flight commanders,' Pirius Red said without preamble. 'So you can guess why I called you here.'

Burden and Pirius Blue glanced at each other.

Burden frowned. Again he seemed oddly evasive. But he said, 'It's not a responsibility I want. But I wouldn't turn it down.'

Pirius Red nodded. He turned to Blue. 'And you?'

Blue was contemptuous. 'Do I have a choice?'

Red snapped angrily, 'More choice than you gave me when you came back from that magnetar. Look, from my point of view you're neither of you ideal candidates. Burden, frankly, I'm suspicious of what's going on in your head.' Burden looked away. 'And Blue – I know you too well, and we'll never get on. But I need you both; you're the best I can find. Blue, you of all people know that.'

He waited. At length, Burden accepted the job, but distantly. Blue nodded curtly.

Red was relieved beyond words.

Now he was able to bring both Blue and Burden further into his confidence. All they had known up to this point, like the other candidates, was that the mission would involve difficult flying with novel technology. He began to explain what the target would be.

'You're insane,' said Pirius Blue. 'We're going to strike at Chandra itself?' But Red saw that his eyes were alive with excitement.

Red said carefully, 'You want me to take you off the mission? I could do that, though you know too much now; you'd have to be kept in custody until the flight was over.'

'And let *somebody else* fly this?' Blue grinned; he looked feral. 'Not a chance.'

Pirius turned to Burden. 'What about you?'

Burden seemed more troubled. 'This could shorten the war.'

'Or lengthen it,' Blue said, 'if it goes wrong badly enough.'

'Either way,' said Burden, 'things must change.'

Pirius nodded. 'Does that trouble you?'

'Whatever we do doesn't matter. Not in the long run. And it's a noble action.'

Pirius had trouble decoding that glimpse of an alien mindset. 'Does that mean you're in?'

Again Pirius perceived a flash of fear. Blue saw it too, and glanced at Burden, worried.

But Burden straightened his shoulders. 'Yes, *sir*!'

Once the last transport had docked, Pirius Red brought his recruits to 492's largest pressurised dome and had them draw up in good order before him. With Pila at his side, he stood awkwardly on a crate, the only rostrum he could find.

He looked along their lines, at Jees's clunky artificial torso, at the anomalously old like Burden, at damaged children like Three – and, Lethe, at his own sullen, other-timeline face. He found it hard to believe that there had been such a rabble drawn up anywhere on the Front in all this war's long history.

Nevertheless they were a squadron, and they were his.

384

'Forty of us,' he said. 'Forty, including Pila, here, my adjutant. And this is our base. It isn't much, but it's ours. And we're about to be transferred into Strike Arm. We're a squadron now. And we're special,' he said.

There was a guffaw, quickly suppressed.

'So we are,' Pirius went on. 'We are a special generation, with a special duty, a privilege. The Galaxy centre engagement with the Xeelee began three thousand years ago. And we are the *first* generation in all those long years to have a chance of winning this war – of winning the Galaxy itself. Whether we succeed or we fail, they will remember us, in the barracks rooms and the shipyards and the training grounds, and on the battlefields, for a long time to come.'

The crews stood silently and stared at him. His words had sounded empty, even to him. His self-doubt quickly gathered.

Enduring Hope spoke up. 'We need a name.'

'What's that?'

'A name. For the squadron. Every squadron needs a name.'

Pila murmured a suggestion in his ear, and he knew it was right. 'Exultant,' he said. 'We are Exultant Squadron.'

They continued to stare. But then Pirius Blue, his own older self, raised his hands and began to clap, slowly, deliberately. Burden joined in, and Hope, and others; at last they were all applauding together.

When he had dismissed them, Pirius turned to Pila. 'Thank you,' he said fervently.

She shrugged. 'Next time you make a speech I'll draft it for you.' A sheaf of Virtuals whirled in the air before her. 'In the meantime, *Squadron Leader*, we have work to do.'

CHAPTER 45

A mong the cultures of matter and antimatter, clinging to their evanescent quark-gluon islands in a sea of radiation, a crisis approached.

As the universe cooled, the rate of production of quarks and antiquarks from the radiation soup inevitably slowed – but the mutual destruction of the particles continued at a constant rate. Scientists on each side of the parity barrier foresaw a time when no more quarks would coalesce – and then, inevitably, *all* particles of matter would be annihilated, as would the precisely equal number of particles of antimatter, leaving a universe filled with nothing but featureless, reddening light. It would mean extinction for their kinds of life; it was hardly a satisfactory prospect.

Slowly but surely, plans were drawn up to fix this bug in the universe. At last an empire of matter-cluster creatures discovered that it was possible to meddle with the fundamental bookkeeping of the cosmos.

Human scientists would express much of their physics in terms of symmetries: the conservation of energy, for instance, was really a kind of symmetry. And humans would always believe that a certain symmetry of a combination of electrical charge, left- and right-handedness, and the flow of time could never be violated. But now quark-gluon scientists dug deep into an ancient black hole, which had decayed to expose the singularity at its heart. The singularity was like a wall in the universe – and by reaching through this wall the quark scientists found a way to violate the most fundamental symmetry of all.

The imbalance they induced was subtle: for every thirty million

386

antimatter particles, thirty million and *one* matter particles would be formed – and when they annihilated, that one spare matter particle would survive.

The immediate consequence was inevitable. When the antimatter cultures learned they were to be extinguished while their counterparts of matter would linger on, there was a final, devastating war; fleets of opposing parity annihilated each other in a bonfire of possibilities.

Enough of the matter cultures survived to carry through their programme. But it was an anguished victory; even for the victors only a fraction could survive.

Another metaphorical switch was pulled.

Across the cooling cosmos the mutual annihilation continued to its conclusion. When the storm of co-destruction ceased, when all the antimatter was gone, there was a trace of matter left over. Another mystery was left for the human scientists of the future, who would always wonder at the baffling existence of an excess of matter over antimatter.

Yet again the universe had passed through a transition; yet again a generation of life had vanished, leaving only scattered survivors, and the ruins of vanished and forgotten civilisations. For its few remaining inhabitants the universe now seemed a very old place indeed, old and bloated, cool and dark.

Since the singularity, one millionth of a second had passed.

CHAPTER 46

Running behind a grav shield was like flying into an endless tunnel.

From her pilot's blister Torec looked ahead, through the usual clutter of Virtual warning flags, at a wall of turbulence. The result of the gravastar shield's spacetime distortions, it was like a breaking wave front, roughly circular, blue-white Core light mixed up and muddled and somehow stretched out in a way that hurt her eyes. There was something deeply unsettling about it, she thought, something that offended her instincts on some profound level.

When she glanced around she could see bright green sparks arrayed around her field of view. They were the other greenships of her flight, which was led today by Pirius Blue, high up there in Torec's sky – Blue, the weird, embittered future-twin version of her own Pirius, who had unaccountably been made flight commander.

The squadron was learning how to fly in formation, and with the grav shield. This was Torec's second training run of the day, her tenth of the week so far, and in the turnarounds she hadn't caught a great deal of sleep. But she put aside her eyeball-prickling fatigue and peered ahead, trying to stay focused on the peculiar phenomenon that might one day save her life, if it didn't kill her first.

The gravastar shield was something not quite of this universe, and the product of inhuman Ghost technology too. No wonder it looked weird. But the theory of its use was simple. Just fly in behind the grav shield, keep to your formation, follow your leader. The flaw was receding from her at nearly lightspeed, and it was her job to keep her greenship plummeting after it, tucked up into this more-or-less liveable pocket of smooth spacetime, not so close that the tidal stresses and fallout from the shield itself were so severe that they would destroy you, and yet close enough that the Xeelee could have no foreknowledge of your approach, because – and it still took her some hard thinking to grasp this – you were effectively in another *universe*.

At the centre of her field of view was a greenship tucked right in behind the wall of curdled horror. That ship, the 'shield-master' as the crews called it, was laden with the grav field generators. Today it was piloted by Jees, the sullen, determined prosthetic rescued from admin duties by Pirius Red, now proving to be one of the best pilots in Exultant Squadron. There was nobody Torec would have preferred to see up there at point than Jees; if anybody could manage the propagation of a kilometre-wide wavefront of spacetime distortion it was her.

But as Torec watched, that central green pinpoint wavered, just subtly. It was enough to send alarms sounding in Torec's head long before her Virtual displays lit up with more red flags.

Jees was having stability problems. Already Torec could see the shimmering of the grav shield front, and spacetime distortions heading back down the 'tunnel' towards her own ship. They made the images of the more distant stars ripple and swarm, as if seen through a heat haze.

'Here we go again,' she called, 'Brace for impact.'

'Pilot, engineer. I got it. Locking down systems.' That was her engineer, Cabel, very young, very intense.

Torec called, 'Navigator? What about you?' When there was no reply, she snapped, '*Three*. Lethe, girl, wake up.'

Tili Three called back, 'Uh – pilot, navigator, I'm sorry—'

'Don't be sorry. Just do your job.' She glanced at her displays. 'Impact in thirty. Twenty-nine . . .'

Cabel, seventeen years old, was very able, and had completed his training for this flight in days. He was one of Pirius Blue's 'baby rats', as Pirius Red put it a bit sourly, rescued by Pirius's older self from the lethal servitude of Quin. Having worked with Cabel intensely, Torec backed Blue's judgement.

Tili Three was another baby rat – but she was different. If anything she was intrinsically smarter than Cabel. Though she had come into the squadron without having completed her basic navigator training Pirius Blue had insisted on pushing her into Exultant, and now she had wound up in Torec's crew. Torec had no doubt about her basic ability, *in the classroom*. But on these training runs – Lethe, even in the sims – she just couldn't cut it. And so it seemed to be now.

The ripples washed down the tunnel at her. They were intense pulses of gravity waves. Torec saw the lead ships thrown from side to side, like bits of dirt on turbulent water. She braced.

The spacetime wash hit. The stars frothed around her. The ship pitched so violently she could feel it in her gut, even through the inertial shielding. She struggled to hold her line.

The trouble was, the grav shield was fundamentally unstable. No, worse than that, it actually *was* an instability, a fizzing, nonlinear flaw in spacetime. That was why it propagated in the first place, like a breaking wave. So having set it off, if you let it run by itself, it would push up to lightspeed and then disperse in a spectacular, bone-shaking explosion – or else it would collapse back into sublight, dissipating its energy. The propagating grav shield was an edge-of-chaos phenomenon, and had to be tweaked continually by the shield-master if it was to hang together.

But even here, in the calm, flat spacetime around Arches Base, it was all but impossible to hold everything together. Sailing along behind the shield was a constant strain, even when things went well. If the shield so much as wobbled, the little ships in its wake bobbed like motes of dust.

The ships handled badly too. In theory the prototype stage had passed and they were into flight development, and these ships, fitted with the project's new technologies, were the configuration they were supposed to fly into the centre of the Galaxy. But it was only ten days since the first of them had come out of Enduring Hope's workshops; they were lash-ups, and they flew like it.

Torec was having a particularly tough time. She wasn't the best pilot in Exultant Squadron, she accepted that. And she was in Blue's flight. Because of their complicated past, she thought – she had been with him in some other timeline, and was with his own younger self *now* – Torec felt Blue had given her the roughest assignments, the worst ships, the greenest crews. And she knew she was never going to be allowed a crack at the most prestigious assignment of all, which was to pilot the shield-master itself.

Well, she wasn't going to fail, not today.

As red flags flared throughout her cabin, she grasped her controls and tried to stabilise her ship. But it wallowed, its moments of inertia all wrong. Laden with its heavy singularity cannon it was desperately unresponsive; it was like trying to run with a laden pack on her back.

When she thought she had control she called, 'All right. Navigator, this is the pilot. Plot us a way out of here.'

There was no reply. When Torec glanced out of her pod she could see Three sitting in her blister, strapped in like a toy while red-flag Virtuals flared around her and the sky wheeled. 'Three. Three!'

'Give it up, pilot,' Cabel snapped.

'No, damn it. Navigator!'

'She's frozen. We don't have time for this. Aim for altitude ninety. Take us straight up and out of this shit.'

A quick check of her own tactical displays showed he was right. If they weren't capable of plotting an orderly way out, straight up and out of the gravastar wake was the only way to save the ship. She dug her hands into her displays once more, clenched her fists and yelled her anger.

The greenship tipped up and shot out of the turbulent wake of the grav shield, and into the sanctuary of flat, smooth space.

At the end of each day Pirius Red held an 'issues meeting'. Pila was at his side, quietly running the formal side of the meeting. Pirius Blue and Burden were here, along with Enduring Hope, Red's representative among the ground crew.

Today Torec attended too. She was a bit of human warmth alongside his adjutant, a woman from the other side of the Galaxy who hated his guts, and the two flight commanders, a distracted religionist and his own embittered future self. But Torec's flight had crashed out today, and he knew she was bringing him issues, not emotional support.

A lot of the problems right now seemed to centre on the use of the gravastar shield. So he had asked the Silver Ghost, the Ambassador to the Heat Sink, to sit in. The Ambassador's huge, hovering form seemed to fill the little room, somehow sucking out its warmth. Burden was fascinated by the Ghost, but the two hard-faced Guardians who accompanied it everywhere ensured the only contact it had with anybody was formalised and specific.

Over a week of meetings like this, a trick Pirius had learned was to start with positives, and that was what he did now – and they were pretty big positives too.

The main elements of the flight training programme concerned the use of the new CTC processors for rapid tactical response, precision bombing and formation flight in the wake of a grav shield. Well, there had been no significant problems with the CTC technology. Likewise the precision flying was going well. The pilots were getting used to the new dynamics of their clumsily modified ships. The starbreaker sighting technique he had come up with, perhaps because it had been figured out by a pilot in the first place, was fitting in easily with their methodology and instincts.

'The only bad news I can see in these areas,' he said, summing up, 'is that it mightn't be possible to give everybody enough time on the new gear. I've requisitioned as much sim time as I can . . .' But everybody knew simulations were no substitute for hands-on experience in a real craft. Besides, the technology was being modified so rapidly that the sim designs were quite often a day or two behind the real thing anyhow.

Pirius Blue stared at him, as always judgemental, hostile. 'And you think that's a *minor* problem? That we might fly into combat without everybody even having had time to try out the new gear?'

'I didn't say minor,' Red said testily. 'It's something we can minimise. Juggling the schedules, accelerating sim upgrades—'

They argued on about the training issues for a while. Red let it run, trying to pick out positives and identifying actions they could take.

Eventually the talk turned to the gravastar, the centre of most of their issues.

Burden passed Pirius Red a data desk. 'I've a summary of the stats here,' he said. 'To date the longest formation flight we've managed is two hours.' Everybody knew they would need to fly behind the shields for six hours to reach Chandra.

Blue said, 'We just have to go back and keep trying until we get it right.'

'But that's wearing out the crews,' Burden said evenly.

Enduring Hope raised a hand to speak. 'Not only the crews,' he said firmly. 'You have to think about the ships as well. Maybe it isn't obvious to you glamour-boy pilots, but even when you *don't* get a catastrophic failure, every time you fly you're fatiguing the structure and the systems. We are going to have to use at least some of these ships in anger. And if we've worn them out even before we've finished training—'

'I hear what you say,' Pirius Red said. 'What I don't know is what to do about it.'

Blue said, 'Our problem isn't our ships, or our people. It's that damn grav shield. If it stayed stable we could track it for six hours – or ten, or a hundred. But we can't keep it stable. We can fly our ships, but we can't fly the shield.'

'Ah,' said Burden. 'And why? Because it's Ghost technology, not human.'

Pirius Red took a deep breath. He'd been prepared for this moment. 'So,' he said slowly, 'we need a Ghost to fly it.'

In the shocked silence that followed, Torec helped him out. 'That is what we did with the prototype, back in Sol system, and for the exact same reasons. A Ghost has to fly Ghost technology.'

The Ghost, which had been hovering like an immense soap bubble, suddenly drifted half a metre forward. It altered the geometry of the meeting, disturbing everybody.

Pirius Blue rubbed his nose, a gesture Red always found irritating. He said without emotion, 'Are you serious? Are you suggesting that you allow a *Silver Ghost* to fly on a human combat mission?'

Red stared him down. 'I felt the same, remember.' He had told Blue about his experiences on Pluto, how he had felt when first confronted by a Ghost. 'The mission is more important than anything else.' He dared Blue to contradict him.

Blue looked disgusted.

Enduring Hope shrugged. 'A Ghost in the cockpit? So what? If you're going to stop smashing up my ships, you can train rats to fly for all I care.'

Burden's reaction seemed more complex. 'The question is, will our crews fly with a Ghost? We have been trained from birth to despise their sleek hides.'

Pirius Red nodded. 'I understand, believe me. If we do this I'll join the first flight myself. Show the way.'

'Good,' said Burden. 'But also – I have to ask – will a Ghost fly with humans?'

'It did back in Sol system,' Torec said.

'But that was a technology proving exercise. This is combat training. We are enemies, remember.'

Pirius turned to the Silver Ghost. 'Ambassador?'

The Ghost rolled, its subtle change of posture somehow indicating it was listening.

'You've heard what we have to say. Are you willing—?'

'I anticipated the request.' Virtual schematics scrolled through the air in front of it. 'I have taken the liberty of preparing a plan. We could be ready to fly tomorrow.'

That left them all speechless.

Pirius Blue said coldly, 'I wonder whose agenda we are really following.'

Pirius Red broke up the meeting, trusting his people to figure out the actions required to achieve the new plan.

After the others had gone, Torec stayed behind. 'Pirius, I need to talk to you. About Tili Three.'

'I saw your log.'

'She isn't going to cut it.' Torec shook her head, as miserable as if this was her own failure. 'I don't think it's a lack of ability, or courage. And it's nothing to do with her prosthesis. It's just that she's been through too much down on Quin. She's burned out.'

This would be the fourth crew member Pirius had lost like this. The attrition rate was worrying, but there was nothing he could do about that; for some, this assignment was simply too tough.

Torec was upset. 'I hate to raise this. I don't want her hurt.'

'Don't worry. I'll sign her off as unfit for duty.' If he didn't, she could be marked down as 'Lacking Moral Fibre' – in the barracks, one of the worst stigmas you could have attached to your character. 'Talk to Blue,' he told Torec. 'He can break it to her.'

Thanks,' she said. She glanced around; seeing the room was empty, she gave him a peck on the cheek. 'You're a good man, Squadron Leader.'

She hurried out. Pirius stared after her, bemused.

Pirius Red decided to hotfoot it to the refectory while he had a chance. But Nilis waylaid him.

Even here on 492, while the squadron got itself together, Nilis was continuing to work on his multi-faceted studies of Chandra's mysteries. But he was still encountering baffling obstructions. 'It's immensely frustrating,' he would say. 'After all the clock is counting down for me too. At this rate we will have destroyed Chandra before we know what it is!'

To Pirius's relief, though, he didn't want to talk about the black hole today.

'I watched the transcript of your meeting,' the Commissary said. 'Abbreviated, of course.'

Pirius frowned. 'Do you think I'm wrong to allow the Ghost to lead us?'

'I don't know if you're right or wrong – and nor do you, until you try it. But it's certainly a good idea.' Nilis smiled. 'You've come a long way since Pluto, Pirius. I'm proud of you. You are becoming able to rise above your first reactions, your conditioning. I think it's called maturity.'

Well, perhaps. Pirius had thought this over before the meeting, knowing he had to float the possibility. He told himself he had no qualms about using the Ghost: whatever it took to get the job done. Pluto was far away, weeks ago. But even so it had been odd seeing Burden and Hope trailing a Silver Ghost as it headed out of the room; Blue's face, a cold mirror of his own, had been like his own conscience. Had he really matured since Pluto? Or was he compromised by contacts with earthworms, as Blue kept telling him?

Nilis said, 'If I may I'll ride along with you tomorrow, on this remarkable flight. As a Virtual passenger, I mean,' he added hastily.

'Why? Because it's *historic*?' Pirius, over-stressed, over-worked, felt irritated. 'To be frank, Commissary, I don't think many of us are thinking about history right now.'

Nilis winked. 'Ah, but history never stops thinking about *you*, pilot.'

For some reason that chilled Pirius. 'We might not end up with any crew capable of flying anyhow,' he said bleakly. 'We lost another one today.'

'Tili Three? I know. But you did the right thing, Pirius. You showed compassion.' Nilis smiled, his face crumpling slightly. 'I'm no military man, but I believe this is called "leadership". I have the feeling that if you keep this up, you're going to become the kind of stubborn, loyal, dependable, inspirational fool who soldiers have always followed, to glory or their deaths.'

Hotly embarrassed, Pirius looked away. 'I wouldn't know, sir.'

'Of course not, of course not.' Nilis stared at Pirius with his big, moist eyes, and his expressive face was creased with concern. 'And how are you in yourself?'

'I'm fine,' Pirius snapped. He gazed back defiantly for a moment, but when Nilis waited for more, he weakened. 'I'm doing my best,' he said. 'It's just there is so *much* to do.'

Nilis laid his warm, heavy hand on Pirius's shoulder. 'Listen to me. You're doing all that could be asked of you. If you manage to get your hastily assembled crews of veterans and misfits through such a challenging training programme, and in a few weeks – that in itself will be a massive achievement, regardless of how the mission turns out.' Nilis straightened up. 'Remember this, though: *you* are your own most important resource. Make time for yourself. Lean on Pila more. Make sure you rest properly, eat, all the rest of it. Don't neglect the biology. I'm relieved you decided to fly yourself tomorrow. Remember, I pushed for you to be squadron leader in the first place because you're the best pilot I've ever encountered. So keep up your own training. And another thing . . .'

Pirius, his stomach rumbling, resumed his walk to the refectory. Nilis trailed him, advising, hectoring, arguing, his eyes bright and earnest.

So the next day Pirius Red found himself free of his desk, at the controls of a greenship, and 'flying down the tunnel', as the crews were starting to call it. Ahead of him was the oscillating, turbulent, eye-watering disc of a grav shield, and around him were walls of distorted spacetime.

The little constellation of greenship lights was steady. The flight, under Burden's command – Pirius had been careful to relegate himself to a mere pilot's role – was going well.

Right at its heart was the shield-master ship piloted by Jees. The best pilot in the squadron, in this most difficult of environments, was once again flying steady and true. Pirius had assigned Torec to serve as Jees's navigator today – but in her engineer's pod was the massive form of the Silver Ghost, working the grav shield generators.

Unconventional it was, but it seemed to be working. Even Pirius's own flight had been smooth, though he had deliberately taken on board two comparative rookies for his own navigator and engineer. Up to now, the flight couldn't have conformed more to plan if this had been a sim, even though no flight which was a surf along the stitched-up interface between one universe and another, with a Silver Ghost as guest engineer, was ever going to be *routine*.

As the record time of two hours flying behind a shield approached, Pirius felt some of the tension seep out of his body.

Nilis, a Virtual uncomfortably lodged in the cockpit with Pirius, was, after the first hour or so, relaxed enough to dip into the comms loops between the ships. He was particularly intrigued by the conversation between This Burden Must Pass, the notorious Friend of Wigner, and the Silver Ghost in the lead ship. Burden was taking the chance of talking to the Ghost away from its Guardians.

'And so you believe,' came the Ghost's simulated voice, 'that this universe is essentially transient – all you sense, all you achieve, even your experiences of your inner self will pass away.'

'Not transient, exactly,' Burden called back. 'Just one of an un-countably infinite number of possibilities which will, cumulatively, be resolved at timelike infinity, after the manner of a collapse of quantum functions.'

'But in that case what basis for morality can there be?'

'There is a moral basis for every decision,' said Burden. 'To show loyalty to one's fellows – to put oneself in harm's way for the sake of one's species. And while this is only one out of a myriad timelines, we believe that the, umm, the *goodness* in each timeline will sum at the decision point at timelike infinity to gather into Optimality . . .'

'Fascinating,' Nilis said to Pirius. The Commissary whispered, as if he might be overheard. 'They are fencing, in a way. Each knows far more about the other's beliefs than either is prepared to reveal. Fencing, and yet looking for common ground.'

Pirius Red was light on moral philosophy. 'That stuff about putting one's self in the way of harm for others – that sounded like Doctrine to me.'

'So it is,' Nilis said. 'Much of the Friends' "philosophy" is actually recycled Druzism – as you'd expect, given the environment it sprang from. Hama Druz seems to have believed that self-interest is the primary driver of any unthinking human action. He said that soldiers are therefore the only moral citizens of any society because only they have *demonstrated* their selfless morality by putting themselves in harm's way.' He sniffed. 'Of course Druz ignored the plentiful evid-ence of kinship bonds among the animals and insects – an ant isn't driven by simple selfishness – and he certainly ignored Coalescences, human hive societies which were plentiful even in his day. Druz was a good sloganeer, and he obviously was a key figure in human history. But he really wasn't a very sophisticated thinker. I've always found his arguments terribly one-dimensional – haven't you?'

Even now Pirius was horrified by such blasphemy, and he deflected the remark. 'There's more than just Druzism in Burden's beliefs.'

'Oh, of course. The other element is this basic notion that this universe is an imperfect place that can somehow be fixed. It's an expression of a feeling of betrayal, you see, a sense that one's life is irredeemably imperfect and can never be made good. I can quite understand such a creed arising in a society of child soldiers – deliberately kept in miserable conditions as a motivator to fight – whose only escape is either to die young fighting or grow old in shame. No wonder they want to believe things can be made better. They are quite right!

'But what's interesting is that the Silver Ghosts came up with a similar belief. They too were betrayed by the universe, when their sun failed and their world froze over. *They* elaborated such traumas into a belief that the universe is a hostile place that must be tamed. But they sublimated their feelings of anger, not into the passive acceptance of the Friends, but into programmes of exotic physics. They sought ways to change the universe – they tried to make it better!'

Pirius frowned. 'You're saying that the Friends are a Ghost cult?'

'Perhaps not as crude as that. But Ghost philosophy is the most interesting element in the whole volatile mix of this new creed.

'Humans fought Ghosts for long enough, and earlier we worked with them too. Perhaps humans swapped beliefs with Ghosts. And if *that's* so, perhaps the Friends may be the first interstellar religion, the first to fuse the traditions of two species . . . *The Ultimate Observer could plausibly be a Ghost deity!*'

Pirius frowned. 'No human would follow a Ghost.'

'I wouldn't be so sure, pilot. People have followed more bizarre beings in the past, though they were mostly imaginary!' He sipped an invisible drink, not reproduced in the Virtual. 'One has to wonder, though, if some such encounter as this wasn't in the mind of that Ghost up there all the time – perhaps we have been *given* the gravastar technology as a ploy, so that the Ghosts can achieve their own ends, whatever they are. I suppose the great mixing-up that Project Prime Radiant is inflicting on the orderly pools of the Coalition is a good opportunity for subversion . . . I always did intend that we should shake up history, you and I. But one must wonder what great oaks might grow from the seeds we are planting today.'

Pirius didn't like the sound of any of that. It sounded too much like the paranoia Nilis had criticised him for before. With a curt command, he shut down unnecessary chatter on the loops; the conversation between Ghost and Friend immediately stopped.

The little flotilla sailed on, huddling behind its wall of distorted spacetime, with only formal technical communications passing between the ships.

CHAPTER 47

The universe was expanding at half the speed of light. It was small and ferociously dense, still many times as dense as an atomic nucleus.

At least quarks were stable now. But in this cannonball of a cosmos the matter familiar to humans, composed of protons and neutrons – composites of quarks, stuck together by gluons – could not yet exist. There were certainly no nuclei, no atoms. Instead space was filled with a soup of quarks, gluons and leptons, light particles like electrons and neutrinos. It was a 'quagma', a magma of quarks, like one immense proton.

As time wore inexorably away, new forms of life rose in the new conditions.

The now-stable quarks were able to combine into large assemblies; and as these assemblies complexified and interacted, the usual processes of autocatalysis and feedback began. The black holes were still there to provide structure, but larger clumps of matter also served as a stratum for life's new adventures, and there was energy for free in the radiation bath that still filled the universe.

Among the new kinds, ancient strategies revived. There were exploiters and synthesisers. 'Plants' fuelled their growth with radiant energy – but there were no stars yet, no suns; rather the whole sky glowed. 'Animals' evolved to feed off these synthesisers, and learned to hunt each other.

As always the variation in life forms across the cosmos was extraordinarily wide, but most shared certain basics of their physical design. Almost all of them stored information about themselves in their own complicated structures, rather than in an internal genetic data store, as humans one day would: for these creatures their genotype *was* their phenotype, as if they were made wholly of DNA.

Their way of communicating would have seemed ferocious to a human. A speaker would modify its listener's memories *directly*, by firing quagma pellets into them; it was a message carried in a spray of bullets. They even reproduced rather like DNA molecules. They opened out their structures, like flowers unfolding, and constructed a mirror-image version of themselves by attracting raw material from the surrounding soup of loose quarks. These 'quagmites' were not quite like the creatures humans would one day encounter in the Galaxy's Core, but they were their remote ancestors.

There was little in common in the physical basis of human and quagmite; a quagmite was not much bigger than an atomic nucleus. But the largest of the quagma creatures were composed of a similar number of particles to the atoms which would comprise a human body. So humans and quagmites were comparable in internal complexity, and their inner lives shared a similar richness. Many humans would have appreciated the best quagmite poetry – if they could have survived being bombarded by it.

Meanwhile, the quagmite creatures shared their universe with older forms of life.

The ancient spacetime-chemistry creatures, having survived yet another cosmic transition, gradually found ways to accommodate themselves to the latest climate, even though to them it was cold and dark and dead. In their heyday there had been no 'matter' in the normal sense. But now they found they could usefully form symbiotic relationships with creatures formed of condensate matter: extended structures locked into a single quantum state. A new kind of being ventured cautiously through the light-filled spaces, like insects with 'bodies' of condensate and 'wings' of spacetime defects. It was the formation of a new kind of ecology, emerging from fragments of the old and new. But symbiosis and the construction of composite creatures from lesser components were eternal tactics for life, eternal ways of surviving changed conditions.

In the unimaginably far future humans would call the much evolved descendants of these composite forms 'Xeelee'.

The proto-Xeelee were, meanwhile, aware of another species of matter born out of this turbulent broth. This would one day be called dark matter by human scientists, for it would bond with other types of matter only loosely, through gravity and the weakest nuclear force. There was a whole hierarchy of particles of this stuff, even a sort of chemistry. This faint stuff passed through the quark-cluster cities and the nests of the proto-Xeelee alike as if they didn't exist. But it was there – and, like the Xeelee, this dark matter was going to be around for good.

As the endless expansion continued, the quagmites swarmed through their quagma broth, fighting and loving and dying. The oldest of them told their legends of the singularity. The young scoffed, but listened in secret awe.

It seemed to the quagmites that the ages that had preceded their own had been impossibly brief, a mere flash in the afterglow of the singularity. But it was a common error. The pace of life scaled to temperature: if you lived hot, you lived fast. The quagmites did not suspect that the creatures who had inhabited earlier, warmer ages had crammed just as many experiences – just as much 'life' – into their brief instants of time. As the universe expanded, every generation, living slower than the last, saw only a flash of heat and light behind it, nothing but a cold dark tunnel ahead – and each generation thought that it was only *now* that a rich life was possible.

The comfortable era of the quagmites couldn't last for ever; nothing ever did. It was when the universe was thirty times older than it was at the end of the matter-antimatter conflict that the first signs of the quagmites' final disaster were detected.

CHAPTER 48

After five weeks of Kimmer's ten, Exultant Squadron was to be transferred to Orion Rock, from which the assault on Chandra would be mounted.

It took three days for Rock 492 to be evacuated: the living areas emptied out, the squadron's fifteen greenships lifted off the surface. When Pirius Red had first arrived on 492 it had been a garbage heap, but now it was time to leave he was sorry. After all he and Torec had taken this ruin and made it, not just their base of operations, but their home.

And, of his motley assembly of superannuated veterans and misfits, two had died in operations run out of this Rock. So there was blood soaked into its silvery regolith, human bones buried in its loose dirt, as they were buried on a billion other worlds and moons and asteroids across the face of the Galaxy.

On the last night, as the close-out crews did their work, Pirius kept Torec back. In their skinsuits they wandered through the empty chambers, the stripped-out barracks and refectories and dispensaries, the big engineering bays with their floors grooved and shaped to take equipment now removed. They could hear systems shutting down, one by one, the vibrations diminished, the circulation of air and water stopping, as if the Rock itself was slowly dying. As they walked from one chamber to the next the light cut out behind them, so they were always walking out of darkness.

In the last chamber they found a corner where they unzipped their skinsuits. The air was rapidly losing its heat, making them both shiver deliciously. They pushed the seams of their suits together and sealed themselves inside.

The inertial generators shut down. They found themselves rising from the floor. All around them specks of asteroid dust, disturbed by the Rock's residual vibrations, rose up to make the air sparkle.

Deep inside the Cavity, a long way inside the Front, Orion Rock was buried in the North Arm of the Baby Spiral.

To reach it Exultant Squadron formed up into a tight convoy. The ten prime greenships, with five backups, were at the centre. All the greenships had been modified with the gear for Project Prime Radiant, but the equipment was bedded in now, and after the hours of training flights the crew knew how to handle their ungainly craft. The fighting ships were accompanied by equipment freighters, tenders and other support craft, and a handful of command vessels, including Commissary Nilis's corvette. One massive Spline warship loomed over them. Bristling with weapons, its moon-like bulk dwarfed its charges.

It was an unlikely flotilla, Pirius supposed. It was strange to reflect that on this handful of battered, hastily modified old hulks might rest the destiny of the Galaxy.

The group sailed through the Front and made their way down the spine of the Baby Spiral's arm, moving in a series of FTL hops and sublight-drive glides. Despite the time pressure, the only way to proceed was cautiously: the spiral arm was a crowded corridor of molecular dust, drifting rock and young stars, a difficult jaunt. But there was so much noise and clutter here in this tunnel of bombarded gas that there was a good chance they would remain undetected by Xeelee scouts all the way in.

After two sleepless days and nights, with the crews stressed-out and weary, they reached Orion Rock.

Pirius, sitting in his pilot's blister, gaped. He had never seen anything like it. The Rock *shone*.

Like every asteroid of its size, it was an aggregate shape as lumpy as a clenched fist, deeply pocked by impact craters. But on this Rock the surface had been worked, every square centimetre of it. Every crater hosted a landing pad or a dry dock or a portal, and away from the craters the land had a peculiar ridged texture. As they approached Pirius saw it was covered by a dense scribble of trenches and foxholes, zigzagging at precise ninety-degree corners. It was ornate, even decorative, like a maze. You could tell that people had been here for a *long* time.

Orion had been spawned out of random accretions in this spiral arm long ago, and had since drifted down its centre line. As it had required no human intervention to steer it on to a path that directed it straight at the Xeelee concentrations, the Rock was a marvellous natural hide. It had been occupied by humans for a thousand years, and the results of that occupation were visible on its surface – and yet it was still unsuspected as a military asset by mankind's foe.

The greenships and their escorts settled on a landing pad at the centre of the largest crater – all save the big Spline, which took up a watchful position directly overhead, like a fleshy eye.

The crews were eager to get out of their stinking skinsuits, and to eat, bathe, screw, and otherwise get the tension of the flight out of their systems. But Marshal Kimmer came on the loop and ordered the whole squadron from Pirius Red on down to form up before his command corvette. There was nothing for it but to comply gracefully.

They clambered down to a surface of some black, hard substance so smooth and flat it was almost slippery. Near Kimmer's corvette, Pila, Nilis, Kimmer, Guild-Master Eliun and various other command staff and civilians gathered in a loose circle. Captain Marta was here, the stern training officer from Quin Base who Pirius had drafted at the suggestion of his older self to oversee the set-up of operations on this Rock. Their skinsuits looked bright and fresh, and the military types were adorned with animated decorations.

And a Silver Ghost rolled complacently above the polished ground, unperturbed by the vacuum and hard radiation of the Core.

Pirius had practised no parade drill with his squadron; there had been no time for such luxuries. Still, he drew them up in good order, though he accepted a little assistance from Commander Darc, who helped get the rows spaced out and lined up properly. Compared to the glittering gathering of commanders and civilians, the greenship crews looked shabby and exhausted. But as they stood to attention – Burden and Torec, Jees with her silvery prostheses returning sharp highlights from the starlight, even his own older self, all of them in scuffed and grimy skinsuits – Pirius felt a burst of pride.

A party approached. In the lead marched a block of soldiers in gleaming white skinsuits, following a track that ran arrow-straight from the crater wall, Pirius estimated there must be a thousand of them. Their commanders stood to attention on discs that hovered a metre above the floor.

On the squadron's comms loop Pirius heard muttering. 'I don't believe it,' Blue said. 'It's a welcoming committee.'

'Belay that,' Pirius Red murmured. 'We're going to have to work with these characters. Let's get off to a good start.' The muttering subsided.

The lead party on those discs slowed smoothly before Marshal Kimmer. The marching troops came to a crisp halt, as precise as bots.

As the welcoming committee clambered down from their discs, Nilis, unmistakable in his antiquated skinsuit, gestured clumsily at Pirius. Reluctantly Pirius abandoned his squadron and walked forward to join Kimmer and the other dignitaries. He stood beside Pila; she looked amused at his discomfiture.

The leader of the party was an extraordinarily tall and skinny man who, despite the careful tailoring of his skinsuit, was stiff and clumsy, and he had some trouble getting down off his disc. This official appeared to do a double-take when he saw a Silver Ghost among the new arrivals.

Wheezing, the official puffed himself up and stepped forward to face Kimmer. The two of them were oddly similar, Pirius thought: tall, thin, elegantly formed. 'Marshal, welcome to Orion Rock!'

'Thank you—'

But Kimmer was taken aback when poles sprouted out of the hover-discs and thrust towards the stars. Virtual flags, adorned with the green tetrahedral sigil of free mankind, began to ripple in a non-existent breeze.

The tall official said, 'My name is Boote the Forty-Third – *Captain* Boote, I should say. I command here, and I place my base at your disposal. I am the one hundred and nineteenth captain of this station, and the forty-third to wear the proud name of Boote . . .' He spoke comprehensibly, but he had a very strong, clipped accent. 'For one thousand and fifty-seven years, sir, we have waited for the call. If today is the day we fight and die for the benefit of the Third Expansion of mankind – if the purpose of this station is to be fulfilled on my watch – then I, Boote the Forty-Third, will be proud to take my place in history.' He struck his sunken chest with his fist.

'Thank you, Captain,' Kimmer said dryly. 'I know you will do your duty.'

The two parties faced each other, motionless. As the delay lengthened, Pirius grew puzzled.

Pila leaned towards him so their helmets touched. 'Go to the backup command loop.'

Pirius tapped his chest control panel, and he heard massed voices. '. . . *Named for a victory / Over Ghosts, a vanquished enemy / Our Rock, as firm as our resolve / Is dedicated to our duty* . . .' Now he saw the faces of the ranks of troops, their moving mouths. They were singing, he realised, all thousand of them, singing a song of welcome to their visitors. They even sang harmonies.

'The lyrics are none too tactful in the circumstances,' Pila murmured through his helmet.

Pirius glanced surreptitiously at the Ghost, but it showed no reaction to this song of triumph about its kind's most terrible defeat.

The song went on and on. By now Nilis had coached Pirius in the need to be diplomatic, but by the fourth verse he had had enough. He switched to the squadron loop and ordered his crews to fall out. Then he confronted Captain Boote the Forty-Third. 'Sir. Thanks for the song. Where's the refectory?'

Kimmer glowered; Nilis looked mortified. Pila laughed.

Once he'd got his skinsuit stripped off, Pirius went straight to work.

In theory, so he'd been told, the base was fully equipped with all they needed to operate the squadron. He told Pila his target for resuming training flights was twenty-four hours. Again she laughed.

Captain Boote led Pirius and Nilis through the guts of the complex that had been dug into Orion Rock.

Boote wore a robe that trailed to the floor in languid, elegant drapes. His face and scalp had been shaved of every scrap of hair, even eyebrows and nostril hair.

If Boote was magnificent, so was the base he commanded. But like him it was odd too. In its layout it was essentially the same as every other Rock Pirius had visited, with the usual barracks rooms, refectories, dispensaries, science labs, training facilities from classrooms to sim chambers, and technical facilities from environment systems to huge subsurface hangars.

But every other Rock had an air of shabbiness; a Rock always looked lived-in, because it *was*, by a bunch of squabbling, randy trainees and troopers who cared a lot more about sack time than about hygiene and neatness – and because, by Coalition policy, every military facility was cut to the bone in resources anyhow. A base was a place you left to go fight, not a place you longed to get back to.

Orion was different. Pirius had never seen a base so *neat*. In the barracks rooms there wasn't a blanket out of place. When they passed, the troops sprang to attention and lined up neatly by their bunks, eerie grins plastered over their faces. Even the walls were smooth to the touch – worn at shoulder-height by the passage of millions of young bodies.

Neat it might have been, but everywhere was dark, lit by only a few hovering globes. Pirius thought the air was a little cold, though it tasted fresh enough. Not only that, everybody – even the youngest children in the junior cadres – crept about quietly, treading softly and murmuring. Boote said it was always like this.

'Ah,' Nilis said. 'Silent running.'

'What's that?' They were both whispering; it was contagious.

'This is a covert base, remember. The crew are sailing towards the Xeelee, who must not suspect they are here. And they strive to keep everything below the level of the background noise of the Baby Spiral – their energy expenditure, their signalling. As for the whispering and creeping about, I don't imagine it makes much practical difference, but, though I'm no expert on motivation, I should think it is good psychology – a constant reminder to *keep your head down.*'

Pirius peered around curiously at the wide-eyed children who smiled hopefully at him. He tried to imagine how it must be to have grown up in this claustrophobic environment of darkened corridors and whispers. But these kids had never known anything different; to them this was normal.

As they walked on, Boote proudly explained the origin of his name.

Of course there were no true families here, no heredity; that would be far too non-Doctrinal. This was a place of birthing tanks and cadres, like most military bases. But a tradition had grown up even so. The first Boote, centuries back, had been a fine captain who had inspired loyalty and affection from all. When her successor had taken her name on his accession, to become Boote the Second, it had seemed the most natural thing in the world, a tribute that had become a badge of honour to the captains who had followed, right down to this fine fellow, Boote the Forty-Third. Similarly there were 'dynasties' among the engineers and medics, comms officers and pilots, and other specialist corps.

Nilis raised his eyebrows at Pirius, but said nothing. Wherever you went a little deviance was inevitable, it seemed.

They were taken out on to the surface in a covered walkway. Nilis cringed from the crowded sky, but after that gloomy enclosure Pirius was relieved to be out under the healthy glow of the Core.

They surveyed earthworks dug into the ground. Teams of troopers in skinsuits were working in the trenches. They weren't digging so much as refurbishing, Pirius saw. He had never seen earthworks so regular and neat: their walls were precisely vertical, their edges geometrically straight and dead neat. And he couldn't see a trace of stray dust anywhere. The troops smiled as they worked, in precise formation.

In one part of the works the troops suddenly lunged out of their trenches and flopped on to the surface, across which they began to wriggle.

'They're manoeuvring,' said Pirius, 'But it's not an exercise. It's more like a game.'

'Yes,' said Nilis. 'And these earthworks are an ornamental garden. These folk have been isolated too long, Pirius. A trench is a place to fight and die. They have *domesticated* these trenches.'

Pirius slowly pieced together an understanding of this place.

Rocks were an essential element in most attacks on Xeelee concentrations; they provided cover, resources, and soaked up enemy firepower. But while most Rocks were purposefully deflected on to their required trajectories, Orion Rock, and a number of others, had natural orbits that took them into useful positions in the Core without deflection. So they could be used as cover, to mount covert operations.

But as the Core's geography spanned light years, travel times were painfully slow. The planners behind this place had been forced to think ahead, across no less than a thousand years – for that was how long Orion Rock would have to travel before it was in a position to be useful.

Nilis said gravely, 'This is the scale of this war, Pirius. Orion Rock is like a generation starship sent to war: forty, perhaps fifty generations doomed to these dark tunnels, all the possibilities of their lives sacrificed to one goal, a strike on the Xeelee, a *single assault* that might be carried out in their children's time, or their children's children.

'A thousand years, though. On pre-Occupation Earth, a thousand years was a long time: time enough for empires to rise and fall, time enough for history. To us it is just a tick-box on a war planner's chart!'

As the troops dug and marched and played at manoeuvres, their mouths moved in unison, Pirius saw. They were singing again. But, thanks to some fault in the systems, he couldn't hear their song.

They had been assigned a hangar, a huge one, beneath that paved-over crater where they had been landed. Pirius went to inspect it. The hangar was big enough for a hundred greenships, let alone fifteen, and it was fully equipped with repair and maintenance facilities. Criss-crossed by walkways, full of hovering bots, the hangar was fully pressurised, although sections could be opened to vacuum when necessary. The working areas had been kept at microgravity – greenships were built for lightness, and were too frail to support their own weight under full gravity – but the floor and walkways were laced with inertial adjusters. Brightly lit by hovering globe lamps, it was a stunning facility by any standards.

But it didn't have the feel of a workplace. It was too clean, too orderly. It didn't even *smell* right; there was no electric ozone stink, or tang of lubricants, or the hot burning smell of metal that had been exposed to vacuum. It was like a museum, a place where you looked at greenships rather than got your hands dirty working on them.

Pirius joined Enduring Hope, his ground crew leader. But Hope was accompanied everywhere by Eliun of the Guild of Engineers and a couple of that worthy's aides. Since he had been out-manoeuvred back on Arches, Eliun had barely let Hope out of his sight.

The party watched as their precious greenships, crudely modified, nestled into their graving docks.

Eliun punched Pirius in the shoulder, none too gently. 'Look at that!' he said. 'Pilot, these docks were built more than a thousand years ago. These greenships, on the other hand, are barely five years old – some of them younger than that. And yet dock and ship fit together hand in glove, every surface contoured to match, every interface locking, just as these ships could be lodged in any similar dock across the Galaxy. And why? Because of the Guild: I am talking about uniformity, sir, uniformity on galactic scales of space and time. How do you imagine such a war can be fought without this epic *sameness*?'

Pirius was short on sleep and over-stressed. 'Engineer Eliun, I don't know anything about procurement policy. You'll have to talk to Commissary Nilis.' The Engineer wasn't satisfied with that, but Pirius turned deliberately to Enduring Hope. 'So what do you think?'

Hope shrugged. 'Technically the hangar's perfect. But look at this.' He led Pirius to one of the graving docks, where the battered hulk of an Exultant greenship now rested. He ran his bare hand over the massive cradle of fused asteroid rock, metal and polymer. 'It's *worn*,' Hope said, wondering. 'It's the same everywhere. Every bit of equipment in this place is worn smooth, until you can see your face in it. For a thousand years they've done nothing but polish everything in sight.' Hope grinned nervously. 'This is the strangest place I've ever seen.'

Pirius grunted. 'Well, I don't care about the last thousand years. All I care about is the next twenty-four hours, because at the end of it I want this place set up for our operations. Now. What about the cannon gear? Do you think you'll have to cut through that roof to get it in here? . . .'

They walked on, talking and planning. Engineer Eliun tailed them for a while, but Pirius didn't acknowledge him further and after a time Eliun gave up and stomped away.

After the first twenty-four hours, they had achieved only a fraction of what Pirius had demanded. He called a crisis meeting in Nilis's office.

Boote's staff were an uninspiring bunch, soft, flabby-looking administrators and clerks who seemed to have no ambition save to replace the Captain one day. Boote at bay, though, had a glint in his eye, and Pirius had the feeling that he had a bit of steel in him and would put up a fight.

It was yet another obstruction, just as they had encountered all the way from Earth. Pirius was hugely weary, impatient to get back to his ships, and he felt like biting somebody's head off. The only thing he wanted, he kept reminding himself, was to get the job done.

He turned to Enduring Hope. 'Engineer, why don't you sum up how far we've got in twenty-four hours?'

Hope consulted a data desk. He looked as ticked-off as Pirius felt. 'The priorities are, one, setting up a manufactory on the far side of the Rock for producing the point black holes we will need for the cannon; two, modifying the hangar for our upgraded greenships.' He snapped the data desk down on the tabletop. 'So far we've argued a lot and we've laid down the foundations for the manufactory. And that's it.'

Pirius said, 'I wanted to be flying by' – he checked the Virtual chronometer that hovered over Pila's head – 'two hours ago. You all committed to that yesterday. What's gone wrong?'

Hope took the bait. He jabbed a finger at Captain Boote. 'It's those people. They block everything we propose. Or they "defer" it for "discussion" further up the "chain of command".' His tone, dripping with sarcasm, was deeply insolent. 'They're blocking us, Pirius.'

Captain Boote sputtered. 'I won't be spoken to like that!'

'Quite right,' Nilis murmured. 'Why don't you tell us your perception of the problem here, Captain?'

The Captain turned his magnificent hairless head to Pirius. ' Squadron Leader, we support your project. That's our function. But you must recognise the practical difficulties. For a thousand years – *a thousand years*, sir! – we have worked and polished and honed this base until it is perfectly fit for its purpose, which is to strike a great blow against the enemy. Now you are asking us to change that. To rip holes in our walls – to install equipment so new it won't even interface to our kit!' He held up his hands. 'Of course we must accept the challenge of the new. But all I'm asking for is time, while recognising the pressure of your schedule, a measured and thoughtful response . . .'

He talked smoothly, liquidly, one sentence blending into another so seamlessly that Pirius couldn't see a way to cut into the flow. And he was so plausible that after a while Pirius found himself helplessly agreeing. Of course these new things couldn't be done here; what other point of view was possible?

In the end Nilis managed to break into the monologue. 'If I may say so, Captain, I think there is a failure of imagination here. You and your antecedents have been here so long, loyally following the dictates laid down long ago, that I don't think any of you quite grasp that some day *all this must end*.'

Boote's mouth dropped open. But then he shook his head. 'If it is my generation that has the privilege of fulfilling the mission of Orion Rock, I will grasp the opportunity with both hands . . .' Once again he talked on. But it sounded like another rehearsed speech, and Pirius saw that he himself didn't believe a word he was saying.

With a smooth motion Captain Marta produced a handgun. Darc

made a grab for the weapon, but Marta fired off her shot. Boote was hit in the arm. It was a projectile weapon, and the impact threw him backwards off his chair and against the wall. For a moment his spindly legs waved comically in the air, while his aides flapped around him.

When they got him upright and back on his chair again, he had his hand clamped over a spreading patch of blood on his upper right arm. His face was florid with anger and fear.

Nilis was shocked into pallid silence. Pila hadn't so much as flinched when the shot was fired; looking faintly annoyed, she brushed blood spots off her sleeve. Hope and Torec were trying hard not to laugh.

Boote pointed a shaking finger at Marta. 'You shot me!'

'A flesh wound,' she said. 'A half-hour in sick bay will fix that.'

'I'll have the hide flogged off your back for this.'

'That's your privilege, sir,' Marta said evenly. 'But I thought I should introduce a little reality into the discussion. *This is real*, Captain. The sky really is falling.'

Pirius stared at her. Then, as the silence lengthened, he realised it was his cue. He turned to Boote. 'Captain, I'm not in a position to adjourn the meeting. Time is too short. I'll ensure Captain Marta answers any charges you care to raise later. Commander Darc, would you accept her custody for now?'

Darc inclined his head ironically.

'Captain Boote, you need to be excused to get that graze seen to. In the meantime, who would you nominate to represent you in the continuing negotiations?'

After that, things went much better.

CHAPTER 49

The trouble started in the most innocuous, most mundane of ways: problems with waste.

For many quagmite kinds, eliminated waste was in the form of compressed matter, quarks and gluons wadded together into baryons – protons and neutrons. You could even find a few simple nuclei, if you dug around in there. But the universe was still too hot for such structures to be stable long, and the waste decayed quickly, returning its substance to the wider quagma bath.

Now, as the universe cooled, things changed. The mess of sticky proton-neutron cack simply wouldn't dissolve as readily as it once had. Great clumps of it clung together, stubbornly resistant, and had to be broken up to release their constituent quarks. But the energy expenditure was huge.

Soon this grew to be an overwhelming burden, the primary task of civilisations. Citizens voiced concerns; autocrats issued commands; angry votes were taken on councils. There were even wars over waste dumping. But the problem only got worse.

And, gradually, the dread truth was revealed.

The cooling universe was approaching another transition point, another phase change. The ambient temperature, steadily falling, would soon be too low to force the baryons to break up – and the process of combination would be one way. Soon all the quarks and gluons, the fundamental building blocks of life, would be locked up inside baryons.

The trend was inescapable, its conclusion staggering: this extraordinary implosion would wither the most bright, the most beautiful of the quagmite ecologies, and nobody would be left even to mourn.

As the news spread across the inhabited worlds, a cosmic unity developed. Love and hate, war and peace were put aside in favour of an immense research effort to find ways of surviving the impending baryogenetic catastrophe.

A solution was found. Arks were devised: immense artificial worlds, some as much as a metre across, their structures robust enough to withstand the collapse. It was unsatisfactory; the baryogenesis could not be prevented, and almost everything would be lost in the process. But these ships of quagma would sail beyond the end of time, as the quagmites saw it, and in their artificial minds they would store the poetry of a million worlds. It was better than nothing.

As time ran out, as dead baryons filled up the universe and civilisations crumbled, the quagma arks sailed away. But mere survival wasn't enough for the last quagmites. They wanted to be remembered.

CHAPTER 50

On Orion Rock, time flowed strangely for Pirius Red. The days seemed to last for ever, but his nights seemed very short. And the sum of those long days, as they accumulated into weeks, amounted to no time at all.

Pirius hammered home the ten-week target every time he spoke to his crews, and as the training schedule was compressed and the technical development work accelerated, the effort everybody put in was more and more frantic. But the calendars wore down regardless.

Suddenly deadline day was here.

And it went, with no word from the Grand Conclave. One day passed, two.

Pirius figured they may as well use the time productively. The flight crews and ground staff continued their training. By now, as well as flying the modified ships on endless low-level loops past hapless target Rocks, they were running full-scale simulations with flight crews and a fully staffed operations room, everybody working together to iron out procedures. Commander Darc's experience was vital in this – and to Pirius's surprise Pila proved observant and helpful, pointing out ways to improve the information flows between ships and the base. Even she seemed finally to be committing herself to the great effort.

All this was useful, as far as it went. Behind the scenes, though, those in the know became increasingly anxious. Even now it was possible that the Grand Conclave would, for its own inscrutable reasons, withhold final permission to fly the mission.

Up to now Nilis had remained remarkably calm. His design of the mission had been largely conceptual – 'a mere data desk sketch,' he said – and now they were down to operational details there was generally little he could add. He kept himself busy with his continuing analysis of the true nature of Chandra. He said he wanted to make sure they understood what it was they were attacking before they 'blew it to smithereens' – although he continued to complain about obstruction and a baffling lack of cooperation from the military authorities who were his hosts. 'It's almost as if they don't *want* me to learn about Chandra!' he told a distracted Pirius.

But after the deadline expired, Nilis became increasingly agitated. He started to make lurid threats about how he would return to Earth and storm his way into the sessions of the Grand Conclave itself.

Then, two days after the formal deadline, an 'Immediate Message' was handed to Pirius. It had come through the office of Marshal Kimmer, and was signed by the Plenipotentiary for Total War herself: 'Operation PRIME RADIANT. Execute at first available opportunity.'

That was all. Pirius read the note again, hardly able to believe what he was looking at. He said, 'Suddenly we are no longer a project but an operation.'

Pila was watching him, her beautiful, cold face intent. She seemed fascinated by his reaction. 'How do you feel?'

'Relieved,' he said. Then: 'Terrified.' He glanced at a chronometer. It was evening. *First available opportunity*. One more full day to prepare, then; after that, they would fly at reveille. 'Thirty-six hours,' he breathed. 'We go in thirty-six hours.' He stood up. 'Come on, Pila. We've work to do.'

That night he called in Pirius Blue and This Burden Must Pass, his flight commanders, for a final operations meeting. With Pila at his side, he locked the door of his office, set up a security shield, and showed them the order. Red watched Burden carefully, still not quite trusting him. But neither he nor Blue showed shock, surprise or fear. Maybe they didn't quite believe it, Red thought.

At this point it was their job to go over every detail of the mission, and to talk through tactics regarding the resistance they might en- counter, and how they would recover from any foul-ups at various points in the mission profile. After they were done, Pila would draft the final Operation Order that would be disseminated to the flight crews.

As they got to work Red said, 'Maybe this session will be quick. We've war-gamed this a dozen times.'

'You'd be surprised,' Burden said dryly. 'The imminence of real action has a way of focusing the mind.'

Pirius Blue was watching his younger self curiously. 'How are you feeling? You haven't flown a combat mission before.'

Red said, irritated, 'Yes, I'm the rookie; thanks for reminding me.'

'That may help,' Blue said awkwardly. 'I mean it. There's no substitute for going through it for real. When you lead crews into a situation where they're likely to buy it, it frightens you – the responsibility – and that gets mixed up with your own personal fear. You can't help it. It's stomach-churning. But experience is one thing; the residual shock is another. You never quite recover. You have enough on your plate today. It may be better that you're fresh.'

Red said, 'I'm not frightened of dying. I'm not even frightened of the responsibility for other people's lives.'

'But you're frightened of screwing up,' said Burden.

'Yes,' Red admitted.

'Don't worry,' Blue said. 'We're at your side.' He sat stiff in his chair, and he couldn't meet Red's eyes.

Red knew this was the closest Blue could bring himself to pledging loyalty to his own younger, less experienced, over-promoted self. It would have to do, he thought.

Red pulled a data desk towards him. 'Let's get on with it,' he said gruffly. 'First, the launch sequence. We will go in two waves . . .'

The next morning, as he began his day, Enduring Hope immediately knew something was up.

He made his usual inspection walk through the bomb dump, a hangar that had been modified as a store for the point black holes. And he walked into the big main hangar, where fifteen heavily engineered, thoroughly worn-out greenships were being treated with tender loving care by his technicians. Everywhere he went he sensed a heightening of activity, and of tension. For one thing there were more flight crew around than usual, working with the ground crew on the ships they would fly. But there was more to this atmosphere than that. He'd been through this before, back on the other side of the magnetar incident that had cut his life in two, when he had flown his one and only combat mission.

Everybody understood the need for security. Generally you had no idea until a day or so before the launch of a mission exactly what your target was to be. This mission had been no different – save only for the novel bits of technology they had all had to become used to. As always there had been much speculation. The advantages of the new super-fast processors and the formidable black hole cannon were obvious. But nobody could figure out what the grav shield, difficult and temperamental, was actually *for*. And nor could anybody come up with a convincing target. It was sure to be something big, though – big and therefore exceptionally dangerous. But all this was scuttlebutt.

This morning, though, it was clear that things had changed: from somewhere in the higher echelons, it was being said, orders had arrived to proceed. Right now Pirius Red was probably briefing the senior staff, and everybody else was supposed to be in the dark. But it was astonishing how these things got out, how people picked up on almost imperceptible cues, if it really mattered to them – and this was an issue of life or death.

Hope knew his duty, anyhow. He was going to make sure each of these dinged-up greenships was ready to do whatever its crew demanded of it, if he had to crawl into the guts of every one of them himself. He went to work with a will.

In the middle of the morning, Virtual images of Pirius Red appeared around the hangar, summoning the flight crews to a general briefing in one of the big conference rooms. The crews gathered in little knots, talking quietly, and began to drift out of the hangar.

It's real, Hope thought; it really is happening. He felt an odd pull. It wasn't so long since he had been flight crew himself.

He walked quickly around the hangar. Work was going well. In fact, he told himself, if he hung around watching over his technicians' shoulders he would get in the way. He could be spared for a couple of hours.

So, as the last crews walked down the short corridor to Officer Country, Hope followed them.

Torec was on security duty at the door of the conference room. Hope found his way blocked by her arm. 'Where do you think you're going?'

'The briefing.' Through the open door Hope glimpsed the thirty-odd flight crew milling, finding seats. They all seemed to be here, both primary crews and reserves. On a dais at the front sat the two editions of Pirius, Burden, Commissary Nilis and others. As the officers prepared their briefing material Virtual images flickered tantalisingly over their heads.

'Flight crew only,' Torec said. 'I can't let you in.'

'Come on, Torec,' he whispered. 'I used to fly, remember?'

'I don't know why you want to be here.'

Neither did Hope, quite. He looked into the room. 'Because it's history.'

'Yes,' she said. 'There is that. OK.' She lifted her arm. 'But if anybody spots you I'll say you slugged me.'

He grinned his thanks and hurried into the room.

The atmosphere in there was even stranger than out in the hangars. The tension in the air was like ozone. All the flight crew seemed to be talking at once, and the air was full of noise. But the talk was meaningless, just banter, ways to drain off stress. Hope spotted pilot Jees, who sat a little apart, as always, like a half-silvered statue; with no apparent nerves, she watched the platform and waited for the show to start.

Hope found space at the back, between two burly navigators. Of course everybody in this audience knew who he was, but they had all worked with him on their ships and seemed to accept him.

Pirius Red stood up on the platform. He raised his arms for silence, but he needn't have done; the hubbub died away instantly. Pirius looked out over the crews, a complex expression on his face. 'You know why we're here.' He spoke without amplification, and his voice, gruff with tension, was precise, determined. 'Operation Prime Radiant is *on*.' There was a rumble of appreciation at that; one or two stamped their feet. 'I know it's still not much more than a name for most of you, but that's about to change.

'I've already had briefings with the flight commanders, and representative specialists pilots, navigators, engineers – and we've put it all together, as best we can. Commissary Nilis here will give you an overview of the objectives and strategy, and then Blue, Burden and I will go through the operation in more detail. At the end of this briefing you'll be given copies of the draft Operation Order by the adjutant. After that we'll split for briefings in your specialist groups. We have more detailed Virtuals of the mission profile, including sims if you've the time to sit through them.

'At every stage I want you to answer back. What we're going to attempt is something nobody's done before. So if you spot a screw-up waiting to happen, or can see a better way to do things, say so. At the end of the day the adjutant and I will pull all that feedback into a fresh draft of the Op Order, and we'll hold another update session in here. Is that clear?'

There was no reply. He paced, as if suddenly uncertain, and gazed out at them; the crews watched him silently.

Pirius said, 'I'll tell you what we're going to do tomorrow, in a sentence. We're going to strike a blow at the Xeelee from which they cannot recover. And I'll tell you something else. Tomorrow is our best chance, but it's not the only chance. If you screw up tomorrow, you'll go back out there as soon as we can patch up the ships, and patch *you* up, and do it again. And you'll keep on going out until the job is done. So if you don't want to go back, do it right first time.' He glared at them, as if daring them to defy him. Then, to silence, he sat down.

Enduring Hope glanced around cautiously. Pirius wasn't the kind of leader who cracked jokes or expected you to applaud him. But Hope saw no frowns, no pursed lips, no scepticism. If you were a flyer you didn't expect coddling. These crews knew Pirius by now, and his older self, and they respected him. They were ready to follow him wherever he was about to lead them. Lethe, Hope thought, *he* would follow Pirius, either of them, just as he had before, if given the chance.

Nilis was next up. The Commissary, bulky and much older than the flight crews arrayed before him, was dressed in a black Commission robe that was frayed at the cuffs. He fumbled with his data desks and coughed to clear his throat. Nilis seemed a lot more nervous than Pirius had been – or maybe it was just that Pirius hid it better.

Nilis began by summarising the novel technical elements of the mission: the grav shield, the CTC processor, the black hole cannon weapon. 'That's as much as you know, I suppose,' he said. 'That and, as Pirius said, the name of the mission: Operation Prime Radiant. Now I can tell you that the name refers to the most significant Prime Radiant of all: *the base of the Xeelee in this Galaxy.*' There was an audible gasp at that. He looked out at them, squinting a little, as if he couldn't quite make out their faces. 'I think you understand me. After three thousand years of inconclusive siege warfare, we – *you* – are going to strike at the very heart of the Galaxy, at the supermassive black hole known as Chandra, the centre of all Xeelee operations.'

Enduring Hope felt numb. He couldn't quite believe what he was hearing.

Nilis began to go through a bewildering array of Virtuals, but gradually, the outline of the mission became a bit clearer.

Very shortly, after a billion years of drifting down the arm of the Baby Spiral, Orion Rock would erupt into the open. Emerging deep inside the Cavity, this heavily armed Rock was an immediate threat to the foe, who would surely attack. But Orion was a diversion. While the local Xeelee firepower spent itself on the Rock's defences, Exultant Squadron would slip away.

The greenships would fly deeper into the Cavity behind their grav shield, whose purpose, Nilis now revealed, was to thwart the Xeelee's ability to gather FTL foreknowledge about the mission. Later the CTC processors would be used so they could penetrate the Xeelee's final layers of defence. And then the black hole cannon would be used to strike at Chandra itself, and the Xeelee concentrations that swarmed there.

As Nilis spoke on, the crews began to mutter. Hope knew what everybody was thinking. It was well known that nobody had flown so close to the Prime Radiant and lived to talk about it; even Pirius Blue hadn't gone in that deep. All this novel technology was hardly reassuring either. A crew liked to fly with proven kit, not with the product of some boffin's overheated brow.

But I would go, Hope thought helplessly.

Nilis got through his technical Virtuals. He said, 'Your commanders will take you through the operational aspects of the mission in detail. But I want to tell you *why* it's so important to strike at the Prime Radiant – no matter what the cost.'

He spoke of strategic theory. The Galaxy was full of military targets, he said, full of Xeelee emplacements of one kind or another. But those which were 'economically upstream' in the flow of resources and information were more valuable. 'It is cheaper, simple as that, to strike at the dockyard where greenships are constructed, to destroy it in a single mission, than to run a hundred missions chasing the ships themselves.' He brought up images of the Prime Radiant, heavily enhanced. Somehow the Xeelee used the massive black hole as a factory for their nightfighters and other technologies, he said, and as their central information processor. He spoke of the damage he hoped black hole projectiles would do to such mighty machines as must exist around Chandra.

Hope thought it was very strange to hear this obviously gentle man talk of such profound destruction.

Nilis closed down his last Virtuals. He faced his audience, hands on hips. 'You may say to me, *why* must this be done? And why *now*? Why *you*? After all the war is not being lost. We and the Xeelee have held each other at bay for three thousand years. Why should it fall to you to strike this blow – and, I'm afraid for many of you, to pay the price?

'I'll tell you why. Because, after twenty thousand years of the Third Expansion, the majority of mankind are soldiers – and most are still children when they die. *Most people don't grow old*. They don't even grow old enough to understand what is happening to them. To our soldiers war is a game, whose lethality they never grasp. This is what we are: this is what we have made ourselves. And the numbers are terrible: in a century, more people die in this war than *all* the human beings who ever lived on Earth, before mankind first reached the stars.'

He stalked around the dais. He was an old, overweight man walking back and forth, almost comically intense. 'The Prime Radiant is central to everything the Xeelee do in this Galaxy. To strike at Chandra will be as devastating to the Xeelee as if they turned their starbreaker beams on Earth itself. And that is what we will do. We will stop this war. And we will stop it now.'

When he had finished speaking, there was a cold, stunned silence.

Marshal Kimmer stood; he had been seated among the flight crews, at the front of the room. He said simply, 'I know that you will make this attack succeed. I know you will inflict a tremendous amount of damage. And I know, yes, that you will make history.' Where Nilis had been received in silence, Kimmer won a cheer. He finished, 'The first launches will be at reveille tomorrow.' And with that he turned on his heel and walked out of the room.

When Pirius's detailed briefing was over the crews dispersed quickly.

Hope hurried to the hangar. There was much to be done. But word had already filtered back to the ground crews about the nature of the mission, and the atmosphere was dark and silent. It was like working in a morgue. But they got the job done anyhow.

At the end of the day Enduring Hope went to find This Burden Must Pass.

Burden was in a barracks room, surrounded by a small circle of sombre-faced flight crew – and not all of them were Friends. Hope joined the little circle and listened to Burden's gentle conversation of love and hope, fear and endurance, and the consoling transience of all things.

But though his voice was steady, strain showed on Burden's face, like a dark shadow.

CHAPTER 51

The universe was now about the size of Sol system, and still swelling.

And even before baryogenesis was complete, another transition was approaching. The new baryons gathered in combinations of two, three, four or more. These were atomic nuclei – although nothing like atoms, with their extended clouds of electrons, could yet exist; each nucleus was bare.

These simple nuclei spontaneously formed from the soup of protons and neutrons, but the background radiation was still hot enough that such clusters were quickly broken up again. That would soon change, though: just as there had been a moment when matter could no longer evaporate back to radiant energy, and a moment when quarks no longer evaporated out of baryons, soon would come a time when atomic nuclei became stable, locking up free baryons. This was nucleosynthesis.

For the last quagmites, huddled in their arks, it was hard to imagine any form of life that could exploit such double-dead stuff, with quarks locked inside baryons locked inside nuclei. But from a certain point on, such nuclear matter must inevitably dominate the universe, and any life that arose in the future would be constructed of it.

The quagmites wanted to be remembered. They had determined that any creatures of the remote future, made of cold, dead nuclear stuff, would not forget them. And they saw an opportunity.

At last the moment of nucleosynthesis arrived.

The universe's prevailing temperature and pressure determined the products of this mighty nucleus-baking. Around three-quarters of the nuclei formed would be hydrogen – simple protons. Most of the rest would be helium, combinations of four baryons. Any nuclei more complex would be – ought to be – vanishingly rare; a universe of simple elements would emerge from this new transition.

But the quagmites saw a way to change the cosmic oven's settings.

The fleet of arks sailed through the cosmos, gathering matter with gauzy magnetic wings. Here a knotted cloud was formed, there a rarefied patch left exposed. They worked assiduously, labouring to make the universe a good deal more *clumpy* than it had been before. And this dumpiness promoted the baking, not just of hydrogen and helium nuclei, but of a heavier nucleus, a form of lithium – three protons and four neutrons. There was only a trace of it compared to the hydrogen and helium; the quagmites didn't have enough power to achieve more than that. Nevertheless there was *too much* lithium to be explained away by natural processes.

The scientists of the ages to follow would indeed spot this anomalous 'lithium spike', and would recognise it for what it was: a work of intelligence. At last cold creatures would come to see, and the quagmite arks would begin to tell their story. But that lay far in the future.

With the subatomic drama of nucleosynthesis over, the various survivors sailed resentfully on. There were the last quagmites in their arks, and much-evolved descendants of the spacetime-condensate symbiotes of earlier times yet, all huddling around the primordial black holes. To them the universe was cold and dark, a swollen monster where the temperature was a mere billion degrees, the cosmic density only about twenty times water. The universe was practically a vacuum, they complained, and its best days were already behind it.

The universe was three minutes old.

CHAPTER 52

That night, the last night before the action, Torec came to the bed of Pirius Blue. She stood at the side of his bunk, silhouetted in the dark.

He hesitated. He had lost Torec before the magnetar action, on the day his life split in two, and since this younger copy of his own Torec had come into his life he had avoided her. But when she slid into his arms, her scent, her touch, were just as they had been before.

They came together once, quickly; and then again, more slowly, thoughtfully. Then they lay together in the dark.

Around them the barracks was half-empty. A lot of crew were unable to sleep. Pila had arranged for the refectories to stay open, so some were eating, and elsewhere people were gambling, joking, playing physical games, all looking for ways to let off the tension.

Torec lay with her head on Blue's chest, a firm warm presence. She whispered, 'I thought you weren't going to let me in.'

'I didn't know if I should.'

'Why?'

'Because—' He sighed. 'It's been a long time since the day I left you on Arches, on that final mission. And you've been to Earth! You've *changed*. You always were full of depths, Torec . . . And I've changed too. I've had a chunk deleted out of my life, and been thrown back in time. I'm not me any more.'

'You're the same person you were before you left.'

'Am I?' He turned so he could see her shadowed face. 'Think about it. In the timeline I came from, I was with you for *two years* after the point at which I returned to the timeline of Pirius Red, and everything got skewed. You see? We spent all that time together, you and I. But *you* never lived through those two years, did you?'

'I did,' she murmured. 'A copy of me did. But that copy has gone, or never existed – gone to wherever deleted timelines go . . . It's so strange, Pirius Blue.'

'I know. And sad.'

'Sad? Oh. Because I'm not *your* Torec.' She snuggled back down to his chest. 'But there's nothing we can do about that, is there? So we may as well get on with things.'

'Get on?'

'What else is there to do?'

Pirius Blue laughed. 'As Nilis would probably say, we haven't evolved to cope with time-looped relationships.

'I know what your real problem is,' she said. 'And it's got nothing to do with time paradoxes.'

'What, then?'

'I've been with *him*. Your evil time-clone rival.'

He stifled a laugh. 'He thinks the same about me.'

'Well, you both resent each other. But you're not the same. I think he's in awe of you.'

'But he's *your* Pirius.'

'I don't think it works like that. You're growing apart, becoming different people. But you're still both *you*.'

'Does he love you? . . .'

It was the first time either Pirius had used that word to her.

She sighed. 'You know I love you. Both of you.'

He stroked her back, a spot between her shoulder blades where her skin felt like the smoothest, softest surface he had ever touched. 'It's a mess. A stupid triangle. I don't know how we will sort it out.'

'Wait until the mission is over,' she said.

And see if any of us come back – that was what she left unsaid.

After a time she drew away from him.

'You're going to him,' he said.

'He needs me too. And I need him.'

'I understand,' he said, though he wasn't sure if that was true.

When she had gone Blue rolled into the part of the bunk where she had been lying, still warm from her body, and tried to sleep.

*

Two hours before reveille, Cohl was already on the surface of Orion Rock, In her massive, armoured skinsuit, she was propped up in a foxhole with the members of her platoon around her. The monopole-cannon emplacement they were ordered to protect was a couple of hundred metres away, a complicated silhouette against a shining sky.

As it had been since its chthonic birth, this Rock was still immersed in the glowing molecular clouds of the North Arm of the Baby Spiral. But if she looked ahead she could see a gaggle of stars through the mist, like light globes hanging in smoggy air. That was IRS 16, the cluster of very crowded, very bright stars that coalesced out of the Baby's infalling material as it poured into the crowded space that surrounded Chandra.

Orion Rock itself was probably almost as old as the Galaxy itself, and for all that time it had been swimming helplessly along this lane of gas. For a thousand years humans had dug their way into this Rock. Now both those immense intervals of time were coming to a close, for, in two hours from now, this Rock would burst through the last veils of cloud that separated it from IRS 16. It was hard to believe that Cohl should be *here* at a moment like this.

What was even harder to believe was that at least half her platoon were asleep, and the rest were eating. But that was life in the infantry. Your priority was eating and sleeping, and you took whatever chance you had to do either – even now, on the brink of battle.

Cohl was an ambassador. Her mission, given her by Pirius Red, was to ensure that the two halves of the operation, the Navy fliers who would take the greenships to Chandra and the Army infantry down here on the Rock, communicated properly, shared the same objectives, and worked well together when the crunch came. That was what she had been working towards in the weeks since she had been brought here from Quin.

The senior staff and civilians were going to evacuate Orion before the action and go back to Arches. Even Captain Boote the Forty-Third had chosen not to stick around to witness this climax of his beloved Rock's destiny. Pirius Blue had pulled strings to ensure Cohl could go if she wanted to. But she couldn't bear the thought of running out on the people she had worked with for so long. There was only one place she wanted to be – on the surface, waiting for the sky to fall in, along with the rest of the troopers. And so here she was.

Blayle wasn't asleep, though. Blayle, her platoon sergeant, was a good bit older than her, in his mid-twenties. She could see his eyes on her, bright blue eyes visible behind his faceplate, a cold blue like the light of IRS 16.

He asked, 'How are you bearing up, Lieutenant?'

'Fine,' she said uneasily. Her rank was basically honorary, and it made her uncomfortable.

'I'm proud to be here,' he said, without affectation. 'There's a lot of tradition, here on Orion.'

'I know.'

'My own birth cadre – Cadre 4677 – is mentioned in the Rock's first operational order, which is preserved in the archives. Of course we never knew what our mission would turn out to be. And nobody ever knew when it would end. But now it's turned out that it's *me*, my generation, who has the responsibility – no, the privilege – to be here at the climax.' He sighed. 'A thousand years culminates here and now, in what *I* do today.'

Blayle was a disciplined soldier and a good sergeant; as she had worked with this platoon she had learned to lean on him. But he was a thoughtful, soft-bodied, soft-spoken man who seemed to lack the spirit of camaraderie of some of the other troopers, the loyalty that impelled them to fight so hard. Rather, Blayle seemed to embrace the larger mission of Orion Rock, and had to argue himself into fighting. And, like most people on this Rock, Blayle was a combat rookie.

'Might be best not to think too hard about that stuff, Sergeant. Combat is difficult enough without the feeling that forty generations are looking over your shoulder.'

'Yes. What would Hama Druz say if he was here? "Focus on the moment; the present is all that matters." '

'He might say, shut your flapping mouth while some of us are trying to sleep,' somebody called to a ripple of laughter.

Cohl knew little about the mission of Exultant Squadron. What she *did* know and her platoon didn't, however, that all their elaborate preparations, all the lives that would be lost on this Rock today, were not even the point of the operation. After a thousand years of planning, preparation and silent running, Orion Rock was to be sacrificed as a diversion. She wasn't going to say a word about that.

Cohl tried to relax, letting the Rock's microgravity cushion her. She closed her eyes, and tried to shut out the situation, to think back to less complicated times, when she had been just another trainee on Arches Base . . .

*

Even reveille sounded sombre that morning.

It didn't make any difference to Enduring Hope, who hadn't slept anyhow. He had spent those last hours checking and rechecking everything he could think of, but the novel systems grafted on to these wretched greenships were about as integrated as a third arm growing out of his own back, and he knew that the paltry weeks of developments, trials and modifications had not been enough.

What he was really scared of was that he might be responsible for the mission's failure. He knew his crews felt the same. So they kept on working, right up until the moment the first flight crews began to arrive, trying to be absolutely sure that this mission wouldn't screw up because of something they had missed.

At last the crews of the first wave arrived. And Pila was with them. As the flyers clambered out of their little transporter, Pila stood to one side and began making checks on a data desk she carried. Nobody approached her.

Everybody still found Pirius's adjutant more than a little intimidating – this woman from Earth was cold, and *strange*. But her duties included such mundanity as ensuring that the crews had been served the breakfast they wanted, that the transports had been laid on correctly, a hundred tiny details to make sure that nothing got in the way of the crews doing their jobs. She carried out those duties with calm, invisible efficiency, and people had slowly granted her respect.

Everybody knew a Ghost was flying this mission. Hope was relieved that *it* didn't show up this morning.

The crews, meanwhile, did what flight crews usually did. They allowed the techs to check over their suits, but ran double-checks themselves – if you were flight, you never trusted ground crew with something like *that*. Some of them quizzed their engineers on the state of their ships, as if anything they could ask now would make a difference. Others indulged in various superstitions, such as walking around their ships, or kicking at their landing rails. One man vomited up his breakfast. A tech cleaned it up for him. The atmosphere remained tense, quiet.

Hope saw one stocky pilot pull open the front of his skinsuit to squirt a jet of urine over his ship's landing rail.

'Pirius,' he called.

The pilot turned, his face shielded by his visor. 'I'm Blue, by the way, to save you making a fool of yourself.'

'I knew it was one of you from the lumpy shape of your dick,' Hope said, walking over to him. 'Where's your clone?'

Pirius pointed. Another copy of Pirius, in his own skinsuit but with a commander's red flashes on his shoulders, was working his way around the hangar, shaking hands, having a final word with his crews. 'Red's doing his job,' said Pirius Blue.

'Just what you'd do,' Hope said.

'I'm glad I don't have to.'

'I bunked into the briefing. I heard Nilis speak.'

'Nilis, yes,' Blue said uncertainly. 'What an oddball the man is. Red claims to understand him; I never will.' He regarded Hope. 'I don't think he gave us the truth about what he's thinking, in that briefing.'

'The truth?'

'He has all these ideas about how Chandra is hosting antique life forms, and if we were to keep on burrowing into it we'd find more and more. He's becoming fascinated with Chandra for its own sake, I think. Falling in love with the damn thing.'

'How does that help us destroy it?'

'It doesn't,' Blue said. 'You can't control these Commissaries, though. We had better get the job done before he digs so far he comes up with a reason for us not to attack it in the first place.'

'Pirius—' *I know how scared you are*, he thought. But he could never say such a thing.

Blue held up his hand. 'You know how it is. The fear goes away. I'll be fine once I lift.'

'I won't be, though,' Hope said fervently.

Pirius Blue grasped his hand briefly. 'I wish you were flying with us.'

'Me too.'

'Just don't steal my stuff until *after* I've lifted. Show some respect.' And with that Blue turned and clambered up a short ladder to his cockpit.

It took only minutes for the crews to load themselves into their blisters. The last maintenance hatches were closed, the last bomb trolley withdrawn. The ground crew pulled out of the hangar floor.

The roof of the hangar cracked open, and the air vanished in a shiver of frost. The harsh blue light of the Galaxy's heart flooded into the chamber, overwhelming the glow of the globe lamps that hovered around the ships.

Hope watched from the hangar's observation area. Here was Marshal Kimmer and Captain Marta, and the reserve crews who weren't making this flight, and others like Tili Three who hadn't made the grade, and many, many of this strange base's child-soldier inhabitants, all come to see the launches. Hope suspected that the military types longed to be in those ships, as he did, rather than be stuck here watching them leave. But he wondered how many were here because, morbidly, they expected these crews not to return.

Pirius Red's own ship was to be the first to lift. As they worked through their final preparation the crew's comms were piped into the observation areas.

'Waiting for the red flag to power up sublight . . . We've got a red, we're clear.'

'Start number three.'

'Primed.'

'Engage three . . .'

The greenship raised itself a hand's breadth above its cradle. Hope could feel a pulse in the asteroid's own inertial field as it tried to compensate for the shift in mass.

'Pressure rising in the generators.'

'Copy that. Watch the compensation for the bomb pod, engineer.'

'On it.'

'Waiting on the green for take-off, crew. Waiting on the green. Green acquired, we're cleared.'

As the greenship lifted, its main body bulkily laden with its unfamiliar technology, it wallowed a little.

'Passing through the roof.'

'Turn to port, port on my 129. Let's give them a show, crew.'

Beyond the hangar's open roof, in clear space, the greenship spun once, twice, its three crew blisters whirling about the craft's long axis, an exultant gesture. Then it squirted out of sight.

There was a hand on Hope's shoulder. It was Marshal Kimmer. 'Fifteen hours,' the Marshal said. 'Six hours out, three on station, six back. Then it will be over, one way or the other.'

'Yes, sir.'

All over the hangar now the greenships were rising.

*

Cohl hadn't believed it was possible she would sleep. But she needed a nudge in her ribs from Blayle to jar her awake.

When she glanced up at the sky those shining gas clouds were burning away, and a shoal of bright blue stars, hot and crowded, swarmed above her. After billions of years of flight through the glowing clouds of the Northern Arm, Orion Rock, obeying the blind dictates of celestial mechanics, was at last emerging into the open. And for the humans who crawled over and beneath its surface, the moment of destiny was coming.

CHAPTER 53

The impoverished universe expanded relentlessly.

Space was filled with a bath of radiation, reddening as the expansion stretched it, and by a thin fog of matter. Most of this was dark matter, engaged in its own slow chemistry. The baryonic matter – 'light' matter – was a trace that consisted mostly of simple nuclei and electrons. Any atoms that formed, as electrons hopefully gathered around nuclei, were immediately broken up by the still-energetic radiation. Without stable atoms no interesting chemistry could occur. And meanwhile the ionic mist scattered the radiation, so that the universe was filled with a pale, featureless glow. The cosmos was a bland, uninteresting place, endured with resentment by the survivors of gaudier eras.

Nearly four hundred thousand years wore away, and the universe inflated to a monstrous size, big enough to have enclosed the Galaxy of Pirius's time.

Then the epochal cooling reached a point where the photons of the radiation soup were no longer powerful enough to knock electrons away from their nuclear orbits. Suddenly atoms, mostly hydrogen and helium, coalesced furiously from the mush of nuclei and electrons. Conversely the radiation was no longer scattered: the new atomic matter was transparent.

The universe went dark in an instant. It was perhaps the most dramatic moment since the birth of light itself, many eras past.

To the survivors of earlier times, this new winter was still more dismaying than what had gone before. But every age had unique properties. Even in this desolate chill, interesting processes could occur.

*

The new baryonic atoms were a mere froth on the surface of the deeper sea of dark matter. The dark stuff, cold and gravitating, gathered into immense wispy structures, filaments and bubbles and voids that spanned the universe. And baryonic matter fell into the dark matter's deepening gravitational wells. There it split into whirling knots, that split further into pinpoints, that collapsed until their interiors became so compressed that their temperatures matched that of the moment of nucleosynthesis.

In the hearts of the young stars, nuclear fusion began. Soon a new light spread through the universe. The stars gathered into wispy hierarchies of galaxies and clusters and superclusters, all of it matching the underlying dark matter distribution.

Stars were stable and long-lasting fusion machines, and in their hearts light elements were baked gradually into heavier ones: carbon, oxygen, nitrogen. When the first stars died they scattered their heavy nuclei through space. These in turn were gathered into a second generation of stars, and a third – and from this new, dense material still more interesting objects formed, planets with rocky hearts, that swooped on unsteady orbits around the still-young stars.

In these crucibles life evolved.

Here, for instance, was the young Earth. It was a busy place. Its cooling surface was dotted with warm ponds in which a few hundred species of carbon-compound chemicals reacted furiously with each other, producing new compounds which in turn interacted in new ways. The networks of interactions quickly complexified to the point where autocatalytic cycles became possible, closed loops which promoted their own growth; and some of these autocatalytic cycles chanced upon feedback processes to make themselves stable; and, and . . .

Autocatalysis, homeostasis, life.

Shocked into awareness, humans mastered their environment, sailed beyond the planet of their birth, and wondered where they had come from.

It seemed to the humans that the ages that had preceded their own had been impossibly brief, a mere flash in the afterglow of the singularity, and they saw nothing but a cold dark tunnel ahead. They thought that it was only *now* that a life as rich as theirs was possible. It was a common mistake. Most humans never grasped that their existence was a routine miracle.

436

But they did learn that this age of stars was already declining. The peak of star formation had come, in fact, a billion years before the birth of Earth itself. By now more stars were dying than were being born, and the universe would never again be as bright as it had in those vanished times before.

Not only that, humans started to see, but other forces were at work to accelerate that darkening.

For humans, the universe suddenly seemed a dangerous place.

CHAPTER 54

Suspended over the glistening surface of Orion Rock, bathed in the fierce light of the Cavity's crowded stars, Pirius Red formed up his squadron.

Jees was the shield-master, of course, his best pilot – with a Silver Ghost in her engineer's blister. Pirius Red himself tucked in just behind and to Jees's starboard; Commander Darc, the backup shield-master, took the matching position to port. The rest of the ships took their places behind him, one by one calling off, making a formation after all the training that had become as familiar as the inside of Pirius's own head.

Pirius felt a peculiar, nervous thrill. Despite the training, this was the first time the squadron, *his* squadron, had formed up to fly in anger – the first and, if it went well, the last.

But he was too busy for such reflections. Scout drones were already returning warnings of a Xeelee response to the Rock's sudden emergence from the spiral-arm clouds. If the squadron didn't get out of here *now* it wouldn't be going anywhere, and the preparation would have been for nothing.

He went around the loop one last time. The familiar voices called in from the ships: Jees herself, Darc, Torec, This Burden Must Pass, even his own older self, Pirius Blue, all ready to go.

He called, 'Squadron. Go to sublight.'

He felt a subtle push as his ship's drive cut in. The stars ahead swam, blue-shifted. In seconds the squadron's ten ships reached ninety per cent of lightspeed, the optimum for setting up the grav shield. The formation still looked good; the hours of training were paying off.

'On your call, Jees,' he said.

Directly ahead of Jees's tiny ship the grav shield coalesced. It was like an immense lens that muddled the fierce light of the Galaxy's heart.

'Shield stable,' Jees called.

'Good work. Form up, form up.'

The squadron edged forward, perfecting the formation.

Already they were no longer even in the same universe as Orion Rock, Pirius thought; tucked up in this pocket cosmos, streaming through the prime universe at a fraction below lightspeed, the Xeelee would be quite unable to see them. That, anyhow, was the theory.

Before going to FTL, his last duty was to check with his own crew. His engineer was Cabel, the best of the bunch. His navigator was a kid called Bilson. A promisingly bright boy but woefully inexperienced – for one reason or another he hadn't been able to get the flying hours of some of the others – which was why Pirius had pulled rank and insisted he fly in his ship.

They were as ready as they would ever be.

If you had to ride behind a grav shield, the first FTL jump was the worst. During the endless training flights that had been learned the hard way. You had to go into the jump at ninety per cent light – and come out at the same velocity, smoothly enough to keep the grav shield stable – *and* keep your formation. They had done it in training; now they had to do it for real.

'OK,' Pirius called, keeping his voice steady with an act of will. 'On my command . . .'

Locked together by a web of artificial-sentient interactions, the ships jumped as one.

Cohl had seen the squadron rise out of its hangar. The greenships clustered in a tight little knot, right at her zenith.

She had done her duty, here on the surface, forging her links between infantry and flyers. She knew how important she had been to the overall mission, and she had welcomed Pirius Red's trust in her. But now that it was about to start, she longed to be up there, in those ships where she belonged. And she wondered if it could be true, as the barracks gossip had it, that there was a Silver Ghost somewhere aboard one of those ships.

The greenships seemed to shimmer, as if she was looking through heat haze. She had never seen anything like it before. Perhaps it was the grav shield, she thought, wondering.

She whispered, 'Three, two, one.'

The greenships, ten of them, squirted out of sight, arrowing towards the very centre of the Galaxy. Exultant Squadron was gone.

But a cherry-red glow was rising, all around the horizon.

Her platoon tensed, taking their positions. She gripped her weapon harder, and tried to keep her voice light. 'Get ready,' she called.

The ground shuddered, and little puffs of dust floated up before her, immediately falling back. The Xeelee assault had begun.

Pirius felt the familiar FTL inertial lurch, deep in his gut, and the shining sky blinked around him.

He hastily checked his displays. His ship had come through fine, he saw immediately, and had fallen back into the universe with its ninety per cent lightspeed vector maintained.

Jees reported that the shield remained stable. The plan was to hold their positions for fifteen seconds, while they checked the functioning of the shield and other ships' systems, and see if they had been able to hold their formation in these unique conditions.

But there were only nine ships in the sky, not ten.

'We lost Number Six,' called Bilson.

'I see that,' Pirius snapped. He barked out unnecessary orders for the ships around the gap to close up. The ships were already moving into their well-practised nine-ship formation, just as they had rehearsed for eight and seven and six, and on down.

One jump, they had barely left the hangar, and already a ship was lost. This mission was impossible.

The others seemed to sense his hesitation. 'We go on,' Pirius Blue barked.

'Yeah,' Torec growled. 'Nine out of ten through the jump is better than we war-gamed.'

They were right, of course. 'We go on,' said Pirius.

'Lethe.' That was Bilson. 'Look at that.' He brought up a Virtual feed of Orion Rock, already light hours away.

The Rock was under attack. A swarm of black flies was drifting down over its surface, obscuring the earthworks and weapons installations. Human weapons spat fire in response.

'It doesn't matter,' Pirius said. 'Don't think about it. Let's just make it worthwhile. Kick in the jump programme. Number One—'

'The shield is still nominal, commander,' Jees called.

'On my command.' Again the sentients locked the ships together; without sentient support, the slightest inaccuracy in such enormous and complicated leaps would have left the squadron scattered over the sky. But the ships' limited sentience, like every weapon in this immense battlefield, was subservient to human command; this was a human war.

'Three, two, one.'

After the second jump the flight got rougher, and nobody had time to look back anyhow.

Cohl's own monopole-cannon bank had begun to fire. From its muzzles point lights swarmed into the sky, and at its base she could make out human figures running back and forth, tending its ferocious machinery. This bank was one of hundreds emplaced on the Rock's surface, all firing now, and looking up she could see streams of sparks, each a minuscule flaw in spacetime, washing up towards the bright blue stars of IRS 16. As its great engines of war opened up, the Rock shuddered and shook. It was almost joyous, as if the Rock itself welcomed this sudden conclusion of its own long genesis.

Ships were rising too, disgorged from underground hangars. Most of them were greenships, but of the standard design, lacking the modifications of Pirius's squadron. They hastily gathered into tight formations and hurled themselves after the monopole fire. But Xeelee nightfighters came barrelling out of the blue starlight, and those brave green sparks flared and faded, starbreaker light stitching through them.

A whistle sounded on the general comms loop, a sound she had learned to dread. She couldn't hesitate. She had to lead the way.

Her rifle gripped in one hand, she hauled herself over the earthwork's lip. She didn't get the move quite right. Her body was a clumsy, ungainly mass with too much inertia in a gravity field that was too weak, and she sailed perilously high over the churned-up asteroid ground. Light flared ahead of her, a battle already underway around the cannon emplacement. But though a few starbreakers flickered nearby nobody was shooting at her right now. She didn't look back. It was up to Sergeant Blayle to ensure the rest of the platoon followed her lead.

She careened down into the dirt, face-first. She was still alive, still in one piece. She was huddled in a shallow crater that afforded her a little cover, a few seconds' breathing space.

She raised her head cautiously. The monopole cannon emplacement was still firing. But shapes drifted around it, spheres and ellipsoids, all of them jet black. They were Xeelee drones, and they swarmed around the weapon emplacement like bacteria around a wound – as black as night, chillingly black, in a sky that glowed bright as day. The Xeelee would often send in drones like this as a first wave to try to neutralise a Rock before deploying the heavier weaponry of the nightfighters and other ships. Even the Xeelee conserved their resources, it seemed.

But already the infantry were doing their job. Shadowy figures threw themselves towards the drones, firing as they arced on their short hops from one bit of cover to the next. Their weapons fired pellets of GUT mass-energy that shimmered as they hurled themselves towards their targets, and then burst open like miniature Big Bangs.

One lucky shot took out a drone – but it exploded, a booby trap. Debris showered, a vicious rain that lanced through the bodies of several troopers before digging itself into the churned-up dirt. The endless chatter on the comms loops was interrupted by screams, the first of the action, before the morale filters cut them out.

Cohl's platoon caught up with her. She checked her telltales. One trooper had fallen already, hit by a bit of shrapnel from that drone. Nine left, then, nine huddling in shallow pits in the broken ground.

'Let's go!' She dug her hands and feet into the dirt and thrust herself forward again, firing as she flew.

Most of the drones sailed through the fire unperturbed. Xeelee construction material was tough stuff. The trick was to hit a drone at a point of weakness, at a pole of an ellipsoid, or an edge or vertex of a more angular shape. The spheres were toughest of all, but you still had a chance if you could get your shot close to one of the little windows that dilated open to allow the drones' weapons to fire. Aiming was pretty much out of the question, though; all you could really do was add your rounds to the general fire that washed down over the drones. Cohl never even knew if her shots hit the target.

And meanwhile the Xeelee were firing back, with lances of some focused energy that were invisible except where they caught the churned-up asteroid dust.

Another of Cohl's platoon fell in that hop. Still another was hit after they landed, her left arm sheared neatly off. The trooper was left alive but stunned, and blood briefly fountained, turning to crimson ice. A medical orderly was soon on her. He slammed his palm against her skinsuit's chest panel. The wound was cauterised with a flare of light, and her skinsuit sealed itself up and started to glow a bright brick red, the colour of distress. The medic began the process of hauling the wounded back to the earthworks she had just come from.

Cohl could see troopers all over the surface of the Rock, firing, falling, dying. There was a constant attrition, a hail of killings and terrible wounding that somehow seemed banal. The medic teams were working between the waves of advancing troops, right up to the front line. As casualties began to flow back from the lines all over the Rock, the strange industry of processing the wounded and the dead had already begun. And they still had a hundred metres to fight through before they closed on the weapons station.

Cohl checked her platoon once more. Three down, seven up. 'Let's go,' she called again. 'On my mark. Three, two, one—'

And she threw herself into the fire.

Then there were eight.

Two hours in, Number Three suffered an instability in its GUT-energy generator: it had to turn back and run for home base. Pirius suspected that this failure had been human rather than technical. A major challenge in these bastardised ships was to keep the systems balanced to avoid excess stress on the power systems; a better pilot or engineer might have held it together.

But they were all feeling the strain. His own eyes were gritty, his face pooled with sweat that his skinsuit's conditioning systems didn't seem able to clear, and his hands were locked into claws by the effort of applying just the right touch to his controls, as he tried to balance the FTL jumps and sublight glides. But he couldn't afford to let his concentration lapse, not for a second, not if he was going to get his own laden, lumbering ship through this, and not if he was to keep his squadron together.

As they inched their way towards Chandra the astrophysical geography was slowly changing. The squadron was now tracing a feature the planners called the Bar: it was the pivot of the Baby Spiral, a great glowing belt of molecular gas that marked the bridge that joined the

East and West Arms. Pirius could see the lane of gas like a shining road beneath him. He knew that road led straight to the system surrounding Chandra, the supermassive black hole itself, though that central mystery was still invisible to him.

And if he looked up, through a cloud of lesser stars he could see the bright blue lamps of the IRS 16 cluster. Orion Rock was somewhere up there, its human cargo fighting and dying.

Pirius, tucked into the shield's pocket universe, saw this in a Virtual display. The light which fell on them through the grav shield was heavily stirred and curdled, but with tough processing you could get some information out of it.

As the fourth hour wore away, the squadron began to attract more attention. Suddenly they had an escort – Pirius counted quickly – a dozen, fifteen, twenty nightfighters, flying in loose formation around them. The Xeelee probed the squadron's formation with starbreaker beams that folded, wavered and dispersed as they penetrated the pocket universe. The greenships were able to evade these random thrusts easily enough without bending their formation too far. But the Xeelee weren't serious; for now they seemed to be more intent on simply tracking this strange new development.

'That's got to be good news,' Torec called. 'They are surveilling us, not attacking. We're something new, and they don't understand.'

'Just as well,' Pirius Blue growled. 'These lumbering beasts couldn't defend themselves anyhow.'

'The grav shield is working,' Torec insisted. 'The Xeelee don't have FTL foreknowledge of what we're up to.'

Commander Darc called, 'I think you're right. And maybe Orion is doing its job; they may not have the resources to spare for—' But he was cut off.

Pirius, immediately anxious, glanced up and to his right. The green spark that was Darc's ship was falling away from the formation.

'Darc! Number Four, report!'

For an agonising second there was silence. Then Darc came on the loop. 'Leader, Four. A lucky shot, I'm afraid. I lost my engineer. Lethe, Lethe.'

'Can you hold formation?'

'Not a chance. I'm wallowing . . . Dropping out now.'

Pirius's heart sank. Losing Darc was like a punch to the heart.

But even as he was wrestling with whatever was left of his ship,

Darc was watching *him*. 'Squadron Leader. Snap out of it. Call the seven.'

Pirius shook his head. 'Form up the seven, the seven,' he ordered. Around him the surviving ships swam into the seven-strong formation they had practised against this eventuality. 'But, Lethe,' Pirius snapped, 'we just lost our reserve shield-master.'

'In that case,' Jees said dryly, 'we'll have to get by with one. Sir.'

Darc called, 'Remember my final instruction, Squadron Leader.'

Darc had sworn to kill the Silver Ghost on Jees's ship immediately, if it gave him the slightest excuse. Pirius said, 'I won't forget, Commander.'

Darc laughed defiantly. 'Get it done, Pirius! I'll see you when it's over.'

Pirius Red could see the Xeelee had triangulated on Darc: he was at the tip of an arrow-head sketched out by lancing crimson light. It was an oddly beautiful sight, Pirius thought, beautiful and deadly.

Blue said, 'He's taking on our escort. Trying to draw them away.'

'A brave man,' Burden murmured.

'He's showing us the way,' Pirius Red said firmly. 'Form up – Six, you're slack! What do you think this is, a joy ride? Form up, form up.'

He tried to settle down once more to the steady strain of nursing his ship and his squadrons in the wake of the imperturbable Jees. But another distracting display showed him what was happening at Orion Rock, which was now under heavy and concentrated attack. The Rock was fulfilling its primary purpose in the operation, which was to divert Xeelee fire. But such was the energy poured over it that the Rock glowed like a star itself.

Around the cannon emplacement, Xeelee drones still soared and spat. The fire from both sides had churned up the asteroid dirt, and all signs of the earthworks over which generations had laboured had been erased in hours.

For a moment the action was washing around to the emplacement's far side, and Cohl had nothing to fire at. She threw herself into a trench, panting. She lay as still as she could, locked in with the stink of her own shit, piss, sweat, blood and fear, trying to let the fatigue work out of her limbs, and sucked water and nutrients from nipples in her helmet. Even here the fire of the continuing battle lit up the furrowed surface of asteroid dirt before her, and glared off the scars on her faceplate.

The morale filters seemed to have been overwhelmed. The comms loops were dominated by wailing now, the massed crying, screaming, pleas for help from thousands of wounded troopers. But the wounded were far outnumbered by the dead. The noise was harrowing and useless.

There were only four left of Cohl's platoon, four including herself. They had fallen back to a final perimeter just outside the platform on which the monopole cannon stood. She stole a glance over the lip of the trench. The cannon were still firing, but fitfully; Cohl had no idea how many gunners were alive. But still the Xeelee drones swarmed, a cloud of swimming black forms that seemed to grow denser the more you fired into it.

She knew it was only chance that had kept her alive long enough to be seeing this.

Cohl had been sealed up in her suit for four hours already. It was too long, of course. Every soldier knew that if an action took too long it had gone wrong, one way or another. And if the casualty rates inflicted on her own platoon were typical, soon those drones would get through and shut down the cannon for good.

But there was scuttlebutt on the comms loops that worse was to come: that in the angry sky above the nightfighters were breaking through the picket line of greenships, and were moving in to finish off the Rock altogether.

Blayle was beside her, his face an expressionless mask. 'A thousand years,' he murmured. 'A thousand years of building – of *belief*. Blood lines forty generations deep that were for nothing but to throw a handful of soldiers into Xeelee fire—'

'Don't think about it, ' Cohl muttered.

'I can't help it,' he said, almost wistfully. 'The more tired I get, the more I think. A thousand years devoted to a single purpose, gone in *hours*. It defies the imagination. And what is it for?' He craned his neck to peer up at the brilliant blue lamps of IRS 16. 'I don't know if the action is succeeding. Why, I don't even know what the Xeelee are doing here, let alone why we're attacking them.'

'We don't need to know,' Cohl said, falling back on Doctrine. Then, more thoughtfully, she said, 'But it's probably always been that way.' If you were a soldier, war was small scale. All that mattered was what was going on around you – who was shooting at you, which of your buddies was still alive and trying to keep *you* alive. Whatever you knew of the bigger strategic picture didn't matter when you were at the sharp end.

And as the enemy's fist closed around this Rock, she could see no end point but defeat.

She had long burned off her initial adrenalin surge, long gone through her second wind. Now she was like an automaton, going through the motions of the fighting and keeping herself alive almost without conscious thought. She had trained for this, been burned hard enough by her instructors on Quin for this strange condition to be familiar. But it was as if she was no longer even in her own head, but was looking down on her own hapless, dust-coated form in its failing skinsuit, scrunched down in a ditch in the dirt, trying to stay alive.

She glanced at the chronometer in the corner of her faceplate display. She'd had five minutes' break; it felt like thirty seconds.

'It shouldn't have been me,' Blayle said now.

'What?'

'Why *me*? Why, after all the generations who lived out fat, comfortable lives in this Lethe-spawned Rock, why is it *me* who has been pushed out here to fight and die? It should have been those others, who died in their bunks,' he muttered. 'It shouldn't have been *me*—'

Electric-blue light flared, and asteroid dirt was hurled up before them. Cohl twisted and fired into the blue-tinged fog of dust. She glimpsed Xeelee drones, pressing down on her trench. There was something above her; she felt it before she saw it. She rolled on her back, preparing to fire again.

But the ship was a flitter, small, unarmoured. Its door was open and a ladder hung down.

'Cohl!' She recognised the voice; it was Enduring Hope. 'Evac!'

'No. The cannon—'

'The Xeelee shot the heart out of it. The Rock is finished. There's no point dying here.'

'I have to stay.' Of course she did; that was Doctrinal. You weren't supposed to keep yourself alive, not while there were still enemy to shoot at. ' "A brief life burns brightly," ' she said reflexively.

'Balls,' Hope said with feeling. 'Come on, Cohl; I've risked my ass to come flying around this Rock looking for you.'

She made a quick decision. Reluctantly she turned to Blayle. 'Sergeant . . .'

He didn't respond. There was a small scar on Blayle's faceplate, a puncture almost too small to see. A thousand years of history ends here, she thought. She wished she could close his eyes.

In the end only two of Cohl's platoon were lifted out with her, two out of the nine she had led out of the trench.

As the flitter lifted, she saw the landscape of the Rock open up. Its whole surface crawled with light as Xeelee drones and human fighters hurled energy at each other, all in utter silence. It was an extraordinary sight. But already the nightfighters were closing in, to end this millennial drama for good.

The flitter squirted away. Cohl, still locked in her skinsuit, closed her eyes, and tried to control her trembling.

Pirius tried not to watch the chronometer. And he tried not to think about his own fatigue.

He felt as if he had been walking a high-wire for six hours. He tried to concentrate on the moment, to get through the next jump, and the next, and the next. If you didn't survive the present, after all, future and past didn't matter; that old earthworm Hama Druz had been right about that much. For all their training and sims, however, they hadn't figured out how exhausting this was going to be, this tightrope walk through the centre of the Galaxy. He hoped he would have the physical and mental strength actually to fight at the end of it.

He shut the passage of time out of his mind. So he was surprised when a gentle chime sounded on the comms loops. But he understood its significance immediately.

Ahead the grav shield was dissolving, and in the sky around him the stars and gas masses of this shining, complex place were swimming back to where they should be.

'No sign of our escort,' Bilson said.

'We got through,' Pirius murmured.

'Yes, sir,' Even Jees's steady voice betrayed an edge of fatigue now. She should have been spelled by Darc, and Pirius knew that for the last hour she had been nursing one failing system after another. Still, she had delivered them here, just as the operational plan had dictated, and with no more losses: seven ships had survived out of ten who had started.

Somebody called, 'What's *that*?'

It was a star, a hot, bright, blue star, a young one – not part of the IRS 16 cluster, though; they were far from that now. And there seemed to be a cloud around it, a flattened disc, like the shields of rock from which planets formed.

'That,' said Bilson, 'is SO-2. We're exactly where we are supposed to be, sir.'

Engineer Cabel was less clued in. 'And SO-2 is—'

'The innermost star in orbit.'

'In orbit around *what*?'

'Chandra,' said Bilson simply.

Pirius, for all his fatigue, felt a thrill of anticipation.

Blue called. 'And what is that cloud around the star? Dust, rock—'

'Wreckage,' Bilson said. 'The hulks of human ships – greenships, Spline. Some other designs I can't recognise. Older ones, perhaps.'

Burden said grimly, 'Even here the Galaxy is littered with corpses.'

'Xeelee in the scopes,' Bilson said softly. 'They know we're here. Pilot, we don't have much time.'

'So we're not the first to come this way,' Pirius said crisply. 'Let's make sure we're the last. Defensive formation, seven-fold – come on, you know the drill.'

The greenships slid into place around him and the squadron edged forward. Pirius scanned the sky, looking for Xeelee fighters, and for Chandra, the strange black hole that was his final destination.

CHAPTER 55

In this age of matter the proto-Xeelee found new ways to survive. Indeed, they prospered. They formed new levels of symbiosis with baryonic-matter forms. The new form – a composite of *three* ages of the universe – was the kind eventually encountered by humans, who would come to call them by a distorted anthropomorphic version of a name in an alien tongue: they were, at last, *Xeelee*.

But soon the new Xeelee faced an epochal catastrophe of their own.

They still relied on the primordial black holes, formed in the earliest ages after the singularity; they used the holes' twisted knots of spacetime to peel off their spacetime-defect 'wings', for instance. But now the primordial holes were becoming rare: leaking mass-energy through Hawking radiation, they were evaporating. By the time humanity arose, the smallest remaining holes were the mass of the Moon.

It was devastating for the Xeelee, as if for humans the planet Earth had evaporated from under their feet.

But a new possibility offered itself. New black holes were formed from the collapse of giant stars, and at the hearts of galaxies, mergers were spawning monsters with the mass of a million Sols. Here the Xeelee migrated. The transition wasn't easy; a wave of extinction followed among their diverse kind. But they survived, and their story continued.

And it was the succour of the galaxy-centre black holes that first drew the Xeelee into contact with dark matter.

There was life in dark matter, as well as light.

Across the universe, dark matter outweighed the baryonic, the

450

'light', by a factor of six. It gathered in immense reefs hundreds of thousands of light years across. Unable to shed heat through quirks of its physics, the dark material was resistant to collapse into smaller structures, the scale of stars or planets, as baryonic stuff could.

Dark and light matter passed like ghosts, touching each other only with gravity. But the pinprick gravity wells of the new baryonic stars were useful. Drawn into these wells, subject to greater concentrations and densities than before, new kinds of interactions between components of dark matter became possible.

In this universe, the emergence of life in dark matter was inevitable, in their earliest stages, these 'photino birds' swooped happily through the hearts of the stars, immune to such irrelevances as the fusion fire of a sun's core.

What did disturb them was the first stellar explosions – and with them the dissipation of the stars' precious gravity wells, without which there would be no more photino birds.

Almost as soon as the first stars began to shine, therefore, the photino birds began to alter stellar structures and evolution. If they clustered in the heart of a star they could damp the fusion processes there. By this means the birds hoped to hurry a majority of stars through the inconvenience of explosions and other instabilities and on to a dwarf stage, when an ageing star would burn quietly and coldly for aeons, providing a perfect arena for the obscure dramas of photino life. A little later the photino birds tinkered with the structures of galaxies themselves, to produce more dwarfs in the first place.

Thus it was that humans found themselves in a Galaxy in which red dwarf stars, stable, long-lived and unspectacular, outnumbered stars like their own sun by around ten to one. This was hard to fit into any naturalistic story of the universe, though generations of astrophysicists laboured to do so: like so many features of the universe, the stellar distribution had been polluted by the activities of life and mind. It would not be long, though, before the presence of the photino birds in Earth's own sun was observed.

The Xeelee had been troubled by all this much earlier.

The Xeelee cared nothing for the destiny of pond life like humanity. But by suppressing the formation of the largest stars, the birds were reducing the chances of more black holes forming. What made the universe more hospitable for the photino birds made it less so for the Xeelee. The conflict was inimical.

The Xeelee began a grim war to push the birds out of the galaxies, and so stop their tinkering with the stars. The Xeelee had already survived several universal epochs; they were formidable and determined. Humans would glimpse silent detonations in the centres of galaxies, and they would observe that there was virtually no dark matter to be seen in galaxy centres. Few guessed that this was evidence of a war in heaven.

But the photino birds turned out to be dogged foes. They were like an intelligent enemy, they were like a plague, and they were everywhere; and for some among the austere councils of the Xeelee there was a chill despair that they could never be beaten.

And so, even as the war in the galaxies continued, the Xeelee began a new programme, much more ambitious, of still greater scale.

Their immense efforts caused a concentration of mass and energy some hundred and fifty million light years from Earth's Galaxy. It was a tremendous knot that drew in galaxies like moths across three hundred million light years, a respectable fraction of the visible universe. Humans, observing these effects, called the structure the Great Attractor – or, when one of them journeyed to it, Bolder's Ring.

This artefact ripped open a hole in the universe itself. And through this doorway, if all was lost, the Xeelee planned to flee. They would win their war – or they would abandon the universe that had borne them, in search of a safer cosmos.

Humans, consumed by their own rivalry with the Xeelee, perceived none of this. To the Xeelee – as they fought a war across hundreds of millions of light years, as they laboured to build a tunnel out of the universe, as stars flared and died billions of years ahead of their time – humans, squabbling their way across their one Galaxy, were an irritant.

A persistent irritant, though.

CHAPTER 56

The seven surviving greenships of Exultant Squadron formed up into a tight huddle. In the sudden calm the crews gazed around at the extraordinary place they had come to.

Of all the Galaxy's hundreds of billions of stars, SO-2 was the one nearest the black hole. And now they were within its orbit. This central place, a cavity within a cavity light weeks across, was free of stars – because any star that came closer than SO-2 would be torn apart by black hole tides. It was filled with light and matter, though, with glowing plasma, but Pirius's Virtual filters blocked that out. It was as if the seven of them hovered within a great shell walled by crowded stars, like flies inside a Conurbation dome.

And at the very centre of this immense space was a pool of light. From this distance it was like a glowing toy, small enough to cover with a thumbnail held at arm's length. It was a floor of curdled and glowing gas, as wide as planetary orbits in Sol system. This was the black hole's accretion disc, the penultimate destination of debris infalling from the rest of the Galaxy – the place where doomed matter was compressed and smashed together, whirling around the hole like water around a leak in a bucket, before it fell into the black hole.

Of the monstrous black hole itself Pirius could see only a pinpoint spark, an innocent light like a young sun, set in the centre of the disc. Somewhere in there was an event horizon that would have engulfed ten Sols side by side; indeed in Sol system it would have stretched to the orbit of the innermost planet, Mercury. The glow was the final cry of matter, compressed and heated as it fell into the hole, the flaw in the universe into which the Galaxy was steadily draining.

And it was Pirius's target.

453

Cabel was studying magnified images of the accretion disc. He found a bright arc, traced across the churning surface of the disc, glowing brightly. 'What's that?'

'I think it's a star,' Bilson said. 'A star that came too close. Lethe, there is still fusion going on there.'

Cabel said slowly, 'A *star*, being torn to pieces. Lethe, what a place we've come to.'

Blue called, 'Heads up. Take a look at your tactical displays.'

Pirius Red's Virtual maps of the region lit up with virulent crimson sparks, the locations of Xeelee concentrations. Most of them were around the rim of the accretion disc itself.

Blue reported, 'The good news is that I don't see any nightfighters or other combat ships in this region – none within the orbit of SO-2. So the feint with the grav shield worked. The Xeelee really didn't anticipate we would get this far, and their reactions are slow. We have some time. But those red points in the accretion disc are Xeelee emplacements, Sugar Lumps, probably used as flak batteries. They are static – they aren't going to come after us – but they pack a punch.'

So, Pirius thought, studying his display, to get at the black hole his greenships were going to have to fly through a hail of Xeelee flak as well as pushing through the hazardous zone of the accretion disc.

'Let's get it done before they wake up,' he said. 'I'll go in first. Engineer – navigator – are you with me?'

'Ready, pilot,' Bilson said, his voice tight with tension.

Cabel called, 'It's what we came here to do.'

'Prep the weapons.'

Pirius worked through his checklist quickly, trying to set aside his own doubts, his fear. He knew they only had a few chances to make this work. Each of the ships carried only one pair of black hole bombs: they would be able to deliver just one blow each. And this first run, with the Xeelee totally unprepared, was their best chance of all. If he succeeded on this very first strike, they could go home. He desperately hoped he could make it happen.

The other crews were quiet as they worked. He didn't want to speak to Torec: he felt it would help neither of them. But he couldn't forget she was there. Even if he got himself killed, he told himself, if he did his job, nobody else had to die today – *she* wouldn't have to die.

It occurred to him he hadn't heard a word from This Burden Must

Pass since they had arrived in this cathedral of stars. It was a troubling, niggling thought, but he had no time to deal with it.

Green flags lit up. The ship was ready for the attack run. Pirius said, 'Let's do it.' He clenched his fists around his controls.

With Cohl and the rest of the final evacuees from Orion, Enduring Hope was lifted to Arches Base. The journey took two hours, so Hope arrived six hours after the greenships had been launched – when, he realised, Pirius should be arriving at Chandra.

Hope's feelings were complex. The weeks he had spent preparing for the moment of the launch were over. He felt a great sense of relief, even anti-climax, that he had managed to get his ships away with only one major foul-up, only one ship lost; it had been better than he had expected, in his heart of hearts. And he was pleased to have been able to pull a few strings to get Cohl off Orion.

And yet frustration was knotting up inside him. He was after all a flyer, and his crewmate from the last, fated mission of *Assimilator's Claw* was at this moment flying into a pit of Xeelee fighters at the centre of the Galaxy, and *he*, Hope, wasn't there. He was stranded here on Arches Base, and until and unless those ships came home there wasn't a thing he could do about it.

Some consolation his creed was now, he thought dismally. He did believe intellectually that all he lived through was just one road among many, all to be resolved at the confluence at the end of time. But it certainly didn't *feel* like that, not at moments like this. He wished he could talk it over with This Burden Must Pass – but Burden too was fighting at Chandra.

Lacking a better alternative, Enduring Hope made his way to his barracks. Perhaps he could get some sleep. He had a duty to keep fresh; when the ships came limping home again the skills of himself and his engineering crews would be crucial.

But at the barracks a runner found him. He was to report to Officer Country. Hope was even more surprised when the runner led him to Arches' main operations room.

He stood in the doorway, mouth agape. The room was a broad, deep arena, with walkways on several levels surrounding a huge Virtual display at the centre. Today the main display was a diorama of the centre of the Galaxy, with a brilliant pinpoint that must be Chandra itself surrounded by an accretion disc and other astrophysical monstrosities. This main display was surrounded by more Virtuals, graphs, diagrams and scrolling text that were, he recognised, diagnostic data on the Exultant ships themselves. Some of the walkways crossed the pit so that you could walk through the displays, studying them as closely as you liked. Around this pit of ever-changing information staff worked, talking rapidly, tapping bits of data into the desks they carried. On one high balcony Hope glimpsed Marshal Kimmer himself, standing gravely with his hands clasped behind his back, surrounded by a cluster of aides.

It was a Navy ops room at the height of a major operation; it was a nest of tense, coordinated activity. But the discipline and organisation were obvious, and despite the complexity of the task and the tension of the hour, not a voice was raised.

And the information displays changed constantly. The central diorama had obviously been based on the information retrieved by Pirius Blue during his earlier pass through the central regions. But Hope saw now that sections of it were changing all the time, evidently updated with data returned from the ships of Exultant themselves.

Which meant they got through, he thought hotly. Exultant Squadron had survived, and had pushed through to its target, the very centre of the Galaxy. He clenched his fists.

And now he looked more closely he saw a little cluster of brave green sparks, hovering above the accretion disc. One of those green gems broke from the cluster and was swooping down towards the accretion disc. It was utterly dwarfed, like a fly dropping towards a carpet, but it was advancing anyway. It had begun, Hope realised, thrilled; they were going in for the raid. And if he had survived, that lead spark must be Pirius Red himself.

'I know you.'

A woman approached him. She wore a plain white robe, and was short, shorter than he was. The skin of her face was smooth, but it was not the smoothness of youth, and her eyes were hard and sharp, like bits of stone. She said, 'You're Tuta. Who calls himself Enduring Hope.' She opened her mouth and laughed. It was an ugly, throaty noise, and her teeth were black.

He replied, 'I think I know you too. After he returned from Sol system Pirius told me about you.'

'My fame spreads across the Galaxy,' Luru Parz said dryly. 'I'm sure Pirius is much happier now he's away from Earth's politicking and scheming, and is able to fly his toys around the centre of the Galaxy again.'

Enduring Hope stared at her; he couldn't help it.

Luru snapped, 'Speak, boy! Tell me what you're thinking.'

Hope licked his lips. 'I'm thinking I don't know whether I should offer you a chair, or report you to the Guardians.'

She laughed again. 'You have a better sense of humour than Pirius, that's for sure. I think I like you, Tuta.'

He asked hesitantly, 'And is it true?'

'Is what true?'

'That you are' – he glanced, around and spoke quietly – 'immortal?'

'Oh, I doubt that very much. I just haven't got around to dying yet.'

'Why are you here? And *how* are you here?'

'As it happens I played a major part in initiating this project in the first place – as Pirius ought to have told you, though I doubt he understood it himself, Pirius or his bed-warmer, those poor baffled children. I've come here to see the climax of what I started. I think I'm entitled to that much. As to *how* I got here, I leaned on Nilis to arrange it. Even so detached a Commissary as that bumbling oaf can still pull strings.'

'Where is the Commissary?'

'Frankly he was getting so anxious he was making a nuisance of himself, and the officer in command of the room sent him away. But he was distracted anyway. He's still analysing his fragments of data about Chandra, still seeking to discern what he calls its "true nature". No doubt you know about that. But of course Chandra's importance to the Xeelee is all that counts. And if we get a chance we should smash it, simple as that. That's why I supported this project in the first place. If it was up to me I would stop Nilis's pointless rootling. All he is likely to find is a reason to pull our punches, and what use would that be?'

If this woman was one-tenth as old as Pirius's unbelievable claims, then she must have seen so much, *lived* so much: Hope's imagination failed as he tried to grasp what that must mean. 'I wouldn't have thought you would care what happens today, one way or another.'

'It's a significant day in the long history of mankind, Tuta, whichever way it turns out. And I intend to be here to see it, triumph or disaster – or, more likely and a lot more fun, a bit of both – eh?' And she opened that hideous mouth again.

A bustling form emerged on to one of the higher walkways. It was Nilis himself, back despite his banishment. The Commissary recognised Hope and summoned him with a wave. Hope climbed a staircase and found himself, dauntingly, on the balcony with Marshal Kimmer himself.

It turned out that it was Nilis who had called for Hope to come to the ops room during this crucial hour. 'I think I know you people by now. You would rather be *there* – but, given you're stuck out here you will burn up if you don't know what is becoming of your friends. I asked for Cohl too, but she's in sick bay. I arranged a data feed for her though.' He smiled at Hope almost fondly, and again Hope had thought how strange it was that such a gentle, thoughtful man should be responsible for a weapons system of such stunning destructive power.

Kimmer said softly, 'Commissary. The moment approaches.'

Nilis looked at the display, 'So it does. Oh, my eyes . . .' He went to stand with the still, statuesque form of Marshal Kimmer.

The room grew silent. That lone green spark was creeping towards the centre of the main display. The Commissary's hands were folded over each other, his knuckles white with tension.

In a series of short FTL hops, Pirius flew low over the surface of the accretion disc. He and his crew were alone now, the rest of the squadron lost in the glare behind him.

Below him fled a broadly flat, curdled surface, glowing white, a pool of gas that rotated visibly, churning like storm clouds on Earth. This was all that was left of the mass of stars and planets and living things that had been unlucky enough to fall into this lethal pit. He knew that a black hole destroyed all information about the matter it took into its event horizon, everything but spin, mass and charge; but whatever the turbulent plasma below had once been, it was already reduced to nothing but fodder for the endlessly voracious Chandra.

He had long passed the closest approach achieved by his older self, Pirius Blue, on his scouting jaunt. Nobody in human history had ever approached the event horizon of a supermassive black hole so closely – and he had to go in a lot closer yet.

Nothing he saw was real, of course. All he saw was a Virtual rendering, reconstructed in wavelengths he was comfortable with, the glare turned down; if he had looked out of his blister he would have been blinded in an instant. But he thought he could sense the churning of this dish of plasma the size of a solar system, perhaps even the gut-wrenching gravities of the event horizon itself. He could *feel* the vast astrophysical processes around him. He was a mote trapped inside an immense machine.

'One minute to closest approach to the horizon,' Bilson warned.

Pirius felt his heart beat faster, but he tried to keep his voice light. 'Remember your training. We practised on Rocks a couple of hundred kilometres across. Today we're hitting a target a hundred *million* klicks wide. It ought to be easy.'

'But,' Cabel said dryly, 'it's a hundred million klicks of black hole event horizon.'

'Shut up,' said Bilson, the fear sharp in his voice.

'No flak,' Cabel said. 'They still haven't seen us. We might actually live through this.'

'Thirty seconds,' the navigator called.

'Stand ready.'

And suddenly it was ahead of him, the centre of everything, a sphere of glowing gas like a malevolent sun rising from the curdled accretion disc. The event horizon itself was invisible, of course: dark on dark, it was a surface from which not even light could escape. The glow he saw was the final desperate emission of infalling matter.

Under the control of its CTC processor, the ship rose up from the plane of the disc.

Pirius looked down as the accretion disc fell away. At the disc's inner edge the infalling matter, having been spun and churned and compressed in its final frantic orbits, at last reached the event horizon. Wisps and tendrils, gaudy and pathetic, snaked in from that inner edge, glowing ever more feverishly.

He looked ahead into the ball of churning gas that surrounded the event horizon. The horizon was a sphere, but vast, a sphere as wide as Mercury's orbit. The greenship's path should take it skimming up towards its pole, kissing the surface tangentially at the point of closest approach, a precise one hundred kilometres from the mathematically defined surface of the event horizon itself.

A shining, electric-blue path appeared in the complicated Virtual sky before Pirius. Projected by navigator Bilson it was his computed course, designed to take him to the hundred-kilometre closest approach distance. Though they would pass vanishingly close to the event horizon of a supermassive black hole, there was nothing to fear from tides: Chandra was, paradoxically, too big for that, and in fact they could fall all the way down through the event horizon without feeling a thing.

Seconds left. The last million kilometres fell away, the immense curved surface started to flatten beneath the prow, and the mist of tortured matter cleared ahead of him—

To reveal a shining netting.

'Pull up!' Bilson screamed.

Pirius dragged at his controls, but the ship's proximity sensors had reacted before he did. The ship climbed up and away. The electric-blue path disintegrated and vanished.

Suddenly the texture of that wall was fleeing beneath his prow. He made out an irregular mesh of shining threads, spread out like the lights of an immense city, all of it obscured by a storm of infalling plasma. This close he could see no signs of curvature; the event horizon was effectively a plain above which the greenship fled.

Bilson started to bring up magnified images. That structure really was a kind of net, a mesh of silvery threads. Small black shapes crawled along those threads – but they were 'small' only on this tremendous scale; the shortest of those threads must have been a thousand kilometres long. The dominant structure was hexagonal, but the hexagons were not regular, and the effect was more like a spider's web than a net.

Bilson breathed, 'A web big enough to wrap up the whole of the event horizon. I think those black things are ships.'

Cabel asked, 'Xeelee?'

'I guess. Not a design we've seen before. They seem to be trapping the infalling matter. Feeding off it. And look, there are more ships coming up from inside the mesh.'

'Then this is the central Xeelee machinery,' Bilson said. 'What they use to make their nightfighters, to run their computing. This netting is the engine of the Prime Radiant. It must have taken a billion years to build.'

Lethe, Pirius thought. What have we got ourselves into?

Cabel called, 'I hate to hurry you. But those flak batteries are waking up.'

Pirius called, 'Bilson—'

'Understood, pilot.'

A new path was laid in, a shining blue road that ducked down into the netting. The ship started to track the new course – but it bucked and swept up again.

'It's that mesh,' Bilson shouted. 'We weren't expecting *structure* over the event horizon. The netting is actually under our hundred-kilometre ceiling, but the ship's fail-safes won't let us get close enough.'

Pirius thrust his hands into the controls. 'I'll override.' Even as he pushed the ship's nose down, the systems fought back, and the ride was bumpy. 'But I can't hold this for long. Cabel, get the range finder working.'

Two cherry-red beams lanced out beneath the fleeing ship. Their paths were deflected in arcs, extraordinarily elegant, by Chandra's ferocious gravity. Pirius, glancing down, saw the triangulating starbreakers slice through the netting as they passed, like burning scalpels passing through flesh. The intersection point should have been at about the level of the event horizon, but he couldn't make it out.

'We're doing a lot of damage,' Cabel reported. 'Those flak batteries are definitely growing interested.'

'Never mind the flak,' Pirius growled. 'There's nothing we can do about the flak. Prepare the weapon. Bilson, are we at the right altitude?'

'I can't tell,' Bilson said. 'It's not working – not the way it's supposed to. There's some kind of distortion when the beams pass through that netting.'

Cabel said, 'We're running out of time—'

To have come all this way and to fail . . . He held the ship steady on its course. 'Do your best.'

'Yes, sir.'

Cherry-red light flooded Pirius's cockpit.

'They found us!' Cabel yelled.

He was right; the ship was about to be triangulated by two, three, four starbreakers. Pirius snapped, 'I need an answer, navigator!'

'Now!' Bilson screamed.

'Engineer! Fire!'

Cabel didn't acknowledge, but Pirius felt the shudder, familiar from training, as the cannon was fired, and twin point black holes shot out of the heavy muzzles mounted on the greenship's main hull.

Once the shells were away Pirius relaxed his grip on the manual controls. The ship lifted itself up and away, twisting to evade attack, its CTC processor enabling it to respond faster than any human reaction. The cherry-red starbreaker glow dissipated.

Pirius lay back and sucked in a deep breath. Still alive.

The greenship shuddered, as if it were a toy boat bobbing on a bathtub.

'That was the detonation,' Cabel said.

Bilson was silent for a few seconds, gathering data. Then he said, 'No damage. The weapon worked, but we must have missed the horizon.'

Pirius felt a heavy despair descend, 'All right,' he said. 'Keep gathering data. Maybe we can figure this out yet.'

'I didn't screw up, pilot,' Bilson said miserably. 'I gave you the best I could.'

'I know,' Pirius said wearily. He believed him. But he knew that Bilson would blame himself for this for the rest of his life. 'We still have work to do. We have six more chances, six more ships. The others will need our help. Keep your heads up. All right?'

'Yes, sir,' Cabel said blankly.

'Navigator?'

'Sir.'

The mood among the remaining crews, at their station high above the plain of the accretion disc, was bleak.

Torec tried to make the best of it. 'Whoever went in first was almost bound to fail. But we learned a lot.'

Bilson remained very down. 'We didn't know about that mesh. We can't see through it, and our starbreakers are distorted by it somehow, so we can't aim. And we haven't got time to rewrite the attack plan.'

'He's right,' said Pirius Blue. 'Those flak batteries didn't see you coming in, but they chased you back out, Red. And the ops room say there are nightfighters on the way.'

'We have to go back in,' said Pirius Red. 'Now, before it gets any worse.'

'I'll go,' said Jees abruptly. It was the first time she had spoken since Pirius's return.

Pirius Red said, 'But your ship's configured to carry the grav shield.'

'We don't need it on the way back. We'll just be running for home.'

'No, but your bird will wallow even more than the rest.'

'Then I'm expendable. And I'm your best pilot,' she said simply. 'If anybody can make this work, I can.'

Torec pointed out: 'Pirius. She has a Silver Ghost on board.'

'That's irrelevant,' Jees snapped, 'Its presence doesn't affect the operation of the weapon. And now we've done with the shield its usefulness is at an end. The Ghost is just cargo now; it has no say.'

'She has a point,' Pirius Blue said.

But, Pirius Red thought, the Ghost was probably listening to every word.

He called his second flight commander. 'Burden? What's your recommendation?' But, though his comms channel was clearly open, Burden didn't reply. Again Pirius felt a flicker of unease.

'Come on, Pirius,' Jees said evenly. 'We need a decision.'

Enough. 'Go,' he said.

Jees had evidently been waiting for the go-ahead. Her ship immediately looped out of formation and streaked down towards the accretion disc.

She got about as far as Pirius had. Then starbreaker beams from those Sugar Lump flak stations, four of them, triangulated on her. She held her position, got her own range-finding starbreakers working, and reported doing a little more damage to the net. But her green spark winked out before she even launched her bombs.

When it was over, just minutes after Jees had left the formation, Pirius forced himself to speak.

'OK. OK. Maybe there's another way.'

Enduring Hope was still on the balcony with Nilis, Kimmer, Luru Parz.

When the news of the second failure, and the loss of Jees and her crew, filtered through to the ops room, Nilis was distraught. He wandered along the walkway, wringing his hands and wiping the soft flesh of his face. 'Oh no,' he said, over and over. 'Oh no, oh no. It's my fault. We are failing, and their lives are burning up like sparks, and all for nothing . . .' It was a distressing sight. But Enduring Hope reminded himself that Nilis was, at heart, a civilian, with a civilian's lack of understanding of war.

Marshal Kimmer did not react, either to the bad news from the target or to Nilis's loss of control. There was little he could do to shape the course of events, but in this difficult time he was a pillar of rectitude, Enduring Hope thought, a model of strength and determination. Hope had never thought much of Kimmer as a commander, what little he had seen of him; but this dark moment seemed to be bringing out the best in him.

Pila came hurrying along the walkway. She whispered to the Commissary, something about results concerning the nature of Chandra. Nilis looked shocked, and immediately followed her off the walkway and out of the ops room.

Enduring Hope was simply baffled. What in the universe could be more important than to be here, in these next few crucial minutes? But he felt relieved Nilis and his emotional turmoil were gone.

Luru Parz watched suspiciously.

The Marshal himself tapped Hope on the shoulder. 'Engineer. Look. Your friend is going back in – Pirius.'

Hope was a bit overwhelmed to be prompted by a marshal. But he asked: 'Which one? Sir.'

'Both of them.'

'This time we send two ships in,' Pirius Red said. 'Not just one at a time. I'll go first.'

Torec said, 'You've used up your weapon.'

'I know. I'll go in to guide. Bilson, you've been there. We know we've breached that netting; maybe Jees managed to make the hole bigger. What if we could pass the starbreakers *through* that breach? We'd have a short time of free flight, not blocked by the net. We might see enough to hit the event horizon. What do you think?'

Bilson was very subdued. 'It's possible. It would be a *very* short time. Less than a second.'

'All right. Which is why whoever is going in will need a spotter.'

Torec said, 'So who makes the bomb run?'

Pirius took a breath. He wondered how long he could keep making these decisions; he felt as if he was sentencing another crew to death. But he had to make a choice. 'Burden – are you ready?'

There was no reply. And as the seconds ticked by, Pirius suddenly understood that there would be none. He brought up a Virtual image of Burden's face. Behind his skinsuit visor Burden's face was ghost pale, as if drained of blood.

Burden's navigator whispered, 'He's been like this since we passed SO-2. I didn't want to say—'

Pirius Blue said, 'Burden. *Burden*. Quero!'

Burden's eyes flickered. He licked his lips, and forced a smile. 'I'm sorry.' His voice was a hoarse croak, his throat evidently closed up.

Red said, '*He's frozen*. Lethe. Blue, did you know about this?'

Blue sighed. 'No. But I wondered . . . It happened before, didn't it, Burden?'

Burden seemed to be loosening a little. 'Yes. It happened before.'

'And that's why you got busted down to the penal divisions on Quin. Cohl was right to be suspicious of you.'

'I never lied to you—'

'But you never told me the full truth, did you? It was nothing to do with your unorthodoxy.'

'That didn't help. But, yes. I froze up. Just like this. People died, you know. Because of me, because I froze. I don't understand it. I can fight on a Rock. I can fight my way out of those blood-soaked trenches. I can save lives. But up here, in a greenship—'

'And that's why you kept busting your balls in combat missions? You were punishing yourself.'

'Lethe,' Torec snarled. 'And that garbage about timelike infinity – did you mean *any* of it?'

'I gave hope,' he said quietly. 'And it gave me hope. That some day it will all be put right. *People died because of me.*'

Blue said, 'Down on the Rocks, you saved far more.'

'The arithmetic of death doesn't work like that,' Burden said.

'No, it doesn't,' Torec said.

'I let you down, Squadron Leader.'

'Yes,' Red said with feeling. 'Yes, you did.'

'When you asked me to join you, and then to be a flight commander, I couldn't refuse. It was such a noble thing to attempt, such a *right* thing. I wanted to be part of it. I just hoped I'd be able to get through it.'

'Well, you haven't,' Torec said bitterly.

Red said, 'Guys, we don't have time for this.'

'I'll make the run,' said Blue immediately.

Red said, 'Why? To save your buddy's face?'

'No. Because I'm the better choice anyhow for a two-ship run. Think about it, Red. We're the same person. If we go in together, communication's going to be essential. If we can't understand each other, who can?'

Red said, 'But—'

'I know what you intend to do,' Pirius Blue said, 'While I drop my bombs, *you'll draw the flak*. That's what you're really planning, isn't it, Red? You see, I told you I understood you.'

Pirius sighed. 'All right. Cabel – Bilson – yes, I intend to draw the flak away from Blue. Maybe that way we'll give him a chance of succeeding with the mission. But you've been down there already. If you don't think you can do this again—'

'Count me in,' Cabel said immediately.

Bilson was clearly having a lot more difficulty. But the navigator sighed raggedly. 'You did say that if we screwed up today we'd be back tomorrow. Let's get it over.'

'Good man,' Pirius said warmly.

'Let's do it,' Blue said. His ship broke immediately out of the formation.

Pirius grasped his controls, and the two ships settled side by side.

Burden said, 'I just want to say—'

'Later,' Red snapped.

Torec whispered, 'Godspeed.'

Blue asked, 'What does that mean?'

'Something I learned on Earth. Very old, I think.'

'No goodbyes,' Pirius Red said. 'Ten minutes we'll be back.'

Torec forced a laugh. 'Knowing my luck, both of you. Or neither . . .'

In formation, the two ships swept down through the great hollow towards the shining puddle of the accretion disc.

Once again Red found himself flying low over the accretion disc; once again the event horizon itself rose like a malevolent sun before him. But this time Blue's ship was a green spark off his port bow.

Blue opened a private loop to Red. 'Of course,' he said, 'if we *both* get killed down here, then nothing will be left of me – of you.'

'That would be simpler,' Red said.

'That it would. Take care of Torec if—'

'And you,' Red called. 'Good luck, brother.'

'Yes – Lethe! I'm in flak!'

Pirius Red glanced across. Two, three, four starbreaker beams were raking the sky, trying to triangulate on Blue's ship. Red yanked his ship sideways, cutting between. To his satisfaction, two or three of the beams started to track him, while the others lost Blue, who ducked below his nominal course. But if one of those beams touched him, however briefly, he would be done.

Red began to weave back and forth, the CTC pulling the ship through a rapid evasion pattern faster than any human pilot could – faster than a Xeelee, Pirius thought. But the starbreakers tracked after him.

Cabel growled, 'I think I'm going to lose my breakfast.'

Pirius shouted, 'But it's working. Bilson! Keep tracking – it's your job to guide Blue in.'

'Understood, pilot.'

'Coming up on that netting,' Pirius Blue reported. 'Wow – I don't think I believed it – a contiguous structure light minutes across! The Xeelee have been busy . . . Red, I'm in flak again.'

Pirius, following his evasive course, had drifted too far from his temporal twin. No time to get back under sublight.

He punched his controls. The ship *jumped*, a big FTL jump of a light second or so. He heard the blister hull creak, and his displays lit up with red flags; you weren't supposed to make such jumps in spacetime this turbulent. But it had worked, and he had lodged himself just in front of Pirius Blue.

And once again the flak beams were focused on him. He laughed out loud. 'Bring it on!'

Bilson said, 'I lost the lock.'

'Then get it back,' Pirius shouted. 'Come on, navigator, we're almost there.'

'I have it. I have it!' A starbreaker speared out from the greenship's weapons pod, and hit a stretch of netting some distance before the two fleeing ships.

'I've got it,' Blue called. 'Good work, Bilson. But we need to have a word about your flying, Red.'

'Have you got the event horizon?'

Blue said quietly, 'We have a fix.'

Pirius's cabin flared with cherry-red light. The starbreakers were close. He ignored the glow, overrode the automatics, and held the ship to its line. 'Only a few seconds more, crew—'

The blister shuddered around him, and a telltale blared. He had lost one nacelle, one crew blister: it was Cabel, probably the best engineer in the squadron, gone, burned away, a scrap of flesh in this tremendous tumult of energy. Regret stabbed, but he had no time now, no time. Still he stuck to his line. 'Blue, drop the damn bombs—'

'Gone!' Blue called.

Pirius hurled the ship sideways. But the starbreakers tracked him, and still the ship shuddered.

Blue reported, 'Gone and – Lethe—'

'What? Blue, I can't see.'

'The black holes converged – we picked up the gravity wave pulse, right on the event horizon. And the Xeelee – Lethe, it's working . . . Oh.' He sounded oddly disappointed.

Pirius wrenched his ship around once more. 'Blue! Report.'

'The flak has got me. I can't manoeuvre – I'm wallowing like a hog—'

'Blue!'

'I always did want to be remembered,' Blue said.

'So did I.'

'Maybe we will be after all. Goodbye, brother. Tell Nilis . . . But his voice winked out, and Pirius heard no more, nothing but Bilson's quiet sobbing.

In the ops room the cheering was loud.

That netting around the event horizon looked as if it had been punched open by a vast fist. The surface beneath, a mist of sheets and threads of plasma falling into the event horizon, was awash with waves of density that flared brightly – some were so dense, the monitors said, that hydrogen fusion was briefly sparking. These waves were caused by oscillations of the event horizon itself, where it had been struck a mighty punch by the coalescing black holes of Blue's cannon. All around this part of Chandra intense pulses of gravitational waves were washing out, and it was those waves that were wreaking such damage on the netting structure, far overwhelming the feeble human efforts.

It was Nilis's moment of triumph. When Enduring Hope looked for the Commissary, he was nowhere to be seen.

Luru Paz watched, her eyes cold.

'Lethe, Nilis was right,' Marshal Kimmer said. 'It worked! Where is that oaf? Commissary!'

At last Nilis came running on to the walkway. He was carrying a data desk which he waved in the air. He hurried up to Kimmer. 'Marshal! I have it at last. Those final images of the web structure were the key – I knew there was more to this black hole than we suspected!'

Kimmer evidently didn't know what he was talking about, and didn't care. He wrapped one arm around Nilis's shoulders. 'Commissary, you old fool! Unlike you I have no imagination, I had to see it with my own eyes to believe it. But you've done it! You've ripped a hole in that peculiar Xeelee nest – and we still have four armed ships left to finish the job. By the time we're done that black hole will be as naked as the day it was formed, and the Xeelee will have nowhere to hide. I tell you, if you told me you had found a way to beat the Xeelee in a bare knuckle fight I'd believe you now!'

Nilis pulled away forcibly. When he spoke, it was practically a shriek. 'Marshal – listen to me. *We have to call off the attack.*'

Kimmer, shocked, was silenced.

Luru Parz said, 'And the remaining ships—'

'Call them home. Let no more lives be lost today.'

Kimmer looked thunderous. 'You had better explain yourself, Commissary.'

Nilis waved his data desk, 'I told you. I have it!'

'You have *what*?'

'The truth about Chandra. The Xeelee live off the black hole. But *the Xeelee aren't alone* . . .'

CHAPTER 57

The monads cared nothing for humans, of course, or for quagmites, or Xeelee, or photino birds, or any of the rest of the universe's menagerie at this or any other age. But they liked their universes to have *story*; and it was living things that generated the most interesting sagas.

And so in the time before time, when they picked out their seedling universes from the reef of possibilities, the monads, midwives of reality, exerted a subtle selection pressure. They chose for enrichment only the brightest bubbles in the cosmic spindrift: bubbles with a special, precious quality. A tendency to complexify.

Thoughtful beings, human and otherwise, would wonder at the endless fecundity of their universe, a universe that spawned life at every stage of its existence – and wonder *why* it had to be so.

Some of them came to understand that it was the universe's own innate tendency to complexify that had created the richness of structure within it.

Simple laws of molecular combination governed the growth of such intricate, inanimate forms as snowflakes and DNA molecules. But autocatalysis and homeostasis enabled simple structures to interact and spin off more complex structures still, until living things emerged, which combined into ever more complicated entities.

The same pattern showed in other aspects of reality. The hive structures of ant colonies and Coalescent communities emerged without conscious design from the small decisions of their drones. Even in the world of human ideas, the structures of religions, economies and empires fed back on themselves and became ever richer. Even mathematical toys, like games of artificial life run in computer memories, seemed to demonstrate an unwavering tendency to grow more complicated. But then, human mathematics was a mirror of the universe humans found themselves in; that was why mathematics worked.

Complexifying seemed inevitable. But it was not. A universe could be imagined *without* this tendency.

If the ability to complexify had suddenly been turned off, the universe would have seemed very different. Snowflakes would not form, birds would not flock, ants and Coalescents would have tumbled out of their disintegrating hives, baffled. On larger scales, economic and historical cycles would break up. Ecosystems would fail; there would be no coral reefs, no forests. The great cycles of matter and energy, mediated by life, on a living world like Earth would collapse.

But of course there would be no observers of such catastrophes, for without complexity's search for feedback loops and stable processes, hearts could not beat, and embryos could not form.

Humans had the good fortune to exist in a universe in which there was no law of conservation of complexity, no limit to its supply.

But it didn't have to be that way. That the universe could complexify, that richness of existence was possible at all, was thanks to the monads, and their subtle pan-cosmic selection. The monads had selected, designed, nurtured a universe that would be fruitful for ever, in which there was no limit to the possibilities for life and energy, for life and mind, as far ahead as it was possible to look.

While empires rose and fell, while the universe continued its endless unravelling of possibility after possibility, the monads slumbered. They had done their work, made their contribution. Now they waited for the precious moments of the farthest future when this universe, in turn grown old, spawned new fragments of chaos, and they could wake again. But in their epochal sleep, even the monads could be drawn into history. And even they could be harmed.

CHAPTER 58

Luru Parz watched the Commissary with blank hostility, Enduring Hope with bafflement.

Nilis tried to tell his complex story too quickly, too briefly. For months he had been trying to assemble all the data on Chandra that he could find: on the Xeelee and quagmites and other denizens, on cosmological data like the relic Big Bang radiation, on the astrophysics of the black hole itself and the knotted-up singularity at its heart – and now even on the extraordinary artefact the Xeelee had wrapped around the event horizon. And he had come to a new conclusion.

Nilis said triumphantly, 'Do you see? Do you see *now*?'

'No,' snapped Kimmer.

There was a story in this information, said Nilis. And that story was the secret history of the universe.

Nilis said he had looked deep into the structure of Chandra, and had found life infesting even the singularity at its heart. 'These deep ones – the ones I call "monads", it is a very antique word – they are older than all of us. Older than the Xeelee, older than the universe itself! It will take a lot of study to figure it all out. But it's clear that the monads are responsible for life in this universe. Or rather for the tendency of this universe to complexify, to *produce* life. It is a level of deep design about the universe nobody ever suspected. And in their nests of folded spacetime, huddled inside the event horizons of black holes, they slumber – waiting for our petty ages to pass away – until the time comes for a new universe to be born from the wreckage of the old.'

'And the Xeelee—'

'They live off Chandra, the black hole. Their net structure is the

472

great machine which allows them to achieve their goals: to birth nightfighters, to use the black hole as a computing engine, all of it. But that's trivial. It's what's *inside* the black hole that counts. The Xeelee are just parasites. Secondary. They don't matter!'

Kimmer said dangerously, 'They matter rather a lot to me.'

Enduring Hope thought he understood, 'And if we attack the black hole,' he said doggedly, 'we could destroy the monads. Is that what you fear?'

'Yes,' Nilis said gratefully, sweat beading his brow. 'Oh, my boy – yes! That is precisely what I fear.'

Kimmer said, 'But even if you are right there are other galaxies. Other nests of monads.'

Nilis insisted, 'We can't make any simple assumptions about this situation, Marshal.' He spoke rapidly about levels of reality, of interconnectivity in higher dimensions. 'By striking a blow in this one place we may wreak damage everywhere, and for all time . . .'

Luru Parz said slowly, 'The Commissary fears that if we destroy the monads we will break the thread – don't you, Nilis? – the shining thread of life, of creativity, that connects this universe to those that preceded it, and to those that will follow. To kill them would be patricide – or deicide, perhaps.' She smiled. 'Ah, but I forgot. In this enlightened age you don't have gods, or fathers, do you? It's entirely appropriate of humanity that when we do find God we try to turn Him into a weapon, and then kill Him.'

'Shut up, you old monster,' Kimmer said.

Luru Parz said coldly, 'But this is why I've been trying to stop you, Nilis. To stop this pointless research.'

His jaw dropped. 'You – it was *you*? You obstructed me, you blocked me from the data, the processing resources I needed? I thought you were my ally, Luru Parz, It was you who said we must study the black hole in the first place!'

'Study it sufficiently to destroy it – that's all we needed. Not this! Knowledge is a weapon, Nilis. That's *all* it is. I always feared that if you rooted around for long enough you'd find some reason *not* to complete the project. Over-academic fools like you always do.'

Maybe she was right to block him, Enduring Hope thought. He recalled his conversation with Blue, who had foreseen exactly this outcome: that sooner or later Nilis would find a reason to fall in love with Chandra, and would try to stop the attack.

Nilis said darkly, 'Listen to me. My analysis is hasty. And it contains more questions than answers. Regardless of any pan-cosmic responsibility, if we were to destabilise this monad complex, we don't know what the result would be. The damage could be huge. I can't begin to estimate it—' He shook his head. 'Damage on a galactic scale, perhaps.'

Luru Parz pushed past Nilis to face Kimmer. Her face was alive, intense, but Hope thought it had the intensity of a sharpened blade, not a human expression. 'Then let it be so. Marshal – *we must do it regardless of the consequences*. This is our one chance, don't you see?'

Kimmer said, 'But if we cause such devastation – if the Galaxy centre detonates—'

Luru shouted, 'What of it? Let the Galaxy be cleansed! Marshal, I have seen the human race populate a galaxy once; we can do it again. And this time it would be a galaxy free of Xeelee. *We must do this*.'

Nilis laughed, a brittle sound. 'Marshal, you aren't listening to her? Why, you fool—'

Kimmer's reaction was immediate. He swung around and swatted the Commissary aside with one gloved fist. Nilis fell backward, clattering clumsily against a bulkhead, blood seeping from his mouth.

Enduring Hope ran to him and cradled his head. 'Commissary, Commissary,' he whispered. 'You can't go around calling a marshal a fool!'

Luru Parz seemed to have recovered her detachment. Breathing hard, she said, 'Our debate here is irrelevant anyway.'

Kimmer, confounded by the rapid turning of events, glowered at her. 'What do you mean?'

'The decision to go on doesn't belong to us. It belongs to Pirius Red. Who has heard every word we have said. Haven't you, pilot?'

The voice from the centre of the Galaxy was sepulchral. 'I have, Luru Parz.'

Pirius Red pressed his gloved hands to his temples.

He and Bilson, his surviving crewmate, had made it back to the rump of his squadron. But he was grateful that he was alone in his blister. He was still trying to absorb the shocks of the last few minutes – the death of his engineer and the sudden loss of his own older self. He had no idea how he was supposed to feel about that. And now *this*, a questioning of the whole basis of the mission by the man who had instigated it all.

He found it difficult even to speak. He knew he was close to burn-out.

This Burden Must Pass said, 'It's your decision, Squadron Leader.'

Pirius's laugh was bitter. '*Now* you have something to say.'

Torec, her voice strained by grief, snapped at Burden, 'Yes. And for you it doesn't matter because, right or wrong, everything will be put right at the end of time, won't it?'

'Perhaps not this,' Burden said softly.

'We should wait,' Bilson said hesitantly. 'We need time. If Nilis is right . . . We need time to check.'

Torec said, 'But we won't get as good a chance to strike again. We know that. The Xeelee will be waiting for us next time.'

'We will find another way,' Bilson said. 'People are smart like that.'

'Yes, we are,' said Burden.

Pirius was anguished. If Nilis was even half right, they could be committing a terrible crime, a crime that might transcend the universe itself. How could he possibly know the right thing to do? Who was *he* to have such a decision thrust upon him?

And yet the choice seemed clear.

Pirius said, 'Enough of us have died today.' Including half of myself, he thought. He tried to rehearse the words. *We pull back* . . .

'Pilot.' Bilson's voice was full of wonder.

Pirius looked down at the accretion disc. A kind of cloud was rising above that puddle of light, a black cloud. When he increased the magnification of his images, he saw they were ships, a horde of them, rising like insects.

'It's the Xeelee,' Torec said. 'They're streaming out of the cavity. I don't believe it. They are abandoning Chandra.'

Burden said, 'It looks as if they agree with Nilis. There are some things just not worth destroying, whatever the cost.'

'Let's go home,' Pirius said.

The five battered ships swivelled as one, and turned away from the heart of the Galaxy, where the Xeelee ships were still rising, countless numbers of them.

When Pirius Blue came to, he was embedded in darkness, unable to move. Impact foam, he realised.

To his own surprise, he was still alive. He had survived the flak assault, and the destruction of his ship. He wasn't even injured, as far as he could tell.

With voice commands he brought up sensor data, which flickered before his eyes inside his visor. Drifting at the centre of the accretion disc, he learned, he was rather a long way away from any possible pick-up. And nobody knew if he was alive or dead. Suspended in darkness, locked into the foam, he came to a quick decision. He uttered a command.

His foam shell burst and flew apart, leaving him in his skinsuit. He was falling in a cloud of fragments, and a bath of brilliant Galaxy-centre light. His visor turned jet black, and its inner surface immediately lit up with red warning flags.

He checked his suit's systems. All overloaded, all on the brink of failure. A skinsuit wasn't designed to withstand the ferocious conditions of the centre of the Galaxy, and it knew it. But it didn't matter. This would be over soon, one way or another.

With more commands he coaxed his visor to leak through a little of the hard light that battered it. Soon he could see again, if sketchily.

He was floating through a forest of shining threads, silvery lines as straight as laser beams – but some of the threads were broken, twisted.

With a jolt, he understood. He was falling *through* the net structure around the black hole. There was no sign of those vessels they had spotted crawling over the net, however. And there was no sign of his ship, or his crewmates, who, if they had not died immediately, must be drifting as helplessly as he was.

To his surprise, one comms loop was still working. He couldn't talk to the squadron, but there was a line to the ops room on Arches. With brisk commands, he set it to transmit only, and patched in a visual feed from his visor. He was happy for them to watch what he watched. There might be much for them to learn, however the operation worked out. But he didn't want to talk to anybody. *No goodbyes*. Not when there was another version of himself who could do all that for him.

Still falling helplessly, he swivelled in space and looked down at the event horizon.

Though infalling plasma crawled across its surface, reddening as it fell out of existence, *it was dark*, a dark plane beneath him. The ferocious light that bathed this place was either absorbed by the event horizon or else was deflected by the black hole's immense gravity field; he was in the shadow of the black hole, a strange relativistic shadow left by bent and distorted light.

He lifted his head. The event horizon was like a monstrous planet, so vast it was a plain beneath him that cut the universe in two. Everywhere redshifted plasma writhed and crawled, raining into the hole, and immense auroras flapped. But at its straight-line horizon he saw bands of light, one, two, perhaps three stripes, running parallel with the edge. The rings were another product of the hole's huge gravity field, as light was not simply deflected but pulled through one orbit, two, before being flung away.

But now he was falling ever more rapidly towards that fatal surface. Telltales warned him that his signal lock to Arches was being lost: the increasing redshift he must be suffering was affecting the frequency control. It was a secondary effect of the distortion of time itself by the black hole's gravity. He tried to divert some of his processing power to adjusting the signal, to keep the lock as long as possible.

Time, time: from the point of view of his own younger self in the outside universe, time would pass more and more slowly for Blue as he approached the event horizon, until at last duration ceased altogether, and he was pinned against the horizon like a fly embedded in glass. It wouldn't be long, he thought, before relativity played a final trick on his tangled lifeline, and Pirius Red became the older twin after all.

Blue would know nothing of that. He probably wouldn't feel anything when he passed through the event horizon itself. This far out from such a massive object, tidal forces had not yet begun to pluck at a body as small as his. Once inside the horizon, though, his fate would be determined.

Inside a black hole space and time pivoted about the constancy of lightspeed, and exchanged roles. Outside, time proceeded inexorably forward, but you could move back and forth in space. But inside a hole it was space that was one-directional. No matter how hard he struggled, his progress would be one way towards the singularity at the geometric centre of the hole – the singularity was now his only future. And there, long after the tides had torn his body apart, the strings and membranes that underlay the very particles of his body would be stretched and torn before being crushed out of existence altogether.

The telltale acknowledgement signal from Arches turned to a

high-frequency chirp that disappeared into inaudibility. He turned the comms system off; it was no use now.

He glanced back the way he had come. Though the crowded sky directly above him seemed unaffected, towards the hole's horizon his view was blue-shifted and muddled. It was as if he was looking out through a shallow, mirrored cone: even light was being pulled into the hole's gravity field, and was starting to rain down on him. As he fell further the light would fold up behind him, and eventually all the light in the universe would be pulled tight into a pencil-thin cone, spearing down after him as he fell into darkness.

Of course the most likely cause of his death would be his suit's failure. But perhaps he could juggle its systems, force the hole itself to kill him. He grinned fiercely. It would be a challenge.

CHAPTER 59

On the long journey back to Arches they saw no sign of Xeelee. Ops told them that when the black hole web was abandoned, the Xeelee appeared to have ceased their operations right across the face of the Galaxy, from Core to rim. Pirius found it hard to believe that this one action had made such a difference. But he was glad that they weren't harassed; they would have been easy targets.

He was only bringing back four ships, though. This Burden Must Pass had volunteered to stay at Chandra for an additional day. He would record what he could of the field of action, and search for any survivors of the lost ships. Pirius agreed to this reluctantly. It was standard operating procedure, and as the sole surviving flight commander Burden was the right man for the job. But Pirius knew that this offer had more to do with the contents of Burden's own head.

Besides, he didn't like the idea of leaving anybody behind. He made sure Burden's crew were happy with the idea before he agreed, but they seemed loyal to Burden.

Four ships left, then – and then another was lost. It was another systems failure – catastrophic, as the containment of the point black hole bombs failed and the ship was immediately torn apart. After that Pirius ordered the crews to dump their remaining bombs. He knew he would regret for the rest of his life not having thought of this precaution earlier.

So in the end only three ships returned to Arches Base. They were directed to a hangar with enough cradles to hold the ten that had flown out from Orion Rock fifteen hours before.

Pirius was the first down. He made a shaky landing, dropping his ship too hard into its cradle. There were dozens of ground crew on standby, and they came swarming around immediately. But of course there was only Pirius and Bilson to help out of their blisters; the stump of Cabel's nacelle was a mute testament to the loss.

Enduring Hope and Cohl were both here. Pirius was unreasonably pleased to see their familiar faces. They embraced, stiffly, in their skinsuits. But he could see their distress at the loss of Blue, 'their' Pirius.

Marshal Kimmer, in a bright skinsuit adorned with badges of command, came striding forward. 'Well done, pilot, well done!'

Pirius allowed his hand to be shaken. But when Kimmer demanded to know how the operation had gone, Pirius just said, 'Wait for the debrief,' and turned back to his crew. You didn't speak to a senior officer like that, but he was too tired to care.

Pirius sent Bilson to the sick bay. But he fought off the medics who tried to lead him away too; he wasn't about to leave the hangar until the other surviving ships made it home.

In they came, one at a time. Neither made a landing much better than he had, but both got down safely. The crews in their skinsuits clustered on the floor of the hangar, while medics and reserve flight crew crowded around them and Hope's technicians moved in on the ships.

Everybody talked at once. Relief was the first emotion, relief to be alive. The release of nervous energy was almost like elation. But those empty cradles told a harrowing story. People would wander off alone and glance at the sky, as if expecting one of the lost ships to come limping home even now.

Pirius's most difficult meeting was with Torec. She hugged him, but her small face, inside her visor, was closed with grief. 'I've got you back,' she said, 'but I've lost you as well. How am I supposed to cope with *that*?'

'I don't know,' he murmured.

Once inside the base, the crew were taken through standard post-operation processing. First the medics checked them over. All but one, a navigator with a broken arm, were released. Then they were taken to a refectory, where food and drink were heaped up. They suddenly discovered how hungry they were. But there was enough food for thirty, and it was uncomfortable to be surrounded by empty chairs.

After that, though Pirius felt so exhausted he thought he would sleep for a week, they were taken away for preliminary debriefs, individually, in crews, and then as a whole. That went on for six wearying hours, until at last a consensus Virtual record of the operation was put together, combining all their viewpoints and the logs of the surviving ships. The crews accepted this as necessary. Details about the mission could be argued over for years, but these first moments, when memories were fresh and unclouded by sentiment or denial, were essential for an accurate record. It was gruelling work, though.

Marshal Kimmer sat silently throughout these sessions. The only emotion he showed came when Pirius described how he had taken his ship back for a second run on Chandra, to guide Blue and to deflect the flak.

When the debrief was over, Kimmer approached Pirius. 'You were right,' he said gruffly. 'I should have waited for the debrief. But I'll say it again. Well done, pilot.' He seemed to want to say more, but his small, mean-looking mouth appeared incapable of expression. He bowed and walked away, his entourage of aides at his heels.

By now Pirius was so tired he felt numb, detached, as if he was still wearing a skinsuit. But he knew he had one more duty.

Commissary Nilis was in his room, deep in Officer Country. Pila sat with him. They were sorting through data desks, and Virtual images of Chandra and its surrounds floated in the air. Nilis actually shied away from Pirius when he came in, a kind of shame showing in his broad, rumpled face.

Pila, though, gazed at Pirius. 'Well done,' she said softly.

He wondered what she was feeling. This strange, cold woman from Earth had been on her own journey, he supposed. He said, 'I couldn't have done it without you, Pila. I won't forget that.' He turned to Nilis and said formally, 'Commissary – I was glad to have taken part in the final experiment that proved your theories.'

That took Nilis by surprise. 'Oh, my boy, my boy. Thank you! And you validated my faith in you, in spades. You have come a long way from that mixed-up child on Port Sol and Venus, my boy, a long long way. You are a man – you poor wretch!'

'And of course it *has* been a great technical achievement.' He smiled, his rheumy eyes wet. 'Who would have thought, when we were limping around in Sol system, that we could have brought it off?

Well, I always had faith in you, Pirius; I knew you could do it, if anybody could.'

'And we made history today.'

'Oh, yes, there's that too. How remarkable to think that of all the galaxies we see in the sky only ours is clear of the Xeelee – and all thanks to human endeavour! And it is a historic moment in other ways. It's a fallacy, you know, that communication is always possible between alien cultures. The dismal records of the Assimilation prove that. Sometimes perceptions of our common universe simply diverge too much. In an awful lot of first contacts "communication" is primal: only to be ignored, eaten, or attacked. And there is no record of the Xeelee attempting *any* form of communication with any lesser species, save extreme violence. But in this incident they *did* respond. We threatened Chandra, they withdrew, we did not attack; information, of a sort, passed between us, and a kind of agreement was reached.' He sighed. 'If only it were possible to build on this breakthrough! Perhaps the perpetual war could be ended. But I fear that may be Utopian.'

Pirius knew how important this sort of philosophical stuff was to the Commissary. 'A triumph in many ways, then.'

'Yes.' But Nilis's face crumpled. 'But too many people were lost – too many young lives rubbed out because of me and my dreams. Those moments when the first two runs failed, and I thought that despite the sacrifices I had demanded I had failed, were almost more than I could bear.'

Pirius tried to find words about the proportionality of the losses compared to what had been gained. But Nilis, he saw, was inconsolable for now. After a time he left him to his work.

In their barracks, Torec was already asleep. She hadn't even taken off the coverall given her by the medics after they peeled her out of her skinsuit. Pirius crawled in with her. She stirred, mumbled, and turned into his arms, a bundle of soft warm humanity.

He had thought he would be too agitated to sleep. Besides, he felt guilty about lying down to sleep when others had died, or were still out there. If he slept this long day would finally end, and he would somehow lose it, lose them.

But sleep rose up like a black tide, regardless.

The next day, his first priority was his crews.

He toured the base. They were in their barracks, or the refectories, or the sick bays, or the gyms and training rooms where they had gone to work out the tension from their systems. A couple of them had gone back to the ships to help the ground crews with their own investigations and debriefing.

Some just accepted what had happened. It was a gamble worth taking, they said; you win some, you lose some. Others were bitter at the stupidity of the commanders, including Pirius himself, who had sent them into the Cavity with such poor intelligence. He absorbed their anger. And some just talked. They went over and over what they had done, telling and retelling their own small war stories as part of the whole. That was all right. It was part of the healing, and Pirius's job now was to listen. And it wasn't going to stop here, he knew. The shock of what they had gone through, and the guilt at having survived where others hadn't, would never leave them.

Pirius had lost a temporal twin, a part of himself, and he wondered which way his own damage would work out – and how Torec, who had lost her lover and welcomed him home at the same time, would sort out her own complicated, guilt-ridden grief.

More than twenty-four hours after Pirius's return, This Burden Must Pass brought his own battered ship home.

Pirius hurried to meet him, and walked with his crew to the sick bay. With his visor cracked open, Burden's face was drawn, dried sweat was crusted under his shadowed eyes and his hair was plastered to his head. Burden said that they had encountered no Xeelee harassment on the way back, 'It looks as if it really is true,' he said. 'They have abandoned the Galaxy to mankind. And because of *us*.'

'Quite a story to add to that end-of-time confluence of yours,' Pirius said.

'Yes, quite a story.' Burden said more slowly, 'Pirius, about what happened out there—'

'Forget it,' Pirius snapped.

'I can't do that,' Burden said. 'If I'd gone into Chandra as you ordered, as was my duty, maybe Blue would have survived.'

'We'll never know. We've all come home with regrets, Burden. Now we move on.'

Burden nodded, his eyes downcast. 'We move on.'

Burden said he had found traces of Jees's ship. It was smashed up.

Two of the crew nacelles were more or less intact, but the systems had failed before the safety cut-ins could work.

'They didn't survive.'

'We sent the crew blisters into the black hole.' Burden smiled thinly, exhausted. 'It seemed fitting.'

'That it does.' Pirius was thinking over what Burden had said. His thoughts were muddy; already the events of the flight seemed remote, as if they had happened a decade ago, or in another life. But there was something missing from Burden's report. 'You didn't mention the third nacelle. Jees rode with the Silver Ghost.'

Burden grinned. 'I wondered if you'd ask about that. I'll have to report it, I suppose. Of the Ghost's nacelle I found not a trace. Not only that, it looked to me as if it had been sheared off – 1 mean, deliberately.'

'The Ambassador escaped,' Pirius said, marvelling. Once more there was a Silver Ghost loose in the Galaxy. 'But what different can one Ghost make?'

'The Ghosts are remarkable creatures, and very resourceful. I don't think we've heard the last of the Sink Ambassador. And you have to wonder if, from the Ghost's point of view, this whole operation was set up – if *we* were set up – just to give the Ghost a chance to get free.'

'That's impossible.'

Burden glanced around. 'I'm not going to repeat this in the debrief. But I want to go back out there again.' He spread his gloved hands. 'After all, the war is over, it seems. They don't need me to fight any more. Not that I was much use at that in the first place. I want to go back to the centre again, to look for the Ambassador.'

'Why?'

'Because we never finished our philosophical discussions. Things are different now. Perhaps we can learn from the Ghosts about how we're going to live our lives from now on. Oh, Pirius – one more thing.' He dug out a data desk and showed him some complicated schematics. 'Something the sensors picked up.'

Burden had observed structures of dark matter drifting through the centre of the Galaxy. Invisible to human senses, passing through even the crowded matter around Chandra as if it was no more substantial than a Virtual, the shadowy forms had settled around the central black hole.

Burden said, 'I remember what you said about Nilis, and Luru Parz, and their interpretation of history. The Xeelee cleaned these dark matter creatures, the "photino birds", out of the Core. Now the Xeelee are gone – and in less than a day the birds are back.' He put away the data desk. 'Silver Ghosts loose – dark-matter creatures swarming through the Core – we have planted many seeds, as Nilis would say. Something tells me the future suddenly got a lot more complicated.'

A week after the crews returned from the Core, Arches Base received visitors from Earth. The scuttlebutt in the dorms was that one was a member of the Grand Conclave itself, the highest body of governance in the Coalition: one of just twelve people who governed a Galaxy, and she was *here*. Not only that, the scuttlebutt went, she had come to give them all medals.

The day after that, the crews of Exultant Squadron and everybody connected with Operation Prime Radiant were called to the hangar. The hangar was covered by a translucent dome that gave a view of the sky, and the hot white light of the Core beat down into the interior of the pit. All ten of the ships' cradles were empty now; the surviving ships would perform a flyby, piloted by reserve crews.

Everybody was here, brought together for the first time since they had dispersed after their debriefing. With Pirius were Torec, Burden and the rest of the surviving crews. Cohl was here, and Enduring Hope brought a gaggle of grinning ground crew techs. The more senior officers, including Captains Marta, Seath and Boote, kept apart, resplendent in new dress uniforms.

Others came out for their share of the limelight. Aside from civilians like Commissary Nilis and Pila, there were much more lowly types: workers, techs, administrators. Many of them were older than the flight crews, and their ranks gleamed with metallic implants, for this was the Navy's way of using its surviving veterans. But they performed the various unglamorous but essential jobs that kept the base running and the ships flying, and with Pila's help Pirius had made sure that they would be here.

A piping sounded, a tradition, it was said, dating from a time when man's ships sailed only the seas of Earth. The officers muttered quiet orders. The military staff and civilians alike drew their ranks up a little tighter and stood rigidly to attention.

A party swept from the shadows into full Galaxy light. Marshal Kimmer and Minister Gramm accompanied a much more imposing figure. Philia Doon, Plenipotentiary for Total War, tall, slender, was dressed in a long golden cloak that swept around her feet. Her gait was graceful – and yet it was not quite natural, as if she used prosthetics, and her footsteps were loud and heavy, abnormally weighty. Kimmer was speaking to her, but she was looking into the sky, and Pirius had the impression that even as she took in Kimmer's words, she was listening to some other voice only she could hear.

The skin of her slender face shone a subtle silver-grey. There wasn't a hair on her head.

Doon took her place on a low platform. One by one the staff of the base were presented to her. Marshal Kimmer himself went up first, followed by Nilis, who bowed as he was handed some kind of elaborate data desk. Then Doon began to work her way through the officers, down the ladder of superiority.

When it was his turn, Pirius found his heart thumping as he approached this strange creature. She towered over him.

'Congratulations, pilot,' the Plenipotentiary murmured. Her voice was rich, but too precise – artificial, he thought. She said, 'Your squadron – "Exultant" – was well named.' But even as she talked there was no expression in that silvered face, and she didn't even seem to be looking at him. She beckoned him closer, and he smelled a faint scent of burning. She pressed her hand to his chest, and when she lifted it away a bright green tetrahedral sigil glowed there, his new battle honour.

Pirius was very glad when the ceremony was over and they were allowed to break ranks.

Nilis approached Pirius. 'Well, pilot, now you have seen right to the very heart of our marvellous Third Expansion – and *that* is the type of creature that festers there.'

'You mean Plenipotentiary Doon?'

'She is what is called a "raoul",' Nilis said. 'Do you not recognise the texture of her skin?'

'I don't know the technology.'

'Not technology. Not even biology – or at any rate, not human biology. That stuff is the hide of a Silver Ghost. The Plenipotentiary is a symbiote; she has the internal organs of a human, but the flesh of a Ghost. Oh, and she has implants tucked into her belly, I believe: more symbiotes, another conquered alien species living on within the bodies of our rulers, a group-mind entity that once, it is said, conquered the Earth and is now used to provide instantaneous links between the Plenipotentiaries and their circle of chosen ones.

'There is plenty of justification for all this surgery and genetic tinkering: the Plenipotentiaries have such responsibility that they *need* such powers, such dispensations from the Doctrines that are supposed to govern us all. But I hardly think Hama Druz would approve, do you? He would say she is a monstrosity, perhaps. But that monstrosity is what you have been fighting for.'

A monstrosity? Watching the Plenipotentiary, Pirius remembered Nilis's talk of an eleventh step in human evolution. Were those prostheses no more than cosmetic – or would Doon somehow breed true? Perhaps this extraordinary woman really did represent the future, whether she made him comfortable or not.

They joined Pirius's friends. Nilis told them high-level gossip he had heard about the impact of the operation on Earth. 'Do you know, on Earth, for the first time in millennia the Library of Futures is *blank*? The future is unknown.' For a moment he sounded almost gleeful, 'I hear that a lot of people are *very* scared. We really have shaken everything up, haven't we, pilot? All the way back to the corridors of Earth itself! Who can say what is to come? Oh, we face a great dislocation, of course. I suspect our greatest challenge will be to keep mankind from tearing itself apart, now that it has no one else on whom to vent its anger and frustration. We don't need warriors any more, but we do need peacekeepers, I fear!

'But isn't it refreshing?' he said, and he bounced absurdly on his toes. 'Think of it! Can we not now place Hama Druz in the grave which he so richly deserves? Druz in his neurotic terror longed to keep mankind static, unchanging. But that denies the basic creativity of the universe in which we are embedded – a creativity, indeed, which flows from the creatures inside that spectacular artefact you attacked, Pirius. Now we need no longer deny our essential nature: now we can swim with the flow of the universe rather than against it – and perhaps, at last, uncover our true destiny as children of the cosmos.'

All that sounded a bit vague to Pirius.

Enduring Hope said, 'But, Commissary, when we get up tomorrow morning – what shall we *do*?'

Nilis laughed, avuncular, and spread his hands to the sky. 'Why, there is a whole universe out there waiting for you – now that you don't have to die before you grow up.' He pointed to the senior officers, to Kimmer and Seath and Marta. '*They* are too old to change. No doubt they hoped to die before the war ended – well, *bad luck*! For young people like you the future is suddenly opened up. Perhaps some of you will come with me to Chandra, to study that remarkable nest of transcosmic life. And perhaps some of you will go sailing beyond the bounds of the Galaxy itself. Why not? We've always been so busy battling to survive in *this* Galaxy, for twenty thousand years we haven't so much as sent a probe out *there*.'

Cohl said seriously, 'But the Xeelee are still out there – they are everywhere but *here*.'

'The Xeelee will keep for another day,' Nilis said gently. 'And in the meantime you have families to build.

There was a stunned silence.

Pirius was shocked. 'Families?'

'Well, why not? The old machinery has always been there, even if we don't use it any more. And now the rules have changed. It will do you good to have a real family, you know, to put down roots. You really don't know how it feels.' He winked. 'And I always did want to be a grandfather – honorary, at least!'

Pirius stared at Torec. Her face was flushed, but he could see generations of conditioning warring with even more ancient impulses. He hadn't yet got over the loss of Pirius Blue, but a part of him had been *glad*, guiltily, that his temporal twin had gone, that his life had simplified a little. Now it looked as if it was going to get a lot more complicated again. He felt a sudden, warm rush of joy.

From out of the crowd, Luru Parz approached. She was wearing a simple white robe. To Pirius, Luru Parz was a nightmare of his difficult time in Sol system. He felt unaccountably afraid. He wondered what possible justification she could have used to crash this event – but if she wasn't shy even of a Plenipotentiary, she was powerful indeed.

'Congratulations, pilot. Quite a feat of arms.'

Nilis said warningly, 'Luru Parz, this is hardly the time for more of your antique strangeness. Let these young people enjoy their moment.'

'Their moment?' Luru Parz smiled coldly. 'Their moment, yes, the moment of vivid brightness that makes a mayfly life worthwhile.' She glared up at the sky. 'And we have won the Galaxy! When I was born – when mankind was restricted to a single planet and was under the heel of an alien conqueror – nobody would have believed this day would come. For now we are briefly the biggest fish in this puddle of stars. But what is one galaxy? Out there, on scales beyond our very perception, is an ocean of wonders and dangers we can't even imagine.'

Nilis snapped, 'What do you want, Luru Parz?'

She turned on Pirius. 'I want to make sure you understand what you have done, pilot. For better or worse, you have broken open the strange madness that gripped humans for so long. Now the iron law of the Druz Doctrines will weaken, and mankind, scattered over a billion worlds, will begin to explore the limits of the possible. You have brought on us a new age, Pirius, an age of bifurcation. Perhaps you think that's a good thing – I know this fool Nilis does.

'But at least we were united in our madness. You see, we will never again be strong enough, never united, never determined enough, to strike as you could have struck.' She pointed her finger at Pirius. 'You could have destroyed it – destroyed that monstrous thing at the centre of the Galaxy – but you turned back.'

Pirius frowned. 'Do you believe the Xeelee will return?'

'Of course they will. It's only a matter of time. And we will not be able to push them out again. They will be back – just as the photino birds have returned, and another ancient conflict resumes. *And you turned back.*'

Torec asked, 'Where will you go now, Lura Parz?'

'To Earth, of course.'

'Why?'

'To prepare its defences.' With that she walked away, small, closed in, unimaginably ancient.

Hope gasped, and pointed up. 'The flyby!'

Pirius looked up. Far above the surface of the asteroid, the surviving ships of Exultant Squadron sailed across the sky, their graceful human engineering silhouetted against the glare of the Galaxy's heart.

Do not remember heroes. Do not speak their names.

Remember my words, but do not speak *my* name.

I have a vision of a Galaxy overrun by mankind from Core to rim. Of four hundred billion stars each enslaved to the rhythms of Earth's day, Earth's year. I have a vision of a trillion planets pulsing to the beat of a human heart.

And I have a vision of a child. Who will grow up knowing neither family nor comfort. Who will not be distracted by the illusion of a long life. Who will know nothing but honour and duty. Who will die joyously for the sake of mankind.

That is a hero. And I will never know her name.

Always remember: a brief life burns brightly.

– Hama Druz